Madeleine Wickham was born in London in 1969. She read PPE at Oxford and published her first novel, *The Tennis Party*, while working as a financial journalist. Since then she has written five more novels, two of which, *The Gatecrasher* and *The Wedding Girl*, are being adapted for television. She lives in London with her husband, a singer, and their two small sons.

D0715980

www.**booksattransworld**.co.uk

Also by Madeleine Wickham

THE TENNIS PARTY
A DESIRABLE RESIDENCE
SWIMMING POOL SUNDAY
THE GATECRASHER
THE WEDDING GIRL
COCKTAILS FOR THREE

and published by Black Swan

SWIMMING POOL SUNDAY

and

THE TENNIS PARTY

Madeleine Wickham

BLACK SWAN

SWIIMMING POOL SUNDAY and THE TENNIS PARTY
A BLACK SWAN BOOK : 0 552 77099 X

Copyright © Madeleine Wickham 2001
This edition published 2002

1 3 5 7 9 10 8 6 4 2

including

SWIMMING POOL SUNDAY
Originally published in Great Britain by Black Swan,
a division of Transworld Publishers
Copyright © Madeleine Wickham 1997
Set in 11/12½pt Linotype Melior by
Phoenix Typesetting, Ilkley, West Yorkshire.

THE TENNIS PARTY
Originally published in Great Britain by Black Swan,
a division of Transworld Publishers
Copyright © Madeleine Wickham 1995
Set in 11pt Linotype Melior by
County Typesetters, Margate, Kent.

The right of Madeleine Wickham to be identified as the author
of this work has been asserted in accordance with sections 77
and 78 of the Copyright Designs and Patents Act 1988.

All the characters in this book are fictitious,
and any resemblance to actual persons, living or dead,
is purely coincidental.

Condition of Sale
This book is sold subject to the condition that it shall not,
by way of trade or otherwise, be lent, re-sold, hired out or
otherwise circulated in any form of binding or cover other
than that in which it is published and without a similar
condition including this condition being imposed on the
subsequent purchaser.

Black Swan Books are published by Transworld Publishers,
61–63 Uxbridge Road, London W5 5SA,
a division of The Random House Group Ltd,
in Australia by Random House Australia (Pty) Ltd,
20 Alfred Street, Milsons Point, Sydney, NSW 2061, Australia,
in New Zealand by Random House New Zealand Ltd,
18 Poland Road, Glenfield, Auckland 10, New Zealand
and in South Africa by Random House (Pty) Ltd,
Endulini, 5a Jubilee Road, Parktown 2193, South Africa.

Printed and bound in Great Britain by
Cox & Wyman Ltd, Reading, Berkshire.

SWIMMING POOL SUNDAY

For Gemma and Abigail

I am grateful to Dr Stephane Duckett of The Children's Trust, Tadworth, and to Anna Lordon, for their expert advice.

Chapter One

It was only May, and it was only ten o'clock in the morning. But already the sun was shining hotly, and the grass in the garden sprang warm and dry underfoot, and the breeze under Katie's cotton dress felt friendly and caressing. Katie gave a little wriggle. She felt like doing some ballet jumps, or rolling down the slope of the lawn until she landed in a heap at the bottom. But instead she had to stand, still as a rock, with elastic round her legs stretched so tightly it was going to give her red marks. She bent down and shifted the elastic slightly.

'Katie!' Amelia, who had been about to jump, stopped, and regarded her crossly. 'You mustn't move!'

'It hurts! It's too tight!' Katie bent her head round until she could catch a glimpse of the backs of her calves. She spotted a small pink line. 'Look! It's making marks on my skin!'

'Well, stand nearer the chair, then. But keep the elastic tight.' Katie gave a melodramatic sigh and shuffled nearer the chair.

They were playing with a chair because you needed three people for French skipping, and there were only two of them. Sometimes Mummy played with them, but today she was too busy, and had got cross when they asked. So they'd had to drag a chair out into the garden, and thread the elastic round its legs, just like human legs. Now it stretched, two white springy lines, a few inches above the grass. The very sight of it filled Katie with an excited anticipation. She *loved* French skipping. They played it in every single break at school; during lessons she would often put her hand into her pocket and check that the tangled mass of elastic was still safely there.

'Right.' Amelia sounded business-like. She began to jump efficiently over the taut elastic, biting her lip, and planting her feet carefully in exactly the right places. 'Jingle, jangle, centre, spangle,' she chanted. 'Jingle, jangle, out.' She jumped out without even touching the elastic.

'My go,' said Katie hopefully.

'No it isn't,' retorted Amelia. 'Don't you know how to play French skipping?'

'In my class,' said Katie, raising her eyebrows expressively, 'we play so that everybody has one go, and then it's the next person. Mrs Tully said that's the fairest way.' Amelia wasn't impressed.

'That's just for little ones,' she said. 'We play until the person makes a mistake.'

'But you'll never make a mistake!' cried Katie. She scratched the place on her leg where the elastic had been too tight.

'Yes I will, I expect,' said Amelia kindly. 'And anyway,' she added, 'at least you know it's your turn next; I don't think the chair will want to play.' Katie looked at the chair, standing benignly on the grass. She giggled.

'We could ask it,' she began. But Amelia had started jumping again.

'Jingle, jangle, centre, spangle, jingle, jangle, out.'

They had been sent out to play in the garden until their father came to pick them up. Nobody could quite remember what time he'd said he was coming. Amelia thought it was ten, and their mother thought it was ten-thirty, and Katie had been convinced it was quarter to nine, like school, and had actually stood by the door, ready to go, until nine o'clock had come and gone and it was obvious he was coming later.

Amelia had suggested, sensibly, that Mummy should ring Daddy and ask him. But for some reason she didn't want to. She never wanted to ring Daddy. It was always Daddy who rang. He'd rung during the week, and talked to Mummy, and said he was going to take the girls fishing this Sunday. Fishing! Katie had never even *been* fishing. They'd both got very excited and gone down into the cellar and brought up all the nets and buckets they could find. Amelia actually had a fishing-rod that Grandfather had given her, and she'd generously said that Katie could hold it with her if she wanted. Mummy had washed out two jamjars for them, in case there was anything small that they wanted to bring home, and they'd chosen a chocolate bar each as a special treat for their packed lunch.

But all of them, even Mummy, had forgotten that this Sunday was Swimming Day at the Delaneys' house. They *couldn't* miss the Swimming Day. Everyone was going from the village; even people who didn't really like swimming. Amelia briefly wondered what it must be like, to be a person who didn't like swimming. She simply couldn't imagine it. Everyone she knew liked swimming: her, Katie, Mummy, even Daddy when he was really hot.

They'd only remembered about the Swimming Day yesterday, when they bumped into Mrs Delaney at the shops, and she asked if they were coming, and Mummy said that she thought this year, unfortunately, the girls would have to miss it. Katie had nearly started crying right there in the street. Amelia was more grown up than that, but as soon as they were in the car, she'd asked in a desperate voice, 'Couldn't we go to the Swimming Day tomorrow and go fishing another time?' At first Mummy had said no, of course not, in an angry voice. Then, when they got home, she'd said no, but it really was a

11

pity. Then, later, she'd said maybe Daddy wouldn't mind. And last night, as she tucked them into bed, she'd said that as soon as Daddy arrived, she would ask him, and she thought he was sure to agree.

'Jingle, jangle, *out*.' Amelia thumped heavily onto the grass. 'I'm boiling,' she added.

'So'm I,' said Katie quickly. 'I can't *wait* to go swimming.'

'I'm going to dive straight in,' said Amelia. 'I'm not even going to feel it with my toe or anything.'

'So'm I,' said Katie again. 'I'm going to *dive* in.'

'You can't dive,' said Amelia crushingly.

'I can,' retorted Katie. 'I learned it in swimming. You sit on the side and . . .'

'That's not a proper dive.'

'It is!'

'It isn't.'

'It is!' Katie's voice rose in fury. 'It is a proper dive!' Amelia smirked silently. 'I did it the best in my class,' shrilled Katie. 'Mrs Tully said I was a little otter.'

There was a pause. Then Amelia wrinkled her nose superciliously and said, 'Yuck.'

'What?' Katie looked discomfited. 'Why is it yuck?'

'Being an otter is yuck.' Amelia looked at Katie challengingly, and Katie met Amelia's gaze silently for a moment, then she looked away. Amelia's eyes glinted.

'You don't know what an otter is, do you?' she said.

'Yes, I do!'

'What is it, then?'

Katie stared crossly at Amelia. Her mind scrambled over half-imagined pictures. Had Mrs Tully ever actually told her what an otter was? *Otter*. What did it sound like? Into her mind came an image of blue-green water; of silvery streaks of light and a lithe body shooting through the water in a perfect dive.

'It's like a flower fairy,' she said eventually. 'It's a

water fairy. It lives in the water and it's all blue and green.'

Amelia started to crow. 'No, it's not! Katie Kember, you don't know anything!'

'Well, what is it then?' shouted Katie angrily. Amelia brought her face up close to Katie's.

'It's an animal. It's all slithery and hairy and its feet are all webbed and slimy. That's what you are. You thought you were a water fairy!'

Katie sat down on the grass. It didn't occur to her not to believe Amelia. Amelia hardly ever made things up.

'I haven't got slimy feet,' she said, her voice trembling slightly, 'and I'm not all hairy; I've just got normal hair.' She pushed her bright brown fringe off her forehead and looked at Amelia with worried blue eyes. Amelia relented.

'No, but otters are really good at swimming,' she said. 'I expect that's what Mrs Tully meant.'

'Yes, that's what she meant,' said Katie, immensely cheered. 'I'm the best swimmer in my class, you know. Some of them still have *arm-bands*.'

'One boy in my class still has arm-bands,' said Amelia, giggling, 'and he's *nine*.'

'Nine!' echoed Katie scornfully. She was only just seven, and she'd been swimming without arm-bands since last summer.

Suddenly there was the sound of a car pulling up outside the house.

'Daddy!'

'Daddy!'

They both ran around the side of the house. There was their father getting out of the car, as tall as ever, wearing a pair of shorts and a very old-looking blue checked shirt. There was a combination of familiarity and strangeness about the sight of him which made Amelia stop momentarily in her tracks and look away. Katie pushed past her.

'Daddy!' she cried. Their father turned and smiled. And immediately, predictably, Katie burst into noisy, copious tears.

Louise Kember sat in her pretty kitchen and waited for Barnaby to come in. She'd heard the car pull up, heard the girls run out to greet him, and could now hear Katie's muffled sobs. It was nearly five months since Barnaby had moved out, and still Katie wept every time he arrived or left. And every time, a hand seemed to squeeze Louise's heart until fresh painful guilt filled her chest.

Hadn't she been told that it was far better for parents to separate than to stay together, arguing? In those awful few weeks over Christmas, when the rows between her and Barnaby had reached their height, when her frustrations and his suspicions had spilled over into everything they did, contaminating every gesture and giving every seemingly innocuous remark a double-edged meaning, she'd been convinced that when the split did come, it would be a relief for all of them. For her and Barnaby, certainly, but also for the girls.

Larch Tree Cottage wasn't big enough for two shouting parents and two sleeping children; more than once she and Barnaby had been interrupted mid-flow by a white-faced, white-nightied little person at the kitchen door. They would shoot accusing looks at one another as they quickly adopted soothing voices, proffered glasses of water and spoke gaily to Mr Teddy or Mrs Rabbit. And then they would inevitably both go back upstairs with whichever of the girls it was, in a self-conscious togetherness – tucking in and tiptoeing out as though they were once again the young married couple besotted with their first baby.

For a few moments the pretence would last. They would float down the stairs together in a cloud of deliberate good nature, fulfilling the image of the happy, loving, contented parents. But downstairs in the kitchen, the air would be thick with lingering, remembered jibes. The smiles would fade. Barnaby would mutter something incomprehensible about popping to The George for a quick half, and Louise would run a hot bath and weep frustratedly into the foamy water. By the time Barnaby got back she would be in bed, sometimes pretending to be asleep, sometimes sitting up, having formulated in her mind exactly what she wanted to say. But Barnaby would wave her speeches aside.

'I'm too tired, Lou,' he'd say. 'Busy day tomorrow. Can't it wait?'

'No, my life can't wait,' she once hissed back. 'It's been on hold for ten years already.' But Barnaby was already in his automatic, unseeing, unthinking, undressing and going-to-bed mode, and he didn't even reply. Louise stared at him in exasperated anger.

'Listen to me!' she screeched, forgetting the children, forgetting everything but her need to communicate. 'If you really loved me you'd listen to me!' And Barnaby looked up, baffled.

'I do love you,' he said in a low resentful voice, folding up his trousers. 'You know I love you.' And then he stopped and looked away.

And Louise looked away too. Because the truth was that she *did* know that Barnaby loved her. But knowing that Barnaby loved her was no longer enough.

Katie was sitting on the grassy bank outside the cottage next to Barnaby. His arm was round her, and she was juddering slightly, but her tears had dried up. On the other side of Barnaby was Amelia, who felt a bit like crying herself, but was far too grown up.

'That's better,' said Barnaby. He squeezed them both

15

tightly so their faces were squashed against his shirt. After a moment Katie started to wriggle.

'I can't breathe,' she gasped dramatically. Amelia said nothing. She felt safe, all squashed up against Daddy, smelling his smell and hearing his laugh. Of course, Mummy hugged them all the time, but it wasn't the same. It wasn't so . . . cosy. Her face was pressed up against a shirt button and her neck was a bit twisted, but still she could have stayed safely inside Daddy's hug all morning.

But Barnaby was letting go of them and reaching into the car.

'Here you are, you two,' he said, tossing a package into each lap. 'Vital equipment for the day.' The two girls began to unwrap their parcels and Barnaby watched, a pleased smile on his face. He'd bought each of them a present. For Katie he'd bought a small collapsible fishing-rod, and for Amelia, who already had a fishing-rod, he'd bought a smart little fishing-tackle box.

Katie unwrapped hers first. She squealed in delight and leaped up.

'Goody gum drops! A real fishing-rod! You can keep your smelly old rod, Amelia!'

But Amelia looked up from her tackle box in sudden realization, and said in dismay, 'What about going swimming?'

'What about it?' said Barnaby easily. 'I'm afraid you'll have to leave that to the fish. You might be able to paddle, though.'

'No, silly!' Katie dropped her fishing-rod on the ground and rushed over to Barnaby. 'Swimming Day, at Mrs Delaney's house! Can we go instead of fishing?'

Barnaby tried to hide his surprise.

'What! Don't you want to go fishing?'

'I want to go *swimming*,' said Katie coaxingly. 'It's so *hot*!'

By way of illustration she began to fan her legs with

the skirt of her dress. It was a familiar-looking pink and white striped dress; a cast-off of Amelia's, Barnaby abruptly realized. He had a sudden memory of a small Amelia wearing it, leaving for a birthday party, excitedly clutching a present, while an even smaller Katie jealously watched from the stairs.

'Mummy said you wouldn't mind,' offered Amelia. She tried to signal to Katie to shut up. She would make Daddy cross if she wasn't careful, and then they'd never be allowed to go swimming. 'We could go fishing next week,' she suggested. Abruptly, she remembered. 'And thank you for the lovely present,' she added.

'Yes, thank you, Daddy,' said Katie quickly. She picked up her fishing-rod and stroked it tenderly. 'For my lovely fishing-rod.' She looked up. 'But can we go swimming? Please? *Please?*'

'I don't know yet,' said Barnaby, trying to keep his temper. 'I'll go and talk to Mummy.'

Louise had begun rather self-consciously to make some coffee, waiting for the moment when Barnaby would come in. She moved gracefully around the kitchen, a careless half smile on her lips, noting with pleasure the pretty citrus-tree stencils which she had carefully painted onto the pine back door the week before. Those, and the new curtains, splashed brightly with orange and yellow flowers, had really lifted the kitchen, she thought to herself. Next she intended to stencil the bannisters, and maybe even the sitting-room. Larch Tree Cottage had, in the ten years they'd lived there, always been pretty, in a predictable old-fashioned sort of way, but Louise was now determined to transform it into something different and beautiful; something which people would look at with admiration.

As she heard Barnaby's heavy tread in the hallway, she glanced quickly around, as though to reaffirm in her mind the image which she presented. A happy, fulfilled, independent woman, at home in her own beautiful kitchen.

Nevertheless, she turned away as he got nearer, and turned on the coffee-grinder. Her hand trembled slightly as she pressed the top down, and the electrical shriek meant that she couldn't hear his greeting.

'Louise!' As she released the pressure on the coffee-grinder and the noise died down, Barnaby's voice sounded aggressively loud. Louise slowly turned. A jerk of fearful emotion rose up inside her, then almost immediately subsided.

'Hello, Barnaby,' she said in carefully modulated tones.

'What's all this nonsense about going swimming?'

As he heard his own rough voice, Barnaby knew he was playing this wrong; rushing in angrily instead of asking reasonably, but suddenly he felt very hurt. He'd planned this fishing expedition carefully; he'd been looking forward to it ever since he'd had the idea. The cheerful disregard with which his daughters had abandoned the idea wasn't their fault – they were only kids; but Louise should have been more thoughtful. An angry resentment grew inside him as he looked at her, half turned away, feathery blond fronds of hair masking her expression. Was she trying to sabotage his only time with the girls? Was she turning them against him? A raw emotional wound, deep inside him, began to throb. His breathing quickened.

Louise's head whipped round. She took in Barnaby's accusing expression and flushed slightly.

'It's not nonsense,' she said, allowing her voice to rise slightly. 'They want to go to the Delaneys' to swim.' She paused. 'I don't blame them. It's going to be a boiling hot day.'

She tipped ground coffee from the grinder into a cafetière and poured on hot water. A delicious smell filled the kitchen.

'Mummy!' Katie's piercing voice came in from the hall. 'Can we have a drink?' There was the sound of sandals clattering against floorboards, and suddenly the girls were in the kitchen.

'I'll pour them some Ribena,' said Barnaby.

'Actually,' said Louise, 'we don't have Ribena any more.' Barnaby stopped still, hand reaching towards the cupboard. 'Water will do,' added Louise.

'What's wrong with Ribena?' demanded Barnaby. He flashed a quick encouraging grin at Amelia.

'What's wrong with Ribena?' Amelia echoed.

'It's bad for your teeth,' said Louise firmly, ignoring Barnaby. 'You know that.'

'What's wrong with Ribena?' Amelia repeated, lolling against a kitchen cupboard.

'I want Ri-bee-na,' said Katie.

'I can't blame them,' said Barnaby.

'Or Tango,' said Katie, encouraged. 'Or Sprite. I *love* Sprite . . .'

'All right!' Louise shouted. There was a sudden silence. Louise scrabbled inside a jar on the work-surface.

'Go on, both of you, along to Mrs Potter's shop, and buy yourself a fizzy drink.' Katie and Amelia stared at her uncertainly. 'Go on,' repeated Louise. Her voice trembled slightly. 'Since it's such a hot day. As a treat. Stay on the grassy path and come straight back.'

'And then will we go swimming?' said Katie.

'Maybe,' said Louise. She handed some coins to Amelia. 'It depends what Daddy says.'

When they'd gone, there was silence. Louise slowly pushed down the plunger of the cafetière, lips tight. She stared down into its gleaming chrome surface for a minute, formulating words. Then she looked up.

'I would appreciate it, Barnaby,' she said deliberately, 'if you would try not to undermine *everything* I do.'

'I don't!' retorted Barnaby angrily. 'I wasn't to know

you'd suddenly taken against Ribena. How the hell was I supposed to know?' There was a pause. Louise poured the steaming coffee into mugs.

'And anyway,' added Barnaby, remembering, with a sudden resentful surge, the reason for his anger, 'I'd appreciate it if you didn't muscle in on my time with the girls.'

'I'm not! How can you say that? They're the ones who want to go swimming, not me!'

'What, so you aren't going swimming?'

'I probably will go, as a matter of fact,' said Louise, 'but I wasn't planning to take them.'

'Planning to take someone else, were you?' said Barnaby, with a sudden sneer. 'I wonder who?' Louise flushed.

'That's unfair, Barnaby.'

'It's perfectly fair!' Barnaby's voice was getting louder and louder. 'If you want to go swimming with lover boy, then I don't want to get in your way.'

Louise's eyes swivelled, before she could stop them, towards a new shiny photograph, freshly pinned up on the notice-board behind the door. Barnaby's gaze followed. His heart gave an unpleasant thud. The picture was of Louise, smiling, standing next to an elegant young man with smooth brown skin and glossy dark hair, on the steps of some grand-looking building that Barnaby didn't recognize. They were both in evening dress; Louise wore a silky blue dress that Barnaby had never seen before. The man wore a double-breasted dinner jacket; his patent-leather dress shoes were impeccably polished and his hair had a confident well-groomed sheen. As he stared, unable to move his eyes away, Barnaby's chest grew heavy with despair and loathing. He scanned the picture bitterly, as though searching for details, for clues; trying not to notice the excited happy look in Louise's face as she stood, with a strange man, in a strange place, smiling for a strange photographer.

Abruptly, he turned to Louise. 'You've had your hair cut.'

Louise, who had been expecting something more aggressive than that, looked surprised.

'Yes,' she said. Her hand moved up to her neck. 'Do you like it?'

'It makes you look . . . sexy.'

Barnaby sounded so gloomy that Louise smiled, in spite of herself.

'Isn't that good? Don't you like me looking sexy?' She was moving on to dangerous ground, but Barnaby didn't take the bait. He was staring at her with miserable blue eyes.

'You look like someone else's idea of sexy, not mine.'

Louise didn't know what to say. She took a sip of coffee. Barnaby slumped in his chair as though in sudden defeat.

For a few minutes they sat still, in almost companionable silence. Louise's thoughts gradually loosened themselves from the current situation and began to float idly around her mind like dust particles in the sunshine, bouncing quickly away whenever she inadvertently hit on anything too painful or serious. Sitting, sipping her coffee, feeling the sunshine warm on her face, she could almost forget about everything else. Meanwhile Barnaby sat, in spite of himself, blackly imagining Louise in a pair of strong dinner-jacketed arms; dancing, whirling, laughing, being happy, how *could* she?

Suddenly there was a rattling at the back door. Louise looked up. Katie was beaming in through the kitchen window, triumphantly clutching a shiny can. The door opened and Amelia bounded in.

'We had a lift,' she said breathlessly, 'from Mrs Seddon-Wilson. She said, were we going to the swimming?'

'And we said, yes we were, nearly,' said Katie. She danced over to Barnaby. 'Are we going, Daddy? Are we going swimming?'

'We haven't talked about it yet,' said Louise quickly.

'You *must* have!' said Katie in astonishment. 'You were talking all that time, when we went to the shop and got our drinks . . . They didn't have any Sprite,' she added sorrowfully, 'but I got Fanta.' She offered her can to Louise.

'May you open my drink for me?'

'In a minute,' said Louise, distractedly.

'Are we going swimming, Mummy?' asked Amelia anxiously. 'Mrs Seddon-Wilson said it was going to be tremendous fun.'

'*Tremendous* fun,' echoed Katie, 'and I told her about my new swimming-suit and she said it sounded lovely.'

'What about it, Barnaby?' Louise adopted a brisk businesslike voice. 'Can they go swimming?' Barnaby looked up. His face was pink.

'I think the girls and I should go fishing as planned,' he said stoutly. He looked at Katie. 'Come on, Katkin. Don't you want to use your new rod?'

'Yes, I do,' said Katie simply. 'I want to go fishing, but I want to go swimming, too.'

'But you go swimming every week at school,' said Barnaby, trying not to sound hectoring.

'I know we do, Daddy,' said Amelia, in an attempt to mollify, 'but this swimming is different. It's the Swimming Day. It only happens once a year.'

'Well, tell you what,' said Barnaby, giving her a wide smile. 'I'll speak to Hugh, and get him to invite us over to swim another day; just us. How about that?' Amelia looked down and swung her foot.

'It won't be the same,' she said in barely audible tones. Barnaby's good humour snapped.

'Why not?' he suddenly bellowed. 'Why is it so important that you go swimming today? What's wrong

22

with the lot of you?' Louise's eyes flashed.

'There's nothing wrong with the girls,' she said icily, 'just because they want to spend a nice hot day swimming with their friends.' She put a proprietorial hand on Amelia's shoulder. Amelia looked at the floor. Suddenly Katie gave a sob.

'I'll go fishing, Daddy! I'll go fishing with you! Where's my rod?' She fumbled with the back door and rushed out into the garden.

'Oh great,' said Louise curtly. 'Well, if you want to blackmail them into going with you, that's fine.'

'How dare you!' Barnaby drew an angry breath. His cheeks had flushed dark red, and his forehead had begun to glisten. 'It's nothing to do with blackmail. Katie wants to come fishing. So would Amelia, if you hadn't . . .'

'If I hadn't what?' Louise's grip tightened on Amelia's shoulder. 'If I hadn't what, Barnaby?'

Barnaby looked at the two of them, mother and daughter, and suddenly a defeated look came into his eyes. 'Nothing,' he muttered.

Then the back door opened and Katie was in the kitchen again. She was holding her rod in one hand and a piece of tangled elastic in the other. 'I nearly couldn't find my French skipping,' she said breathlessly.

'Are you sure you want to go fishing?' said Louise, ignoring Barnaby's glance.

'Yes, I'm *quite* sure,' said Katie grandly. 'And anyway, I've got my swimming-suit on under my dress, so I can go swimming with the little fishes.' Barnaby began to say something, then stopped.

'All right,' said Louise. 'Well, we'll see you later, then.' She looked at Barnaby. 'Not too late.'

Barnaby looked at Amelia. He gave her a friendly smile.

'How about you, Amelia? Want to come fishing?'

23

Amelia blushed. She looked up at Louise, then back at Barnaby.

'Not really,' she said in a small voice. 'I want to go swimming. Do you mind, Daddy?' Barnaby's cheerful expression barely faltered.

'Well,' he said slowly, 'of course I'd love you to come with us, but not if you'd rather go swimming instead. You should just do what you enjoy the most.'

'I enjoy *fishing* the most,' announced Katie, brandishing her rod. 'I hate nasty old swimming.'

'You love swimming,' objected Louise.

'Not any more,' retorted Katie. She looked up at Barnaby. 'Me and Daddy hate swimming, don't we, Daddy?' Louise's lips tightened.

'Well, Katie,' she said, 'you're a big girl now, you can make your own decision. I just hope you don't regret it.'

'What's regret?' asked Katie immediately.

'It's to look back on something you've done,' said Barnaby, 'and wish you hadn't done it. You won't do that, will you, Katkin?' But Katie wasn't listening. She had begun to do her birdcage dance around the kitchen, using the fishing-rod instead of her birdcage. As she danced, she began to hum the tune.

'We won't regret going swimming,' said Amelia bravely. 'Will we, Mummy?'

'No,' said Louise, 'I shouldn't think we will. Katie, stop dancing, and go with Daddy.' Katie stopped, foot still pointed out.

'I don't regret going fishing,' she said.

'You haven't been yet,' pointed out Amelia.

'So what?' said Katie, rudely.

'Come on,' said Barnaby, impatiently. 'Go and get in the car, Katie.' He grinned briefly at Amelia. 'I'll see you this evening,' he said, 'and we'll tell each other about our day.'

When he had left the kitchen, Amelia's chin began to wobble. She suddenly felt very unsure of herself. The

kitchen seemed empty and silent now that Daddy and
Katie had gone, and she wasn't sure that she'd made the
right decision. She looked up at Mummy for a
comforting glance, but Mummy was staring at something on the notice-board. Amelia followed her gaze. It
was a photograph of Mummy and Cassian.

'Is Cassian coming swimming, Mummy?' she asked,
falteringly. Louise's head whipped round.

'No!' she said. Then, at the sight of Amelia's anxious
face, her voice softened. 'No,' she repeated, 'he's in
London.'

'Oh.' Amelia wasn't quite sure why, but this piece of
news made her feel a bit better about going swimming
with Mummy instead of fishing with Daddy. 'Oh,' she
said again. Louise suddenly smiled.

'So we'll have a lovely day, just the two of us,' she
said, 'swimming and getting brown. Mummy and
Amelia. What do you think?'

Into Amelia's mind appeared a blissful image of a blue
swimming-pool glittering in the sunlight, herself
floating effortlessly in the middle of it. She looked
happily up at Louise.

'I think, yes please,' she said.

'Well, go and get your things, then,' said Louise
brightly. 'We want to make all we can out of the day.'

Amelia clattered out of the kitchen and thudded up
the narrow cottage stairs. And Louise followed at a more
leisurely pace, humming gaily to herself and wondering
which sun-hat she should take with her, and trying as
hard as she could to dispel from her mind the lingering
image of Barnaby's indignant, angry, wounded face.

Chapter Two

Hugh and Ursula Delaney had first opened their swimming-pool for charity more than twenty years ago, when their two sons were children and the people at Melbrook Place – the largest house in the village – were refusing to hold a village fête. Devenish House, the Delaneys' own house, was not in quite the same league as Melbrook Place, but it was the second biggest house in the village – and it had a swimming-pool.

The first Swimming Day had been on a blisteringly hot day, at a time when the nearest public swimming-bath was thirty miles away in Braybury, full of chlorine, and housed in an unpleasantly green-tiled building. Parents and children alike, unused to the luxury of an outside heated pool, had thrown themselves into the blue water like joyous seals, tumbling and splashing with the determination of those who know they have a limited amount of time for pleasure. Pictures of the occasion in the Delaneys' photograph album showed women and men in baggy pre-Lycra swimming-suits emblazoned with orange flowers and purple swirls, leaping from the diving-board, or floating on their backs, or sitting round the side of the pool, legs dangling in the depths, unwilling to relinquish the water for a moment. And all around them – in the water, under the water, jumping and diving and ducking and shrieking – were the children. Some, unable to swim, clutched in fearful delight to the edge of the pool, while parents coaxed them further in, others floated in pleasurable torpor, buoyed up by shiny rubber rings and arm-bands. Some had proper bathing-suits; many did not. Many had never been swimming before in their lives.

In the two decades since then everything had changed. The people of Melbrook now benefited from a shiny new leisure centre in nearby Linningford, complete with indoor and outdoor pools, Jacuzzi, steam-room and sauna. All the children of the village could swim as a matter of course. The appeal of a simple swimming-pool – by now rather old, and with no accompanying exercise bikes or health bar – had rather diminished. Meanwhile, new people had moved into Melbrook Place and declared themselves more than happy to reintroduce a Melbrook Place fête. There was really no need for the Swimming Day to happen any more.

But the people of Melbrook were both loyal and conservative. When Hugh and Ursula had tentatively suggested, six or seven years ago, that the Swimming Days had outlived their function, there had been a general outcry. People whom Hugh and Ursula had never met; people who, as far as they were aware, had never even been to one of the Swimming Days, had accosted them in the street, and asked anxiously whether the rumours were really true. The residents of the new development just outside the village had drawn up a petition. One young woman, who had only been living in Melbrook for a few months, had waited for Ursula outside church one Sunday, and proceeded to berate her soundly for eroding the character of the village.

In the end it hadn't been worth the struggle. Hugh and Ursula had capitulated and agreed to carry on; now it seemed as though the Swimming Days would go on for ever.

There was only one year in which they had not held a Swimming Day. Three years before, Simon, their younger son, had died, suddenly, of a brain tumour, at the age of twenty-eight.

He died in February, on a cold grey day, and the coldness stayed inside Hugh and Ursula all year. After the funeral they stayed inside their house, avoiding the world, while outside the blossoms opened and the air grew warm and the sun played on the water of their swimming-pool. Then, when the leaves began to turn and the air grew cooler, they packed up and went to their little house in France. Hugh left his wine-importing business ticking over in the hands of his assistant. Ursula told people not to expect them back for Christmas.

They spoke to nobody. Matthew, their elder son, was in Hong Kong, working hard and coping with his grief as best he could on his own. Their own families, based respectively in Derbyshire and Scotland, were both too far away to have known Simon properly and too close to provide dispassionate comfort.

The only one who understood was Meredith. Their daughter-in-law; Simon's widow.

He had met her at a gallery opening; she was an artist from America, via most cities in Europe. She was slightly older and slightly cleverer than him, and quite a lot richer. Hugh found her fascinating; Ursula found her frightening. The wedding had been at a register office in London; Meredith had worn a black tailcoat and top hat and at the reception had decorated, in dark-red ink, the shirt-back of Simon's enchanted managing director.

After Simon's funeral, Hugh and Ursula looked at Meredith's blue-white face, her long lank hair and shaking hands, and pressed her warmly to stay with them for a while. Ursula filled her room with flowers and pot-pourri, and ran her hot baths; Hugh poured her deep glasses of whisky and offered her cigarettes. But after two days she disappeared. They received a postcard from the airport; Meredith had returned to her native San Francisco.

For months after that they heard nothing from her. They had not had the chance to get to know her very well; there were no grandchildren to be considered; now it seemed that Meredith, too, had left their lives for ever.

Until she turned up in France. 'I didn't realize you guys'd run away too,' were her first words. Her face was still white; she looked worse than she had done after the funeral. 'The States didn't work,' was all she would say.

They spent an uneasy first week all together in the cottage, skirting and hesitating and avoiding the subject of Simon. Then, one evening, as the windows of the little kitchen fogged up with condensation and Hugh built up the fire in the grate, Meredith began to talk. She talked about Simon, about herself, about herself and Simon, about herself and her family. Her hands shook. She smoked furiously. She made challenging assertions about Simon, then stared from Ursula's face to Hugh's face and back again, looking for a reaction. Around midnight, she began to cry. Ursula, strung up, confused and bewildered by most of what Meredith was saying, began to cry too. Hugh leaned across the table and clasped Meredith's hands tightly in his own. 'Please don't stop,' he said shakily. 'Don't stop. And please don't go away again.'

They stayed in France, all together, until the first anniversary of Simon's death had passed. Hugh began to communicate with his assistant in England, Meredith began to draw again, but it was Ursula who decided, with uncharacteristic firmness, as February turned into March and another spring began, that it was time for them to go home.

They arrived back in Melbrook on a bright, clear, sharp morning. While Hugh and Ursula unpacked, Meredith wandered around the house and garden as though she'd never been there before. Eventually she came inside.

'You got two barns here,' she stated.

'That's right,' said Hugh, surprised. 'Although, actually, one's a stable.' Meredith waved her hands at him impatiently. 'What I want to know is', she said, 'which one can be my studio?'

A bubble of joy rose up inside Hugh. Meredith had always been vague about her plans. He and Ursula had felt sure she would soon announce her intention to move back to London – or further. After all, they had reasoned miserably to each other, what on earth was there to keep a young, independent, vibrant woman like Meredith in a village like Melbrook? Now he tried to catch Ursula's eye. She was looking confusedly at Meredith.

'Does that mean . . .' she began. Hugh broke her off.

'Whichever one you want,' he said, unable to keep the delight out of his voice. 'Have both. Have the whole house.'

Meredith had lived with them ever since. When Matthew got married in Hong Kong, she designed an outfit for Ursula and went to the wedding with them. When Hugh took Ursula on a wine-tasting trip around Burgundy, Meredith came too.

Every so often she would take off on her own – to London, or Amsterdam, or New York; once for a month to Sydney. During those times, while she was away, the atmosphere was taut, the shared unspoken fear hanging over the house like an exam result. But she always came back to her red-painted bedroom, and her gold-painted bathroom, and her muralled sitting-room. And relief would flood painfully through Hugh, and he would block from his mind the gnawing truth that, sooner or later, Meredith was going to find someone to share her life with, and was going to leave him and Ursula alone again, to live their lives as they did before, but no longer knowing quite how to go about it.

It was Meredith who had masterminded the first Swimming Day after Simon's death. That year the weather was unremittingly gloomy throughout May; Hugh and Ursula expected that few people would turn up. But they were reckoning without the curiosity of the village. Everyone had heard about Meredith; few had met her. As family after family trooped in, their faces lit up as they saw the object of their visit sitting at the entrance, smiling rather ferociously as donations dropped into the plastic pot. It really was too cold to swim that year; only the hardiest children ventured into the pool. But it wasn't too cold to sit and stare at Meredith and tell each other what a striking girl she was, and what a tragedy the whole thing had been.

And now Meredith was as much part of the Delaneys' Swimming Day as Ursula's elderflower cordial. This year, expecting a large crowd, she had enlisted the help of the vicar's wife, Frances Mold, at the entrance table. After a shaky first meeting at Simon's funeral, at which Meredith pronounced herself 'Agnostic-stroke-Atheist-stroke (if anything) Buddhist, I guess', these two had developed an unlikely friendship, and could often be seen striding the fields together; a tweed skirt and brogues alongside a pair of velvet jodhpurs and riding boots.

Hugh and Ursula were having a cup of coffee in the conservatory when Meredith poked her head through the window.

'Lots of people are here already,' she said, gesturing behind her.

'So we can see,' said Hugh. 'Jolly good. We'll come out in a minute and help.'

'What I came for', said Meredith, 'was that list of people who have paid already.' She looked at Ursula. 'You know the one? You had it yesterday.'

'Ah yes,' said Ursula vaguely, 'the list.' She patted her

31

silvery blond hair, arranged becomingly in a French pleat, and took a sip of coffee.

'Do you know where the list is?' asked Meredith. 'Did you find it last night?'

'Not *last* night, no,' said Ursula, frowning slightly. 'Wasn't it on the dresser?' She looked at Meredith with large blue eyes, bright in the greenish gloom of the conservatory.

'No, Ursula,' said Meredith patiently. 'Don't you remember? We were talking about it last night. I couldn't find it, and you said you'd taken it off the dresser to add a couple of names, and you said you'd look for it.'

'Ah yes,' said Ursula, 'now I remember.'

'Did you look for it?' prompted Meredith.

'I may have had a little search,' said Ursula unconvincingly. Meredith exchanged glances with Hugh. This was the sort of behaviour that used to drive Simon mad with his mother, she thought. And before she could stop it, a familiar series of pictures flashed briefly through her mind: Simon, the wedding, Simon in hospital, the funeral. She felt a short pang of pain, but in a moment her mind was clear again; the memories packaged neatly away. All that was left behind was a strong feeling of fondness for Ursula.

'But you didn't find it,' she suggested.

'I don't think I did,' said Ursula eventually. 'But I'll go and have a look for it now, shall I?' She screwed up her face in thought. 'You know, dear, I'm sure it's on the dresser.'

'It's not on the dresser, Ursula,' said Meredith, grinning at her. 'That's the whole point. I already looked there.'

'Well, dear, you never know; you might have missed it,' said Ursula in gently obstinate tones. She put down her coffee cup on a bamboo table, and stood up. A white and green print crêpe de Chine dress rustled prettily in soft folds around her. 'I'll go and look for it straight away,' she announced.

'OK then,' said Meredith, 'and maybe, Hugh, you could have a look too? Somewhere other than the dresser?' Hugh winked at her.

'I'll see what I can do,' he said.

By the time Louise and Amelia arrived at Devenish House, Hugh had found the list lurking behind an ormolu clock on the dining-room mantelpiece. Meredith had gone to change into her swimming things, and Ursula was presiding over the entrance table, together with Frances Mold.

Frances's husband, the Revd Alan Mold, was, that morning, taking family service in the neighbouring village of Tranton. He was in charge of both parishes – Melbrook and Tranton – and alternated between them every Sunday. This arrangement had been in existence for nearly ten years, and at first the general idea had been that the congregation from Melbrook would follow him to Tranton every other Sunday, and the congregation from Tranton would reciprocate. In practice, however, the arrangement was cheerfully regarded as a good excuse to attend church only once a fortnight.

The only person who regularly accompanied Alan to Tranton was Frances herself. However, this morning, even she had forgone the family service in favour of a quick eight o'clock communion, in order to be free to help the Delaneys. Now she sat, chatting cheerfully to Ursula at the entrance table, looking about her with a pleasant anticipation.

Although labelled 'The Entrance Table', there was, in fact, no obvious place of entrance to the swimming-pool of Devenish House. From the conservatory and French windows of the house, the garden sloped and stepped in a vague Italianate fashion, embellished with carved stone walls, urns and slabs, until the ground flattened out a few hundred yards from the house. And here, framed by a decorative paving area and, beyond, endless smooth lawns, was the swimming-pool – cool, blue and shaped like a kidney bean. It had been installed by the people who lived in Devenish House before the Delaneys, at a time when the kidney-shaped swimming-pool was the ultimate in status symbols. Many times since moving in, Hugh had threatened to fill it in; to replace it with something oblong and functional and further away from the house, or even with nothing at all.

'That pool could be a putting-green, you know,' he would exclaim, on days when the tarpaulin cover flapped in the wind and the very idea of plunging into anything cooler than a hot bath brought on a shiver. 'It could be something useful. Or at least tasteful.'

'Count your lucky stars,' Meredith had retorted the first time she heard him. 'It could be painted black and in the shape of a penis.'

As Louise approached the entrance table, Ursula looked up.

'Louise, dear! How lovely to see you! And Amelia! No Katie?'

'Katie's gone fishing for the day with Barnaby,' said Louise shortly.

'Oh dear,' said Ursula, her face falling slightly. 'Hugh will be sad not to see Barnaby.' She paused. 'But I can quite see that it would be a little awkward . . .'

She broke off and looked from Louise to Amelia. Only recently had Meredith managed to persuade Ursula that it was really true about the Kembers splitting up, not just malicious village gossip, and when finally convinced, Ursula had been most upset. 'I find it terribly sad,' she said vaguely. 'I suppose . . .' She paused and adopted a delicate tone. 'I suppose you find it very *painful* to see Barnaby.'

'Not particularly,' said Louise tightly.

She glanced at Frances Mold, who smiled back sympathetically and said in a hurried, cheerful voice, 'Hello, Amelia! How nice to see you!' But Ursula was lost in her own hazy reflections.

'Poor dear Barnaby,' she said without thinking. Then, realizing what she had said, she gave a little start. 'Oh, Louise! My dear, I didn't mean . . .'

'It's quite all right,' said Louise shortly. She opened her purse and handed Frances Mold a note. 'Here; that's right, isn't it?'

'Yes, exactly right.' Frances gave Louise an apologetic glance. 'See you later.'

'Maybe,' said Louise, discouragingly, and stalked off. She was, she realized, being unfair to poor Frances, who was the most tactful creature in the village. But Ursula's foolish remarks had, today, for some reason touched Louise on the raw. She clenched her fists angrily by her sides as she strode towards the swimming-pool, and felt an angry frown crease her forehead.

'Stupid fool,' she muttered crossly. 'Stupid, stupid, stupid.'

Louise had never been quite as friendly with Ursula as Barnaby was with Hugh. The two men had become friends years before, when Amelia was a baby. Barnaby had overheard Hugh talking in The George about some hedging that needed doing on his land, and immediately offered to help; Hugh had reciprocated with a case of burgundy. After that, the two men had fallen into an easy, relaxed friendship, and Louise had made an honest attempt to forge the same kind of relationship with Ursula. But it had not been a great success. Louise found Ursula rather old, rather dull, and exceedingly stupid. When she started to fuss irritatingly over first Amelia and then Katie, Louise began to find more and more excuses not to accompany Barnaby to Devenish House.

35

And then everything had changed – with the dreadful death of the Delaneys' son, and the year they'd spent abroad, and the arrival of Meredith.

Louise had not taken to Meredith. At their very first meeting, Meredith had scowled at Louise's carefully composed expressions of sympathy and stalked off, black hair streaming behind her. She'd apologized later, but Louise already felt slighted. And ever since then, Louise had always sensed, perhaps unfairly, that Meredith looked down on her, laughed at her, even, for leading such a conventional unchallenging existence.

Since it was not safe to visit Devenish House without coming across Meredith, Louise had found herself seeing Ursula less and less frequently. Barnaby and Hugh were still good friends, but Barnaby often observed, ruefully, that Hugh was in less need of company these days. With Meredith there, the Delaney family had become far more self-sufficient than before.

Daisy Phillips arrived at Devenish House slightly after eleven, reached the middle of the drive, and then stopped, stricken with sudden nerves.

She had never been to the Delaneys' house before. Her parents had only bought the cottage in Melbrook a few months ago, and they hadn't really got to know anybody in the village. But Mrs Mold had told her to be sure to come to the Swimming Day, and said she would introduce her to everyone. Daisy liked Mrs Mold. She was a piano teacher, as well as the vicar's wife, and she had passed by the cottage one day as Daisy was practising. Immediately she had come down the path and knocked on the door.

'A pianist! In Melbrook!' she had exclaimed. 'What luck!'

Daisy was going to the Royal Academy of Music in the autumn. She had spent most of this academic year in Bologna, studying with Arturo Fosci, and picking up a little Italian. But then she'd come back to England, and all of a sudden there had arisen the problem of where Daisy should live. With her busy parents both working from their tranquil London flat, she couldn't really live there and practise. 'It was fine when it was just the school holidays,' her father had explained kindly, 'but if it's going to be for several months on end . . .' And then his mobile phone had rung, and he'd broken off to answer, and Daisy had stood waiting for him to finish, until he put his hand over the mouthpiece and said, 'We'll talk about it later, Daisy.'

One of her brothers lived in London, but in a tiny flat with room-mates and no space for a piano; the other was travelling round the world. In the autumn she would be able to practise at the Academy, but until then, she really needed somewhere of her own, where the noise didn't matter. For a while it had seemed as though she was going to have to find her own flat in London, or maybe rent a studio, and then suddenly, at supper one evening, her mother exclaimed, 'Of course, the cottage!'

'What cottage?' said Daisy.

'The cottage in Melbrook,' said her father. 'We bought it while you were in Italy. It's very pretty.'

'And tax efficient,' added her mother. She took a forkful of baby spinach. 'We don't actually go there very much.'

'We don't actually go there ever, you mean,' said her father.

'We went once,' retorted her mother. 'Don't you remember? It was bloody freezing.' She shuddered.

'Anyway,' said her father. 'What about it?'

'Daisy could live there and practise to her heart's content,' said her mother. Her eyes began to gleam. 'And if she was down on the employee roll . . .'

'She already is,' put in her father.

'. . . then all her expenses would be tax-deductible. What about it, Daisy?'

'You'll never fit Daisy's piano into that cottage,' her father had objected, before Daisy could reply.

'Yes you will!' her mother had retorted. 'Of course you will. That sitting-room's jolly big!'

'And so is a grand piano.'

'Not that big:'

'When was the last time you looked at one closely?'

And so they'd argued all through supper. Daisy's mother went and fetched the floor plan of the cottage and drew a grand piano into the sitting-room, fitting snugly next to the fireplace. Her father leaned back in his chair and roared with laughter.

'What's that supposed to be? A baby grand? Honestly, Diana, you're miles out. Now, *this* is where it could go, but it might be a tight squeeze . . .'

By the end of the evening the floor plan was criss-crossed with outlines of pianos, and the question of whether or not Daisy actually wanted to live in the cottage had been forgotten. And the next evening her mother announced that she'd spoken to the estate agent, who had confirmed that there had indeed once been a grand piano in the sitting-room.

'So there you are,' said her mother triumphantly to Daisy. 'All sorted. Now we just have to move you down there.'

Daisy had been down there now for three weeks and was starting to get used to it. Living on her own was all right – she'd done that in Bologna – and so was practising for most of the day, but not knowing anybody nearby was very strange. All her life she'd been used to having friends about, either at school, or in London; even in Bologna there had always been the other students to talk to. It wasn't as if she was a particularly sociable person. In fact, at school, she'd always been considered a loner. But being a loner when you were surrounded by 400 other girls was, she thought, a different matter from being a loner when you were surrounded by empty fields.

Her parents kept asking her if she'd started talking to the villagers.

'I'm sure they're very friendly,' her mother would say, her voice coming, crisp and familiar, down the phone line. 'Just ask them how the crops are growing, or how their cows are doing . . .'

'Lots of them live in bungalows,' Daisy objected, but her mother wasn't listening.

'And remember, you're *working* there for us, in case anyone asks.'

Daisy had remembered that when Mrs Mold had arrived.

'I'm doing some work for my parents,' she blurted out quickly, as Mrs Mold ran her hands lovingly over the curves of her piano. 'For their company. It's a management consultancy.' But Mrs Mold wasn't listening.

'A Bösendorfer. You lucky thing. Do you mind if I have a play?'

Mrs Mold wasn't actually terribly good at the piano, Daisy thought now, as she looked up at the windows of Devenish House, shiny and opaque in the sun. But she seemed very kind, and it would be nice to see her today.

She took a few steps back, until she was suddenly out of the shade of a huge rhododendron bush, and the sun was beating down on her face. She was sure today was the Swimming Day, but where was it all happening? Was she supposed to go round the side? What if she was somehow at the wrong house? She imagined herself bursting round the side of the house into a stranger's garden, startling some innocent family drinking coffee on the lawn.

She clutched her swimming things more tightly. Her mother's voice, firm and impatient, floated into her mind. 'For heaven's sake, Daisy. Just ring the bell and ask. They won't eat you.'

The dark-blue front door was set in a rather grand porch, with grey pillars and a curved stone pediment and a bell-pull made from wrought iron. While she waited for someone to come to the door, Daisy looked around for clues, but the only other thing in the porch with her was a boot scraper shaped like a hedgehog; nothing about swimming. This was probably the wrong house. There were probably two Devenish Houses, she thought. Or maybe an Old Devenish House and a New Devenish House . . .

'Hello?' It was a man, with grey hair and a brown face and a jolly expression.

'H-hello.' Daisy couldn't prevent her voice from trembling. 'I was told . . .' Suddenly she was lost for words. Was she really about to tell a strange man that she wanted to come and swim in his swimming-pool?

'Have you come for the swimming?' Hugh said, helpfully.

'Y-yes!' said Daisy thankfully. 'My name's Daisy Phillips. Mrs Mold told me . . .'

'Ah, of course! Frances!' said Hugh. 'Well, you're very welcome!'

Daisy looked helplessly at him. Suddenly Hugh's expression changed.

'The signs *are* up, aren't they?' he said.

'S-signs?' Hugh darted out into the drive.

'I might have known it! Ask her to do *anything* . . . Look, I'm sorry about this,' said Hugh. 'There should have been signs telling you where to go. The pool's through there.'

'Oh good,' said Daisy, with relief. 'And w-where should I get changed?'

Hugh looked again at Daisy Phillips. She was a tall girl, about eighteen, he guessed, with clouds of dark hair floating down to her waist, and a pale, pale complexion. Her dark eyes flew downwards at his gaze; her hands rubbed one another anxiously; one whiteespadrilled toe nervously circled the blue and green tiles of the porch. He tried to imagine this girl changing nonchalantly amongst the other ladies of the village in the sweaty, rubbery atmosphere of the changing tent and failed.

'Well,' he said slowly, 'quite a lot of people come already changed, so why don't you use one of our bedrooms?'

'Really? Are you sure that's all right?'

'Quite all right,' said Hugh heartily. He felt an unaccountable need to reassure her. 'Now,' he said, as though to a six-year-old, 'why don't you pop upstairs, and when you come down, you'll find the pool out there, through the conservatory. That way.' He pointed down a passage. Daisy nodded. 'And meanwhile, I'll go and sort out the signs for the drive,' added Hugh.

'Which room should I use?' asked Daisy, as he disappeared.

'Oh, just use any old room,' Hugh called over his shoulder. 'Any room at all.'

It was not Daisy's fault that the first room she should pick on was Meredith's. She cautiously pushed the door open, then gave a horrified, 'Oh!' She was looking at a large corner room, painted a deep red and dominated by a large mahogany bed. On one wall was a carved grey marble fireplace. Propped up against another was a huge gilt mirror. And in the middle was a thin, brown, sinewy woman, with long black hair, a forbidding expression and no clothes on.

'Don't you usually knock?' she said in a casual American accent, starting to pull on a black many-strapped swimming-costume.

'I'm so sorry,' Daisy said, bright red and trembling. 'I thought . . . I just . . .' Her words dried up. Why hadn't she knocked? 'I-I was looking for somewhere to change.'

'Well, how about the changing tent?' suggested

Meredith drily. 'That's where you're supposed to change.' Daisy gaped at her.

'He didn't say . . .' she began. 'He told me . . . to come upstairs.'

'Who?'

'Mr . . .' Daisy broke off. She didn't know his name; or did she? Had Mrs Mold told her? Was it Devenish, like the house?

'Look, never mind,' said Meredith abruptly. 'Since you're here, you can help me get into this thing. See these straps? I can't get them right.'

Cautiously, Daisy advanced towards Meredith. A web of interlaced black Lycra straps lay untidily across her back.

'Just yank them into place,' instructed Meredith. Daisy put up her hand awkwardly towards Meredith's back. She pulled one of the straps downwards and another upwards. 'I have a picture of it somewhere,' said Meredith. 'That might help.' She strode over to a small Victorian wash-stand in the corner of the room, piled with papers, magazines and books. 'Here!' She tossed a glossy magazine at Daisy, who, startled, dropped it on the floor.

'Butter-fingers,' said Meredith, coming over. She caught a glimpse of herself in the big gilt mirror as she passed. 'I guess it looks OK now.' She shook back her hair and looked at Daisy with glinting green eyes.

'So,' she said casually, 'what's your name? And what do you do? Nothing that needs co-ordination, I hope?'

'My name's Daisy Phillips,' said Daisy, blushing awkwardly. 'And I . . .' She stopped as a sound made Meredith's head rise suddenly. From outside came the purring and crackling of a car coming down the drive. Meredith quickly strode over to the window. Looking past her, Daisy could see a dark-green car and a slim man with dark eyes and greying temples getting out of the driver's seat. Meredith remained motionless for a

42

moment. Then she turned around and gave Daisy a distracted look.

'Look, you can change in here if you like,' she said. 'Just take your stuff with you when you go, and pay at the entrance table. All right, Daisy Phillips?'

'Yes,' said Daisy. 'Thank you.' Meredith turned to her reflection in the gilt mirror and tossed back her hair.

'How does my suit look?' she demanded.

'Fantastic,' said Daisy honestly.

'It ought to,' said Meredith, 'it cost enough.' She picked up a deep-red towel, slipped her feet into a pair of black leather sandals and closed the door behind her.

Outside, on the landing, Meredith paused and allowed a small dart of delight in her chest to flower a little. Through the circular window above the stairs she could still just see the corner of Alexis Faraday's car. He was here; Alexis was here. Downstairs, maybe, or outside, already lying back and soaking up the sun. Meredith threw back her shoulders and began to walk down the stairs. Then she remembered: sunglasses. Abruptly she turned back and threw open the door to her room. Daisy looked round, startled. She was down to only a pair of knickers.

'Forgot my shades,' said Meredith. 'You don't mind, do you?' Daisy blushed; a delicate pink which spread down as far as her full white breasts. Meredith watched, interestedly, as the colour gradually faded. 'Got sun block?' she enquired, picking up a pair of opaque black sunglasses.

'Y-yes,' stumbled Daisy.

'Good,' said Meredith, 'you need it.' And without further comment she left the room, put on her dark glasses and made her way out to the swimming-pool, and to Alexis.

Ten miles away, in an unbearably hot, dusty and clogged line of traffic, Barnaby finally lost his temper.

43

'All right, Katie!' he shouted. There was sudden silence in the car. 'Stop whining! If you've really changed your mind; if you *really* want to go swimming, then we'll go swimming.'

With a suddenly heavy heart he brutally changed into reverse gear and, ignoring the irritation of the other drivers on the road, swung the car round. He changed gear again, put his foot down, and sped off down the clear side of the road, back towards Melbrook, the Delaneys' house, and the swimming-pool.

Chapter Three

Amelia and Katie were doing somersaults in the shallow end of the pool. Katie *loved* doing somersaults. She whirled round in the water, clutching her nose tight, feeling breathless and blue and shiny, then emerged into the warm sunny air with triumph.

'There!' She pushed her wet hair out of her eyes. 'I went round twice.'

'No you didn't,' said Amelia, who was bouncing up and down on the floor of the pool. 'I was watching.'

'I did! It felt like twice.'

'It was a very long once,' conceded Amelia, 'but it wasn't twice. Even I can't go round twice; I always run out of breath. Now,' she instructed, grabbing Katie before she could plunge into the water again, 'I'll do a handstand, and you see how long I stay up. Count like this, one thousand, two thousand.'

'OK,' agreed Katie. 'Then me.' She watched, swimming breathlessly on the spot, as Amelia disappeared under the blue water. A moment later a pair of wavering legs appeared.

'One thousand, two thousand, three thousand, four thousand, five thousand,' counted Katie rapidly. Then she stopped. Was she going too fast? 'Six thou–sand,' she enunciated carefully, 'sev–en thou–sand.' On the other hand, perhaps that was too slow. She trailed a finger in the bright iridescent surface of the swimming-pool. The water was just right; cold enough so that she'd squealed when she jumped in, but not so freezing that she had to keep moving. It was perfect.

Now that she was in the pool, she couldn't think why she'd *ever* wanted to go and do boring old fishing with Daddy. It had been horrible in the car; all boiling hot and smelly, and the car seat had burned her legs, and then when they got in the traffic jam, Daddy had started getting cross and shouting; not at her, at the other drivers, but still it wasn't very nice. And she'd started thinking about Amelia and Mummy, and started wishing she was with them, running and jumping with a huge refreshing splash into the pool. And the more she wished, the hotter she felt, and the longer the car journey seemed.

At first she hadn't said anything; she'd been very quiet and good. Then she'd just said a few things like, 'I'm hot,' and, 'Can we stop for a drink?' and, 'How much further is it?' But then, when Daddy started getting cross, she'd said in a half sob, half sigh, 'I wish we were going swimming.' She'd said it a few times, and at first she'd thought Daddy wasn't listening, so she'd said it with more and more feeling, until eventually he'd suddenly shouted very loudly and turned the car round. And when she'd started crying, he'd said that he wasn't really angry, and maybe, after all, a swimming-pool was the best place to be on such a hot day.

He was right, Katie now thought, leaning back and admiring her shiny starfish-decorated swimming-suit. She wanted to stay in here all day, and all night; for the rest of her life, maybe. She lay her head lazily against the surface of the water and felt cool blue wavelets lap into her ears.

Then, with a start, she realized she'd stopped counting Amelia's handstand. 'Eight thousand, nine thousand, ten thousand,' she said quickly, watching Amelia's legs. The legs faltered and fell back into the water.

'How many?' Amelia's wet face appeared in front of her.

'Ten thousand.' Amelia frowned.

'Is that all?'

'My go,' said Katie quickly. She plunged down, clutching her nose, feeling for the bottom of the pool with one outstretched hand. But balancing on a single palm wasn't easy, and after only a few seconds she collapsed back into the water.

'Only three thousand,' said Amelia. 'You should do it with two hands.'

'But it hurts my *nose*,' wailed Katie. 'All the water goes up it if I don't hold it.'

'Can you open your eyes underwater yet?'

'Of course I can.' Katie was scornful.

'OK then, let's dive for coins. We'll go and get them off Mummy.'

Louise was lying on her back, enjoying the sensation of the sun burning into her face. She had deliberately chosen a spot on the grass slightly apart from the group of chatting women which she would normally have joined. Now, above the sounds of splashes and shrieks from the pool, she could hear Sylvia Seddon-Wilson beginning on some long, no doubt exaggerated, and no doubt highly amusing anecdote. But Louise didn't feel like chatting, or even listening. She felt like being on her own and thinking.

If she lifted her head very slightly and swivelled her eyes to the right, she could see Barnaby, ensconced in a deck-chair next to Hugh Delaney. In spite of herself, she felt a pang of pity for him as she watched him. He should have known better than to expect Katie to last even a short car journey without vociferous complaint, Louise thought. If he'd just ignored her, and managed to get to wherever the fishing was, Katie would soon have forgotten her woes and they would probably have had a lovely day.

As it was, he'd arrived twenty minutes ago, a

disconsolate miserable sight, made even more so as Katie sprang free of his grasp, yelling, 'Mummy! We're here! We came swimming, after all!' Everyone had looked up; everyone had taken in the situation at a glance; eyes had swivelled from Barnaby to Louise and back to Barnaby.

Barnaby had come over and explained, in a few sentences, what had gone wrong. Louise had mustered a sympathetic word or two of reply. And then, as the surrounding eyes watched, Barnaby had made his way over to the other side of the swimming-pool where Hugh – stalwart Hugh – had already pulled over a chair in preparation for him. The entertainment for the village was almost complete, thought Louise bitterly. Now all that was needed for their delectation was an appearance by Cassian, village anti-Christ.

Louise knew the village's opinion of Cassian. She knew the village's version of events. No-one had asked; everyone had assumed. They had assumed that when Louise popped over to Cassian's cottage and ended up spending the evening there, something suspicious must be going on. They had assumed that when Barnaby arrived at The George, silent and angry and without Louise, he had found some sort of confirming evidence. No-one – and here Louise wriggled angrily on her towel – no-one had noticed that the problems between her and Barnaby stretched way back before Cassian had arrived in the village.

Louise and Barnaby had married soon after she left university. The wedding was a large glittering affair – only right for the only daughter of a man who, until recently, had been the local MP and, at one time, a cabinet minister. Louise Page – as she was then – had been a well-known figure on the local political campaign circuit. She had started to help out her father while she was at school and became even more involved after her mother died. When an election fell during her first year at university, she motored over from Bristol every weekend to put up posters and go from house to house with her clipboard, blue scarf and cheerful smile.

When she rang Barnaby's doorbell, she found a group of agricultural college chums watching the football, drinking beer, and unwilling to be disturbed.

'What does it matter?' said one of them, offering her a can. Louise stared.

'What does it *matter*?' she echoed in disbelief. 'It matters . . . it matters . . .' Her hands started to whirl helplessly in the air. 'It affects your whole life! If you don't vote for the right people . . .'

'I'm not going to vote,' said one of them. 'Bloody waste of time.'

'You must vote!' Louise's voice sounded through the house like a clarion. 'You must! My God! You're young, don't you care?'

'I'm going to vote.' Barnaby's voice came from the back of the room. Louise turned and looked at him. He's huge, was her first thought. He sat on a smallish wooden chair that looked as though it might break under his weight, and cupped a can of beer in a huge paw of a hand. But his voice was gentle and Louise smiled at him.

'Good,' she said.

'Not for your lot, though,' said Barnaby, gesturing to her rosette. 'I'm voting Green.' He took a swig of beer while his friends exchanged derisive glances.

'Green?'

'You're a bloody hippy, Barn.'

'Going to join the hunt sabs too?'

Louise ignored them and met his eye.

'Well, good for you,' she said. 'At least you care.'

And that would have been that had Barnaby not come to vote while Louise was on poll-monitoring duty. She smiled as he approached the polling station, and put her pen next to his name, ready to tick.

'Well,' she said, as he got near. 'I don't have to ask you who you're voting for, do I?'

'Not for you, if that's what you mean,' said Barnaby.

'I didn't expect you to,' said Louise. 'In fact, I would have been disappointed if you had.' Barnaby looked at her.

'How long do you have to stand there?'

'Another couple of hours.'

'And then?'

'Home, to wait for the results.' She flushed slightly. 'My father's the Conservative candidate.'

'John Page, I know.' Barnaby grinned at Louise's look of surprise. 'We're not all unaware yobs.' He looked at her clipboard. 'And is he going to win?'

'I should think so. It's closer run than last time, but still . . .'

'And then you celebrate madly?'

'Then we celebrate madly.'

'And tomorrow?'

Louise shrugged.

'Hang-over.' Barnaby grinned.

'You know, it just so happens, I've got a very good cure for hang-overs.'

His cure had been to take her to bed, with a directness that sent Louise, who was accustomed to sensitive thoughtful undergraduates, into slight shock. When they had finished, he went to make her a cup of tea, and she lay in his single bed, clutching the sheet up to her chin as though afraid of attack, shaking slightly, while thoughts, protests and attempts at indignation batted round her mind like butterflies. From his bedroom window was a view of some school playing-fields, and as she lay there, completely silent, a group of rugby players came running onto the field, dressed in bright-red kit. With their big burly legs, they reminded her of Barnaby, and suddenly she began to cry.

'I thought you'd gone away,' she wailed, as he came back into the room, and then stopped short, for this was not what she had meant to say at all. But it was too late. Barnaby, who, he later told her, had been pacing the kitchen anxiously, wondering if what he had just committed was an act of love or an act of violence, hastened to her side with a relieved solicitude. His tea was so strong it made Louise shudder, but she said it was lovely, and smiled at him with tears still dancing on her eyelashes, and Barnaby, feeling a sudden unfamiliar surge of tenderness, went straight away and carefully made her another cup, just the same.

Since then they had never really talked very much about politics. Louise's father stood down at the next election, which was a year before Louise and Barnaby married, and then, a couple of years later, was made a peer.

'If only we'd *known*,' Louise would say at regular intervals. 'We could have been married in the House of Lords.'

'But then we would have had to wait,' Barnaby would reply, 'and I would have had to move to Melbrook on my own.'

Barnaby had accepted a job running a medium-sized estate, ten minutes' drive from Melbrook, which he started two months after they married. He had been in the same job ever since. Louise had long ago given up suggesting he look for a more senior, more challenging, or more lucrative job.

'We're happy here,' he would say, 'that's all that matters.'

And for a long time they were happy. They moved into Larch Tree Cottage, and Louise commuted into Linningford for her job as marketing executive with a small publishing firm. Then she had Amelia and gave up her job, and then she had Katie. She was no longer involved in politics, her father wasn't an MP any more,

51

and besides, Melbrook was in a different constituency. Besides which, she no longer felt quite as fervent about it all. For a few years, the minutiae of the children, the school run, village gossip and church fêtes kept her going. I'm lucky, she would tell herself at frequent intervals, I may not have a career, but I have a loving family and a happy life.

It never occurred to her to question why she needed to reaffirm these facts to herself quite so regularly. Nor did she understand why, as the tenth anniversary of her marriage to Barnaby approached, she began to get edgy and irritable; to attack Barnaby with unreasonable complaints and heap bitter criticisms on the village, her life, his job, Britain. It didn't help that her brother had recently moved with his family to a reportedly exciting new life in New York; nor did it help that Barnaby couldn't begin to understand or, it seemed, sympathize.

'But you grew up in the country!' he once shouted, when her impatience with Melbrook had spilled over into a suppertime diatribe.

'I know!' she retorted angrily. 'But it was different! It was exciting! We had important people to stay, and we had interesting discussions, and we had a flat in London, and we went to parties at the House of Commons, and . . .' she broke off, feeling foolish. 'You just don't understand,' she finished feebly.

'I do understand,' said Barnaby bitterly. 'You wish you'd married someone intelligent and important and glamorous. Not a country bumpkin like me.'

'No!' exclaimed Louise, a little too late. 'No, don't be silly.'

And then Cassian Brown had moved into the village. Smooth and sophisticated and intelligent and charming. Barnaby had distrusted him on first sight. But Louise had been enchanted when, at a welcoming drinks party at the vicarage, Cassian revealed, first that he was interested in politics, and then that Lord Page had always been a particular hero of his.

Cassian was a young lawyer with the biggest law firm in Linningford, a huge prestigious concern with offices in London and all over the world. He had been seconded to the Linningford office for two years to run the commercial litigation department, and had, he said charmingly to Frances Mold, decided to take the cottage in Melbrook as soon as he saw its exquisite view of the church. He smiled at Frances, revealing perfect white teeth against tanned, not quite English-looking skin. Frances said faintly, 'How nice,' and Barnaby nudged Louise. 'What a creep,' he whispered in her ear.

But Louise didn't think he was a creep. On the way home from the drinks party she'd been full of exhilarated chatter.

'He actually remembered that speech of Daddy's,' she said, striding ahead into the darkness. 'That one about housing.'

'It's a famous speech,' said Barnaby brusquely. But Louise wasn't listening; her thoughts had moved on.

'His grandparents were Italian,' she said. 'Did you know that?'

'Whose grandparents?' said Barnaby, feeling a deliberate angry need to misunderstand.

'Cassian's, of course,' said Louise. Her voice sounded, to Barnaby, light and happy. 'Bruni, they were called, but they changed it to Brown when they came to England. It's a shame, don't you think? He went to Oxford,' she added irrelevantly, 'like Daddy.'

Barnaby couldn't bear it any more.

'Do we have to keep talking about this chap?' His voice thundered through the dark street. Louise turned back, unsure how to react.

'Well . . .' she began, in hesitant mollifying tones. But as she marshalled her thoughts, her initial instinctive desire to pacify was taken over by indignation. 'Well!' she repeated. 'So now I'm not allowed to talk to

53

anybody, is that it? One interesting person comes to live in Melbrook and we're not allowed to talk about him. Well, fine. What shall we talk about? Oh, I know, the lambing. We haven't talked about that for at least an hour.'

Her voice held an unfamiliar sarcasm, and Barnaby stared at her through the darkness for a few moments, unable to read her expression. Then he shrugged and walked on.

'What?' demanded Louise, grabbing him as he went past. 'What? Aren't you going to *say* anything? Talk to me!'

Barnaby paused and looked at her. Then he said, 'I haven't got anything to say,' and strode on ahead.

Maybe, thought Louise now, turning over onto her front and resting her sunbaked cheeks on her hands, maybe if Barnaby had talked to her a bit more, instead of listening to all those silly rumours; maybe if he'd trusted her a bit more, then they wouldn't have had all those awful rows. With a painful jolt, she remembered the last one they'd had. She'd been pink and outraged; he'd been obstinately determined. He'd actually told her, *commanded* her, to stop seeing Cassian. She'd shrieked back, in frustrated anger, that she was going to see whoever she wanted, whenever she wanted, and if he didn't like it he could bloody well move out.

She still wasn't sure where those last words had come from, but once they had burst out into the air, there was no taking them back. Barnaby had gazed at her, a look of disbelief on his face, and the air had seemed to resonate with shock. And Louise had slumped heavily into a chair, wanting to say, sorry, she didn't mean it, but, somehow, unable to.

'Mummy!' Drops of water pattered onto Louise's back, and a shadow fell over the sun. 'Can I have a two-penny piece to throw?'

'Can I have one, too? Can I have a pound coin?' Louise reluctantly looked up. There were Amelia and Katie, standing over her in breathless excitement, dripping water onto her bathing-suit and leaving wet footprints on her towel.

'Did you see me do a handstand?' asked Katie. 'Did you see when I did cycling in the air? Did you see when Amelia nearly did a backward somersault?' She hopped up and down, so that her hair flew out and sprayed Louise with water.

'Careful!' said Louise, sitting up. 'You'll get people all wet. Now, where's my purse?'

'Here,' said Amelia, promptly, holding it out. She watched carefully as Louise unzipped it. 'A two-penny piece,' she said. 'Or a penny.'

'And a pound coin for me,' said Katie, doing a quick bunny jump on the grass.

'Don't be *stupid*,' said Amelia. 'A pound coin will never show up. And what if you lost it?'

'I wouldn't lose it,' said Katie, giving Amelia a disdainful look.

'Here you are,' said Louise. 'A tuppenny piece each. Now go and play.'

'Watch me dive,' begged Amelia. 'I've got a really good dive.'

'Maybe later,' said Louise. 'After lunch I'll come and watch.'

Daisy stood at the edge of the grass and wondered where to sit. She had hastily changed into her swimming-suit as soon as Meredith had gone, then hurried down the stairs and out into the sunshine. Mrs Mold had been very welcoming at the entrance table, and had said, unfortunately, she was a bit tied up at the moment, but why didn't Daisy introduce herself to a few people; she'd soon find that everybody was *jolly* friendly.

And Daisy had smiled and nodded. Now she peered

anxiously around, trying to ignore the spasms of nerves in her stomach; trying to look confident, and wondering who she could approach. To the right was a group of women, all gaily laughing at something. But most of them seemed much older than Daisy. She wouldn't know what to talk to them about. Only one looked anywhere near Daisy's age, and she was busy with a baby.

Dotted round the pool were more little groups of families and friends, as well as a few loners, stretched out on chairs or on towels. None of them looked up at Daisy, or smiled, or waved her over. In desperation, Daisy looked around for the American woman whose bedroom she'd walked into, but she was nowhere to be seen, and neither was the friendly owner of the house.

Daisy took a hesitant step forward. She was going to have to sit down somewhere. People would start to stare at her if she stayed hovering on the edge of the lawn all afternoon. She would simply find her own spot now, she decided, and then perhaps talk to people a bit later on.

Slowly, self-consciously, she wended her way through the chattering groups, stepping over beach-mats and bags, apologizing whenever she came within six inches of someone's towel, until she reached a quiet patch of grass some way from the swimming-pool. Quickly she spread out her towel and lay down, trying to ignore the latent blush of embarrassment that was spreading over her cheeks.

From his steamer chair at the side of the pool, Alexis Faraday watched Daisy's progress with slow lazy amusement. His eyes followed her, swivelling under brown lizard lids, taking in her hair, her eyes, her pale skin and her gawky grace. She moved, with painful awkwardness, between the prone bodies on the grass, apologizing where there was no need, biting her soft pink underlip anxiously. When she reached her destination, she looked around, hesitated, then abruptly spread out her towel and lay down, as though avoiding gunfire.

Alexis stared at her for a few more seconds, and when it was obvious that she was not going to sit up again, he looked away. For Christ's sake, what was he doing, staring at a child like that? She couldn't be more than eighteen. Less than half his age, he realized, with a sobering thud, and he deliberately closed his eyes and leaned back in his chair.

A few moments later, he heard a cool attractive American voice beside him.

'So this is how the esteemed lawyer prepares his cases. Lying flat out in the sun.' Alexis opened one eye and grinned.

'So this is how the great artist composes her canvases,' he parried. Meredith shrugged, pulled up a deck-chair, and sat down.

'This is work,' she said. She smiled conspiratorially at him, and her eyes gave a tiny challenging glint. 'We all have to take inspiration from somewhere,' she elaborated.

'Aha! Yes.' Alexis shifted on his chair, and regarded Meredith quizzically. 'Inspiration. So should I expect to see *Man sleeping by swimming pool* in your next collection? And will I recognize myself?' Meredith grinned.

'I shouldn't think so. But you never know, you might get into one of Ursula's water-colours.'

'Of course.' They both involuntarily looked towards the terrace, where Ursula stood happily, an old paint-stained smock of Meredith's over her bathing-suit, gazing at the scene before her, with brush in hand. 'Tell me,' Alexis added casually, 'how is Ursula's painting going?' Meredith looked away.

'She paints a lot,' she said distantly.

'And, no doubt, she's improving as she goes,' suggested Alexis gravely. Meredith bit her lip.

'Something like that.' There was a short pause, then suddenly Meredith emitted a strange snuffle that sounded a bit like a laugh. Alexis looked at her in mock-surprise.

'Something wrong?' Meredith shook her head and clutched her mouth. Her shoulders shook.

'She's terrible!' she whispered suddenly, and gave a half-suppressed, half-hysterical giggle. She leaned closer to Alexis. 'I can't *tell* you how bad she is! I thought she'd get better; I even encouraged her, but . . .'

Alexis began to chuckle.

'And the thing is,' Meredith continued, wiping her mirth-filled eyes, 'everybody in Melbrook thinks she's a fucking genius! She's even had a show!' She began to shake again. 'And I bought the first picture!'

Suddenly she sat up. 'And where were you at the show?' she demanded. 'We sent you an invitation.'

'I know you did,' agreed Alexis. 'I was working, I'm afraid.'

'You work too hard,' said Meredith accusingly. 'We never see you.' She pushed back her long dark hair, and a pair of green eyes shone at him out of a tanned vibrant face. 'I thought country lawyers were supposed to take every afternoon off to play golf.'

'They do,' said Alexis. 'Unfortunately I don't play golf.' Then his expression changed and he sighed. 'You're right, I don't come over here enough. I should do, it's really not very far. But then, you know, these days I don't really seem to do anything enough.'

He seemed about to elaborate, and Meredith leaned forward interestedly. But suddenly Ursula's voice broke in from behind.

'Oh, Meredith dear,' she said. 'My painting's going so well today! You must come and have a look. And, look, it's Alexis! When did you get here? Hugh never said.'

'Ursula!' Alexis stood up, an elegant man with a slim figure which belied his greying temples and slightly hooded eyes. 'It's lovely to see you. Now let me come and look at this painting. Meredith, you can give us your expert opinion.'

He linked arms with each of the women, giving Meredith a little conspiratorial squeeze. And as he did so, and as they began walking together towards Ursula's easel, bare arm linked with bare arm, bare leg brushing against bare leg, Meredith felt her stomach leap, and her cheeks pinken and, in spite of herself, her heart begin to beat just a little more quickly.

Chapter Four

As morning turned into afternoon, the air became more still, the sun seemed to expand, and the heat intensified. Voices around the pool became lower, as though confiding secrets; many people fell asleep in a post-picnic torpor.

Barnaby and Hugh sat side by side on their deck-chairs, in a companionable silence. By the diving-board, Louise was standing with her arms folded, watching Amelia and Katie diving, and sporadically offering help and encouragement. Their cries of, 'Watch me!' rang through the sleepy, subdued, heat-filled air, along with the squeals of some younger children splashing in the shallow end. Hugh glanced at Barnaby and gestured towards Louise.

'Hard for you,' he said succinctly. Barnaby shrugged. 'I'm all right. It could be worse . . .' He broke off.

Hugh nodded understandingly. There was another silence between them. Then Hugh said, 'If you ever feel like getting away . . .' Barnaby exhaled sharply.

'I do,' he said, 'frequently.' Hugh leaned back a little; shifted himself in his deck-chair.

'There's always our cottage in France. Use that; you can drive over.' He turned his head towards Barnaby. 'I mean it. If you feel you need some time on your own.' He paused. 'We went there, after Simon . . .' He broke off.

'Of course,' said Barnaby. 'I remember.' He turned his head towards Hugh.

'I'm very grateful,' he said simply. 'It's good of you to offer.' Hugh shrugged.

'It's extremely difficult to get things in perspective when you rub up against them every day. Difficult for both of you.' There was a pause, and Hugh looked over towards Louise. 'Can't be easy for Louise, either,' he said.

Barnaby felt a sudden spurt of indignation, as though Hugh had suddenly changed sides halfway through the match. But he managed to say, 'No, I'm sure it's very difficult for her, too.'

Hugh eyed Barnaby with amusement.

'I don't think you really mean that. And, fair enough, why should you? But I believe I'm right; that you're both suffering at the moment.' He leaned back and closed his eyes. 'At any rate, it's you I'm offering the cottage to. Take it any time, we haven't any particular plans this summer.'

'Thank you,' said Barnaby. He suddenly wanted to say more; to confide in Hugh; to ask his advice; to relate the story of his betrayal with the anger and pain which he had so far shown to nobody save Louise. But instead, he said again, 'Thank you,' in a voice that faltered slightly. Then he lay back, closed his eyes, and waited, miserably, for the onslaught of his own tangled, anguished, unavoidable thoughts.

Louise was unwillingly standing in the heat of the sun, watching Amelia and Katie cavorting in the water. Every time she attempted to leave, they called desperately to her again, requesting her to witness yet another obscure acrobatic feat. As she stood, she saw Barnaby and Hugh talking quietly and gesturing towards her, and felt a surge of hot embarrassed fury. She could guess what Hugh thought of her. The Delaneys had always been more Barnaby's friends than hers; no doubt

Barnaby was now pouring out some tale of woe to overly sympathetic ears.

'Hurry up,' she said sharply to Katie, who was dithering on the diving-board. She could feel Hugh's quizzical eyes on her, and determinedly ignored them. What was he thinking? Probably notching up even more black marks against her, for venting her frustrations on an innocent child. Katie looked up, surprised.

'I'm just making it bouncy,' she said.

'Yes, hurry up,' said Amelia, who was waiting behind to have her go. 'You always take ages.'

'I don't!'

'Yes you do! Slowcoach!'

'Mummy!' Katie's shrill voice appealed to Louise. 'She called me a slowcoach.'

'Well then, get on with it,' said Louise firmly.

'Yes, come on!'

Still Katie remained at the end of the board, and suddenly Amelia impatiently ran a few steps onto the diving-board, stamping hard. Katie gave a shriek and jumped off the end of the diving-board. When she surfaced, she was squealing angrily.

'That's not fair! Amelia, you . . .' But she didn't have time to finish before Amelia leaped off the diving-board, curled into a ball and dive-bombed her with an enormous splash.

Ursula, walking by the pool, looked at these goings-on with alarm. She quickly approached Louise.

'Dear, I think perhaps you should calm the children down a bit; they seem terribly excited.' Louise turned round at her voice. Bloody Ursula. Another censorious face, another voice of disapproval. So now, not only was she a heartless hussy for splitting up with Barnaby, she was also an inadequate mother.

'They're fine, Ursula,' she said tightly. She waited for Ursula to come out with another tactless comment about Barnaby. Perhaps, this time, she would say,

Oh, wasn't it a shame for the children.

But Ursula's eyes were on Katie.

'Hello, Katie!' she called.

'Hello, Mrs Delaney,' Katie called back. 'Do you want to watch Amelia swimming under my legs? It's really clever.' Ursula glanced hastily at Louise, who allowed herself the satisfaction of a small smile.

'Yes, why don't you watch the girls?' she said, with distant amusement. 'You'll find it's tremendous fun.' And quickly, before Ursula could protest, she stalked off.

Meredith had fallen asleep, lying on a chair next to Alexis. For a while, from behind his sunglasses, he affectionately watched her sleeping. His eyes ran idly over her face, and then over her tanned skin, and her long legs, and her strong narrow feet, and her determined hands. He paused, staring at Meredith's hands, and counted to ten. Then, holding his breath and without moving his head, he shifted his attention away from Meredith and towards the young girl with the pale skin and dark clouds of hair.

She was sitting up on her towel, now, pushing her heavy hair off her neck as though she were too hot, looking around cautiously. The patch of grass on which she was sitting was, by this hour of the afternoon, partially shaded by a tree, and as she moved, lacy, leafy shadows gently dappled her white skin. Slowly she rose to her feet, tugging awkwardly at her bathing-suit and pushing her hair back again. She glanced nervously at the family group sitting near her, then, as the father of the family rose his head questioningly, flushed and looked away again.

Alexis watched in fascination as she traced a halting solitary path towards the swimming-pool. She paused by the edge and looked at the water doubtfully, as though not entirely sure whether it was meant for her.

Then, slowly, she dipped in a toe. As she did so, her long milky-pale leg was reflected in the glimmering blue water, so that it briefly appeared to be one long swan-neck limb.

'Daisy!' A voice came from the other side of the pool, and at once the girl retrieved her toe, looking round in sudden apparent guilt. Alexis looked for the source of the voice. Waving from a garden chair, attired in a jolly scarlet bathing-suit, was a woman whom he recognized as the vicar's wife. She was now gesturing reassuringly at Daisy.

'It's absolutely lovely in the pool!' she was calling. 'Have a good swim, and then come over and have a chat with us!'

Alexis looked back towards the girl. Daisy. Suddenly, unexpectedly, she smiled at the vicar's wife; a shy, uncertain smile. Alexis felt a strange pang under his ribs. He watched her dive into the pool, dark hair streaming out behind her, white feet pointed. And as he did so, he suddenly wanted to see her smiling shyly again; this time, at him.

'So, Louise,' Sylvia Seddon-Wilson smiled charmingly, and drew on her cigarette, 'where's that sexy man of yours?' Louise shrugged hesitantly.

'Who do you mean?'

'Oh, Louise! You don't think I mean Barnaby!' Sylvia's playful voice rang out with a calculated reson-ance, and Louise shrank slightly into her chair. She had not meant to be drawn into Sylvia's coterie today, but after snubbing Ursula there had been nowhere else for her to go and sit. And Sylvia was, to be fair, a long-term acquaintance – if not exactly friend – of Louise's. Some years older than Louise, and with her teenage sons away at school, she lived a leisured life in the old vicarage, redecorating herself and the house at frequent intervals and observing the affairs of the village through sharp, if slightly jaundiced eyes.

As her voice rose provocatively over the sounds of the swimming-pool, Louise glanced hesitantly over towards Barnaby, but he was too far away to hear Sylvia's remarks.

'No, I mean your delicious toyboy,' said Sylvia. Louise blushed scarlet, but Sylvia appeared not to notice. 'Cassian. Gorgeous Cass. Is that what you call him? Cass?'

'No,' said Louise discouragingly. It had been, she acknowledged to herself, a mistake to sit down with Sylvia.

'Well, I must say', said Sylvia, leaning comfortably back in her chair, 'that I think he's divine. So sexy. That hair . . . He's Italian, is that right?'

'Half Italian,' mumbled Louise. She felt that she was being misrepresented; that she should somehow try to correct Sylvia's assumptions. But then, what would she say? What exactly *was* going on between her and Cassian? She wasn't, herself, entirely sure. And while she struggled in her mind to define, in simple terms, their relationship, she was also aware of a slight flowering pride at Sylvia's admiring comments; a desire for the alluring picture of herself and Cassian as a glamorous couple to continue.

She turned her head slightly, so that the reproaching sight of Barnaby vanished from the corner of her vision, and gave Sylvia a secretive smile.

'His grandparents were Italian,' she elaborated, casually laying claim to Cassian's family as well as him.

'Italian men!' exclaimed Sylvia, giving a theatrical shiver. 'To die for!'

'Oh no, you don't mean it! They're awful! Revolting!' Louise looked up. It was Mary Tracey, a cheerful young woman who lived not far from Louise and had often acted as baby-sitter for Amelia and Katie. She was dripping wet from the pool, and holding an equally wet, fat

65

and happy baby. 'We went on holiday to Pisa once, and my bottom got sore from all the pinching! I wouldn't have minded if it had got any smaller,' she added, sitting down, 'but it didn't.' Louise giggled.

'I wasn't talking about peasants from Pisa,' Sylvia said airily. 'I was talking about gorgeous young lawyers.'

Mary glanced swiftly at Louise and her face closed up slightly. Louise looked away, with a small uncomfortable pang. Mary had been demonstrably upset when the Kembers had split up; it had happened just after she came home from the hospital with baby Luke, and Louise had always felt that she had let Mary down in some inexplicable way.

The baby began to grizzle and slither on Mary's lap, and she sighed.

'He's hungry again,' she said. 'He's always hungry.' She jogged him up and down a little, and he affectionately grabbed a strand of her hair.

'Ow!' she yelped. 'Get off!' Sylvia raised her eyebrows at Louise.

'Aren't you glad yours are past that stage?' she asked in mock-horror. Louise laughed, but she was mesmerized by Luke; by his determined, concentrated expression and his waving, grasping hands.

'Amelia and Katie were never like this great lump,' said Mary cheerfully. 'They were little sweethearts.' She sat Luke down on the grass. 'Why can't you be good, like they were?' she chided him. He gazed at her for a few seconds, then screwed up his face, and began to howl.

'I'll have to feed him, I suppose,' she sighed. 'See you later.'

As she retreated, Sylvia took another drag on her cigarette. She pulled out a gold compact and checked her reflection unhurriedly. Then she put it away, smiled, and regarded Louise lazily again from under azure-painted lids.

'Anyway,' she said, 'you must come over to dinner sometime, Louise . . . you and, of course, Cassian.'

'Yes, that would be nice,' said Louise hesitantly. She lay back in her chair, closed her eyes, and tried unsuccessfully to imagine herself actually attending a dinner party with Cassian as her acknowledged partner. The Law Society dinner, a fortnight ago, had been different. That was in London; no-one there knew or cared what their background story was. She'd gone as Cassian's guest, eaten four courses, listened intelligently to the speeches, joined in the discussion, even put one of Cassian's colleagues right on some political point. It had been a wonderful evening. But that had been in London, not here in Melbrook, in front of Barnaby, in front of all of them. Village events – even private dinner parties – were not the same thing at all. To go anywhere publicly with Cassian would be at best uncomfortable, at worst a fiasco. Sylvia should realize that, thought Louise. Then, looking sidelong at Sylvia's faint smirk, it occurred to her that Sylvia already did.

Meredith awoke to find the sun behind a cloud and an empty place beside her. Alexis must have gone for a stroll, she thought. She lifted herself up on her elbows and blinked sleepily. Cast in a sudden shade, the pool appeared chilly; the sleek wet heads of the swimmers bobbed darkly amid dull blue-grey waves, and the splashing and shrieks of the children seemed to have risen in volume.

She pushed her hair back, sat up cross-legged on her chair and stretched out languorously like a panther. Then, mid-stretch, she froze. There, in front of her, was Alexis, in the water. Alexis, who famously never swam. She stared at him. His hair was wet and he was inefficiently treading water, and he was smiling at someone.

Hating herself, Meredith casually lay back down on

her chair and reached for her sunglasses. The black-tinted lenses made everything around her seem even more gloomy, but at least with them on she could stare inconspicuously at Alexis and whoever it was he was talking to; still talking to – and still smiling at.

From the bathing-suit it appeared to be a woman, but her face was turned away from Meredith. Without really intending to, Meredith swiftly catalogued all the women of the village that it could be, dismissing each in turn with a snap judgement. *Too old. Too bossy. Too married.* Then, as the nameless woman began to turn in the water, a sudden realization hit her mind, flooding it with relief. It wasn't a woman, it was the dippy girl; the klutzy teenager. Daisy . . . Daisy Phillips.

Filled with a sudden lightness, she stood up, approached the pool and dived in.

'Hi, Alexis,' she said, surfacing near the pair of them.

'Hi, Daisy.' Alexis gave Daisy a surprised look.

'You know Meredith?'

'Yes,' said Daisy hesitantly. 'At least, I didn't know she was called Meredith; sorry,' she stumbled, turning to Meredith, 'I mean, I didn't know *you* were called Meredith. Thank you very much,' she added, 'for letting me use your room.'

As Daisy came to the end of this halting little speech, Meredith raised her eyebrows sardonically and tried to catch Alexis's eye. But he was still gazing at Daisy in apparent fascination.

'Oh, that's OK,' said Meredith, in friendly playing-along tones. 'Any time.' She registered, in slight disbelief, that Alexis was turning and smiling at her, as though thanking her. What the hell for? Who was this kid to him? A surrogate daughter?

'Feel free to use my room at the end of the day if you want to,' she offered, adding a cheery grin for good measure. The girl, Daisy, smiled gratefully at her. And then, like a fucking mirror image, so did Alexis. What's going on here? Meredith wanted to shout. Next I'll be asking this loopy girl if she wants to come bake cookies with me.

But instead she smiled at Alexis and Daisy, said, 'I'll catch you later,' and swam swiftly, confusedly, away.

The sun sat determinedly behind a cloud for the next half an hour, and eventually the prone sunbathers around the pool gradually began to stand up, stretch, look at their watches and start to gather their belongings together.

Meanwhile, Amelia and Katie, utterly oblivious of the weather, had commandeered the diving-board. Amelia was doing back dives and Katie was doing front dives.

'I'm going to be in the diving team when I go to senior school,' Amelia was announcing proudly, standing with her back to the water. She bounced up into the air, arched her back, and entered the water cleanly, hands in a neat point.

'So am I,' said Katie, as soon as Amelia's head popped up above the water again. 'Look at my star jump!' She leaped high into the air, with legs outstretched and toes pointed, then brought them together sharply before plunging into the water.

'That's not a dive,' said Amelia scornfully.

'Well, nor is a back dive,' said Katie, paddling breathlessly to the side of the pool.

'Yes it is,' retorted Amelia. 'Why do you think it's called a back *dive* if it's not a dive?'

'Dives are facing *forward*,' said Katie. 'Look!' She rushed recklessly past Amelia onto the diving-board, and essayed a cautious forward dive from the end, one hand clutching her nose.

'That was rubbish!' yelled Amelia, as soon as Katie's head was clear. 'I'm going to do another back dive. Get out of the way!'

'So am I!' retorted Katie desperately. 'So am I going to do a back dive! You just wait, Amelia.'

Louise was gathering up her things, preparing to leave, when Barnaby came striding over.

'I thought I'd take the girls out to supper,' he said, with no preamble. 'For a pizza, maybe. They'd like that.'

'They've got school tomorrow,' objected Louise, 'and it's already getting late. Maybe another time.'

'We won't be long,' insisted Barnaby. 'I've hardly seen them today.'

'Yes, you have,' retorted Louise. She paused. 'And anyway, they'll be too exhausted to go out after all this swimming.'

'No they won't,' said Barnaby obstinately. 'It's only five. We'll go straight from here, eat at six, be home by seven. Easy.'

'It's not easy,' said Louise, her voice rising. 'I then have to get them bathed and ready for bed, and check their homework, and make sure they're in a fit state for school tomorrow.'

'Oh, for God's sake!' exclaimed Barnaby. 'What does school matter?'

'Yes, well, I might have expected you to take that attitude,' said Louise. She folded up a towel with abrupt angry movements.

'What's that supposed to mean?' Barnaby glared at her.

'Mummy! Watch!' A piercing voice came from the diving-board.

'In a minute, Katie,' Louise called. She glared back at Barnaby. 'It means whatever you want it to mean.' There was a moment's silence. Then Amelia came bounding up, dripping wet and shivering.

'Where's my towel?' she demanded. Barnaby ignored Louise's gaze.

'Amelia!' he exclaimed. 'Feel like going out for pizza tonight?'

'Yeah! Pizza!' Amelia beamed up at Barnaby.

'Mummy! Amelia! Watch me!' Louise ignored Katie's cry. Her nostrils were white with anger.

'Barnaby!' she hissed. 'If you don't stop doing this, I'll . . .'

'You'll what?' Barnaby whipped round, and stared at her with a deep angry hurt in his eyes. 'What exactly will you do, Louise?'

'Am—ee—lia! Watch me do a back dive!' Katie's final appeal was so shrill that they all turned to watch.

Standing with her back to the water, Katie was bouncing on the end of the diving-board. She bounced and bounced until the board was vibrating vigorously, then, shooting a triumphant look at Amelia, hurled herself backwards into the air.

The last voice Louise heard was Amelia's, saying, 'Katie's never done a back dive before.'

And then there was just the sight of Katie's small body arching inexpertly in the air, looping round too far, until her head was directly above the corner of the diving-board. And then there was the sickening crack as the board smacked upwards, hitting her head with a terrible malevolent force. And then there was the silence, as her apparently lifeless little body slithered quietly down into the water.

Chapter Five

Cassian Brown was driving back to Melbrook from London, in self-congratulatory mood. He had spent most of the weekend in meetings with one of his law firm's most important Middle Eastern clients, striking a complicated out of court settlement worth, in the end, just short of £800,000. Which, he had to admit to himself, was of no great significance, financially, for the client. But still, it had been a triumph of negotiation. And even though he himself had played only a relatively small role in the dealings, his contribution would, he was sure, have been recognized by those that mattered.

Now he wondered to himself whether it would be worth telephoning Desmond Pickering, head of litigation at the London office. A casual friendly call, just to ensure that Desmond was aware of Cassian's part in the proceedings; just to make certain that no-one else was claiming too much of the credit. He could, Cassian thought, perhaps suggest an informal lunch meeting. Or even invite Desmond down to Melbrook for the weekend. Londoners, he'd noticed, were all too eager to come down to the country if it was only an hour or so away on the motorway.

They could drink white wine, sitting in Cassian's pretty little cottage garden, and talk business discreetly, and perhaps stroll around the village. And then he could introduce Desmond to Louise. Desmond would be impressed by Louise. The daughter of Lord Page, no less. The Honourable Louise Kember.

Kember. Cassian frowned. Such an ungainly name, like its owner. Why on earth had Louise taken on the surname of that oaf? And why, more to the point, had she married him in the first place?

Cassian liked to think that he had spotted the potential of Louise even before he'd been informed of her relationship to Lord Page. He'd noticed her immediately, he told himself; he'd seen at once that she was stifled, bored and suffering from a lack of stimulation. She was intelligent and educated, yet she was expected to have no interests above those of her children, the village, and that insufferable boor of a husband.

A picture of Barnaby's face swam into Cassian's mind: dim and brutish, with the suspicious stare of an ill-educated peasant. Those huge hulking shoulders, those clumsy hands, those boots, always caked in mud. And the inarticulateness of the man! Cassian recalled their very first meeting at a drinks party. He had attempted a number of pleasant conversational gambits, and Barnaby had seemed incapable of responding with anything more than a shrug or a grunt or a monosyllable.

Louise, on the other hand, had positively sparkled with wit and charm and important names. Cassian recalled, again, the *frisson* he'd received when she'd casually referred to current cabinet ministers by their Christian names; when she'd spoken, with the disparaging tone of an insider, of Commons food; then, later, after a few more drinks, when she'd related the story of the time the Prime Minister telephoned and she was the only one in, and she thought it was a hoaxer and didn't pass the message on.

Little idiot! Cassian gave a small grin. For all her knowledgeable veneer, Louise had, he'd soon discovered, less of a grip on the world of politics than she liked to think she had. Her mind revolved, he often observed, along the peculiarly feminine parochial grooves which he had noticed in female colleagues at work. They all had the same insistence on knowing irrelevant details; the same ability to take an episode of grave political or legal import and turn it into a trivial anecdote; the same fixation on names, faces and people, rather than issues, concepts and theories.

But no matter. What Louise did have was an effortless ease with the workings of British politics, a grounding in the party political system, an awareness of the lifestyle of a Member of Parliament, and, perhaps most importantly, experience of being involved in a successful political campaign. She had the background, the breeding. She would make an admirable politician's wife. Any selection committee in the country would love her.

At this thought, Cassian began to breathe slightly more quickly. He looked down and saw that his fingers were clenched tightly on the steering-wheel. Carefully, he loosened them and took a deep breath. He mustn't rush things; he mustn't ruin his chances. He knew what people were saying about him: that he was a home-breaker; that he'd lured Louise away from her honest husband. People must think he and Louise had been conducting some kind of torrid affair. At this, Cassian allowed himself a small smirk. As pretty as Louise was, it was a kind of girlish breathy prettiness that held no attraction for him. But that wasn't the point; she would make a lovely suitable bride.

As he began to imagine their smart London wedding, bristling with important people from both politics and law, perhaps with the two little girls as adorable photo-genic bridesmaids, the telephone in his car rang. He switched it on to speaker-phone. A young anxious voice filled the car.

'Cassian? It's Jamie.' Cassian frowned with annoy-ance. Jamie was one of the newest trainees at the Linningford office.

'How the fuck did you get this number?' he snapped.

'I-I phoned your secretary at home. I'm really sorry to bother you. It's just that . . .'

'What?'

'Well, I've been searching all weekend, and I still haven't tracked down that case for you. And I . . . well, I was just wondering, did you have any more information about it?'

'What case?' said Cassian impatiently.

'The one for the letter to Simmons Ltd. Y-you wanted me to check the details.'

'You haven't done it yet?'

'Well, n-no. I've been trying to find the case . . .'

'Jamie, I don't need this crap. That letter was urgent!'

'I know! I've been looking for the case. I'm in the library now, but you didn't give me very much to go on . . .'

'Well, that's just tough! You fucking well find that case, and you have the letter ready on my desk by tomorrow morning. All right?'

'All right.'

'And you don't ring me on this line again, OK?'

'Y-yes. I'm really sorry, Cassian . . .' But Cassian abruptly switched off the phone, cutting Jamie off mid-flow.

For a moment he couldn't remember what he had been thinking about. Then, gradually, a series of pleasant images began to filter back into his mind. A collage of blue eyes, feathery blond hair, a bright giggling laugh, a title, an important father and an easy entry into the world of high-flying politics.

As he neared Melbrook, Cassian decided he would go straight to see Louise, to relate to her the triumph of the weekend. Perhaps, he thought, taking the turning for her house, it was even time to move their relationship on to a new level. The rush of adrenalin from the weekend's deals had not completely faded; there lingered inside him still a faint frustrating arousal. He would get rid of it by taking Louise to bed, and simultaneously would get rid of the ambivalence still hanging over their relationship. It had surely been long enough by now. Barnaby had been out of the house for months. Louise must be ripe and ready; she wouldn't refuse him.

Filled with a faint anticipation, he sauntered up the path, rang the doorbell, and pushed a hand back through his glossy dark hair. When the door opened, he began a sexy half smile, and stepped forward to give Louise a kiss.

But it wasn't Louise who stood in front of him in the doorway, it was Mary Tracey, holding her baby. Automatically, Cassian frowned. Then, with sudden horror, he saw that her face was red and swollen, with bloodshot eyes and tear-stained skin. Immediately he thought of Louise.

'Has something happened?' he began in an alarmed voice. Mary's face crumpled up and she gave a little sob.

'It's Katie,' she managed, before dissolving into fresh, shuddering streams of tears. 'She's had an accident.'

Barnaby stood, clutching the door of the Accident and Emergency ward of Braybury Hospital, and shook with terror. Fifteen feet away, in a cleared space, lay Katie, unconscious, on a hospital bed. A plastic contraption was in her mouth; a battery of transparent tubes ran from her body to flashing green television screens; and now, looming over her immobile form, was a huge monster of a machine. Someone had explained to him in a clear careful voice, that this was the portable X-ray machine, and that he would, briefly, have to move away from the area of Katie's bed. Louise was allowed to put on a lead jacket and stay, together with one of the nurses, but everyone else moved out of the radiation zone, leaving the small form of Katie briefly marooned, like a leper or a corpse.

'OK.' The machine began to move away; the voice of

the X-ray operator resonated through the tense silence and immediately, as though on starting blocks, the team of doctors and nurses waiting on the sidelines rushed forward again, each sure of where to go, what to do and how to do it. Only Barnaby remained motionless. A paralysis of helplessness anchored him to the ground. He could not think what to do, or what to say, or what to feel. Pictures circled again and again in his mind, and with them billowed clouds of pain and disbelief.

He'd got to Katie first. Amid the screams and shouts and – from those who hadn't seen properly – giggles, he'd somehow got to the pool, dived in, and desperately groped in the water for her little body, and eventually managed to scoop her out and place her tenderly by the side of the pool. She hadn't drowned; she'd seemed to be breathing, and everyone had said, 'Thank God.'

Then the ambulance crew had arrived. And it was then, as Barnaby watched them wedging her head into a wooden frame, and placing her on a stiff board, and covering her face with an oxygen mask, and heard them radioing ahead to the hospital, saying, 'Please alert trauma team', that this feeling of unbearable, inarticulate panic had begun.

None of the ambulance crew had smiled at him, or said, Not to worry, or We'll soon have this little lady on her feet again. They'd worked quickly and efficiently, while the taut silence around the pool grew heavier and heavier. Louise had kept her head, to some degree, organizing Mary Tracey to look after Amelia, and talking soothingly to Katie. But Barnaby had stood mute, still dripping from the pool, unable to speak; unable to look, almost, as these calm professionals packaged up his daughter and swiftly took her away from him.

Only one parent in the ambulance, they'd said. And Barnaby had stared back at them, in numb, stupid incomprehension. But Louise had turned, pale-faced and hesitant, to Hugh, and even before she could ask, he was insisting on driving Barnaby to the hospital, behind the ambulance all the way. When they'd got here, the trauma team had been waiting for them at the door. And as the doctors leaped into their frantic work over his daughter's unconscious form, Barnaby had stood still and watched, while water dripped down his neck and a terrible, unspeakable fear seeped through his body.

Mary Tracey sat at the table in Louise Kember's kitchen, clutched baby Luke to her chest and surreptitiously watched Cassian. He had led her gently into the kitchen, sat her down on a chair, and was now making them both a cup of tea. As he waited for the kettle to boil, he leaned casually against a kitchen cupboard, an elegant figure, even in off-duty clothes. Slowly Mary took in his tanned muscular arms, his thick glossy hair, his curved lips and white teeth. He was, she admitted to herself at last, quite something to look at.

Mary had always been fond of both Barnaby and Louise. When the rumours had begun she had stoutly disbelieved them; when they had actually split up, she had felt devastated. If such a wonderfully happy couple could break up, she had thought to herself, what hope was there for the rest of them?

And at the bottom of her heart she had blamed Cassian Brown. If he hadn't moved into the village, she had decided, none of it would have happened. Never having met him properly, she had conjured up in her mind an image of him as an evil, lecherous character, preying on a happily married woman. Italian blood in him, she'd thought. No wonder. He was probably all mixed up with the Mafia. He was probably setting Louise up for some horrible life of crime.

Now she looked at him uncertainly, as he poured out a nice cup of tea for her and gave her a charming

78

smile. He didn't seem such a bad person after all, she thought unwillingly. He was being very kind to her — he'd listened carefully as she told him all about the accident — and he was so good-looking. No wonder Louise . . .

'Do you like sugar?' Cassian's voice caught Mary by surprise.

'Oh, yes please,' she replied. She looked down at Luke, and hastily wiped away a dribble from his little chin. What must she look like herself? she suddenly found herself thinking. All blotchy and crumpled . . . Then, with a sudden emotional swoop, her thoughts returned to poor little Katie. Her heart gave an unpleasant thump and she began to shift uncomfortably in her chair. It didn't seem right to be sitting doing nothing.

'I'll take a drink up to Amelia in a minute,' she said quietly. 'Ask her what she wants for supper, poor little pet.'

'I suppose Louise might stay at the hospital all night', said Cassian, 'if things are really bad.'

Mary looked at him in alarm.

'H-how bad', she faltered, 'do you think they might be? Do you think . . .' She tailed off, unable to say the words. Cassian looked at her soberly.

'Head injuries are no joke,' he said. He put the tea down in front of her. 'Here,' he said, 'drink this.'

'Thank you,' mumbled Mary. She felt sudden respect for Cassian, a serious professional man. He was young, but he knew about things. He had the answers to her questions.

She sipped her tea and felt its sweet warming strength spread through her body. Cassian was still standing up, drinking his own tea. Suddenly he seemed to make a decision.

'I think I'll go along to the hospital,' he said. 'Unless you want me to help you here?'

He gave her a brief questioning smile, and Mary shook her head dumbly.

'No, of course not,' said Cassian smoothly. 'I'm sure you can manage. And I'd very much like to er . . . make myself useful to Louise.'

'Give them my love,' said Mary. 'And lots of love to Katie.' Her voice began to shake, and she felt her nose start to prickle again.

'Oh, sure,' said Cassian, picking up his jacket. 'Absolutely.'

Louise and Barnaby had been shepherded into a tiny room off the side of the ward, which was furnished with an oatmeal-coloured three-piece suite and a vase of plastic flowers. They sat in a white-faced silent blur, each battling with their own shocking, tormenting emotions.

Louise's thoughts skittered through her mind in a circular, repetitive cycle. Katie bouncing on the board, Katie shrieking, Katie falling; that scream. A knife-like pain in her heart, then, rushing tantalizingly into her head before she could stop them, the crowding unbearable what-might-have-beens. If she'd told Katie to get out of the pool earlier. If she'd told the girls not to go on the diving-board. If Katie had gone fishing after all. If they'd all gone fishing. A picture of them all happily eating pizza. A fleeting, deceiving sensation of relief, and then, with a flash, the icy stab of reality; of Katie's little body, unconscious, wired up. And immediately back to Katie bouncing on the board, Katie shrieking, Katie falling.

For the moment she could not wrench her mind from its repeating, circular pattern. Lurking in the shadows of her mind, waiting to pounce, towered emotions that were huge and frightening; that would consume and destroy her. For the moment they must be kept out. And so her mind raced around, lingering on no thought long enough for it to develop; allowing no conclusions to be drawn; no speculations to be made.

She avoided the very sight of Barnaby. One word; one look from him, and the vulture emotions would smash down the door and she would be no good to anybody. So she stared downwards, with an ashen face and a desperate inward absorption, and waited for the doctors to come, while her mind raced round and round, faster and faster and faster.

Mary was starting to trudge upstairs to Amelia's room when she heard a knock on the door. Startled, she went to open it. It was Cassian, back again already.

'Sorry to trouble you, Mary,' he said, and gave her a charming smile. Mary's heart gave a little flutter.

'Oh, no trouble,' she said breathlessly. 'Did you forget something?'

'Not exactly,' said Cassian casually. 'I just wanted to check something very unimportant. Something I was wondering about.' He smiled sympathetically at her. 'When the accident happened, there were still lots of people present, weren't there?' He spread his hands vaguely. 'Witnesses, if you like. People who saw what happened.'

'Oh,' said Mary in surprise. She hefted Luke up further on her chest and stroked his downy hair. 'Well, yes,' she said, 'I suppose there were. Heaps of people were there. All the village, really. Although, of course, not everybody was looking when it . . . when it actually happened.' Her face began to crumple.

'Yes, of course,' said Cassian quickly. 'Well, that's all I wanted to know. Thanks.' And he began to stride back towards his car, while Mary looked after him in slight puzzlement.

When the door of the little room opened, Louise jumped and looked up fearfully. A face peered round. It was a

81

young man, wearing round spectacles and a white coat.

'Mr and Mrs Kember? My name's Michael Taylor. I'm the consultant dealing with Katie.'

He came into the room, sat down, and looked earnestly at Louise and Barnaby.

'As you know,' he began rapidly, 'Katie has sustained an injury to the head. She was hit quite hard when she . . .' he consulted his notes . . . 'crashed down on the diving-board. Now,' he paused, 'we've just had back the results of Katie's scan. And we've found what we suspected might be the case, that a blood clot has formed, which is pressing on Katie's brain.' He looked from Barnaby to Louise. 'I don't want to appear to be rushing you,' he said, 'and I know it's difficult to take all this in, but we're going to have to remove the clot as soon as possible to maximize her chances of recovery.'

There was a silence. Barnaby looked away. Louise met the consultant's eyes.

'Brain surgery,' she faltered.

'I know it sounds frightening,' said the consultant earnestly. 'In actual fact, it's a fairly straightforward operation, and we need to give the brain as much chance as possible to heal.' He paused. 'We'd like to take her into theatre as soon as we can.'

There was another silence. Louise could hear her breaths coming quick and shallow. She felt as though she might be hallucinating. Suddenly Barnaby spoke, in a husky, almost inaudible voice.

'But she will be . . . all right.' The consultant's gaze did not flicker.

'There is a strong chance that once the pressure on her brain has been relieved, Katie will make a good recovery,' he said. He paused. 'But you must remember, she has received a considerable injury to the brain; not merely from the blow to the head, but also from lack of oxygen during the time spent underwater.' He looked at Barnaby. 'I gather she wasn't

82

under for more than a few seconds?'

'I got to her . . .' Barnaby's voice was hoarse and cracked. 'I got to her as quickly as I could.'

'Well then,' said the consultant gently, 'you may well have saved her from serious brain damage.'

'But you don't know?' Louise's voice was high and brittle.

'I'm afraid we don't,' said the consultant. 'Not yet. After surgery, things may be clearer.' He flipped to another page of his notes. 'There are several encouraging factors. There seems to be no paralysis, and her spinal cord appears undamaged, and the swelling of her brain is less severe than we might have expected.' He looked at them. 'Until Katie regains consciousness, we won't know exactly what sort of damage has been done, if any.'

'And when will that be?' Louise tried to control her voice.

'I'm afraid that's something else that we don't know.' He looked at Louise. 'You're shivering, Mrs Kember. Would you like the nurse to bring you a cup of tea?'

Louise shook her head numbly.

'I'd like to see Katie, before she has her operation.'

'Of course. Do you have any more questions?'

Suddenly there was a knock on the door. A nurse poked her head into the room.

'Excuse me,' she said. 'A Mr Cassian Brown's here. He said he didn't want to disturb you, but he's brought a change of clothes for Mrs Kember and some bubble bath.' She looked at Louise. 'He thought, if you had to spend a long time here, you might want to have a bath.'

'That's a good idea,' said the consultant. 'When Katie's gone into theatre, one of the nurses will take you to a nice quiet bathroom. You'll want to be rested and refreshed for when she comes out.' He looked at the nurse. 'You can sort that out, can't you, Sandra?'

'Of course,' said the nurse sympathetically. 'Just tell me when you want it,' she said to Louise, 'and I'll run you a nice hot bath.'

Louise looked at the kindly face of the nurse, and to her horror, felt her shoulders heaving. She gave a single, involuntary, anguished cry; heavy hot tears began to splash onto her hands.

'You're very kind,' she struggled to say. Then, unable to stop herself, she gave way to pent-up juddering sobs. The nurse exchanged looks with the consultant.

'I've got to go, I'm afraid,' he said, 'but Sandra will look after you. Sandra,' he added, on his way out of the door, 'they'd like to see their daughter before she goes into theatre.'

'Of course,' said the nurse. She crossed the floor, sat down beside Louise, and brought out a tissue.

'Thank you,' managed Louise. For a moment she seemed to be calming down. She sat up and wiped her eyes. Then, suddenly, she began to weep again in a frenzy of gasping and shuddering.

'I know,' said the nurse soothingly. 'I know.' She put an arm round Louise, and Louise suddenly turned her sobbing face, burying it in the nurse's ample shoulder.

Barnaby stared blackly ahead, immobilized by grief, fear, and an impotent anger. Everybody seemed able to do something to help except him. Someone else was comforting Louise; someone else was operating on his daughter; someone else had even thought to bring bubble bath for Louise. A picture of Cassian's smug face passed briefly through Barnaby's mind, accompanied by a black, suspicious, envious resentment. Why had Cassian been the one to bring bubble bath for Louise? What was he doing at the hospital? What right did he have to interfere?

A cloud of despairing misery fell down upon Barnaby, and his head drooped lower until all he could see was the oatmeal fabric of the sofa. But even that was too much for him, so he shut his eyes and listened to the sound of Louise weeping, and found himself wishing, in a stark, hopeless way, that they could go back to the beginning of the day and start all over again.

Chapter Six

The next morning Meredith woke late, with a looming, menacing feeling in her head, and a painful dream about Simon slipping out of her mind before she could remember it. She got shakily out of bed, pulled back the curtains to reveal another shining bright day, and regarded herself in the mirror. Her face was pale and puffy, and down one side of it ran a deep red crease where she had slept, pressed up against the seam of her nightdress. Like a scar, she thought dully.

And then, in a flash, it all came back to her: the accident, the ambulance, the endless hours afterwards; hours of persuading people to go home, and fending off phone calls, and turning away visitors who had got hold of a garbled version of the story. They'd stayed up until midnight, until someone phoned to give them the news: Katie's operation had gone well, but she was in a coma.

Lightning visions of hospital wards, machines and nurses passed through Meredith's mind. Simon had only been in hospital for a day and a half before he had died, but that time had magnified in Meredith's mind until it seemed a lifetime; a lifetime of sitting by his bed, talking to him, holding his hand, battling with the dragons of fear and pessimism; trying always to keep her voice warm and positive, just in case he could hear. Now, she thought, she would never know if he really had heard any of the things she'd said; if he had taken in any of the love, the respect and the belief in him that she'd tried so desperately to convey.

They'd switched off his life-support machine early in

the morning, and for a few seconds afterwards she'd stared in desperation at his face, believing that if she willed hard enough, he would open his eyes and wake up. But of course, he hadn't, and he never would, and perhaps, Meredith thought, with a sudden stab of fearful pain, little Katie never would either.

She quickly dressed and opened her bedroom door. From downstairs she could hear the voices of Hugh and Ursula . . . and Frances . . . and a voice that sounded like Alexis. In spite of herself her spirits quickened slightly, and for a moment she battled with the desire to shut her bedroom door, choose a new outfit and check her appearance in the mirror. But a stern sense of priorities stopped her from doing so. Now was not the time for thinking of herself.

She came down to find Hugh and Ursula sitting in the kitchen. It was a large sunny room, with yellow-painted walls and a huge oak table. At one end of the table was the remains of breakfast; at the other end was Alexis, drinking a cup of coffee and looking concerned; and at the back door was Frances, wearing an unbecoming beige print frock and an anxious expression.

Meredith looked from face to face.

'Have you heard anything?' she said.

'She's still in a coma,' said Frances.

'Oh, God,' said Meredith. She sank onto a chair and poured herself some coffee.

'I just feel,' said Hugh miserably, 'so . . . so *helpless*.'

'I can't bear to think about it,' said Ursula. 'Poor Louise. Poor Barnaby.'

'Poor Katie,' said Meredith soberly. She looked at Frances. 'And they don't know what the prognosis is?' Frances shook her head.

'I don't think they do. I think they're just waiting for her to wake up.'

'Waiting,' said Meredith. 'That's the worst part. Just sitting there, with that feeling that there's nothing you can do.' There was a short silent pause. From the hall came the sound of the grandfather clock ticking quietly and steadily along.

'Well, actually,' said Frances eventually, 'there is something that you can do, if you wouldn't mind. Alan's holding a service for Katie tonight at six o'clock. We expect that quite a lot of people will come, so we're going to need extra chairs from the church hall, and I was wondering if you could help me move them.' She looked around. 'If we all move a few it won't take long.'

'Of course we'll help,' said Hugh. He sighed. 'It's the least we can do.' He looked at Frances. 'Do you think Louise and Barnaby will come to the service?'

'I don't know,' said Frances. 'It all depends, I suppose, on what happens . . .' There was a brief sobering silence.

'OK,' said Meredith. She put down her coffee-cup. 'Let's go.'

'I don't want to rush you,' protested Frances. 'Have some breakfast first.'

'No, I'm not having breakfast,' said Meredith. Alexis looked at her.

'Your not eating breakfast', he said seriously, 'is not going to help young Katie.'

'I know,' said Meredith impatiently. 'I know it won't help, but still . . . it seems like an insult – to be *eating*, when she's . . .' She tailed off.

'Meredith!' interjected Ursula in alarm. 'You mustn't starve yourself.'

'I'm not going to starve myself,' said Meredith, 'but you know what I mean.' She looked at Alexis. There was a pause, then he nodded.

'Yes,' he said slowly, 'I know exactly what you mean.'

When the others had gone off to the church, Ursula began to clear the breakfast things away, picking up plates and cups, and stacking them haphazardly by the sink. Despite what Meredith repeatedly told her, Ursula could never quite believe that the three of them ever used enough china to make it worthwhile using the dishwasher. And so the usual pattern was that, after every meal, she would put on a pair of rubber gloves and attempt to begin washing-up by hand, while Meredith furiously grabbed the plates from the sink and thrust them into the machine. But today there was no Meredith to stop her. And so, for a while, Ursula stood, diligently scrubbing each plate by hand, rinsing it free of foam and checking its shiny surface in the sunlight. It was a slow process, but she had done all the plates and nearly all the cups and saucers before she was interrupted by the sound of footsteps on the gravel.

At first she thought it was the others returning from the church, but there only seemed to be one pair of feet. And instead of making confidently for the back door, they were hesitating, swivelling around on the gravel, stopping altogether, then starting again. Ursula put down the cup she was holding, took off her apron, patted her hair, and went out of the back door. It was probably somebody from the village, wanting news of Katie.

But when she reached the drive, she stopped in surprise. There, standing with his head tilted back, surveying the house with a full and frank stare, was the young man with the dark hair whom everybody said had broken up the Kembers' marriage. What was his name, now? The only name that came to her mind was Dawn Treader, and that couldn't be it, surely?

'Hello,' said Ursula hesitantly. The young man started, then regained his composure, gave Ursula an unctuous smile and held out his hand.

'Good morning, Mrs Delaney,' he said smoothly. 'I don't know if you remember me. Cassian Brown.'

'Of course!' exclaimed Ursula. 'Prince Caspian!' Cassian stared at her.

'No,' he said, 'not Caspian, Cassian. And I'm afraid I'm not quite a prince.' Ursula blushed.

'No,' she said, 'I mean in the book. *The Voyage of the Dawn Treader.* C.S. Lewis, you know,' she added feebly. 'Prince Caspian. That's where I remembered you from. Although of course the name isn't *quite* the same . . .' She tailed off foolishly as she saw Cassian's blank face. He waited for her to finish, then smiled again, a very brief smile, before adopting a solemn expression.

'I was wondering whether you would allow me to have a look at the swimming-pool where Katie was hurt yesterday,' he said, in grave tones. 'Since I wasn't actually there, I'd just like to see it for myself . . .' Ursula's face crumpled slightly.

'Yes, of course,' she said. 'Poor Katie. Do you know how . . .?'

'She's still unconscious, I'm afraid,' said Cassian. He began to lead the way round the house, and Ursula followed him timidly, feeling that this seemed a little wrong, but not quite sure why.

When they got to the pool, Cassian made his way straight to the diving-board. He looked at Ursula.

'This is where she slipped?'

'Yes,' said Ursula, in a distressed voice. 'I can hardly bear to look.' There was a pause. 'Actually,' she amended, 'I'm not sure whether she actually slipped . . .' But Cassian didn't seem to be listening. He was bending down and running a finger along the surface of the board.

'How old is the pool?' he said.

'Well, I don't really know,' said Ursula. She looked around vaguely. 'It was here when we moved in, and that was over twenty years ago.'

'The diving-board too?'

'Well, yes,' said Ursula. She looked at the diving-board and shivered. 'I'd like to get rid of the horrid dangerous thing.' Cassian looked up sharply.

'Why dangerous?' Ursula looked at him in puzzlement.

90

'Well, dear,' she said gently. 'Katie had her accident trying to dive off it, you know, and I believe professional divers quite often have accidents too.'

'Yes, but you said *this* board was dangerous,' persisted Cassian. 'Why would this particular board be dangerous?' Ursula looked at him confusedly.

'Is it?' she said. 'I don't think it is, really.' Cassian gave up. He stood up and looked around.

'Do you remember how many people were here yesterday?' he asked conversationally. Ursula screwed up her face.

'I suppose . . . about a hundred,' she said. 'I could tell you if we'd counted the donations, but we haven't yet. It didn't seem, somehow . . .' She broke off and clasped her hand to her mouth, her eyes shining slightly. 'Of course,' she said. 'The money must go to Katie. And we must start an appeal. We can begin at the church tonight.' She looked at Cassian expectantly, but he didn't seem to be listening.

'And who was supervising the children?' he said.

'Well,' said Ursula slowly, 'no-one was actually *supervising* them. But they were all here with their parents, you know, and there was always someone watching them. Louise was watching Amelia and Katie for quite a long time, I remember, and then I watched them for a bit . . .' She broke off and looked at him, tears bright in her eyes.

'You know, I find this rather distressing,' she said. 'Would you mind if we went inside?' She paused. 'Perhaps you would like a cup of coffee. The others should be back soon and you can chat to them.' She regarded him sympathetically. 'You must be terribly upset.'

Meredith and Alexis arrived back at the house to find the kitchen empty and the back door open.

'I wonder where . . .' began Meredith.

Then they heard Ursula's voice from outside, saying, 'Ah, that sounds like them!'

She appeared at the back door, looking a little flustered. Meredith opened her mouth to speak, then stopped in surprise as she saw, hovering behind Ursula, the unlikely figure of Cassian Brown, wearing an immaculate suit and carrying a dark heavy-looking briefcase. Her initial temptation was to ask what the fuck he was doing there, but instead she took a step forward and smiled at Cassian. He beamed charmingly back, and nodded his head politely towards Alexis with a smooth deferential courtesy which Meredith, in her mind, labelled creepy.

'Hello,' she said. 'We have met before. I'm Meredith.'

'I remember very well,' said Cassian. 'The artist.' His eyes briefly met Meredith's, and to her astonishment she felt herself staring back at him, unwillingly mesmerized by his deep dark gaze. Briskly, she tore her attention away. 'And this is our friend Alexis Faraday . . .' Suddenly she interrupted herself. 'Is there some news about Katie? Is that why you came?' Cassian shook his head gravely.

'Cassian wanted to have a look at the swimming-pool,' put in Ursula.

'But I'm afraid I've got to go now,' said Cassian smoothly. 'Thank you very much for your kindness.'

He held out one hand to Ursula. She hesitated, then took it, smiling falteringly back at him with the foolish gaze of a fascinated rabbit. Meredith watched Cassian distrustfully, and felt a sudden obscure need to protect Ursula. But against what? A young man with mesmerizing eyes?

They all watched as Cassian made his exit out of the kitchen door, and listened in silence as his feet crunched away on the gravel of the drive. When the sound had faded to nothing, Ursula looked at Meredith with an animated expression on her face.

'I've had an idea,' she said. 'We should give all the donations from yesterday to Katie, and we should start an appeal.'

'Good idea, Ursula,' said Meredith vaguely, but her face was still wary. 'What exactly did that guy Cassian want?' she asked.

'To look at where poor Katie had her accident,' said Ursula. She frowned. 'Something like that.'

'Who is he?' said Alexis. He screwed up his face in thought. 'I'm sure I know him from somewhere.'

'Louise Kember's lover,' said Meredith succinctly.

'Now, Meredith,' chided Ursula, 'we don't know that.'

'But why do I recognize him?' said Alexis. 'Have I met him?'

'Well,' said Meredith, 'he's a lawyer. Maybe he hangs out in the same joints you do.'

'A lawyer?' said Alexis. He looked at Ursula's innocent expression and his face darkened slightly. 'Did he tell you why he wanted to look at the pool?'

'Well,' began Ursula, 'no, not really. He just said that it was because he hadn't been here yesterday. I thought he was probably very upset.'

'He didn't look very upset to me,' observed Meredith. 'He looked . . .'

'You didn't say anything to him,' interrupted Alexis, 'did you, Ursula? Anything about the accident?'

'Well, no,' said Ursula. 'I mean, yes.' She looked from Alexis to Meredith with puzzled eyes. 'What do you mean? Is anything wrong?'

'No, nothing,' said Alexis, quickly. 'I hope not.'

Later on, as Meredith came up the stairs, she heard a voice from Hugh's study. It was a subdued voice, and it was saying, 'Shit.' She gently pushed the door open. There was Alexis, standing at Hugh's open desk, holding some sort of brochure open in front of him.

'What's wrong?' said Meredith lightly. 'Hugh owe you

money?' Alexis whipped round and gave Meredith a rather hesitant smile.

'No, nothing's wrong,' he said, in a voice that wasn't quite cheerful. He quickly put the brochure back in a drawer and shut it. Meredith stared at him sternly.

'Something's wrong, isn't it? What? Is Hugh's business in trouble?'

'No, honestly, Meredith,' said Alexis. 'I was just . . . just checking something.' He began to move towards the door. 'Now,' he said, giving her a charming crinkled smile, 'how about some Meredith-strength coffee to set me up for the rest of the day?'

He took her arm, and as he did so, she felt a sudden foolish tingle of pleasure. But even as she allowed Alexis to lead her down the stairs; even as she glimpsed, with a pang of delight, the reflection of the two of them together in the landing mirror, she could feel a faint web of anxiety anchoring itself throughout her body, tugging gently at her thoughts and causing her face to wrinkle with an unspecified alarm.

Cassian arrived at the hospital at four o'clock. He had spent much of the day loitering in the village grocery store, the post office, outside the church and in The George. And by the time he arrived at the hospital, he had talked to over twenty people in the village about the accident, carefully taking notes and writing down names after each conversation.

As he entered the ward where Katie lay, he adopted a sober expression and looked around gingerly. It was a very small, very quiet ward, with only four beds, all shrouded, to some extent, by floral curtains. One bed was completely shrouded, and from it came the sound of murmurings, then a small cry of pain. A nurse in a blue uniform appeared from behind the curtains, carrying a bowl of something. Cassian averted his eyes.

'Cassian!' A faltering voice attracted his attention. It

was Louise, looking up from where she was seated beside Katie's bed.

'Louise,' said Cassian, in smooth sympathetic tones. She looked, he thought, absolutely terrible; her face was pale and suddenly seemed much older than before; her eyes were bloodshot; her hands were wringing anxiously together.

Then he glanced down at Katie, and his stomach flipped over unpleasantly. Katie's head had been partially shaved; her tiny white face was obscured by a tube; every bit of her seemed connected to one of several television monitors, along which green lines were merrily flickering. On the wall beside her high clanking metal bed was a laminated chart, labelled Glasgow Coma Scale.

'How is she?' he asked. Louise swallowed.

'She's still in a coma, but it isn't as deep as it was, apparently.' She ran a hand distractedly through her hair. 'The blood clot's gone, and they scanned her this afternoon and, so far, no more clots have formed. They were pleased about that.' She looked at Cassian beseechingly. 'It could be a lot worse,' she said, as though to reassure herself.

Cassian stared at Katie, unconvinced, and gave a little shiver.

'Perhaps', he said, 'we could go and have a cup of coffee? Is there a canteen or something?'

The hospital corridors were warm and pastel-coloured, and reminded Cassian of the inside of a smart motorway service station. An impression which was borne out further when they reached the hospital's Four-Grain Eaterie and were given, along with their cups of coffee, a questionnaire to fill in on aspects of the menu, service and decor.

Louise took a sip of coffee and winced.

'I've drunk so much coffee today,' she said. 'That's all I've done. Sit with Katie and drink coffee.' She took

95

another sip. 'I keep talking to her, and singing to her, and rubbing her feet, and none of it does any good.' She looked at Cassian. 'She could be in a coma for weeks!' Her voice was trembling. 'Or months! I mean, she could, couldn't she? What if she never wakes up?'

Cassian looked at Louise silently for a moment. Then he reached out, put her coffee cup down, and took her hands in his.

'You mustn't think like that,' he said. 'You must think positively. She might wake up any moment.'

'I know,' faltered Louise, 'but . . .' Cassian interrupted her.

'On the other hand,' he said solemnly, 'there's no point in denying the facts. Katie has been badly hurt. We don't know when or how well she's going to recover.' Cassian clasped Louise's hands a little more tightly and looked deeply into her eyes. 'And I believe', he continued, in a low sincere voice, 'that it's up to you and Barnaby – and even me –' he dropped his eyes modestly downwards, 'it's up to all of us to do as much for Katie as we can. Whatever that means.'

Louise gazed back at him with a worried, uncomprehending expression.

'We're . . . we're doing everything we can,' she faltered. 'Barnaby's coming along as soon as he's finished work, and then we're going to the special service they're holding at the church. And the doctors have said all they can do now is wait. One of the nurses said . . .' she swallowed '. . . that Katie's body has put itself into a coma just because she needs a good rest, and that everything will be healing while she sleeps.' A tear glistened at the corner of Louise's eye.

'Of course, of course,' soothed Cassian. 'I'm sure that's right, but, you know, there's more you could be doing than that.' He pulled his briefcase onto the table and opened it discreetly. 'I've been doing a bit of research into this accident,' he said. 'I don't want to upset you, but it seems that someone, somewhere, was negligent.'

At those words Louise froze, and her already white face became whiter. Into her tired mind, before she could stop them, flowed the memories that she'd been trying to stave off until now. The vision of Ursula, warning her that the children were overexcited. The picture of herself, ignoring Katie's shrieks; of her and Barnaby, thoughtlessly arguing while their daughter hurled herself into injury; into what might have been death.

It was all her fault; her fault. A violent putrefying guilt exploded inside her, making her shudder with nausea. She clutched at her stomach and looked despairingly at Cassian.

'It was an accident,' she said weakly, pleadingly. She could feel her insides wrenching painfully, and feel a self-loathing rising swiftly through her body.

'Of course it was an accident,' said Cassian briskly, still head-down in his briefcase. 'But even so, there may well have been negligence. In fact, I'm almost sure there was. And so . . .' He broke off suddenly and looked up at Louise. 'You'll have to think about it,' he said, 'and, of course, talk to Barnaby.' He paused, as though for effect. 'But what I recommend, Louise, is that you go to court.'

Louise looked at him through a blur. 'Go to court?' Black shadows were dancing in front of her eyes. 'Be pro-prosecuted?' She took a deep gasp of air. 'I didn't mean . . . I didn't think . . . I'm sorry, I'm sorry . . .'

'Louise, what are you talking about?' Cassian's voice pierced her consciousness. 'I'm not talking about prosecution. I'm talking about a civil case. From what I've discovered, I think you've got very good grounds for suing Hugh and Ursula Delaney.'

Barnaby arrived at the hospital at five o'clock and went straight to the ward, clutching the piles of cards

97

and toys which had arrived at Larch Tree Cottage that day. The chair by Katie's bed was empty and he couldn't see Louise anywhere on the ward. As he gazed around uncomprehendingly, a nurse whom he didn't recognize saw him looking, and said, 'I think Mrs Kember went to the cafeteria. With . . . her husband, is it?'

Barnaby stared, speechless for a moment. Only when he had recovered his composure could he ask where the cafeteria was. He bent down, stroked Katie's hair and whispered, 'I'll be back in a minute, Katkin.' Then he strode off down the corridor with a burning face and a thumping heart.

When he reached the cafeteria, he saw them instantly, sitting back, relaxed, as though nothing was wrong. He was immediately filled with a bleak fury.

'Louise!' he called.

'Barnaby!' She looked up and smiled; she actually smiled. Barnaby strode over.

'Katie's all alone,' he said, aware that his voice sounded accusing, yet unable to stop himself. 'She's been all alone for half an hour.'

'She's not all alone,' protested Louise. 'She's being looked after by a team of trained medical experts.' She took a sip of coffee and Barnaby, suddenly enraged, thumped his huge fist on the table with a bang.

'That's neither here nor there!' he exclaimed. 'The doctors said that *our* voices would help to bring her round! My God, if you can't even sit and talk to her . . .'
Louise stood up, her face pink with anger.

'I've been with her all day. I've been talking to her and massaging her feet and doing everything I can for her. I came here for one cup of coffee! One cup of coffee, Barnaby!' Her distressed voice rose through the room, and various members of the cafeteria staff began to look in their direction. 'And anyway,' added Louise, calming down slightly, 'Cassian and I have been talking about the accident. You should listen to what Cassian's got to say.' She sat back down on her chair and, with slightly trembling lips, took another sip of coffee.

'What?' Barnaby looked at Cassian with black suspicion.

'Perhaps later,' murmured Cassian to Louise.

'No, now!' thundered Barnaby. 'Tell me what he's said, that's so important it's kept you from being with Katie.'

'All right,' said Louise. She took a breath. 'He says we should sue Hugh and Ursula. On Katie's behalf,' she added.

'What?'

'I'm not really sure this is the time or place for this discussion,' said Cassian smoothly. 'Perhaps the two of you could talk, and . . .' He stood up, then flinched as Barnaby roughly pushed him back into his seat. Louise looked anxiously at Barnaby; his face was bright red and his whole body was trembling.

'Talk?' he roared. 'Talk about what? Are you serious?'

'Apparently we could prove they were negligent,' began Louise. Barnaby gazed at her, aghast.

'Hugh and Ursula? Are you saying Hugh and Ursula are to *blame*? My God . . .'

'It's not a matter of blame,' put in Cassian swiftly. 'It's a matter of . . . compensation.'

'Compensation?' echoed Barnaby. 'You mean money! You're just talking about money, aren't you?' Louise looked down awkwardly at the table. 'Katie's been in hospital for less than a day,' Barnaby shouted, 'and already all you can think about is *money*!'

He looked from Louise to Cassian, with an incredulous pent-up expression. All the misery, worry and despair of the last twenty-four hours seemed to be building up inside him like a furnace.

'You're sick,' he suddenly shouted. 'You're both sick!' And with an abrupt savage movement, he kicked over a chair. It hit the table noisily as it fell, and the cups and saucers clattered. From the other side of the cafeteria began some interested murmurings. Cassian smiled apologetically in the direction of the staff, keeping one eye on Barnaby.

'Barnaby, don't be like this,' said Louise. She looked anxiously around the cafeteria. 'This isn't helping Katie either.'

For a few seconds Barnaby stared back at her. Then he sighed, bent down, and righted the chair. Louise and Cassian watched in a nervous silence.

'I'm going, now,' said Barnaby at last, 'to see my daughter, and then I'm going to church to pray for her.' He looked at Louise. 'You can do what the hell you like.'

'Barnaby . . .'

'Leave it, Lou,' Barnaby said in a shaky voice.

And before Louise could say anything more, he left; picking his way clumsily between the tables and chairs and customers; barging out of the door without looking back, with his shoulders hunched up and a stray glittery get-well card for Katie sticking out of the back pocket of his jeans.

The little church was packed when Barnaby arrived. People were milling around, talking and whispering, pulling chairs into line, depositing gifts of toys and flowers on a side-table that seemed to have been set aside for the purpose. The air was tight with uncertain anticipation, and as he surveyed the scene from the porch, Barnaby found himself hesitating like a nervous bride. When he heard his name being called, he gave a startled jump.

'Barnaby!' It was Frances Mold, coming through into the porch and pulling the door behind her. She didn't smile, but took his arm and squeezed it. 'I'm glad you could come,' she said simply.

'There are so many people here,' said Barnaby uncertainly. He gazed down at Frances. 'I don't know half of them.'

'Lots of them seem to know Katie,' said Frances. 'Friends from school, I think.'

'I suppose Louise knows them,' said Barnaby, scowling in spite of himself. The mere thought of Louise still sent a thudding anger through his body. 'Is she here yet?'

Frances looked up at him.

'Louise isn't coming to the service,' she said. 'She phoned from the hospital. She feels she should stay with Katie, just in case she wakes up.'

'Oh,' said Barnaby dully, 'I see.' And suddenly he felt a sense of abandonment. He was going to have to do this on his own.

Frances looked at her watch and reached for the porch door. 'We should really be going in. I've saved you a seat next to me.'

'Wait,' said Barnaby suddenly. 'I'm not . . .' He swallowed and looked away. 'Just give me a second.' Frances waited silently, watching him compose himself, take a few deep breaths and push his fingers through his dark springy hair.

'Right,' he said at last. 'I'm ready.'

As they walked in there was a rippling effect along the pews, as people gradually realized that Barnaby had arrived, and turned to see. Many immediately turned back, but some remained, staring at him with expressions of sympathy ranging from mild compassion to deep distress. Somebody somewhere was quietly crying, and as Barnaby made his way to the front of the church, a baby began to wail.

Alan Mold was already standing at the front of the church, and he gave a kindly nod to Barnaby as he took his seat.

'Let us pray,' he said.

There was a moment's silence. Then, from behind

Barnaby, came a rustling sound, as, wordlessly, the congregation sank together to their knees. And as Barnaby himself slowly knelt down, he felt, through the stillness, the silent support of a hundred people flowing towards him in a single strengthening wave.

It was a short simple service. Alan Mold addressed the congregation in warm tones, read prayers full of love and hope, and led the singing of 'All Things Bright and Beautiful'. When the service had ended, Barnaby stood up to leave, but Frances tugged at his sleeve.

'If I were you,' she said, 'I'd stay here for a bit. Unless you want to have to talk to everybody.'

Barnaby looked down at her. Throughout the service he had felt unable to open his mouth; unable to join in the prayers; unable to sing the hymns. Talking to people was unthinkable. So he nodded gratefully and sank back down next to Frances.

Behind him he could hear the chatterings and murmurings of people leaving; there were many voices that he recognized or half recognized. Several times he heard his name, but he didn't turn round.

'Barnaby?' Suddenly somebody was right beside him. 'Barnaby?'

He looked up. It was Ursula, peering at him in mild concern.

'Hello, Ursula,' he managed. Ursula smiled hesitantly at him.

'I don't know what your plans are,' she said, 'but we wondered whether you'd like to come back to our house for some supper.' She paused, then added anxiously, 'You really must eat properly.'

Barnaby tried to give a jovial smile and failed.

'Don't worry,' he said. 'I'm eating fine.'

'Just for the company, then?'

'To be honest, Ursula,' said Barnaby, 'I'm not much good in company at the moment. It's very kind of you, but I think I'll head back to the hospital.'

'Of course,' said Ursula in slightly crestfallen tones. 'I understand.' Barnaby took her hand.

'I'm very grateful for the offer,' he said, 'but I've got to be with Katie. She might . . .' He swallowed. 'She might wake up any minute.'

'We'll pray that she does,' said Ursula fervently.

'Yes, I know you will,' said Barnaby, and he squeezed her hand. 'I know you will.'

Chapter Seven

Three days later, Barnaby woke early, with a start. He immediately sat up with a beating heart, hoping that he had been woken up by the sound of the telephone ringing. But the phone beside his bed was silent. Another night had passed with no summons to the hospital; no joyful announcement that Katie had woken up. His excitement subsiding, Barnaby got out of bed, padded into his little kitchen and put the kettle on to boil.

Since moving out of Larch Tree Cottage, Barnaby had been renting a tiny ground-floor flat in the new development on the other side of Melbrook. There was only one bedroom and no space for the girls to play when they came to visit, but it was all he could afford, on top of supporting Louise and the girls.

Now he looked around morosely. He suddenly felt weary and depressed. Every night, since the accident, he had fallen into bed hoping, like a child on Christmas Eve, that by the time he woke up, something would have happened. Katie would have woken, smiled, perhaps even asked for him . . .

And every morning he awoke to find no news. No change. She was still stable, the nurses would tell him. No, they couldn't say when she might wake up. No, they couldn't say what damage her injuries might have done. It was early days, they kept saying. All they could do was wait and see.

Until now, Barnaby had quietly obeyed the nurses; had agreed with them that there was no point in thinking the worst; had avoided probing them for the alarming thoughts he could see behind their eyes. Like a coward, what they didn't want to tell him he hadn't wanted to know. But today he did want to know, he suddenly thought, pouring boiling water onto a tea-bag. Today, at the meeting with the consultant, he would demand some answers. He would write out a list of questions and ask them, and would keep asking them until he found out what he wanted to know.

He sat down with his cup of tea and shuffled through the pile of letters he had opened the night before. Many were cards for Katie; letters of concern and sympathy – as though she were dead, he thought savagely to himself. Why was everyone being so bloody gloomy about it? She was going to get better. She was.

At the bottom of the pile were all the other letters. Day-to-day correspondence, mostly bills. Since moving out of Larch Tree Cottage, the bills had been coming thick and fast, like angry rain. There seemed no end to them; no controlling them. Every time Barnaby thought he'd managed to work out a monthly budget, something else came along to surprise him. This week it had been the bill for servicing Louise's car – £300, out of the blue. He was going to have to dip into his savings again.

Why was life suddenly so much more expensive? Living together with Louise in Larch Tree Cottage, his salary had seemed ample for all their needs; now it seemed stretched beyond endurance. None of his sums seemed to add up; however careful he was, at the end of every month he found himself with an overdraft. Despite the fact that he was living in the cheapest accommodation he had been able to find; despite the fact that he'd cut back on practically everything that wasn't essential.

Of course it was his duty to support Louise and the girls, he thought dejectedly to himself, taking a sip of tea and pushing the bill from the garage underneath the pile of cards. They were dependent on him. It was only right. But did that mean he was never going to be able to afford a life of his own?

At ten to eleven, a nurse came over to Katie's bed and tapped Louise on the shoulder.

'Yes?' She turned, startled.

'Sorry,' said the nurse. 'Didn't mean to alarm you. I just thought I'd remind you that you've got a meeting with the consultant at eleven. Just in case . . .' she paused tactfully, '. . . in case you wanted to comb your hair or pop to the loo or anything.'

'Oh, yes,' said Louise dully. 'Yes, thank you. I expect I look dreadful.' She paused. 'Not that it matters what I look like,' she added, slowly getting to her feet. 'I mean, the doctor won't care what I look like, and I shouldn't think Barnaby will, either.'

Since Monday, Louise had barely talked to Barnaby. She had barely talked to anyone, except the nurses and the odd doctor and, of course, all day long, Katie. She spent hours at a time wearily staring at Katie's little face; uttering encouraging words; peering in exhausted desperation for some kind of response. And when there was none she found herself irrationally beginning to doubt her own powers of communication. Sometimes she felt as though she were retreating into a detached light-headed world of her own, in which only she and her own whirling thoughts existed; in which she had been sitting by the same bed for an eternity, staring at Katie's face, willing her to wake up.

On the locker beside Katie's bed was a notebook, which one of the nurses had given to Louise, suggesting she keep a journal of Katie's progress, and of her own thoughts and emotions. So far it was empty. Louise's thoughts were too wild and random to be written down. When she slept, her head filled with dark menacing dreams, which lingered on, like looming shadows, after she woke. Her mind felt stretched; wrung out like an old cloth. Sometimes she thought she might open her mouth and find she had forgotten how to speak.

She hadn't been able to bring herself to attend the church service on Monday evening. The official reason was that Katie might wake up while she wasn't there, but the real reason was that she wasn't sure she could face it. She shuddered as she imagined sitting there, under the glare of all those curious eyes – benevolent and sympathetic, maybe, but curious too, without a doubt. Somehow forcing herself to tell people again and again how Katie was doing; somehow managing to express a suitable gratitude for everyone's interest. Hearing, out loud, the prayers for Katie; trying not to crumble; trying not to cry; trying not to break down completely.

And then there had been the matter of Hugh and Ursula. They had helped to organize the service; if she'd gone to it, she would have seen them; she would have had to talk to them. Louise closed her eyes briefly. She didn't know what to think about Hugh and Ursula; she couldn't think about them rationally; couldn't dissociate them from the accident; from the malevolent nightmares still looming in her mind. Sometimes, as she sat, endlessly replaying the accident in her mind, she would begin to shake with a black nauseous hatred for them; a hatred for their stupid swimming-pool and evil dangerous diving-board. And she would feel a desperate need for them – someone – to be punished for what had happened to Katie. But then something would click in her mind and she would suddenly have an image of a benign smiling Ursula; a kindly Hugh. Old friends of the family, who loved Katie; who would never want to harm her. Tears would well up in her eyes, and suddenly the idea of taking them to court would seem ridiculous, unthinkable.

To Cassian, however, it didn't seem unthinkable at all. As Louise walked along the corridor to the Ladies, swaying slightly with tiredness, she thought about Cassian's proposal. He really seemed to think they had a case. He'd explained it all carefully to her, the night after Barnaby's outburst, and then had sat back, and in a smooth voice, said, 'It's your decision. I won't say another word about it if you don't want me to.'

'No,' Louise faltered. 'It's all very interesting. I'll speak to Barnaby, I don't think he understands properly.'

'You're right,' Cassian had replied. 'I'm sure he doesn't understand.' He looked at her hard. 'I won't say this again,' he said, 'but I think that you and Barnaby should see it as your duty to Katie to take the Delaneys to court.' Then he looked away. 'You owe it to your little girl,' he said in a softer voice. And Louise, strung up and weary, had felt tears trickling down her face, and a sudden conviction that Cassian was right; that he was Katie's saviour; that he was prepared to go into battle on her behalf.

Barnaby arrived at the hospital a few minutes early for the meeting, and went straight to Katie's ward. Louise wasn't sitting beside her bed, and Barnaby felt an immediate, unreasonable wave of anger, and a faint sense of relief. He would have a few moments alone with Katie; would be able to talk to her naturally without Louise standing by and watching, making him feel stupid. He had hardly spoken to Louise since the row in the cafeteria. On the few occasions that they had met beside Katie's bed, they had exchanged a few meaningless pleasantries, just in case she could hear them; otherwise Louise seemed almost to be avoiding him.

'Katie,' he said in a low voice, taking her pale little hand carefully, without dislodging the plastic tube taped to it. 'Katie, it's Daddy. Katie, you're going to be fine. Soon you'll wake up and you'll be able to come home . . .' He broke off. She would be going home to Louise, of course, to Larch Tree Cottage; not home to him.

'Barnaby!' A voice from behind made him jump. He turned to see Louise standing by Katie's curtain rail. She looked pale and exhausted.

'Hello, Louise,' said Barnaby. He suddenly felt stilted and unnatural. 'Has anything . . .' He glanced at Katie. 'Have there been any developments?'

'No,' said Louise shortly. 'Nothing.' She looked at her watch. 'We'd better go.'

The meeting was with the same consultant with round spectacles who had spoken to them in the waiting-room, plus Janine, the nurse who had special responsibility for Katie. Barnaby watched as Louise greeted the consultant with a tremulous smile, then sat down next to Janine and began to talk to her in a familiar undertone, as though they were old friends; as though they were keeping some sort of secret together. Without meaning to, he suddenly said, 'What are you talking about?'

'It doesn't matter,' said Louise.

'Was it about Katie? Is there something I should know?' persisted Barnaby. He tried to smile pleasantly at Janine, but he could feel his face turning red, his breath coming more quickly.

'I was asking Janine for some painkillers, actually,' said Louise curtly. 'I've got a splitting headache.'

'Oh,' said Barnaby. 'I'm sorry to hear that,' he added, but Louise had looked away.

The consultant cleared his throat, shuffled the papers in front of him and then looked up.

'I'm glad you could both come in today,' he said. 'We feel it's very useful to have regular meetings with the parents of children in our wards, to update you on any progress, explain what's happening and give you a

109

chance to ask any questions.' He looked down at his notes. 'In Katie's case, it's still very early days, and as I'm sure you're both aware, there's little we can do other than monitor her very carefully and wait until she begins to regain consciousness. We are keeping a very close eye on her, and if there's any change in her condition, we'll let you know immediately.'

'When do you think . . .' began Barnaby. Everyone looked at him and he gave an awkward cough. 'When do you think she'll wake up?'

'I'm afraid it's very difficult to tell,' said the consultant.

'You must have some idea,' said Barnaby. 'In a week? In a month? In a year?' The consultant sighed.

'I don't want to appear difficult,' he said, 'but we really don't think it's a good idea to try and get into predictions.' He smiled kindly at Barnaby. 'Katie will wake up when she's ready.'

'But you must at least . . .' began Barnaby. Louise interrupted him.

'Barnaby, leave it!' she said. 'They don't know, OK? We just have to wait.'

'It may seem to you as though we're hiding something,' said the consultant earnestly, 'but I can assure you, we're not. When it comes to a head injury, very little is certain.' He looked at Barnaby. 'It really is best to try to keep an open mind. Don't build up any kind of expectations at the moment, just take each day as it comes. And when Katie does regain consciousness, a lot of things should become clearer.'

There was a short silence, during which an unarticulated panic began to grow inside Barnaby. What was going to become clearer? What weren't they telling him?

'She will be OK, though,' he said suddenly, in a voice made belligerent through alarm. 'I mean, you said she wasn't paralysed. She will be able to walk and everything? And talk properly? She won't be a vegetable?'

'Barnaby!' exclaimed Louise.

'Well, what's going to become clearer? What are you talking about?'

'Mr Kember,' said the consultant soothingly, 'obviously you're very concerned for your daughter.'

'Yes,' said Barnaby roughly, 'I am. And I want to know what she's going to be like when she wakes up.'

'Of course you do,' said the consultant. 'We all do. However, at the moment, there's very little we can tell you.'

'But you've done tests, haven't you?' cried Barnaby. 'You've done scans and things.'

'Yes, we have,' said the consultant patiently, 'but a scan can't tell us everything.'

'What can't it tell you? What might be wrong with her?'

'Barnaby,' cried Louise suddenly, in a taut voice, 'why can't you just leave it alone? Why can't you just wait and see, like everyone else?'

'I just want to know!' said Barnaby. 'I want to know what might be wrong with Katie! You must have some idea,' he insisted to the consultant. 'I mean, other people must have had injuries like Katie's. Can't you tell us what happened to them?' The consultant sighed. He picked up his silver ball-point pen and began to trace inkless circles on the top of his folder.

'Damage to the brain can have many different consequences,' he said. 'Many victims will, for example, suffer a certain confusion when they wake up; what we call post-traumatic amnesia.'

'Is that all?' said Barnaby. 'A bit of confusion?'

'Well, no, not always,' said the consultant. 'There may perhaps be problems with . . . well, with speech, for instance. Or there may be some form of post-traumatic epilepsy, or changes in personality. But until Katie wakes up . . .'

'What about walking?' said Barnaby. There was a

111

pause. The consultant began to examine the cap of his pen.

'There may initially be problems with balance and co-ordination, yes,' he said eventually. 'Some patients have to learn how to walk again. But only some,' he added firmly. 'And in most cases rehabilitation is a tremendous help.'

'I see,' said Barnaby, trying to stay calm. He felt as though all his worst fears had been confirmed, as though he was finally being let into a secret which everyone else had known about for days.

'If Katie did need rehabilitation,' said Louise in a shaky voice, 'would that happen here?'

'No, probably at Forest Lodge. It's a rehab centre near here.'

'Does it . . .' began Louise.

'Forest Lodge?' interrupted Barnaby. He felt a cold trickle run down his spine. 'That place on the hill? With all the children in wheelchairs?'

'I don't think they're all in wheelchairs,' said the consultant gently. He looked at Louise. 'It's quite a famous centre, you know. You're lucky to be living so close to it.'

'Lucky,' echoed Barnaby bleakly.

'But it's very early days to be thinking of anything like that,' said the consultant briskly. 'At the moment we must concentrate on bringing Katie round.' He smiled at Louise. 'I gather her classmates made a tape for her; that kind of thing always helps.'

'Oh, good.' Louise flushed slightly. 'There was just one other thing,' she said, not looking at Barnaby. 'If we needed medical reports for a . . . for a court case, would you be able to give them to us?'

'Absolutely,' said the consultant. 'We're quite used to that, aren't we, Janine?' He looked at the nurse, who nodded.

'Oh, sure,' she said. 'Will you be going to court, then?'

'No,' said Barnaby, scowling at Louise. 'We won't.'
Louise ignored him.

'We might,' she said.

The consultant looked from one to another.

'It's none of my business,' he said, 'but I've seen quite a lot of parents in your situation, and I'd say that if you do decide to go to court, you should really try to agree to do it together.' He frowned. 'The whole thing can get pretty stressful, as it is, not to mention expensive.'

'Well, that wouldn't actually be a problem,' said Louise, flushing slightly. 'My . . . my father's very generously agreed to help us out with the legal fees. And, of course, if we win costs, it won't actually . . .' She was interrupted by Barnaby.

'Are you telling me that your father thinks we should sue?' His voice was outraged. 'I don't believe it! I just don't believe it!'

Louise's eyes flashed angrily at him.

'You don't believe he would put his granddaughter before anything else,' she hissed. 'His own flesh and blood. Is that so strange to you? Because if it is, Barnaby, it says more about you . . .'

'Ahem.' The consultant politely cleared his throat, and Louise stopped abruptly, mid-flow.

'Sorry,' she muttered. 'Do carry on.'

'Perhaps we should agree', said the consultant, 'to bring this meeting to an end. Just remember, whatever you decide to do, we'll try and help.' He smiled at Louise and got up. 'We'll have another meeting soon. Meanwhile, do ask Janine if there's anything you'd like to know.'

'Wait!' said Barnaby hurriedly. 'Just one more thing. Do people ever . . . do they ever just wake up out of a coma and they're fine? Back to normal straight away?'

There was a pause. Louise muttered something under her breath.

113

'To be honest, not very often,' said the consultant kindly. 'Not very often at all.'

'But it's possible,' persisted Barnaby. The consultant sighed.

'Yes, it's just about possible,' he began. 'But . . .'

'Don't worry,' interrupted Barnaby. 'It's possible. That's all I wanted to know.'

Cassian was waiting for Louise when they came out of the meeting.

'So,' he said. 'Do they know any more?'

'No,' said Louise, rubbing her eyes wearily. 'They don't know anything. They don't know when she's going to wake up, or whether she'll be epileptic, or whether she'll be able to walk, or whether she'll have the same personality as she did before . . .'

'They said all that? They said she might not be able to walk?'

'Barnaby wouldn't stop badgering them,' said Louise curtly. 'They had to shut him up somehow.' Barnaby scowled.

'They also said she might just wake up and be fine,' he said roughly.

'Oh, Barnaby!' exclaimed Louise. 'Get real! That's not going to happen and you know it.' Cassian nodded seriously.

'That sounds most unlikely to me,' he said in a grave professional voice. 'Head injuries can have all sorts of consequences. Katie's life will probably never be the same again. Even if she recovers, rehabilitation might take months. Years.' He paused. 'She's going to have to be your main priority. You're going to have to put her above everything else.'

'Of course,' snapped Barnaby. Cassian raised his eyebrows.

'You say that,' he said coolly, examining his fingernails. 'But if you're not even willing to go to court on her behalf . . .'

'That's different,' said Barnaby fiercely.

'I can't see how,' said Cassian smoothly. 'You have the opportunity to set her up financially, to relieve the burden on your family, to recompense Katie and yourselves for all this trouble and suffering. The chances are, any award would be made by the Delaneys' insurance company, but you're refusing to go ahead simply because the Delaneys are your . . . friends.' His voice was suddenly scathing. There was a pause.

'It's not just that,' said Barnaby eventually, in an uncertain voice. He looked at Louise. 'How can we go into court and say it's Hugh's and Ursula's fault that Katie's in hospital? How can we blame them? It was an accident. An *accident*,' he repeated, with emphasis.

'An accident which could have been avoided,' said Cassian swiftly. 'I went to inspect that diving-board, and, frankly, I was shocked. The surface is all slippery; the tread has worn down . . .'

'It's not that bad,' said Louise uncomfortably.

'Bad enough,' said Cassian. 'Especially where excitable children are involved. By law, a householder has a special duty of care towards visiting children. Hugh and Ursula should have prevented children from using the board, or else issued a warning, or at least hired a supervisor.' His voice was suddenly hard and censorious. 'Who in their right mind allows children to play on a slippery, unsafe diving-board? It's outrageously negligent!'

'Katie didn't hit her head because the board was slippery,' said Barnaby robustly. 'She just didn't know how to do a back dive properly.'

'How do you know that?' countered Cassian. 'How do you know her foot didn't skid as she took off?'

There was silence. Barnaby looked down,

115

discomfited. With an unpleasant pang, Louise again remembered Ursula saying something to her about the children; warning her that they seemed overexcited. A sickening sensation of guilt began to rise up inside her, but she firmly quelled it.

'I think Cassian's right,' she said quickly to Barnaby. 'We owe it to Katie to go to court.'

'You don't know how long she'll be in treatment,' said Cassian. 'She might need special care for years. Nurses don't come cheap, you know. And then, what if she can't look after herself when she's older? You'll want to set her up with some money.'

'She's going to be fine,' said Barnaby shakily. 'You'll see.'

'Barnaby!' exclaimed Louise in frustration. 'Weren't you listening in there? You can't just close your ears and pretend nothing's wrong.'

'You're letting Katie down, Barnaby,' stated Cassian. 'She needs help and support and money, not a parent who won't face up to the facts.'

'Leave me alone!' Barnaby suddenly lashed out. 'I'm going in to see her.' And he disappeared down the corridor.

Cassian raised his eyebrows at Louise, who looked away uncomfortably. She felt torn between Cassian's cool reasoning and Barnaby's honest emotional reaction. Again, the vision of Ursula's anxious face rose up in her mind, and Hugh, stalwart Hugh, who had been the first to offer to take Barnaby to the hospital. Were they really thinking of taking those decent people to court? No, it couldn't be. But then . . . shouldn't they be doing everything they could for their own daughter, no matter whom it hurt? Didn't they owe more to Katie than to Hugh and Ursula?

For a minute or two, Louise stared down at the pastel corridor floor, while the arguments swung backwards and forwards in her mind. The more she thought, the less clear the answer seemed. Eventually she looked up at Cassian, and hesitantly opened her mouth to speak, but Barnaby's voice was suddenly behind her. He sounded gruff and upset.

'I couldn't stay. Some people are in there, moving Katie's arms and legs around, as if she was a doll.'

'Who are?' Louise turned round. Barnaby looked weary and defeated. He shrugged.

'Doctors, or something.'

'Physiotherapists,' said Louise, suddenly remembering. 'They're exercising her limbs to keep some tone in the muscles, and to make sure she doesn't get sore.' She looked at Barnaby. 'It's quite normal, apparently.'

'She looked like a doll,' repeated Barnaby. He looked at Louise, and suddenly there were tears in his eyes. 'She's in a bad way, Lou.'

'I know,' said Louise. She put her hand gently on Barnaby's. But he shrugged it off, blinked hard several times, then abruptly turned and walked off down the corridor.

Chapter Eight

With every day that passed, Barnaby's hopes diminished, and his secret conviction – that Katie would soon wake up and be back to her bright normal self – seemed a little less likely. But if she wasn't going to be back to her normal self, what was she going to be? His mind could not drag itself away from the darkest, most frightening conclusions; he could not stop himself conjuring up pictures of his daughter, a battered, damaged cripple. Confined to a wheelchair, maybe; unable to talk; unable to lead any kind of normal life. How would she cope? How would any of them cope?

He couldn't persuade his thoughts into any kind of middle ground; couldn't seem to attain the sort of positive but realistic outlook that Louise had adopted. He constantly swung from foolish desperate optimism to bleak pessimism and back again to foolish optimism. And underneath it all burned an angry, mortifying, unspecified guilt, which did not abate with time but got stronger.

And so he threw himself into hard outdoor work with no room for thought – tackling all the physical tasks which needed doing on the estate; leaving the paperwork on his desk to mount up.

On the following Tuesday, the ninth day of Katie's coma, he spent the morning checking walls on the estate, and then popped into a nearby pub for lunch. Eileen, the owner's wife, was behind the bar, and clucked sympathetically when she saw Barnaby.

'How's your little girl?' she said, handing him a pint. 'Has she woken up yet?'

Barnaby shook his head and looked around for somewhere to go and sit. He didn't feel like talking about Katie. But the pub was filling up, and all the tables were taken.

'How long is it now?' asked Eileen.

'Nine days,' said Barnaby. He felt a deep gloom falling over him. Eileen clucked again.

'I was watching a programme about people in comas the other night,' she said, leaning forward on the bar and talking straight into Barnaby's left ear. 'This one poor chap was out for two whole years. Can you believe it? Then he woke up, right as rain.'

'Really?' muttered Barnaby.

'Another one was only in a coma for three hours, but when he woke up he'd lost all his memory. Didn't recognize his own wife!'

Eileen looked at Barnaby for a reaction, and he hurriedly took another slug of beer. He would drink up and then go. Forget about lunch.

'But they cured him at the institute,' continued Eileen, opening a packet of crisps and offering it to Barnaby. 'It was marvellous, really.' Barnaby looked up.

'Institute?' he said. 'What institute?'

'The institute in the documentary,' said Eileen patiently. 'The one in America. It was ever so interesting.' She examined her long magenta nails. 'I love that kind of thing,' she added. 'Medical programmes. I'm not squeamish or anything. Graham thinks I'm crazy.'

'Can you remember what it was called?' said Barnaby, trying not to sound too urgent. 'The institute?' Eileen screwed up her face.

'I don't think I can,' she said. 'It was a really famous place, though. I mean, apparently people go there from

119

all over the world. There was this poor lad from Saudi Arabia, couldn't understand a word anyone said to him. I mean, it doesn't really help, does it?' She broke off into peals of laughter.

Barnaby stared at her. Thoughts were buzzing round his head. But before he could say anything, the mobile phone in his pocket rang.

'Barnaby? It's Louise.' He could hardly hear her over the pub noise.

'Hang on a moment,' he said, 'I'll go outside.'

In the car park he blinked a few times in the bright light.

'Hi,' he said. 'What is it?'

'It's Katie.' Louise's voice was trembling slightly and Barnaby felt his heart give a terrified swoop. He had been waiting so long to hear some news; had thought he was desperate for something to happen, but now he felt suddenly frightened; unwilling to leave his haven of ignorance.

'What . . .' He could hardly speak.

'She woke up this morning.'

A flash of relief exploded in Barnaby's mind.

'That's fantastic!' he shouted. 'That's wonderful news! I'll come straight away. Is she OK? Has she said anything?'

'No, she hasn't,' said Louise curtly. 'She only regained consciousness for about thirty seconds.'

'What?'

'Apparently that's normal. It could be ages before she wakes up properly.'

'Oh,' said Barnaby. He felt suddenly deflated. 'Well, I suppose that's good.'

'Of course it's good!' Louise's voice came furiously down the line. 'For God's sake, Barnaby, what did you expect? That she would just sit up and smile and say, "Where's Daddy"?'

'No,' said Barnaby at once, 'of course not.'

'You've got to be realistic.'

'I am realistic,' said Barnaby indignantly.

'You're not! You're completely unrealistic! You constantly go from one stupid extreme to the other, and it doesn't help, Barnaby. It really doesn't help.' Louise sounded rattled, almost tearful.

'OK, then,' said Barnaby hurriedly. 'Well, here's something that might help. I was just talking to Eileen at The Fox and Hounds, and she said there was an institute in America which cures people who have been in comas. She said people go there from all over the world.'

'And?' Barnaby ignored the ominous tone in Louise's voice.

'And we could send Katie there,' he said.

'Oh, for Christ's sake, Barnaby!' shrieked Louise. 'You're in another world, aren't you?'

'I'm not!' Barnaby shouted. 'It sounded really good!' A couple of people walking through the car park looked curiously at him, and he turned away with a scowl.

'Yes, and I suppose you'd pay for it, would you?' snapped Louise. 'I suppose you'd fork out the half a million, or whatever it takes?' Then she sighed. 'Barnaby, we don't even know what's wrong with Katie yet; if anything. She hasn't even woken up properly yet. So now is really not the time to start talking about institutes in America, is it?'

Barnaby stared miserably at the ground. He couldn't think of anything to say.

'I'll see you this evening at the hospital,' said Louise.

'OK,' said Barnaby. 'Thanks for calling.'

'Yes, well, I had to, didn't I?' said Louise. She sounded suddenly bitter, and Barnaby winced.

When he had put his phone away, he went over to a bench at the edge of the car park and sat down shakily. He felt heavy with guilt, with despair, with indignation. Something was going wrong. He was obviously failing

Louise. Maybe he was failing Katie, too. Maybe he was making everything worse for everybody.

He buried his head in his hands and allowed a little of his buried resentment to surface. What else was he supposed to do? Hide his worries? Not speak to anyone? He'd thought the institute in America sounded like a good idea. He wouldn't have mentioned it otherwise.

Again he winced as he remembered Louise's voice. She sounded hard, full of tension and exhausted. And she made him feel completely useless. 'I suppose you'd pay for it, would you?' Her words ran round his brain like busy mice. What if Katie needed money and he couldn't give it to her? How could he let her down? A picture came into his mind of his helpless little daughter, waking up for a confused, bewildering thirty seconds, wondering where she was, perhaps even wondering who she was; perhaps unable to move; perhaps in dreadful pain. And here he was, sitting uselessly in the sun. He couldn't stand it any longer. He had to do something to help. Take some positive action. He had to do *something* . . .

A sudden surprising thought entered his mind like a slippery fish. Before he could focus on it, it had darted away. Then it returned and lingered for a bit longer, wriggling away when he tried to fix his attention on it, only to dance intriguingly at the corners of his mind.

Was he serious? Could he really be contemplating such a thing? What had happened to him? Where were all his objections? His morals? He tried as hard as he could to conjure up the sensation of indignant outrage which had consumed him only days before, but he couldn't. Somehow everything had vanished from his mind but Katie. Katie governed his thoughts, his feelings, his convictions. He had to put her first, he simply had to. Whatever it took; whatever it meant for other people.

For a long time he sat completely still, allowing his

fermenting thoughts to settle down into hard serious intention. Then he took a few deep breaths, reached for his mobile phone, and felt in his pocket for the little white card which had been sitting there for several days. He shut his eyes, counted to ten, and dialled the number.

'Cassian?' As he spoke the name he felt suddenly self-conscious, and glanced around. Could anyone hear him? And if they could, would they realize what he was doing? For a moment he felt a slight faltering.

'Barnaby? Is that you?'

'Yes. Yes, it is.' Barnaby took a deep breath. For Katie's sake. 'I've been thinking hard,' he said, 'about what you said. About suing Hugh and Ursula. And . . .' He swallowed hard. 'And I think, if there's any chance it would help Katie, then we should go ahead.'

There was a short silence. Barnaby realized he was clenching the mobile phone so hard, it was digging into his flesh. What was the bastard going to say? Was he going to make him feel stupid? Had he done the wrong thing yet again?

'Barnaby, I'm so glad!' The warm congratulatory tone in Cassian's voice took Barnaby by surprise. 'I realize what a tough decision it was to make, but I really think you've done the right thing for little Katie. And you know, Barnaby, I'd like to say that on a personal level I have a lot of respect for your thoughtful approach to this whole matter.' He paused, and Barnaby felt a slight flush come to his cheeks. 'You didn't allow yourself to be rushed,' continued Cassian, 'you took your time, and in the end you came to a decision which I'm sure you'll find is the right one. Barnaby, I'm very glad to be working with you.'

'I just did what I thought was right,' said Barnaby gruffly.

'Of course you did,' said Cassian reassuringly, 'and I know these things are never easy. But you really are

123

doing the best thing you possibly can for your daughter.'

There was a pause. Barnaby leaned back and felt a warm sensation of relief pass through him. At last, maybe, he'd got something right.

'So what happens now?' he said eventually.

'If you and Louise just pop into the office this afternoon,' said Cassian smoothly, 'then I can introduce you to our personal injury experts, and we can get the whole thing going at once. Say, three o'clock?'

'This afternoon?'

'The quicker the better,' said Cassian. 'And after that, you won't have to worry about a thing.'

It was teatime the next day, and everyone was outside, when the doorbell rang at Devenish House. Hugh put his cup down and said, 'I'll go.' Meredith looked severely at Ursula.

'Have you asked someone to tea without telling us?' She turned to Alexis. 'She meets people in the street and asks them to tea, and then forgets all about it! I expect right now the whole village is on the doorstep.'

Ursula began an unconvincing protestation. Alexis simply smiled and bit into a crumbly, buttery biscuit. Meredith looked surreptitiously at him; at the way he leaned back elegantly in his chair; at the way his skin creased up when he smiled, and as she watched, a faint yearning pulled at the pit of her stomach. Alexis had been spending a lot of time with them that week. At first, of course, he had been helping out and generally being supportive in the aftermath of the accident. But now . . . In spite of herself, she felt a fluttering of hope.

As if he were reading her mind, he turned and smiled at her.

'Doing anything this weekend?'

'Oh!' Taken by surprise, Meredith gave a sharp intake of breath. Then, tossing her hair back in a determinedly casual fashion, she said, lightly, 'Nothing much.' She took a sip of tea. Jeez, this was ridiculous. She was behaving like some kooky kid angling for a date. 'I thought I'd check out that new movie,' she added, keeping her voice natural. 'That one, *The Grandfather's Tale*. It's supposed to be a bit weird, but . . .'

'I saw it a couple of weeks ago,' said Alexis. Meredith's heart dropped slightly and she smiled at Alexis to cover it. 'It was excellent,' Alexis added warmly. 'You'll love it.'

'Don't say that!' Meredith forced a light-hearted animation into her voice. 'If anyone tells me I'll love a film, I find myself deliberately hating it.' Alexis laughed. 'It's true,' insisted Meredith, 'I'm very protective about what I like and don't like. If people start dictating I rebel.' She sighed. 'The number of perfectly good films which have been ruined for me . . .'

Ursula was listening, a look of puzzlement on her face.

'But Meredith, dear,' she said, 'what about that charming film I took you to see last Christmas? I told you I was sure you'd love it, and when we'd seen it, you agreed. You said you'd enjoyed it very much.' She screwed up her face in thought. 'What was it called, now? It was a *lovely* film. You must remember. Those beautiful period costumes.'

'Uh, yes, Ursula,' said Meredith. 'I remember. I guess that was an exception.' She caught Alexis's eye, and he gave the barest acknowledging flicker of a smile. And suddenly, inexplicably, Meredith felt her heart pounding violently and her face beginning to flush. We would go so well together, she found herself thinking, the thoughts piling over one another in foolish desperation. We enjoy talking to one another, and we have the same sense of humour, and I certainly find him attractive and . . . She pulled up short, hit by a sudden uncharacteristic loss of self-confidence; and looked away quickly. Perhaps that was it; she'd mistaken the signs: Alexis didn't find *her* attractive, after all.

Surreptitiously, she glanced down at her body, lean and tanned and clad today in a clinging black dress made from an expensive stretchy fabric. If he didn't like the way she looked, there wasn't a lot she could do . . . except perhaps blimp out, she found herself thinking. In case he liked larger women. Eat cheeseburgers every day and put on twenty pounds. Would that do the trick? She gave a stifled giggle, in spite of herself.

Alexis looked up and Meredith's grin died away. Ask him out! she told herself fiercely. Just ask. It isn't such a big deal; he can only say no . . . But for some reason her mouth stayed closed.

Ursula was frowning at the newspaper.

'It says here', she said, 'that women live longer than men.' She put down the paper and gave Meredith a puzzled look. 'That can't be right.'

'Sure,' said Meredith, taking a bite of biscuit. 'They do.' Ursula's eyes flickered doubtfully to Alexis.

'It's true, Ursula,' he said pleasantly. 'Women live longer.'

'But surely that's impossible,' said Ursula in gently obstinate tones. She put down the newspaper and appeared to be thinking. Meredith watched her affectionately, realizing, with a slight shock, that the few remaining blond streaks in Ursula's hair had, without her noticing, vanished into a sea of silver. 'Surely,' added Ursula, 'if it were true, it would mean that there were far more women than men on the earth.'

'Maybe there are,' said Meredith lazily. 'Long may it last.'

'And if that imbalance continued, year after year . . . then eventually there wouldn't be any men left at all,' said Ursula. She gave Meredith an impressive look. 'So I don't think you can be right, dear.'

'Ursula!' exclaimed Meredith, clutching her head in mock-despair. 'Where do you get your logic from?'

'It seems very clear to me,' protested Ursula.

'I'm sure it does,' said Meredith, beginning to laugh. 'Alexis, help me out here.'

'Let's have a look at the article,' said Alexis. He leaned over Meredith to take the paper from Ursula, and Meredith felt a stab of yearning desire.

'Let me see,' she said, without thinking. 'Let me look over your shoulder.'

'OK,' said Alexis easily. He shuffled up so that his chair was next to hers, and shook the paper open on her knee. She could smell his scent; could feel his leg lying against hers; could sense him breathing in and out. For a few seconds she felt pinned down; transfixed by wanting.

'Alexis,' she said softly. He turned and looked at her. 'Yes?'

Meredith took a breath, ignoring the knife-like nerves in her chest. She paused to select exactly the right words; the most noncommittal, yet unambiguous phrase possible. 'Do you think,' she began quietly, shaking back her hair and staring at her hands. 'Do you think—'

She was interrupted by a gasp from Alexis. He was looking over her shoulder.

'Hugh!' Ursula was exclaiming. 'What's wrong?'

Hugh looked back at them. His face looked drained; his eyes had lost their good cheer, and he was holding a letter in his hand. Meredith was suddenly, fearfully reminded of Simon's death.

'This is a registered letter', Hugh began, 'from that chap, Cassian Brown. Louise Kember's friend.'

'Katie . . .' began Ursula in a choked voice. Hugh raised a hand.

'I've just tried to phone Louise,' he said. 'She wasn't there, but the babysitter told me that Katie is making reasonable progress. Apparently she woke up briefly from her coma yesterday morning.'

A sensation of relief flooded through Meredith, and in a tiny corner of her soul, a tinge of envy. Her loved one had never woken up. They were lucky . . .

'Nevertheless,' Hugh was saying, in halting, disbelieving tones, 'it seems that Louise and Barnaby have made a . . . a rather strange decision.' He looked at Alexis and took a deep breath. 'They're going to sue us. For negligence.'

'They're going to *what*?' Meredith's voice rose, outraged, into the afternoon air.

'Sue us, apparently.' Hugh ran a hand through his greying locks. He was still looking at Alexis. 'Can they, Alexis?' Ursula tugged at Meredith's sleeve.

'What exactly do they want to do?' she whispered.

'Take you to court, Ursula,' said Meredith. 'To get some damages out of you. Money,' she added. 'Lots of it.'

'But, Meredith, dear,' said Ursula, 'I don't think that can be right. It was an *accident*, you know. It wasn't our fault.' She looked at Hugh. 'Are you sure he wasn't talking about the appeal? We've raised quite a lot of money, you know . . .'

'Ursula,' said Alexis gently, 'I really don't think the appeal's got anything to do with it. Hugh's obviously right. The Kembers are intending to take you to court.'

'But it was an accident,' insisted Ursula, bewildered. There was a taut silence. Everyone looked at Alexis.

'I'm afraid that won't make any difference,' he said, and exhaled sharply. 'You'll be sued for negligence, under the Occupiers' Liability Act.' He sounded suddenly resigned, and Meredith gave him a hard look.

'But they're our friends,' said Hugh in bleak tones. 'Why do they have to take us to court? Why couldn't they just come and talk to us about it?' He looked at Alexis with a hurt, betrayed expression. 'Wouldn't that be simpler? I mean, don't they realize we want to help

128

in whatever way we can? We'll give them money, if that's what they need . . .'

'It's that smarmy lawyer,' broke in Meredith suddenly. 'He's talked them into it.'

Hugh picked up a teacup, took a sip of tea, then grimaced as he discovered it was cold.

'I'll go and talk to Barnaby,' he said, putting the cup down. 'I'm sure that if we all got together . . .'

'No,' said Alexis firmly. Hugh looked up in surprise. 'It'll be easier all round', said Alexis more gently, 'if you keep away from the Kembers for the moment, just to be on the safe side.'

'Oh, Jesus,' said Meredith. 'Isn't that going a bit far?'

'Wait till you see the claim that the Kembers will make,' said Alexis drily, 'and then talk to me about going too far.'

There was a short frightened silence. Alexis looked around at the worried faces and relented slightly.

'You may find,' he said, 'that when everyone's calmed down a bit, all this talk of legal action comes to nothing. The best thing is not to rush into doing anything that you may regret. Just sit tight and wait to see what happens.'

Meredith gave him a sharp look.

'You don't really think it'll come to nothing, do you?' she said. 'You're just trying to make us feel better.'

Alexis shrugged.

'It all depends. If they're determined to sue, then they'll sue.'

'But we didn't do anything wrong!' said Ursula suddenly. She looked at Alexis with an expression of panic, as though realizing for the first time what was going on. 'We didn't do anything wrong!' she repeated, and looked helplessly at Meredith and Hugh, as though for confirmation.

Meredith took Ursula's hand and gave it a comforting squeeze.

'Of course we didn't,' she said. 'And let's hope that's the way the court sees it, too.'

When Hugh and Ursula had taken the tea things inside, Meredith turned to Alexis.

'You knew, didn't you?' she said in a low trembling voice. 'You knew this was going to happen.'

'I didn't know,' said Alexis wearily, 'but I did have my suspicions. When I saw that young lawyer coming to poke around the swimming-pool for no good reason.' Meredith thought for a moment.

'What were you looking at in Hugh's study?' she abruptly demanded. 'That piece of paper?' Alexis looked at her, a grim unsmiling look. Meredith felt her heart begin to pound nervously.

'I was looking at Hugh's insurance policy,' he said quietly. 'I was checking to see whether the swimming-pool was covered – and whether they were covered for negligence.'

'And are they?' Alexis gave a sigh and looked away.

'They are, and they aren't. They're covered for negligence, but only in the context of domestic use.' He paused. 'Would you call a hundred people, all paying at the door, a domestic use?'

'But it was for charity!' protested Meredith. 'They weren't making any money!'

'I know,' said Alexis. 'but I also know what insurance companies are like. If they can get out of paying, they will . . .' He broke off. 'I'm just afraid that this will prove a good enough excuse.'

'So . . .'

'So if Louise and Barnaby win any damages, Hugh and Ursula will have to pay out of their own pocket. And it could be a serious amount.'

'How much?' Meredith's voice was sharp. Alexis sighed.

'I wish I knew. It really depends on the little girl's

condition, but it could be anything from a few thousand pounds to – I don't know – a hundred thousand pounds, two hundred thousand. Maybe more.' Alexis looked at Meredith, his face clouded with worry. 'Perhaps I should have said something earlier,' he said. 'Warned Hugh. But I really didn't think it would come to this . . .'

Meredith stared back at him, feeling a white anger creeping up inside her.

'How can they do this?' she expostulated at last, keeping her voice low and one wary eye on the house. 'How can they stand up in court and say that Hugh and Ursula were to blame? It was an accident, for Christ's sake. An accident! No-one was to blame. Hugh and Ursula weren't *negligent*. That kid just didn't know how to dive properly.' Alexis shrugged.

'Can you prove that?'

'Well, of course I can't *prove* it, but . . .' Meredith broke off, frustratedly. Alexis gave her a half grin.

'You should be used to this,' he said. 'America's just about the most litigious country in the world.'

'I know,' said Meredith bitterly, 'but somehow I thought it was different here. I thought people valued friendship above money. I thought . . .' She broke off, suddenly pushed back her chair and got to her feet, full of angry energy. Alexis watched as she paced a few aimless steps, then abruptly turned around. 'Well, they're not getting Hugh and Ursula's money,' she said defiantly. 'I mean, I'm very sorry for them and everything, and I know what they're going through.' She paused. 'I mean, believe me, I really know.'

'Yes,' said Alexis quietly, 'I know you do.'

'But I'm not going to let them walk all over Hugh and Ursula. They're innocent. They don't deserve this.' She looked determinedly at Alexis. 'We're going to fight this, and you'll help us.'

'I'll do my best,' said Alexis, 'but it'll be hard. I've been asking around and I gather this Cassian Brown is a very sharp customer.' He looked at her and lowered his voice. 'This isn't going to be pretty, Meredith.'

'None of it's pretty,' said Meredith. 'Life isn't pretty.' She looked away, her expression suddenly bleak. Alexis stood up and began to put on his jacket.

'I'll come round tomorrow evening,' he said, 'to talk about it properly.' He caught Meredith's expression. 'It's OK,' he added, 'there's no rush. Quite the contrary.' He pulled a face. 'Most lawsuits go on for several years, and this one hasn't even started yet. In fact, in my opinion, the Kembers are being very premature, if Katie's condition hasn't even stabilized . . .' He looked at Meredith. 'As Katie's a minor, you see, there's absolutely no rush. They could leave it until she was eighteen before they even think about suing.' But Meredith wasn't listening.

'Aren't you going to stay for dinner?' she asked abruptly, sitting down beside Alexis. 'I know Hugh and Ursula would really appreciate it.'

'I'm sure they would,' said Alexis regretfully, 'and normally, of course, I would. But tonight, I've . . . I've got another arrangement.'

He looked away hastily. And ignoring the crestfallen pang in her chest, Meredith smiled at him, nodded, and said, 'Sure thing,' in a casual, friendly kind of way, and didn't ask him what he was doing. There was a momentary pause, then Alexis leaned over and kissed her quickly, once on each cheek.

'Don't worry,' he said, 'we'll pull through this.'

'I hope so,' said Meredith sombrely.

As he left, she sat completely still, as though in a trance. She hugged herself tightly against the late afternoon breeze, and felt her unwilling disappointment mingle with a sudden vengeful hatred for Louise and Barnaby Kember.

After a while a gust of wind caught her bare arm, giving her goose bumps and making her shiver. And as she pulled her jacket around her and got up to go inside, she suddenly found herself wishing, bleakly, that she could somehow confide in Simon; that she could feel his arms around her once again, and hear his voice, and ask him for some advice and some help and some love.

Chapter Nine

Daisy lay in the bath, watching the green crab-apple leaves fluttering outside the bathroom window, and wondered what sort of an evening it was going to be. Her mother had phoned earlier that afternoon, just to check up on things, and Daisy had foolishly let slip that she had been asked out to dinner.

'How nice!' her mother had said, in the distracted voice that probably meant she was typing something onto the computer at the same time. 'I didn't know there were any boys your age in Melbrook.'

And stupidly, instead of saying nothing, Daisy said, 'Actually, he's not really my age.'

There was an ominous pause. Daisy imagined her mother stopping typing in mid-sentence, then automatically pressing the Save button while deciding exactly what to say.

'Oh?' came her mother's voice at last; a single meaningful syllable, encapsulating both a note of enquiry and a hint that she already knew the answer. 'How old is he, then?'

'Older than me,' said Daisy, cursing herself for having said anything.

'How *much* older, exactly?' Daisy was momentarily silent. She wasn't actually sure how old he was. But thinking about it now, she decided he must be at least forty-something. Nearly as old as her father, she thought, with a little jump.

Her mother sounded as though she was standing up; Daisy imagined her striding to the door of the study, beckoning to her father, mouthing to him to come and listen to this conversation, Daisy was in another pickle.

'He's quite a lot older,' said Daisy at last. 'But it's not . . .'

'Not what?' Daisy blushed.

'You know . . .'

'Are you just going to a dinner party or something?' said her mother, as though suddenly understanding the situation. 'Well, that's quite different.'

'No, I don't think so,' said Daisy. 'I think it's just the two of us. But I'm not quite sure why . . .' She broke off. She couldn't possibly say the truth: that she wasn't at all sure why he had asked her.

'Daisy.' Her mother's voice came crisply down the line in her efficient crisis-management manner. 'Daisy, you're very young and very naïve. Are you sure you really want to go out to dinner with this man?' Daisy flinched. Somehow her mother was making it sound all horrible and sordid.

'It's not like that!' she cried. 'It's . . .'

'What?'

'I don't know,' said Daisy feebly. Her mother was breathing impatiently down the phone.

'Daisy, darling, get a grip. You don't just go out to dinner with people for no reason at all. You have to be careful.' From the background came a sound of electronic bleeping. 'Oh, damn. Look, darling, I've got to go. If you're sensible, you'll cancel this fellow. But if you do decide to go, make sure you ring us when you get back. We worry about you, all alone down there. I don't know what your father will say when I tell him about this . . .' The bleeping sounded again. 'Right, now I really have got to go. Bye, sweetheart.'

'Bye, Mummy,' Daisy had said. And she had put down the receiver and stared into space rather disconsolately for a few minutes.

But now she felt cheered up. She lay luxuriously back

in her bath and listened to the sound of a Beethoven piano concerto thundering through the cottage, feeling a pleasant anticipation steal over her. It would, she thought, be nice to go out to a restaurant and look down a menu and have some wine. What they would talk about, she wasn't sure. But he was such a friendly man, it was bound to be OK. He'd been terribly nice to her at the swimming-pool. And then he'd dropped by one day, while she was practising, and had stayed for coffee, and they'd chatted about the village and her time in Italy and the awful accident. Then he'd phoned up and asked her out to dinner, and she'd said yes.

She turned on the hot tap with her toe, leaned back and felt warm water creeping slowly around her body. That was all very well, she thought reluctantly. But what did it all mean? Her mother's voice echoed in her mind: 'You don't just go out to dinner with people for no reason at all.'

At first, at the swimming-pool, she'd thought he was just being amiable, like Frances Mold, or one of her father's friends. And she had still thought that when he dropped round for coffee. But now – out to dinner? Didn't that mean . . . a date? Was he serious? Would he expect to . . . to come back? To have sex with her? A pang of agitation shot through Daisy and she wriggled nervously in her bath water. But even as she pictured it, pictured him putting his arm round her, or kissing her – let alone anything further – it seemed such a ridiculous idea that she was sure that she must have got it all wrong; that she'd completely misconstrued him. And that would be the worst thing to do, she thought suddenly: to give him the wrong impression; to offend him by making the wrong assumption. If only she could be certain, she thought, reaching for a towel; if only she could be certain *which* was the wrong assumption. It didn't really matter which of them it was, just as long as she didn't pick the wrong one.

*   *   *

Alexis was feeling ridiculously nervous about dinner with Daisy. All day he had been half expecting her to cancel; when he got home to find no winking message on his answer-machine he felt almost caught out. He hurriedly showered, avoiding the sight of his leathery skin in the bathroom mirror; he decided not to shave again, but splashed on a discreet amount of aftershave. He dressed carefully in pale trousers, a pale blue shirt. No tie. A fashionable jacket made from crumpled beige linen.

He put everything on and looked at himself. A middle-aged man stared back at him. A memory of Daisy's young, unblemished, eighteen-year-old skin flickered through his mind and, again, he felt the shock he'd experienced when it had occurred to him just how old he was when she was born. When she was *born*, for Christ's sake. And here he was, dressed up in a young man's clothes, actually contemplating taking her out to dinner. He must be crazy.

When he arrived at her cottage, piano music was coming from within. He rang the bell and stood back on the path, admiring the pretty orchard garden, listening as the sound of a thrush mingled with the sounds of the piano. After a while he rang again. The music continued. Eventually he lifted a cautious hand and pushed at the front door. As he did so, the music increased in volume. It was powerful stirring music that sounded familiar to Alexis, yet which he couldn't identify. For a moment he just stood there in the tiny hall, listening, and looking at his ridiculous reflection in the glass of a carved walnut hall-stand, feeling his heart beat faster and faster. Then, forcing himself to move, he pushed at the sitting-room door.

Daisy looked up from her seat at the grand piano and abruptly stopped playing.

137

'Oh!' she gasped. 'Sorry, I wasn't listening out for the door.'

'Don't worry,' said Alexis. He looked at the piano. 'That sounded powerful stuff.'

'Oh, yes,' Daisy blushed. 'It was Chopin,' she said. There was a pause. 'One of the Etudes,' she added, biting her lip. She blushed again, looked at the book of music in front of her and closed it. Then she looked at Alexis expectantly.

Alexis looked back at her. She was dressed smartly, as though for a school function, in a sleeveless white T-shirt, dark-red flowing skirt and pale tights. Her hair flowed from a velvet band down to her waist in shining dark waves, and she smelt faintly of roses.

Daisy noticed Alexis looking at her and flushed.

'I didn't know how smart . . .' she began hesitantly. 'Do I look all right?'

Alexis stared back at her and nodded. He wanted to say she looked beautiful, but suddenly he felt unable to speak.

'I haven't really gone out much,' said Daisy. 'Since I've been living down here, I mean.'

She got up, awkwardly pushing the piano-stool back, and knocking a pile of music onto the floor. Alexis made a move to pick it up.

'Don't worry,' said Daisy quickly, 'I'll pick it up later.' There was a tiny pause. 'My-my jacket's in the hall,' she added.

'Right,' said Alexis, attempting a cheery tone, holding the door open for her. But his voice sounded strange to his own ears. What the hell was wrong with him? What kind of evening were they going to have, if he couldn't string two words together?

In the dusky hall, Daisy turned suddenly and reached for a jacket hanging on the hall-stand. Alexis, taken by surprise, found himself stepping forward and colliding with her soft warm skin.

'Sorry!' he exclaimed.

'Oh, that's all right,' said Daisy shyly. 'I mean, I got in your way.' Her voice fluttered gently through the air, and Alexis felt a dangerous feeling of desire begin to creep inexorably through him.

'Let me help you with that,' he said. He took the jacket from her and held it up, watching as her pale milky arms slid inside the sleeves. Then, suddenly, Daisy turned and looked at him with questioning eyes.

'I wasn't going to ask,' she said, 'but . . . are we . . .' She broke off. 'Is this . . .' She coloured slightly. 'It's just, this is all a bit new to me, and I was just wondering . . .' She tailed away, her cheeks suffused with an embarrassed colour.

Alexis gazed at her, almost paralysed with longing.

'Well, you know . . . this is all a bit new to me, too,' he managed to say. He relaxed a little. 'This is all a bit new to me, too,' he repeated, 'so, let's just play it by ear, shall we?' He looked down at her and smiled. 'It's not really one thing or the other. I just thought it would be nice for us to have dinner together, that's all.'

'Oh,' said Daisy doubtfully. 'OK, then.' And she allowed him to lead her gently out of the cottage into the scented evening air.

The restaurant Alexis had chosen was relatively new in Linningford. It was bright and bustly, with a pale polished wooden floor, mirrors on the walls, huge ferny plants between the tables and splashy water-colours on the walls. Daisy looked around with a delighted smile.

'I like this place!' she exclaimed, as they sat down. 'It's so pretty!'

A waiter came over and presented two enormous menus with a flourish.

'Mademoiselle; monsieur,' he murmured in deferential tones. Daisy beamed at Alexis, who gave the waiter a sharp look. Was the fellow insinuating anything? But the waiter looked blandly back at Alexis and murmured something about an aperitif. Alexis looked at Daisy's glowing face.

'Two glasses of champagne,' he said quietly to the waiter. Then, 'No, make that a bottle.'

When he had gone, they looked at each other. Daisy carefully unfolded her napkin and lay it across her lap. Alexis glanced around the restaurant, as though in search of a topic of conversation, but it was Daisy who spoke first.

'I saw Mrs Kember yesterday,' she said, 'driving along. She didn't see me,' she added humbly. 'I mean, I just saw her through her car window. But I thought . . . poor them.' Her hands fluttered sympathetically.

'Yes, poor old them,' said Alexis, unable to keep a hostile note out of his voice. Daisy stared at him.

'What . . . why . . .'

'Oh . . . I'm sorry,' said Alexis, 'I do feel for them. But it's just—' Daisy stared at him, eyes wide. He sighed. 'I don't suppose it's any great secret.' He looked at her. 'The Kembers are planning to sue Hugh and Ursula on behalf of Katie.'

'Sue them?' Daisy looked at him, aghast. 'What, because it was their swimming-pool?'

'Yes,' said Alexis, 'and because Louise's lawyer friend has convinced them, no doubt, that they can get lots of money out of Hugh and Ursula.'

'And can . . . can they?' Alexis shrugged.

'Good question. Possibly, yes.'

'But . . .' Daisy hesitated. 'I expect I'm very ignorant,' she said cautiously. Alexis grinned encouragingly.

'I shouldn't think you are,' he said.

'But . . . don't you have to do something wrong to be sued? I mean, they didn't do anything wrong, did they?' Alexis shrugged.

'Define "wrong". Is it wrong to invite people to swim

in your pool without providing a life guard?' Daisy stared at him.

'But that's silly,' she said. 'If it's someone's *house* ...'
Alexis shrugged again.

'If you invite people to your house, you have a duty towards them.' He sighed. 'That's the law.'

There was a pause. Daisy gazed at Alexis, a bewildered look on her face.

'It's really difficult,' she said. 'It was so awful, the accident, and I feel really sorry for the little girl, and it ... it would be really good if she could get some money.' She stopped. 'But going to court seems so horrible. And I thought they were friends.'

'They were,' said Alexis, almost to himself. 'Not for much longer.' He glanced at Daisy. She was staring sombrely down at the tablecloth. 'What are we talking about!' he exclaimed. 'Let's not think about such depressing things.' He looked up and his expression changed. 'Look, just in time!'

The waiter had arrived with the champagne. As he popped it open, a cautious smile reappeared on Daisy's face. She looked at Alexis and blushed.

'Champagne,' she said, looking at her bubbling glass. 'Gosh—'

'You don't have to have it if you don't want it,' said Alexis seriously. 'I should have asked you first. But don't worry, we can order something else. Waiter ...'

Daisy gasped.

'No, I didn't mean ... honestly ...' She broke off as she saw Alexis's face.

'You're teasing me,' she said in surprise.

'Yes,' said Alexis. 'Do you mind?'

'No,' said Daisy slowly. She looked at Alexis, at his brown face and his clever eyes and his crinkly smile, and she smiled back. 'No, I don't ... I don't mind at all.'

*   *   *

Later on, when they had finished eating, Alexis slid his palm across the table and picked up Daisy's hand.

'Look at those pianist's fingers,' he said admiringly. 'I bet you've got more muscle in those than I've got in . . .'

'Your little finger,' suggested Daisy, whose cheeks had become rather pink from the champagne. 'Oh no. That doesn't work.' She looked disparagingly at the hand still on the table. 'The trouble with playing the piano', she said, 'is you never get to have long nails. Mine are horrible, *and* I bite them.'

'They're beautiful,' said Alexis. He looked at her. 'You're beautiful.' Daisy blushed.

'It's been a lovely dinner,' she said in a rather flustered voice. 'I've really enjoyed it.'

'Good,' said Alexis.

He looked at her carefully for a second, then casually relaxed his grip on her hand. An infinitesimal beat of silence passed. Daisy didn't move her hand away. Alexis stared downwards and counted to five. An unspeakable excitement was growing inside him. Slowly he raised his head and looked straight at her. A fiery red had covered her cheeks; her eyes were lowered; her thick dark lashes were casting shadows on her face. Gradually, scarcely daring to breathe, he closed his hand over hers again.

While Alexis ordered the bill and paid it, neither of them spoke very much. Outside in the street it was dark; a warm indigo-blue summer darkness, punctuated by glowing shop signs, and snatches of low laughter, and glimpses of brightly coloured dresses under yellow street lamps. They walked silently to the car. Daisy found that she had begun to shiver. The leather seats of Alexis's car seemed cold and unforgiving as she got in; her legs were trembling and she could think of nothing to say.

'I must hear you play properly some time,' said Alexis

142

conversationally, as he switched on the engine.

'Oh, yes,' said Daisy. 'Well . . . I'm doing a concert in Linningford at the beginning of September.'

'Splendid!' said Alexis. 'What is it?'

'A piano concerto,' said Daisy shyly, 'with the Linningford Symphony Orchestra.'

'Really?' said Alexis. 'I am impressed.' He glanced sideways at Daisy. 'That must be very exciting,' he said.

'Yes, it is,' said Daisy. She could feel her voice trembling and clasped her hands nervously. What was going to happen when they got out of the car? she thought frantically. Was Alexis going to want to come in? Was he going to kiss her? Was he going to want to . . .

'Which piano concerto?' Alexis asked, suddenly breaking the silence. Daisy gave a little jump.

'Oh!' she gasped. 'Er . . . Brahms. The second.'

'I don't know it, I'm afraid,' said Alexis easily. 'I'm not very well up on Brahms.'

'Oh, it's really beautiful,' said Daisy earnestly. There was a pause. Then the car stopped and she looked up, startled, at Alexis. 'Why are we stopping?' she said faintly.

'Because we're here.' Alexis turned and smiled at her. 'Look, there's your cottage.'

'Oh, yes.' Daisy's voice was no more than a husky whisper and she was quivering with nerves. Alexis gazed at her. Her lips were trembling; her dark eyes darted about. He felt as though he had trapped a baby deer inside his car.

Abruptly, he opened his door. Before Daisy could think to move, he was round the other side of the car and gallantly opening the passenger door for her, bowing in a flowery manner that made her giggle, in spite of herself.

'Well, good night,' he said in friendly tones. 'Thank you very much for coming.'

'Well, thank *you*,' said Daisy, feeling her heart

143

pounding painfully in her chest. She looked at Alexis, just visible in the darkness. He took a step forward and she began to breathe a little more quickly.

'It was . . . good fun,' he said.

'Yes, it was,' managed Daisy.

There was a silence. Then, slowly, gradually, Alexis bent his head towards her. He kissed her softly once on the cheek. Then, before she could say anything, before she could even breathe, he was tilting his head slightly, moving a hand up to support the back of her head, and bringing his lips down onto hers. Daisy closed her eyes, and felt his warm lips, and his mouth gently opening hers, and a cool breeze blowing through her hair, and couldn't think of anything else. When he lifted his head, she stared back, slightly dazed, and numb to the nerves leaping in her stomach. I would, she suddenly found herself thinking, if he wanted to . . . I would say yes. A quivering anticipation began to build inside her, but already he was moving away, towards the car.

'I've got to go, I'm afraid,' he said regretfully. He gave her a little smile. 'Have you got your key?'

'Y-yes,' said Daisy confusedly.

'I'll wait until you're safely in,' Alexis said. He opened his door. 'How about', he added casually, 'meeting up again sometime?'

'Yes,' said Daisy. Her words seemed to be struggling to come out. 'Th-that would be nice.'

'I could come round for coffee tomorrow,' said Alexis. 'Unless you're busy practising?' Daisy swallowed.

'No,' she said slowly, 'I'm not busy.'

'Good,' said Alexis. 'See you tomorrow.'

'See you then,' said Daisy.

She crossed the road, walked down the path, waved shyly at Alexis, then opened the door of the cottage and disappeared. Alexis sat quite still for a few seconds, then started the engine of his car, put his foot down, and drove off into the darkness.

Chapter Ten

The news that the Kembers were going to sue the Delaneys over Katie's accident spread quickly through the village amidst a welter of contrary reports and confused opinion. No-one seemed to be quite sure what the details were, or to have more than a vague third-hand account. Eventually, frustrated by hearing a number of conflicting accounts of the story, Sylvia Seddon-Wilson decided to organize a fund-raising coffee-morning in aid of Katie's appeal. She invited all the ladies of the village, including Louise, Ursula and Meredith.

'They won't come, of course,' she said confidently, as she sat at breakfast, licking envelopes. James, her husband, looked politely up from *The Financial Times*.

'Who won't?'

'Well, Louise won't, for a start. She'll be far too busy.' James's brow wrinkled.

'Which one's Louise?' Sylvia sighed impatiently.

'You *know*, James. I told you. The mother of the little girl who had the accident.'

'Oh, yes.' James frowned. 'Bloody awful business. How's she doing?' he added. 'The little girl?' Sylvia paused, mid-lick.

'Apparently, she's woken up from her coma. But . . .' she fixed James with an impressive look '. . . she's been brain damaged. And the latest is that they're taking the Delaneys to court. Suing them. Can you believe it?'

'Jesus Christ.' James shuddered and took a sip of coffee. He looked at Sylvia as though expecting more, but she was licking envelopes again, so he turned his gaze back to the paper. But his attention wandered, and after a few seconds he put the paper down.

'So – how bad is it?'

'What?' Sylvia's eyebrows rose enquiringly.

'How badly has the little girl been brain damaged?'

'Oh,' Sylvia shrugged, 'I don't know.'

'Have you been to visit her?' Sylvia flushed slightly.

'No,' she said shortly. 'And don't look at me like that! You know I'm no good in hospitals.' She finished licking the envelope she was holding and put it down on the pile by her plate. 'I'm holding this coffee-morning instead,' she added, 'as a gesture of support.'

'Support!' James guffawed with laughter.

'It'll be a fund-raising occasion,' said Sylvia angrily, 'so you can stop laughing, James.'

'Oh, a fund-raising occasion.' James grinned derisively. 'I know your fund-raising methods. A sponsored gossip, is it? Fifty pence for every piece of information provided, whether true or not.'

'Oh, shut up,' cried Sylvia. She picked up a piece of toast and bit into it crossly. 'Anyway,' she added irrelevantly, 'I thought you were supposed to be in Antwerp this week.'

'I'm not going till Thursday.'

'Good,' said Sylvia, 'you'll be out of the way for my coffee-morning. How long are you there?'

'Three days. Then I'm flying straight to Oslo.'

'Even better,' said Sylvia. She leaned back in her chair and stretched her arms lazily. 'Well, you needn't hurry back.'

'Don't worry, my darling,' said James, grinning at her, 'I won't.'

By eleven o'clock on the day of the coffee-morning, fourteen ladies had assembled in Sylvia's drawing-room, and all were looking expectantly at the door.

From the hall could be heard the rather flustered tones of Mary Tracey, who had just arrived. Mary, it was tacitly acknowledged by all, must know more about the whole affair than any of them. After all, she seemed to be Louise's closest friend in the village.

And so, in deference to her, nobody began speaking on the subject of the swimming-pool accident until she had been persuaded to entrust baby Luke to the tender care of Mrs Greenly in the kitchen, had been led into the room, and then ensconced on a large Knole sofa in the centre of the room. Sylvia smiled warmly at her and held out a cup of coffee.

'There you are,' she said sweetly. 'I hope it's not too strong.'

'Oh, er, no,' said Mary, turning rather pink. 'I'm sure it's fine. Lovely.'

Mary didn't usually attend Sylvia's coffee-mornings, considering them a bit fancy for her, especially now she had Luke to consider. But Sylvia had been so charming on the telephone that she had felt unable to refuse. Now she looked around in slight alarm; she was probably the youngest woman in the room, and definitely the shabbiest.

There was a pause, as Sylvia returned to her own chair and took a sip of coffee. Then she drew breath. Everybody looked up.

'And so, Mary,' she said in sympathetic tones. 'How is poor little Katie?' Mary swallowed. Every eye seemed to be on her.

'Well,' she began hesitatingly, 'she's woken up from the coma.'

There was a general sigh of relief.

'Thank goodness for that,' said Mrs Prendergast, a large lady who lived across the road from Sylvia.

'That's marvellous news!' said someone else, rather too gaily for Mary's liking.

'Yes,' added Mary quickly, 'but that doesn't mean

147

she's better. She's still very woozy, and they say . . .' she swallowed and took a sip of coffee, '. . . they say she'll probably be brain damaged.' Her eyes suddenly filled with tears. What was wrong with her? she thought furiously. She'd known all about Katie for days. She should be able to speak more matter-of-factly about it, but somehow, telling all these women brought the horror of it back to her all over again. She felt a tear trickle down her cheek.

'Oh, Mary!' Suddenly Sylvia was by her side, stroking her hand. 'Don't talk about it if you don't want to.'

'No, it's all right.' Mary struggled to control herself.

'It's just that we're all so concerned about the poor little thing,' continued Sylvia.

'Brain damage!' murmured one of the ladies sitting by the window. 'How frightful.'

'She won't be a . . . you know, a total . . .' Mary searched for an acceptable word, and gave up. 'You know. And there is a small chance she might recover completely.' She looked around the room hopefully, but none of the other ladies looked convinced by this show of optimism. They exchanged determinedly sombre glances.

'How shattering it must be for them,' exclaimed Mrs Prendergast, giving a little shudder. 'I don't know how I'd cope.'

'Awful!'

'Dreadful!' There was a short respectful pause, then Sylvia turned to Mary.

'But I gather', she said in vague tones, 'that there's some talk of compensation? Damages? A court case?' She cocked her head enquiringly. There was a tiny rustling sound as all the ladies moved forward on their seats.

'Well,' began Mary. She looked around. 'Yes, that's right. Louise and Barnaby are taking the Delaneys to court. Apparently . . .' She paused and wiped her nose.

'Apparently the Delaneys were negligent. The diving-board was dangerous.'

Mrs Prendergast gasped.

'How horrendous!' she cried. 'I mean, my own children used to swim in that pool! They used to dive off that board all the time!'

'So did mine!' chimed in another lady. 'To think it was dangerous all that time! It's criminal!' She looked around agitatedly.

'Terrible!' came another voice.

'They haven't actually proved anything yet,' put in Mrs Quint, a quietly spoken woman who had so far contributed nothing to the conversation. 'I don't think it's quite fair to assume it definitely was dangerous. And I have to say, it didn't look particularly dangerous to me.' The general air of excitement subsided slightly, and Mrs Prendergast looked rather aggrievedly at Mrs Quint.

'Well, they wouldn't be taking them to court if they didn't have a case, would they?' she said in triumphant tones.

There was a pause. No-one seemed able to contradict that assertion.

'Well, I think those Kembers should go for everything they can get,' said Janice Sharp, who had a weekend cottage in Melbrook and had come down especially for Sylvia's coffee-morning. 'Good luck to them! I mean, the Delaneys certainly look as though they can afford it.' Mrs Prendergast nodded.

'Did you know they've got houses all over Europe?' she said, brushing crumbs vigorously off her lap.

'Are you sure?' said Mrs Quint.

'Oh, yes,' said Mrs Prendergast confidently. 'One in France, certainly, and then I think there's one in Italy and one somewhere else . . . They've got all that, but they're too mean to keep their pool safe for our children to swim in! It's outrageous!'

'I don't know,' said Mrs Quint dubiously. 'I'm not sure they're as rich as that, and I assume the Kembers will be suing for a very large amount?'

All eyes turned to Mary, who blushed. She herself had been astounded when she'd heard the sort of sums that were being bandied about by Cassian and Louise. Staggered. But Cassian had been quick to show her exactly why Katie needed so much money and why it would be letting her down to claim any less. Mary blushed even harder as she remembered Cassian sitting next to her at Louise's kitchen table, touching her bare arm with the soft cotton of his shirt; as she remembered the faint expensive scent of his aftershave and the way he smiled at her . . . Then, as she realized everyone was waiting for an answer, she shook her head impatiently to clear her thoughts, took a breath and said abruptly, 'About half a million pounds. Or thereabouts.' There was a sharp intake of breath around her.

'What?'

'You must be joking!'

Even Sylvia was surprised.

'Is that true, Mary?' she said. 'Are they really going to ask for that much?'

'So they say.' Suddenly Mary became aware of the goggle eyes around her, and wondered whether she ought not to have kept some pieces of information to herself. But it was too late, exclamations of astonishment were breaking out all around the room. Mrs Prendergast was nodding at her neighbour and saying repeatedly, 'I'm not at all surprised,' in a defiant voice, as though daring someone to contradict her.

'Imagine,' said Janice Sharp. 'Half a million pounds!'

'That's a lot of money,' said Mrs Quint soberly. 'Let's hope the Delaneys are insured.'

Mary began to feel slightly defensive.

'Well, Katie's been very badly hurt!' she exclaimed.

'She may need special care for years. She deserves the money.'

'Oh, I'm not saying . . .' began Mrs Quint. She was interrupted by the sound of the doorbell. Sylvia stood up.

'Do excuse me,' she said, bestowing a gracious smile around the room, 'and help yourselves to more coffee.'

There was animated chatter while she was gone. Mrs Quint tried to introduce a subject of more general interest into the conversation, but no-one appeared interested in the plight of her garden, nor willing to divulge their holiday plans.

'I just think', Mrs Prendergast was saying as the door opened, 'that if people are actually charging you to use their pool, then they jolly well have a res-ponsibility . . .'

Suddenly she was interrupted by Sylvia speaking from outside the room. Her voice was deliberately raised in a mixture of delight and malice, and she was saying, 'Have you got time for a quick cup of coffee, Ursula?'

A couple of the ladies gasped. Mrs Prendergast's head shot round. There, in the doorway, stood Ursula Delaney, with a benign expression on her face and a cake, sprinkled with almonds, balanced on her upturned hands.

'Hello, everyone,' she said simply. 'I can't stay, I'm afraid, but I wanted to contribute a little something.'

'Not to worry, Ursula,' said Sylvia, giving an amused little grin round the room. 'I'd say it's enough that you've come at all. You know most people here, don't you?' she added.

'I think so,' said Ursula, smiling vaguely around. She walked over to the table and deposited her cake. As she looked up again, there was an embarrassed shuffling. Nobody spoke.

'Dear me!' she exclaimed. 'Please don't stop the

conversation just because of me. What were you talking about?'

There was a dreadful little silence. Mary Tracey felt her cheeks growing hotter and hotter. Then Mrs Quint cleared her throat.

'I was talking', she said firmly, 'about the dreadful state of my garden.' She looked severely at Mrs Prendergast. 'Wasn't I?'

'Oh yes,' said Mrs Prendergast hastily. 'Yes, you were. And . . . and so was I,' she added. 'Mine's in a terrible state, too.'

'So is mine,' chimed in several voices. Ursula looked around, a puzzled expression on her face.

'Oh dear,' she said, 'what bad luck! Our garden seems to be doing quite well.' She gazed out of the window with a thoughtful expression on her face. 'We do have very good mulch,' she said eventually. 'Perhaps that's the answer.'

She looked around with raised questioning eyebrows. But no-one seemed to have a reply.

Chapter Eleven

Two weeks later a letter arrived for Hugh from his insurance company. He opened it at breakfast, read it, then silently put it back into the envelope.

'What?' said Meredith, whose eyes had homed in sharply on the logo on the front of the envelope. 'What did they say?'

Ever since the announcement that Hugh and Ursula were going to be sued, Meredith had found herself waking every morning with an urgent fighting energy which she longed to put to good use. But Alexis had informed her candidly that there was little she could do in such early days, and he'd added again that the case was likely to last a very long time — maybe years.

Years of this tension? Meredith couldn't stand the thought, and she knew she wasn't the only one who was feeling the strain. While she'd been striding around the house with an impotent adrenalin; unable to work; unable to relax, Hugh had retreated silently into himself. His face was subdued and haggard; he'd admitted he wasn't sleeping well.

'What did they say?' Meredith repeated, trying not to sound impatient.

Hugh looked up. He glanced at Ursula, who was peacefully eating a boiled egg and reading the *Daily Mail*, then attempted to smile optimistically at Meredith, but his eyes had a blank devastated look.

'They think it's most unlikely that they would be able to meet any claim for damages arising from a non-domestic use of the pool. They say . . .' he gazed down at the letter, 'they say that if we'd informed them that we were using it for a public function, they could have arranged additional cover. But we didn't.' Hugh put down the letter and looked bleakly at Meredith. 'Basically, they say they're not going to pay.'

'Bastards!' exclaimed Meredith. 'They're just using any excuse to weasel out of it!'

'Maybe,' said Hugh. He rubbed his face miserably. 'But maybe they're right. Maybe I should have given them a call; arranged extra insurance. It just never occurred to me . . .' He broke off.

'Let me see the letter,' demanded Meredith. She grabbed the sheet from Hugh's plate and scanned it. 'It doesn't say they definitely won't pay,' she said, after a few minutes. 'It just says probably.'

'I know,' said Hugh, 'but frankly, I don't hold out much hope that they'll change their minds.'

Meredith looked at the letter again.

'I guess you're right,' she said. She leaned backwards in her chair and looked distantly out of the window. She couldn't quite bear to meet Hugh's gaze; to feel the unspoken implications of this letter flickering fearfully from his eyes to hers – bypassing Ursula, as did so many of their tacit communications. What if Hugh and Ursula somehow lost the case? she found herself thinking. What if they had to pay out huge damages? Hundreds of thousands of pounds? What would they do?

A bubbling fury rose up in Meredith and abruptly she pushed her chair back.

'I'm going out,' she said, and left the room before either Hugh or Ursula could comment.

She stalked out of the drive of Devenish House, and without really knowing what her intention was, strode briskly and deliberately towards Larch Tree Cottage, at the other end of the village. A vision of Hugh's defeated eyes burned in her brain, making her stride more and more quickly, and she reached her destination panting slightly and wondering what she was about to do, exactly. But as she neared Larch Tree Cottage, she saw Louise coming out of the front door, and all hesitation disappeared.

'I just thought you might like to know', she said in a harsh abrasive voice, ignoring Louise's gasp of surprise, 'that it looks like our insurers are pulling out. So if you do win your God-awful case, Hugh and Ursula will have to pay you out of their own pocket and they'll probably be ruined. Just so you know.' She stopped halfway down the path, and looked at Louise for a reaction.

'I'm afraid,' began Louise in a shaky, but rather formal voice, 'I really don't think . . .'

'No, you don't, do you?' broke in Meredith angrily. 'You don't think at all. If you did, you wouldn't be bringing this fucking case to court. You wouldn't be ruining the lives of two perfectly innocent people!'

'I'm not . . .'

'Do you know what this is going to do to them?'

'Well, do you know what this accident has done to us?' interrupted Louise, with sudden indignation. 'Do you know what we've been going through? My God, you haven't even visited Katie in hospital! None of you! You haven't seen what state she's in! So don't start talking about ruining lives. You've no idea what this is like for us!' Louise's eyes blazed, blue and angry, at Meredith.

'The reason we haven't been to the hospital is because you're suing us!' Meredith's voice rose, furious, through the air. 'Did that ever occur to you? We've been advised not to go near you. If you'd only drop the stupid case, we could help! We want to help!'

A smooth voice interrupted her.

'If you want to help, you can leave the premises of my client at once.'

Both women's heads whipped round. It was Cassian,

coming out of the front door. Meredith scowled at him.

'Yes,' said Louise, emboldened by his arrival. 'Just leave me alone, Meredith.'

'Oh, for Christ's sake,' said Meredith scornfully, 'I'll go, then. But just for the record, I do have some idea what you're going through, you know . . .'

'Will you please stop harassing my client,' interrupted Cassian impatiently. Meredith ignored him and looked directly at Louise.

'In case you'd forgotten, my husband went into a coma a few years ago, like your daughter. The difference is, he died.' She broke off suddenly and Louise flushed faintly.

'I can tell you now,' Cassian said, 'this outburst isn't helping your case at all.' He took out a notebook and began to write in it.

'And the other difference is,' said Meredith curtly, 'I just accepted it. I didn't look around for someone to blame, or try to make money out of it.'

'I must request . . .' began Cassian again.

'Oh, fuck off, you little toad,' interrupted Meredith. Louise broke in, without looking at Cassian.

'Well, OK, so your husband died,' she said, in a jerky voice, 'but maybe what's happened to Katie is worse; she could be brain damaged for life!'

'Louise,' snapped Cassian, 'this conversation has got to stop. Go and get in the car.' Louise glanced at him hesitantly, then obeyed.

'Right,' said Cassian. He brought out a mobile phone. 'Now,' he said to Meredith. 'I can call the police – or you can go now.'

Without answering, Meredith began to walk back down the path. She stopped as she passed the car and tried to catch Louise's eye, but Louise frowned and looked away. Meredith shrugged, and carried on walking back to Devenish House.

* * *

Hugh had spent the rest of breakfast patiently explaining to Ursula the meaning of the letter from the insurers, trying to make the situation quite clear, without frightening her. When he'd finished, she looked at him with a face only mildly wrinkled with anxiety, and said, 'Oh dear.'

And Hugh had stared back at her, feeling an uncharacteristic frustration rising through him. Is that all you can say? he wanted to shout. Don't you see what this means for us? But instead of shouting, he clenched his fists under the table and gazed out of the window, and tried to calm his pounding, angry, terrified heart.

Ursula, meanwhile, sat in silence, consumed by difficult and rather perplexing thoughts. She leaned back in her chair and screwed up her face, and when Hugh got up to leave the table, she nodded absently at him as though he were a stranger on a train. She sat for another ten minutes or so after he had gone, then abruptly came to a conclusion. Leaving the dishes for Mrs Viney, who came in twice a week to clean the house, Ursula quickly went upstairs to the pretty satinwood dressing-table which she used as a desk. She sat down, took out a piece of rough paper and, with a missionary zeal, began to compose a letter.

The next day, when everybody had gone out, Ursula left Devenish House clutching a large basket and a pale mauve envelope. She walked briskly through the village, deserted at that hour of the morning, until she reached Larch Tree Cottage.

She was well aware that she was repeating the path which Meredith had taken just the day before; that Alexis would be furious if he discovered what she was doing; that she shouldn't be there at all, but a firm belief in what she was doing kept her step from faltering. Her mission, she thought, was very different from poor Meredith's outburst.

Ursula had been astonished when Meredith confessed to her confrontation with Louise. Yelling in the street! What were they all coming to? It just showed, she thought, that nobody was quite themselves at the moment. Indeed, this was one of the very points she had put in her letter to Louise.

Ursula had great hopes of her letter. She had toiled over it for almost three hours the previous day, then had written it out neatly before hurrying into Linningford to buy a selection of toys. Now she looked at the envelope, addressed to Mrs Barnaby Kember, and felt her heart give a flutter of hope. Alexis might insist, she thought, that they should avoid contact with the Kembers, but what harm could an honest letter do? Surely Louise would melt when she read Ursula's heartfelt appeal – from one mother to another? Surely she would drop this silly case?

She had intended simply to leave the basket in the porch and then go, but outside the cottage, playing on the grassy verge in a rather desultory way, was Amelia. She looked up as Ursula approached.

'Hello, Mrs Delaney,' she said.

'Hello, Amelia,' said Ursula, in surprise. 'Shouldn't you be at school?'

'I've got an earache,' said Amelia, 'so I'm at home.'

'And is Mummy at home, looking after you?' said Ursula, looking, with sudden alarm, towards the cottage. She certainly didn't want to bump into Louise.

'No, she isn't at home,' said Amelia. Ursula relaxed slightly. 'She's at the hospital,' added Amelia grumpily, giving the verge a little kick. 'She's *always* at the hospital.'

'Well, dear, I expect she's worried about Katie,' said Ursula mildly.

'I had an earache,' continued Amelia doggedly, 'and I told her, and all she said was, "Oh, buck up, Amelia." And then it hurt so much I cried in the night, and she

158

took me to the doctor, and all he said was "How's Katie?" And now', she added, with stony emphasis, 'I'm ill too, but I'm being looked after by Mary, and Mummy's gone to see Katie, like she always does.'

Ursula gazed at Amelia in a sudden discomfiture. Poor child. Of course she must be feeling rather left out.

'I hate Katie,' said Amelia, and darted a quick defiant glance at Ursula. Ursula essayed a hesitant smile.

'I'm sure you don't really,' she said. Amelia stared rigidly at Ursula for a few seconds, then flushed and looked away.

'But look,' said Ursula hurriedly. 'Look what I've brought you.' She put a hand into the basket and pulled out the first toy that her hand touched. It was a Barbie doll, dressed in a pink leotard and encased in a shiny wrapper. Amelia stared at it.

'For me?' she said suspiciously. 'You brought this for me?'

'Yes,' said Ursula, hoping she sounded convincing. 'Some of these toys are for Katie, and . . . some of them are for you.' Amelia turned the doll round in her hands for a silent minute. Then, suddenly, she gave a sob.

'I don't want it,' she wailed. 'I want Katie to have it.'

With that she began to cry properly, with splashy tears and a runny nose, and without stopping to think, Ursula sat down on the verge and took Amelia into her arms. Amelia buried her head in Ursula's soft lavender-scented blouse.

'Don't worry,' soothed Ursula, 'everything will be all right.'

Amelia looked up at Ursula, her face red and her eyes wet.

'Katie's all bald on her head, and she's got a horrible tube in her arm,' she said jerkily. Ursula felt an unpleasant twinge in her stomach, but she ignored it and continued stroking Amelia's hair. 'And she can't speak properly,' carried on Amelia, 'and she didn't

159

know who I was.' She gave a small shudder. 'I said, "Hello, Katie, it's me, Amelia," but she just looked at me, as if she didn't even *recognize* me, and then she went back to sleep. She didn't even look at the cards we made for her in Art. Everybody made a card,' she added, 'even Mrs Jacob. And we made a tape.'

Ursula clasped Amelia more tightly. Painful memories of Simon, which she thought she had firmly buried, were beginning to jump to the surface of her mind. To distract herself, she said to Amelia, trying to adopt a reassuring voice, 'Well, now, I wouldn't worry about any of that. Katie's still half asleep, you know.'

'That's what Mummy said,' said Amelia, looking suspiciously at Ursula. 'But Sarah Wyatt, in my form, said she saw a film where the girl had a coma and she died. She said Katie was going to *die*.' She broke into fresh sobs.

'Nonsense,' said Ursula briskly. 'Katie will get much better. You'll see. You'll see.'

There was a short pause. Ursula began to look around anxiously. It occurred to her that Mary must be wondering where Amelia had got to. She shifted slightly, as though to get up, but Amelia still clung to her. Suddenly she said, in a gasping voice, 'It was all my fault.' Ursula jumped, genuinely startled.

'No!' she exclaimed. 'Amelia! You mustn't think that! Whatever gave you that idea?'

'It was my fault,' repeated Amelia hopelessly. 'Katie only tried to do a backward dive because I was doing them. She always copies me.' She looked up at Ursula, entreatingly.

'It was me that wanted to go swimming!' she wailed, and gave a sudden desperate sob. 'Daddy wanted to go f-fishing, but I wanted to go swimming instead, an-and Katie copied me. And then she copied me doing a back dive, too. If I hadn't . . .' She stopped and wiped her nose with her hand. 'If I hadn't done one, then Katie wouldn't have either . . .'

Ursula stared back at Amelia. For a panicked second she could think of nothing to say; her mind was blank and empty. But that wasn't good enough, she told herself frantically. Here was a troubled child, relying on her for comfort and reassurance; she must say something. She *must*.

'That's utter nonsense,' she said at last, trying to adopt an authoritative tone. 'I've never heard anything so silly.' Amelia gazed at her, silent but unconvinced. 'Katie only copies you sometimes,' continued Ursula, cautiously feeling her way, 'but mostly she does exactly what she wants, whether you've been doing it or not. She only came swimming because she wanted to – and she was only doing a back dive because she felt like it.' Ursula scanned Amelia's face for a reaction. 'It was nothing to do with you,' she added for good measure.

Amelia's face was unmoved. Ursula cast round anxiously in her mind for something more persuasive to say.

'I mean,' she added suddenly, 'I'm sure you've both seen professional divers on the television doing splendid back dives, but you're not saying it's their fault, are you?' Slowly, reluctantly, Amelia shook her head. 'Well, then,' said Ursula, with an air of confidence she was far from feeling, 'that proves my point.' She gave Amelia a cheerful distracting smile. 'Now, let's have no more of these silly thoughts.'

She glanced at the doll still in Amelia's hand.

'What are you going to call her? She really is yours to keep, you know.' Amelia slowly looked down at the Barbie doll.

'I'm going to call her Katie,' she said in a low voice. She rubbed her face, took a breath, and began to tear off the packaging.

'Good,' said Ursula. 'Now, why don't you take in the

rest of these toys and show Mary? And perhaps Mummy will let you take them to the hospital.'

She picked up the pale mauve envelope sitting on top of the basket.

'And, Amelia,' she said, 'be sure to give this envelope straight to Mary, or Mummy. Don't drop it or forget about it.' Amelia took the envelope and looked at it.

'What is it?' she said.

'Well . . .' said Ursula hesitantly. 'It's . . . it's some money. For Katie. For all of you really. Just a little present from me, and a letter for Mummy.' She got to her feet. 'Now, in you go,' she said.

She watched as Amelia carried the basket in through the gate. Then, hurriedly, she began to walk away, back home, before anyone saw her.

Later on that day, Alexis sat down with Hugh, Ursula and Meredith in the kitchen of Devenish House.

'Until we actually see a writ and see what claims are being made,' he said, 'we can't begin to prepare a defence.' He looked at Hugh. 'But the earlier we start thinking about it, the better. So I'm working on a few assumptions which I think are safe to make.' He glanced down at a sheet of paper.

'They'll be suing you under the Occupier's Liability Act.' He read aloud. '"An occupier owes to a visitor a duty to take such care as in all the circumstances of the case is reasonable to see that the visitor will be reasonably safe in using the premises for the purposes for which he is invited or permitted by the occupier to be there, except insofar as the occupier has validly extended, restricted, modified or excluded that duty by agreement or otherwise."'

Alexis finished and looked up at his audience. Hugh's face was downcast; Ursula's was bewildered. Only Meredith looked back at him with animation in her face.

'You mean', she said, 'that what we should have had

162

is a notice up, saying, "We do not accept responsibility for your children's safety".'

'Perhaps that would have helped,' said Alexis slowly. 'Although there are some duties you can't simply opt out of by putting up a notice, especially if you've charged at the door.' He sighed. 'This business of taking money for charity confuses the matter.'

'Or else we could have put up a notice saying, "Please do not use the swimming-pool",' said Meredith, in a voice suddenly scorched with sarcasm. 'We could have charged people just to come in and *look* at the pool.'

'Meredith,' began Alexis. She ignored him.

'Or perhaps even that's too dangerous,' she exclaimed. 'Of course! We could have sent everybody a Polaroid of the pool and told them to stay at home. That would have been nice and safe, wouldn't it?' She looked at Alexis with scornful eyes. He sighed.

'You know, you're not being entirely helpful.'

'Well, for Christ's sake!' she exclaimed. 'It's just so . . .' She broke off, as the kettle came to a screeching boil behind her. 'OK, OK,' she said, and gave Alexis a quick grin. 'I'll be helpful. Who wants some coffee?'

As she spooned coffee into the coffee-maker, Alexis turned back to his notes.

'The Act states that an occupier must be prepared for children to be less careful than adults,' he read. Hugh looked up.

'Meaning what, exactly?' Alexis sighed.

'There's nothing exact about it,' he said. 'You're supposed to take into account that children find certain things alluring, and that they haven't got the sense to see that they're dangerous.'

'Oh, come on,' said Meredith impatiently, bringing a cup of coffee over and putting it in front of Alexis. 'A diving-board isn't *alluring*. It's not some kind of ginger-bread house. It's a diving-board, period. Everyone knows what a diving-board is, for Christ's sake.' Alexis looked up at her.

'I'm not giving you my own opinion,' he said patiently. 'I'm just trying to explain the law to you.' Meredith paused and ran an exasperated hand through her hair.

'I know,' she said, exhaling slowly. 'I'm sorry. I'm not mad at you. It just all seems such a load of bullshit.'

'I know,' said Alexis. He gave her a sudden smile. 'Haven't I always warned you, keep well away from lawyers?'

To his surprise, Meredith didn't smile back. She flushed slightly and turned away. But before Alexis could react to this, his attention was distracted by Ursula.

'I did say to Louise, at the time, that the children really should calm down a bit,' she was saying, thoughtfully. Her face crumpled slightly. 'Next time, I don't think we should allow children to go on the diving-board.'

'Next time?' Meredith's voice rang harshly through the air. Ursula looked back at her benignly. 'Ursula,' Meredith said more gently, 'I don't honestly think there'll be a next time. I don't think we'll be having any more Swimming Days. Not for a while.'

'Oh!' Ursula raised a distressed hand to her mouth. 'I hadn't even thought . . .' But before she could finish, Alexis broke in thoughtfully.

'Are you saying you actually gave Louise a warning, Ursula?' Ursula looked at him, surprised.

'Well,' she said hesitantly, 'I wouldn't say it was exactly a warning, but I did say something to her. It was the children, you see,' she explained. 'They were getting rather overexcited. And I said . . .' She stopped and looked at Alexis. He had picked up a pen and was staring at her, waiting for her to continue. 'Is this important?' she faltered.

'It could be,' said Alexis. 'It could be crucial. If you actually *warned* Louise and she took no notice . . .' He looked at Ursula. 'Listen, Ursula,' he said. 'I want you to try to remember exactly what you said to Louise. Your exact words.' Ursula stared back at him uncertainly.

'Well,' she said eventually, her voice quavering slightly. 'I went up to Louise, and . . .' She broke off. 'Or did Louise come up to me?' She looked at Alexis anxiously. Alexis put down his pen.

'I tell you what,' he said kindly, 'you try to remember later on, when it's a bit quieter, and write it all down. And try to remember exactly how you said it. For example, Louise couldn't possibly have thought you were joking, could she?'

'Oh,' said Ursula. 'No, I don't *think* so. Although,' she added doubtfully, 'you never know. Sometimes I make a joke and nobody realizes . . . so it could well have been the other way around, couldn't it?' Alexis looked blank.

'Yes,' he said eventually. 'I suppose so.'

Meredith was looking at him. 'So what are you getting at?' she said slowly. 'That Louise is some kind of irresponsible mother? That *she* was negligent? Is that what we're going to say?' Alexis met her eyes unflinchingly.

'If we need to, then yes,' he said steadily. 'We're going to need all the ammunition we can get. If we can somehow show that Louise was at fault . . .'

'At fault?' Ursula looked up, perturbed. 'Louise wasn't to blame, surely?' She looked anxiously at Hugh, who was still staring downwards. 'Hugh, are you listening to what they're saying? That poor Louise was to blame for Katie's accident.'

'We don't really think she was to blame, Ursula,' said Meredith patiently. 'But Alexis is right. We've got to use every defence we've got. I mean, look at Louise; she's blaming us, isn't she? We can't just stand back and say nothing.'

'Yes, well . . . you know, I think poor Louise is a little upset at the moment,' said Ursula. 'And Barnaby. They probably don't quite know what they're saying, but that doesn't mean we have to sink to the same level.'

She looked at Meredith with suddenly severe blue eyes.

'I think, dear, that it would be very wrong of us to tell anyone that we thought it was *Louise's* fault that poor Katie got injured.' She paused and added informatively, as though clinching the matter, 'It was just an accident, you know.'

'Of course it was an accident!' cried Meredith impatiently. 'And of course it's wrong to blame Louise, but what else can we do? Ursula, you don't seem to understand. These people are taking you to court. To court! They're going to stand up and say the accident was all your fault, and unless you come up with some sort of defence, they'll end up screwing you for every penny.'

There was a short silence. For a moment Ursula stared at Meredith in distress. Then her brow cleared and a complacent expression appeared on her face.

'You know, dear,' she said, 'I don't believe Louise and Barnaby will go to court.'

'What?' Meredith gazed at Ursula, red with incredulous frustration. 'But they're doing it! This isn't some hypothetical case we're constructing here.' She paused, took a breath, and added, in the clearest, plainest tones she could muster, 'The Kembers have informed you, through their lawyer, that they're taking you to court!'

'I know they have,' said Ursula mildly, 'but I'm sure they'll change their minds when they've calmed down a bit.' She nodded at Meredith. 'You'll see, dear, this will all blow over. I've got a feeling about it.' And she gave Meredith a comfortable, almost secretive smile.

Meredith stared at Ursula as though she couldn't believe her ears. Alexis tactfully intervened.

'Let's hope you're right, Ursula,' he said heartily. He

smiled at her. 'And I agree, it is a bit upsetting having to muster evidence against friends. But I'm afraid you can be quite sure that Louise and Barnaby and all their lawyer chums will be putting together as strong a case against you as they possibly can, so the sensible thing is for us to start thinking about a defence.' He saw Ursula opening her mouth again and added quickly, 'Just in case.' Ursula gave a little shrug.

'Well, Alexis dear – you know best,' she said in agreeable, unconvinced tones.

'Yes, he does,' put in Hugh, surprisingly.

Everyone looked at him. Hugh raised his head, and Meredith noticed, with a pang of shock, the weary pockets of flesh drooping under his eyes. This court case was going to be too much for him, she thought with sudden panic. It was going to drive him down into the ground. Simon's death had hit him hard; he was only just beginning to recover from that; this case might go on for years. He was no longer a young man. How was he going to cope? Fucking Barnaby and Louise, she suddenly thought, with a bitterness that threatened to turn into tears. How *dare* they ruin the lives of the most decent people in the world?

Almost immediately, inevitably, her thoughts switched self-reproachfully to little Katie, lying in hospital, and a noisy, fuzzy guilt began to fill her mind. But over the guilt, above its relentless castigating clamour, her thoughts rang out, loud and defiant. So what? So what if they've suffered. Being a victim doesn't give you the right to trample over everybody else. If Katie's life has been ruined, why should Hugh's automatically be ruined too? Why look for blame? Why . . .

Her thoughts were interrupted by Hugh speaking again.

'The best thing we can all do is to listen to what Alexis has to say and help him as much as we can,' he said.

'And, Ursula, if that means you writing down the comment you made to Louise, then I suggest you do it.' Hugh looked hard at Ursula and she nodded meekly. Then he turned to Alexis with worried eyes. 'I spoke to Barnaby myself that day,' he said heavily, 'we were sitting together. But I honestly can't think of anything that either of us said which might be relevant to our defence.' He shrugged hopelessly. 'Sorry not to be more help.'

Alexis smiled warmly at him.

'Don't worry, Hugh. You'll be a help, all right. This case is only just beginning. There's a long way to go yet. You'll see.'

Cassian stared at Louise. He looked at the pale mauve-coloured letter fluttering in his hand, and again scanned a couple of sentences. Then he looked down at the basket of toys sitting on the table. His expression was incredulous.

'Are these people *trying* to lose, or what?'

Louise shrugged uncomfortably.

'First the girl comes and threatens you, and now this!' Cassian picked up the pale mauve matching envelope, pulled out the wad of notes and began to count them.

'The woman's a moron,' he said cheerfully. 'She's a complete fucking moron!' He looked up at Louise and grinned. 'You know, if I were her lawyer, and I saw what's in this letter, I'd be throwing in the towel right now.'

Chapter Twelve

Louise had not told Barnaby about Meredith's visit. Her instinct had been to telephone him straight away, but Cassian had forcefully persuaded her to keep quiet.

'There's really no point in stirring things up,' he said. 'You know what Barnaby's like, he'll completely over-react.'

But news of the scene had already travelled round the village, and when Barnaby arrived at Larch Tree Cottage the following night to discuss the case, he was full of alarmed rage.

'What did she say to you?' he said, as soon as Louise opened the door. 'That girl, Meredith. Did she threaten you? Someone told me she attacked you in the street!'

Louise stared up at his huge angry face, outraged on her behalf, and felt suddenly touched.

'Yes, well, it was quite frightening,' she said in the gently teasing tones which she hadn't used for months. 'She came at me with . . . with five hand grenades and a machete!' Barnaby gave a small astonished start, then his expression changed to an unwilling grin. Louise giggled.

'I was worried!' he said accusingly.

'Of course you were.' Cassian's smooth tones travelled from the back of the hall. Barnaby looked up and scowled. 'But there's no need for alarm,' continued Cassian, gliding swiftly towards the front door and taking Louise's hand, 'I was present when the girl made her attack.' He smiled complacently at Barnaby. 'I was able to get rid of her and note down some of the wilder

169

comments she made. Really,' he added, leading the way to the kitchen, 'these people seem determined to hinder their chances of success.'

Barnaby looked at Louise.

'Why does he say that?'

'Oh.' Louise sighed. 'Ursula wrote me a letter which apparently we'll be able to use in the case. It was a very sweet letter, but she practically admitted liability in it. And she enclosed some money, too.'

'Money? How much?'

'A thousand quid. For a holiday, she said.' Louise looked away uncomfortably. 'Ursula's so stupid. Cassian says her lawyer couldn't possibly have known what she was doing.'

They had reached the kitchen and Louise sat down. In the middle of the table, like an exhibit, sat the mauve letter. Louise glanced down at Ursula's careful loopy writing. Somehow the sight of it made her feel both unbearably touched and horribly guilty at the same time.

She rubbed a hand wearily over her eyes and felt her face droop with fatigue. The past few weeks seemed, in her mind, to have consisted of nothing but the hospital. Driving to and from the hospital, walking up and down the corridors, drinking coffee in the cafeteria, and the endless hours seated by Katie's bed.

She knew every inch of that ward by now; every square of linoleum and every crack in the paintwork. She could have described, from memory, each of the cheery childish paintings which decorated the corridor; could even have listed the names of their creators – Ben, Sam, Lucy M., Lucy B. – written on the paintings in a rounded teacher's handwriting. If she closed her eyes she could hear, over and over in her head, the distinctive tinkling laugh of one of the nurses and the sound of the squeaking trolley which came round every morning. And all the time she could smell that antiseptic hospital smell which lingered on her hands and in her clothes and hair.

Louise's mind felt blurred; her hair felt lank; her face felt robbed of resilience. Her muscles seemed to have forgotten how to smile, and yet there were things to smile about. Katie was improving, everybody said so, and, of course, Louise could see herself that it was true. Katie was opening her eyes now, for quite long periods of time. And each time she seemed to know, just about, who she was and what her name was. But every time she woke, she seemed to have forgotten about the accident and why she was in hospital, and had to be told all over again. Louise's explanations were beginning to sound stale to her own ears; sometimes she could feel a note of unforgivable impatience creeping into her voice. She would break off, abruptly, staring into Katie's confused face, willing her to remember. And then she would silently, uselessly berate herself, as Katie's eyes dulled and she fell back into her heavy unnatural sleep. And Louise would sit back in her chair and begin her waiting again. Waiting either for Katie to wake up, or for it to be time to leave the hospital, drive home, pick up Amelia from whoever was baby-sitting, put Amelia to bed, microwave a quick supper and fall, exhausted, into bed.

Barnaby had offered, a couple of weeks ago, to move back in and give her a hand; since changing his mind on the court case, he'd become enthusiastically, irritatingly helpful. Louise had immediately refused his offer, but now she felt so fatigued that she wouldn't have minded who helped her. And yet, what on earth was she doing all day that made her so tired? Sitting still, pacing about, talking to the nurses, reading magazines. Hardly strenuous stuff. It didn't make any sense, she thought blearily.

Barnaby watched Louise covertly from the other side of the table, and miserably thought how pale and drawn

171

she looked. She needed him, he thought fiercely. She said she didn't, but she did. And a familiar pain began to gnaw at his chest.

'Don't worry,' he said impulsively. Louise looked up and gave him a weak smile. 'I've been doing a lot of thinking,' he continued earnestly. 'I'm sure we're doing the right thing, and I'm sure we're going to win this case. And then we'll be able to give Katie the best treatment there is.'

Louise met Barnaby's honest gaze and wished she could feel so certain. Meredith's furious tirade in the street had affected her more than she had admitted, and Ursula's foolish letter only made her feel more guilty. How on earth would the Delaneys find half a million pounds if they weren't insured? she found herself thinking all the time. What would they do? How would they manage?

The initial thrill she'd had at the thought of going to court had subsided, and hardened into a grim resignation. The more she understood about the case, the less she liked it. And somehow it seemed irrelevant to the real, everyday consequences of the accident. She couldn't make the connection between an abstract half a million pounds' worth of damages, floating uncertainly somewhere in the future, and Katie.

Cassian had uncorked a bottle of wine and now poured out three glasses. Louise relaxed slightly at the reassuring glug-glug sound. She knew she was drinking more now than she had before the accident, but still, she told herself, only a reasonable amount. And if she was always desperate for a drink when she got home from the hospital, well, that was only the same as lots of people with stressful jobs, she reasoned. Nothing to worry about.

'Lu-Lu,' Cassian said caressingly, as he put a glass in front of her. He sat down, then casually took Louise's hand and began to play with her fingers.

172

Barnaby looked away and clenched his fists. A rising anger started to burn inside his chest. Bastard. For a frightening moment, he thought his temper might take over. Desperately, he conjured up in his mind a vision of Katie; of the way she had smiled at him vaguely that afternoon; of her eyes, dulled by the accident but still his Katkin, underneath all the confusion and pain and drugs. I'm doing all this for Katie, he said to himself. For Katie.

'I've been reading up a bit,' he said abruptly, 'in the papers. There was a case just recently about a brain-damaged child who was given six hundred and thirty thousand pounds. Did you see that?' Cassian looked at Barnaby in mild surprise.

'Yes,' he said, 'I believe I did, but that was a rather different case. It was a medical negligence case, rather than occupiers' liability.'

'Oh,' said Barnaby in a chastened voice.

'But there were certainly some relevant similarities there,' added Cassian, kindly. 'And I must say, Barnaby, it's good that you're becoming up to date with recent developments.' Barnaby flushed a dark red.

'I want to do everything I can,' he said in a hoarse voice.

'Of course you do,' said Cassian smoothly. He opened his briefcase and took out a folder.

'Now,' he said, 'I'm about to start putting together draft witness statements. We need as many as possible, and to get them as quickly as possible, before people start to forget what happened.' He passed a list to Louise. 'These are the people who are being contacted by my assistant. Can you think of any others?'

Louise glanced down the list. Suddenly her gaze stopped.

'Amelia?' she exclaimed. 'She can't possibly be a witness!'

'What do you mean?' said Cassian, frowning. 'She'll

be one of the most important witnesses we've got.' He took a sip of wine. 'Don't worry,' he said, 'the courts are very understanding to child witnesses, and she won't have to do very much.'

'But she'll have to remember the whole thing!' Louise's voice was loud and shrill. 'That's bad enough! She'll have to go through it all over again! It'll be terrible for her.'

'Oh, really, Louise!' Cassian was smoothly dismissive. 'She'll be absolutely fine.'

'How do you know?' retorted Louise. 'Barnaby, we can't let Amelia go through all that, can we?'

There was silence. Barnaby said nothing.

'Barnaby!' said Louise sharply. 'You do agree with me, don't you?'

Barnaby slowly raised his head.

'Well,' he said heavily. He took a slug of wine. 'Actually, no. I don't think I do.'

'What?' Louise's voice rang, outraged, round the kitchen.

'I think Cassian's right,' said Barnaby. 'Amelia should give evidence. I mean, she was playing with Katie just before it happened.'

'But think what it'll do to her!'

'She'll be all right,' said Barnaby stolidly. 'She's a sensible girl. And if it helps Katie . . .'

'Well, what if it doesn't!' shrieked Louise angrily. 'What if we put Amelia through all that misery and then lose the case! Or what if we win the money and Katie still doesn't get better? What then?'

'Lu-Lu,' began Cassian smoothly, but Barnaby interrupted him.

'What are you saying, Lou?' he said loudly. 'That you don't want to go to court, after all?' There was a short tense silence.

'No!' exclaimed Louise. 'Oh, I don't know! It's just . . .' Suddenly tears sprang into her eyes and she gave a sob.

'I'm just so tired,' she cried, her voice rising sharply in distress, 'and Katie just doesn't get better, and sometimes I think . . .' she sniffed and wiped her nose with the back of her hand, '. . . I think, well, what good would all that money be to us, anyway?'

Her voice echoed round the kitchen; Cassian and Barnaby said nothing.

'And it'll all take for ever,' continued Louise tearfully, 'and we might not win, and even if we do, the Delaneys aren't insured, so they'll have to sell their house or something, and we all used to be such good f-friends . . .' She gave another heaving sob and buried her head in her hands.

Barnaby looked at Cassian. His expression was sombre.

'I didn't know that,' he said, 'about the insurance.' Cassian took a sip of wine. He didn't look pleased.

'What you must understand,' he said curtly, 'is that the issue of insurance has no bearing on the merits of this case. If you are due damages, then you are due damages. This is justice we're talking about here. Justice! You can't just ignore it!'

'Even if you ruin your friends?' cried Louise.

'Yes!' snapped Cassian, suddenly losing his patience. 'Look, Louise, these people might be your friends, but you owe more to your daughter than you do to them. Don't you?'

Louise didn't answer.

'You can't have it both ways!' continued Cassian. 'Either you sacrifice your friendship – a rather dubious friendship, I might add – or you sacrifice Katie. Which is it to be?' He turned and looked at Barnaby. 'Which is it to be, Barnaby? Which is more important?' There was a pause, then Barnaby exhaled sharply.

'Katie,' he said. 'It's got to be Katie.'

'Exactly,' said Cassian, closing his folder, 'and let me tell you both . . .'

175

He paused, until Louise unwillingly looked up at him.

'Let me tell you,' repeated Cassian, 'that the worst thing you can do for your little girl is prepare this case half-heartedly. If we're going to win some money for her, we need to give it one hundred per cent. Which means using all the evidence and all the witnesses we can muster, whether or not we like it. And if you're not prepared to do that, Louise, then I'm afraid we might as well forget the whole thing.'

'He's right,' said Barnaby suddenly, then flushed a deep red as the two of them turned to look at him. 'He's right, Lou. I mean, if we went through all this and then lost just because we didn't have the right piece of evidence . . .'

'Exactly,' said Cassian, 'Barnaby's got it exactly.'

'Don't you see what I mean, Lou?' said Barnaby in gruff pleading tones. He tried to catch her eye, but she looked away. 'It's not that I'm not fond of Hugh and Ursula, especially Hugh, but now we've decided to go to court, it's all got to be different. It's got to be.'

'But what about the fact that they aren't insured?' said Louise, suddenly, with a note of desperation in her voice. 'Doesn't that affect you? Doesn't that change your mind?'

Barnaby looked at her steadily, with pain in his eyes.

'I never wanted to sue,' he said eventually. 'It was you that wanted to sue. I thought it was wrong.' He paused and took a slug of wine. 'But I thought and thought about it, and eventually I decided that you were right; that we owed it to Katie. That's what I decided, and that stays the same.' He looked down at his huge hands resting on the table, 'that stays the same, whether or not Hugh and Ursula are insured. We still owe it to Katie. We should still sue.'

Louise stared at him for a moment. She picked up her glass and drained it. Then she looked up.

176

'Well, I never,' she said in slow bitter tones. Her cheeks were burning pink and her eyes flickered from Barnaby's face to Cassian's, and back to Barnaby's. 'I never thought I'd see the two of you ganging up together against me. Men know best. Is that it?'

'Of course not,' said Barnaby uncomfortably. 'But you must see . . .'

'I see nothing. Nothing!' Louise stood up, scraping her chair loudly against the floorboards. She pushed her hands shakily through her hair. 'Why don't you just go, Barnaby!' she said, glaring at him. 'We'll have this meeting another day. Or perhaps you don't even need me to come to it, since I'm so obviously in the wrong.'

'Louise,' pleaded Barnaby. 'Why don't you just relax . . .'

'Relax!' Louise's eyes glittered furiously at Barnaby. 'I spend all day at the hospital, I come home, you start lecturing me, and then you tell me to relax!'

'I didn't mean . . .' began Barnaby helplessly.

'I've had enough of all this. Just go, Barnaby! Go!'

Cassian met Barnaby's eyes.

'Perhaps it might be better', he said softly, 'if we all met another day.'

Barnaby nodded numbly.

'Look, Lou, I'm sorry,' he said hoarsely. 'I didn't realize . . .'

'Just go,' said Louise wearily. Barnaby nodded bleakly. He turned slowly away, then looked back, but Louise was staring blankly down at the floor.

'Bye,' he whispered dolefully.

'Bye, Barnaby,' said Cassian. Louise said nothing.

'Bye,' whispered Barnaby again. And with a heavy heart, he tiptoed out of the cottage and made his way back to his lonely empty home.

Much later on Cassian came and sat beside Louise on the sofa, where she was blankly watching the television,

177

turned down low so that it wouldn't wake Amelia. He began to massage her shoulders with a deft expertise.

'I know it's difficult,' he murmured softly into her neck, 'but it'll all be worth it in the end.'

Louise didn't move.

'The important thing is to secure Katie's future,' he added. There was a little pause. 'And our future,' he whispered seductively. 'Together.'

Slowly he pushed aside her hair and kissed her on the back of her neck.

Louise's shoulders froze in uncertain anticipation. There had been so many moments like this since she'd known Cassian; so many times when she'd expected him to make a move, to turn a light kiss into something more intense, to take a casual caress forward into the beginnings of love-making. And, so far, it had never happened. At first she'd felt slightly relieved; let off the hook. After some time, relief had turned into frustrated disappointment. And then, when she heard the rumours going round of her steamy affair, she had begun to feel an ironic amusement. She'd felt a private self-vindication at the knowledge that, whatever everyone thought, she hadn't been unfaithful to Barnaby.

She still hadn't. At least, not yet.

Cassian was still nuzzling the back of her neck. Louise could scarcely breathe. Was it finally going to happen? Now? When she was feeling so tired and groggy?

'I really hate to see you upset,' Cassian said, huskily, against her skin. 'I just want to make you feel better. Darling,' he added.

He felt Louise beginning to unbend slightly, and quickly moved a hand up inside her T-shirt, cupping a breast. With the other hand, he adeptly undid her bra. As it loosened, his fingers slipped underneath it, and he began to caress her soft flesh.

'Cassian,' said Louise weakly. She felt bruised by the

evening's arguments, vulnerable and unsure of herself; unsure of Cassian, even . . . But as she turned to face him, she felt her heart give a little leap. His eyes were gleaming; his expression intense, as though full of ardent fervour.

'Darling,' said Cassian. He looked straight at her with his dark-brown eyes. 'The reason I'm taking this case so seriously', he said huskily, 'is that . . . I love you.'

Louise's battered heart gave a little flutter.

'You must have known how I felt,' said Cassian. 'All this time.' He gave a small self-deprecating smile.

'Well,' said Louise falteringly.

'I've been waiting for the right moment to tell you,' said Cassian. He looked at her, his face suddenly serious. 'Is this the right moment, Louise?'

For a few moments Louise silently stared at him, her lips trembling and her face pale. Then, still silent, she nodded.

Cassian traced a finger down her face, then gently pulled her towards him. As their lips met, a fleeting image of Barnaby's face went through Louise's mind, accompanied by a hazy resentful guilt. But as Cassian's hands began to move with skilful care over her body, the image of Barnaby grew dim and vanished, and her mind and body surrendered, in sudden weary relief, to a blank unthinking pleasure.

Chapter Thirteen

Ten days later the weather broke. Sitting in the children's play-room at the hospital, Louise heard a clap of thunder and saw the first huge splashy drops of rain fall on the window-pane.

She shivered, even though the room itself was warm and bright, and looked at Katie, who was sitting on a play-mat, dispiritedly holding a shoe-lace threaded with wooden beads in primary colours. The play leader had started Katie off, threading the beads onto the shoe-lace herself, and had then surrounded her with more beads to carry on with and make a necklace. But although that was twenty minutes ago, Katie had not managed to add a single bead. She stared dully at the shoe-lace as though she couldn't understand what it was for, and resisted Louise's attempts to encourage her.

Louise sighed and looked at her watch. Still only eleven-forty. At twelve o'clock Barnaby was due to arrive at the hospital to collect them both and take them to Forest Lodge. Katie was now at the rehabilitation stage, it had been explained to them. She was physically independent, although her reactions were still slow; she was able to speak and eat and wash herself, and her memory had, to some degree, returned.

A noise made Louise look up. Katie had scattered the spare beads angrily on the floor.

'I don't like them,' she said, in her new thick heavy voice. Louise smiled encouragingly at Katie.

'Don't you like the pretty beads?' she said. Katie

180

scowled and looked away. Louise smiled again. Sometimes it was only by smiling that she could stop herself from screaming.

Mrs Innes from Forest Lodge had been very encouraging when she had assessed Katie. She had explained the rehabilitation centre to Louise, outlined the individually planned intensive programmes, spoken of multi-disciplinary teams, of reintegration into the education system, of parental involvement.

She had then said, somewhat to Louise's surprise, that she thought Katie should begin at Forest Lodge as a residential patient, to benefit from the twenty-four-hour care. Louise, who for some time had been imagining Katie back at home and everything back to normal, had felt tears come to her eyes and an inexplicable rage, directed primarily against the blameless Mrs Innes.

But now, watching Katie's uncertain progress across the room towards the Wendy house, she could see that everything was not back to normal. Katie was not the little girl she had been. Her speech was blurred; she often seemed to be at a loss for the right word; she grew angry easily, and tired even more easily; and her attention span, which had never been great at the best of times, now seemed non-existent.

They all found it difficult to relate to this new Katie; they all reacted to her in different ways. Barnaby had recently adopted a determined optimism. Every time he visited he relentlessly pointed out improvements in Katie's behaviour, until Louise, who spent more time with Katie than any of them, found herself snapping back – countering each of his optimistic observations with her own pessimistic ones.

She herself found it difficult to gain any perspective. For every achievement there seemed to be a set-back; Katie's progress appeared unbearably slow to her. Buried deep inside her was a foolish wish – belief, almost – that one day she was going to arrive at the hospital to find Katie running down the corridor, cracking the silly jokes she'd loved before the accident, talking in the same voice, back to her old self. The leaden truth – that any progress Katie made would be, at best, gradual – hit her with a depressing thud every day, as she arrived to find Katie only minimally improved from the day before, or not improved at all, or even slightly worse.

Meanwhile poor Amelia, who had pestered and pestered to be allowed to come to the hospital and play with Katie, now often stayed at home instead. Katie wasn't much good at playing with Amelia any more, Louise had soberly come to realize.

A week or so ago, Amelia had insisted on bringing the Noah's ark set to the hospital. She had set out the animals in their twos, then, in a conciliatory voice, said, 'You can have the elephants this time, Katie, because you're ill.' She looked at Katie for some recognition of this generous gesture, but Katie simply grabbed for the elephants. Amelia glanced uncertainly at Louise, then turned back to Katie and said, in a challenging voice that usually presaged an argument, 'Well, I'll have the monkeys then.' The monkeys had always been Katie's favourites, but today there was no shrill reaction from Katie, no cry of 'Am–ee–lia, that's *so* unfair.' Katie didn't seem to care about the monkeys any more. She didn't seem to care about anything any more.

The door opened and Barnaby appeared. He gave Louise a quick smile, then looked around for Katie.

'She's in the Wendy house,' said Louise.

'Kat-kin!' called Barnaby. 'I'm coming to find you!' He glanced down and suddenly spotted the wooden bead necklace, abandoned on the play-mat. 'Did Katie do this?' he asked, his voice suddenly full of pleasure. 'Look at that!'

'Actually,' said Louise gently, 'the play leader did it.

Katie was supposed to carry on, but she wasn't very keen.'

Barnaby's face fell. He turned away from Louise and began to approach the Wendy house, overshadowing it with his hulking frame. Suddenly Katie's head poked out of the window. She was grinning.

'Katie! You clever joker!' cried Barnaby joyfully. He looked over to Louise, as though to say *You see* . . . Louise smiled tightly back.

Had she always felt as irritated as this by Barnaby? she wondered. Or was it just since Cassian had given her a new yardstick to measure him by? Cassian, who was astute and professional, who cared about her and her children. Cassian, who understood that Katie's recovery would take time, who didn't grin at her with that stupid pointless optimism, but talked soberly about Katie and made helpful serious suggestions. Cassian, who came to her tenderly in bed, making her shiver and shudder with delight. Cassian, who . . .

Katie's new raucous laugh rang through the air, breaking her thoughts, and she looked up. Barnaby was standing in front of her, with Katie in his arms and an eager expression on his face. Louise sighed.

'All right,' she said, 'let's go.'

It was some time before they had said goodbye to all the nurses and medical staff on the ward and distributed the presents labelled, 'Thank you, love from Katie.' As she walked with Barnaby, out of the main entrance of the hospital, dodging the rain and watching Katie getting into the car just like any other child, Louise suddenly felt a sense of lifting; a relief. Perhaps things were almost getting back to normal.

Her spirits lifted still further as they entered the gates of Forest Lodge. The centre had been established in a large beautiful country house, surrounded by gardens. Louise turned and smiled at Katie.

'Look, Katie,' she said, 'look at the trees.' She raised

her voice over the sound of rain drumming on the roof of the car. 'Look at the lovely house you're going to stay in.' As she spoke, she looked hard at Katie's face for signs of distress. Mrs Innes had emphasized that if, at any time, Katie became upset at the idea of staying full time at Forest Lodge, they would think again, but to Louise's secret hurt and surprise, Katie had taken the news calmly. Or perhaps, thought Louise, she didn't really understand what was happening.

The entrance hall was large and wood panelled; Mrs Innes was waiting for them as they entered.

'Lovely!' she exclaimed, beaming as though genuinely pleased to see them. 'Well, Katie, you do look better already. I'm sure you're going to make wonderful progress here.' She turned to Louise and Barnaby. 'It's getting on for lunchtime,' she said, 'if you'd like to stay and meet some of the other residents here, and then you can meet the team which will be working with Katie.'

'I've got to go,' said Barnaby regretfully, 'but Louise, you'll stay, won't you?'

'Of course I'll stay,' said Louise. 'Come on, Katie,' she said cheerfully, 'let's meet your new friends.'

The news that Katie Kember was now at Forest Lodge spread swiftly through the village. Mrs Potter, who ran the village shop, heard it from Mary Tracey, and the two of them were discussing it when Sylvia Seddon-Wilson popped in out of the rain for some cigarettes.

'Forest Lodge?' she said, raising her eyebrows. 'The place for disabled children? I didn't realize she was that bad.'

'She's not,' said Mary robustly. 'Not really. She's getting much better. She's talking, and reading a bit, and . . .'

'Well, anyway,' said Sylvia, interrupting her. 'I've got some news! I've been asked to be a witness in the case for the Kembers!' She looked around triumphantly. 'I

184

got a letter yesterday, asking for a statement. Isn't it exciting? I'm going to be a witness! I'll have to buy a new outfit!'

'Actually,' said Mary, 'lots of people have got letters. They wrote to me, too.'

'Oh,' said Sylvia disappointedly.

'They've drawn up a big list of people who were there,' explained Mary, adopting an air of nonchalant self-importance. Rarely had she been in the position of explaining things to Sylvia Seddon-Wilson. 'Cassian says . . .'

'Gorgeous Cass!' broke in Sylvia. 'Isn't he a honey? Perhaps he could come over some time and help me with my statement!' She grinned lasciviously at Mary, who stared sternly back. 'Sorry, Mary, I interrupted you. What does Cassian say?' Mary cleared her throat awkwardly.

'He says, in a case like this, you need as much evidence as possible, as quickly as possible.' Her voice unconsciously imitated Cassian's smooth tones. 'He says they want to know as much as they can before they put together the writ.' She hefted Luke up on her chest. 'But that doesn't mean everybody who gets a letter will be called as a witness in court. They'll only appear if they've got something of crucial importance to say.'

'Something of crucial importance!' exclaimed Sylvia. 'My God, I don't think I've ever said anything of crucial importance in my life.' She gave a sudden guffaw of laughter, and ripped open the packet of cigarettes on the counter in front of her.

'You haven't paid for those yet,' reminded Mrs Potter.

'I know,' said Sylvia impatiently, 'you can put them on James's account if you like. Are you going to be a witness?' she added airily, as Mrs Potter reached down behind the counter for the account book.

'No, I'm certainly not,' said Mrs Potter, emerging red-faced and flustered-looking, 'and I wouldn't, even if I was asked.' She scribbled in the account book and closed it. 'I think it's shocking, the whole thing,' she said with stern emphasis. 'Taking those poor Delaneys to court! What did they ever do wrong? They was only doing their bit for charity and look where it's got 'em.'

'Yes, well, look where it's got Katie,' retorted Mary, feeling a need to defend Louise. 'In hospital.'

'I know that,' said Mrs Potter, folding her arms and leaning against the counter. 'And I'm very sorry. But if you ask me, those parents have got their priorities all wrong. The child's not injured for two minutes, and her parents are already working out how much money they can make out of her! And from friends, too!'

'That's not fair!' said Mary hotly. 'They had to act quickly, otherwise all the witnesses would have forgotten what happened. And she deserves the money! She needs it! If you could see her . . . She could have been killed in that accident.'

'Hmm, yes,' said Sylvia thoughtfully, taking a puff on her cigarette, 'but Mrs Potter's got a point. If it really was just an accident, why should anyone have to pay compensation? Why should Hugh and Ursula be ruined?' Mary looked at her, discomfited.

'Exactly,' said Mrs Potter. 'That's just it. Why . . .'

'On the other hand,' interrupted Sylvia carelessly, 'why *shouldn't* the Kembers do everything they can for their daughter?' She picked up a glossy magazine and began to flip through it. 'I mean, if the diving-board really was dangerous – that's what they're saying, isn't it? And Hugh and Ursula may well have enough money to cover it . . .' Mrs Potter looked at Sylvia, puzzled.

'But you just said . . .' she began.

'Oh, don't listen to me,' said Sylvia cheerfully, 'I never know what I'm talking about.' She brandished the magazine at Mrs Potter. 'Can you add this to the account? I must run. Cheerio.'

She put the magazine over her head and darted out

into the rain. Mary and Mrs Potter watched her getting into her car, a large Jaguar, with a sticker in the back window saying, 'Go First Class – Your Heirs Will.'

'Oh, I don't know,' said Mrs Potter, sighing. 'It seems all wrong to me.'

'Well, I think they're doing the right thing, suing,' said Mary stoutly. 'I really do. I mean,' she said, searching for a comparison, 'if you ate one of my . . . my home-made fish cakes, and it made you ill, you'd want some compensation, wouldn't you? You'd take me to court.' Mrs Potter looked at her in surprise.

'Well, now,' she said consideringly. 'Would I? I'm not sure I would. I think I'd just say, "Oh, that was bad luck," and leave it at that. Or, no, you're right, maybe I would like a little something.' She paused, and appeared to be thinking. 'A Marks & Spencer token, perhaps,' she suggested, 'that would be a nice gesture. But I wouldn't take you to court, not for a fish cake.'

'Well, what if it killed you,' said Mary, unwilling to concede her point. 'Then you'd want something, wouldn't you? You'd want some compensation? Some money?'

Mrs Potter began to laugh; a hoarse bubbling chuckle.

'I'd be dead, Mary, love,' she said. 'If your fish cake killed me, I'd be dead! Money wouldn't be much use to me in my coffin, would it? Nor a Marks & Spencer token, come to that.' Her chuckles increased, and after a while, Mary couldn't help giggling, too.

'Oh, I don't know,' said Mrs Potter at last, wiping her eyes. 'It seems wrong to be laughing. Poor little girl; she didn't deserve this to happen. And I do feel sorry for those Delaneys, too. I'd say they've had enough trouble these past few years, without all of this to-do.' Mary's face fell.

'Yes, I suppose they have,' she said eventually. She looked out into the teeming rain. 'It's a shame. It's a shame for all of them.'

187

*   *   *

Meredith had risen early and spent the morning peering at law books – some newly bought, some borrowed from the library at Linningford. Half a foolscap pad was filled with dense notes before she stopped, stretched and looked out of the window. The rain was still pouring down unremittingly, and her sitting-room was filled with a soft grey light. She reached over, switched on a lamp, then winced as a harsh pool of yellow fell on the sheet in front of her. Better to be in the dark. She switched off the light, leaned back, and tried to make some sense of the facts whirling around in her mind.

Were Hugh and Ursula liable for letting a child dive, unguarded, off their diving-board? Or was it the child's own fault? No-one's fault? The mother's fault? Should Hugh and Ursula put in a claim against Louise for contributory negligence? Should they trump up some kind of counter-suit?

Meredith shut her eyes and pulled a face. All the legal jargon was making her brain ache. She seemed to have read hundreds of accounts of cases of negligence in the British law courts. People who left spilt yoghurt on the floor of their store for people to slip up. People who allowed children to play with dangerous bits of wire. People who didn't fix the bannisters on their stairs.

None of these cases quite appeared to resemble their own situation, and it now seemed to Meredith even more obvious that Hugh and Ursula *hadn't* been negligent, not like some people were negligent. But at the same time, in her heart of hearts, she was beginning to see how Cassian Brown might put together some kind of phoney case against them; how he might even be able to convince a very stupid jury that Katie was a victim of the Delaneys' negligence, and that she was owed damages. And if that happened, how much might Hugh and Ursula have to pay out? Meredith's eyes glanced, unwillingly, down the list of examples of damages claims which she'd compiled. Huge sums stared back at her, and she gave a little shiver. She'd heard the rumour about half a million pounds, which was going round the village, and dismissed it. Now she wasn't so sure. A recent well-publicized case – in which a head-injured child had received nearly £700,000 from a negligent local council – jumped out at her particularly blackly.

Half a million pounds? Hugh simply didn't have that kind of money. Not money sitting around, just waiting for an emergency. His business had dwindled considerably since Simon's death; Meredith knew for a fact that it was bringing in only a small income. Of course, they could sell the little house in France – but that wouldn't fetch much. Not these days. So . . . what? Would they have to sell Devenish House? Sell what little there was of the business? Take out some sort of loan? Declare themselves bankrupt? How on earth would Hugh and Ursula cope with that? Hadn't they had enough?

Meredith stared into the pouring rain and felt an impotent frustrated anger rising through her. Abruptly, she got to her feet. She'd had enough of law books. Enough of the law altogether.

Hugh looked out of the window of his study and saw Meredith walking through the garden, in the rain, wearing her black strappy swimming-costume. She was heading towards the swimming-pool. He waited a few moments, then put down his pen and went outside after her.

The swimming-pool was heated to its normal temperature, and clouds of steam were pouring off it into the rainy atmosphere. Huge raindrops pounded fiercely down onto the surface of the water, which seemed, in this weather, grey and uninviting. But through the misty clouds, Hugh could see Meredith swimming determinedly up and down the length of the pool, efficiently cleaving the water with her strong muscular arms, turning at each end in a seamless movement, purging something out of her system, he guessed. He stood by the side of the pool for a few minutes, sheltering from the loud battering rain under a bright-yellow umbrella. Eventually Meredith noticed him. She stopped swimming and began to tread water, holding her face up to the rain, closing her eyes.

'I fucking hate them all,' she said, above the pounding noise of the rain. Her eyes were still closed. Hugh gave a small grin, and squatted down by the side of the pool.

'I had a letter from the Kembers' lawyers today,' he said, 'requesting permission for some sort of safety expert to come and examine the diving-board.'

They both turned and stared at the diving-board, glistening wet in the rain.

'The diving-board's fine,' said Meredith in a tight voice. 'It's just a diving-board. What's he expect to find? Oil smeared all over it?'

'I really don't know,' said Hugh wearily. 'As far as I'm concerned, it's perfectly safe, but . . .' He tailed off.

'Perhaps we should rip it out,' said Meredith, 'and when this safety expert comes along, we'll say, "Diving-board? What diving-board?"'

She gave Hugh a grin and he smiled reluctantly back. He looked old and defeated. Meredith could hardly bear to look at him. She took a deep breath and plunged under the surface, feeling cold water pour into her ears; hearing the sound of the rain on water suddenly muffled. When she surfaced, Hugh was still there, staring at the diving-board.

'They won't be able to prove anything,' said Meredith, trying to sound confident.

'And what if they do?' said Hugh. He looked at Meredith, a haggard expression on his face. 'What if it's proved in a court of law that it was our negligence that put an innocent child in hospital? That our diving-board was unsafe? How will we live with ourselves?'

'It won't be,' said Meredith uncertainly. 'No way.' There was a doubtful pause.

'It's not the money,' said Hugh suddenly. 'I mean, of course the money is worrying, yes.' He looked at Meredith. 'You know what sort of sums we might be talking about, don't you?' She nodded. 'But even if we had to sell everything . . .' Hugh waved one hand in the rainy air, 'it wouldn't be the end of the world. We'd be able to live with ourselves.' He looked at Meredith. 'What I couldn't live with is the thought that the accident was our fault.' He looked bleakly at Meredith and transferred the dripping umbrella handle from one hand to the other.

'No-one's saying it was your *fault*,' said Meredith, fiercely. 'For Christ's sake, what were you supposed to do? Guard the diving-board against stupid kids? When it's perfectly plain that diving can, yes, can be risky? And when the kid's mother was actually there?'

'Maybe,' said Hugh wearily. 'Maybe that's just what we were supposed to do.'

'What, so nothing's obvious any more?' said Meredith angrily, slapping her hand down on the surface of the water with a sharp splash. 'We have to protect everybody against everything? Whatever happened to common sense? Someone should have told that kid, if you leap high into the air you might hurt yourself. That's a fact of life. It's not anyone's *fault*.' Hugh shrugged.

'But what if the board was dangerous?' he said in a quiet voice.

'It wasn't dangerous,' said Meredith angrily. 'No more dangerous than any other diving-board.'

'Maybe that's enough,' said Hugh. 'Maybe the very fact that a diving-board is dangerous at all will be enough for them to win the case. I just don't know.'

Meredith felt a stab of uncharacteristic fearful panic.

191

She and Hugh looked at each other for a moment, silent, except for the rain.

'Well, God help the world, then,' said Meredith at last, looking away from Hugh's weary face. 'And God save us from the fucking lawyers.'

A pair of sudden hot tears fell from her eyes, mingling with the drips on her face. Quickly, before Hugh could see, Meredith plunged back into the blue-grey depths of the pool, her legs thrusting furiously through the yielding water, her hair streaming out behind her, and the raindrops falling in splashy circles on the surface above her. She swam silently and desperately, holding her breath, until she felt able to surface and talk to Hugh again. But when, eventually, she surfaced, breathless, he had gone. And she was left alone, cocooned from the pounding rain in the warmth of the water, surrounded by steamy clouds, with no-one to talk to.

Chapter Fourteen

By the time the end of term arrived it was baking hot once more, and Amelia was asking, every day, if they could please, *please* go swimming.

They hadn't been swimming at all since the accident; the vision of Amelia plunging again into the forbidding blue water of a swimming-pool made Louise shudder and feel sick. But she couldn't say that to the child, and give her a complex for the rest of her life, so instead she said again, sharply, that they didn't have time. Not at the moment.

Amelia stared resentfully at her mother, then stamped back up the stairs to get her school hat. She hated her mother, and she hated Katie, and she hated everybody. Today was the last day of term, and everybody was taking a present to school for their form teacher. But although she'd kept promising they would go and find something nice at the shops, Louise had forgotten, until Amelia reminded her last night, when it was too late.

'We'll buy something on the way to school,' she'd said hastily. 'Something nice.' But the only shop on the way to school was the garage, and Amelia knew they wouldn't find anything nice there, only jars of coffee and pints of milk and Mars bars.

And it was all because her mother spent the whole time at Forest Lodge. Amelia *hated* Forest Lodge. It was really creepy and it smelt horrible, and all the people in it were weird. Some of them couldn't speak properly and some of them had strange jerky arms, and last time she went there for lunch she'd sat opposite a boy who was much older than her, but dribbled his food. It was *disgusting*. And then he'd smiled at her and tried to take hold of her hand. She'd stared at him in panic, feeling her face turn red and her heart thumping, until a nurse noticed what was happening and hurried over, and said, 'Martin, leave Amelia alone.' And then she'd turned to Amelia and smiled, and said, 'Don't worry! He won't bite!' And Amelia had smiled back, but inside she felt all shaky and frightened.

She didn't see why Katie had to stay there. Katie wasn't a bit like those people. She could walk and talk properly now, and sort of read, and last time Amelia had visited, they'd even played French skipping. Katie had forgotten all about French skipping after the accident, but Amelia had taught her how to do it again, and she'd been quite good – at least, at the very easy jumps.

Everyone kept going on about how well Katie was doing, so much better than they'd expected, and Amelia always said, 'Well, why doesn't she come home, then?' And her mother would say, 'She will, darling, very soon.' But she never did, so they kept having to go to horrible revolting Forest Lodge.

Amelia picked up her satchel and put on her hat, and scowled at herself in the mirror. Nothing was fun any more. She didn't have anyone to play with, and they weren't going on holiday, and everyone seemed cross all the time.

By the end of the morning, however, Amelia's spirits had risen. After they'd had a story, and before they went down for final prayers, Mrs Jacob had taken the star chart off the wall to announce the winner. And it was Amelia!

She was so surprised she just sat still, while Clara, who sat next to her, tugged at her school dress and hissed, 'Go up! Go up and get your prize!'

Mrs Jacob smiled at Amelia and said, 'I've been

awarding stars for good behaviour, as well as the stars I've put in your exercise books, and Amelia has done very well this term! Well done!' And Amelia struggled to her feet and Mrs Jacob gave her a huge tube of Smarties, and everybody clapped.

Then everyone crowded round Amelia's desk for a Smartie, and Amelia handed them out, keeping back the orange ones for herself. And Anna Russet, whom she didn't know very well, said shyly, 'I think you deserved to win the star chart, Amelia.' And Clara, sitting next to her, said at once, 'Yes, so do I. I think you *deserved* to win it.'

Amelia had glowed, pink with pleasure, as she doled out Smarties into thrusting hands, and thought how impressed Katie and Mummy would be when she told them. Then they'd gone down to the hall for final prayers, and Amelia's name was read out, along with all the other star-chart winners, and all the teachers smiled at her. Then they sang Amelia's favourite hymn, and did three cheers for the teachers, and then it really was the end of term.

All the parents were waiting outside, mostly mothers, but a few fathers too, and the playground was filled with children, carrying satchels and pencil-cases and rolled-up paintings and recorders and shoe bags. Amelia looked for Louise in the throng, but she couldn't see her anywhere, so she sat down comfortably on the low wall at the front of the playground and waited for her to arrive.

Half an hour later she still hadn't come. The playground was now nearly empty, with just a few parents and children and a couple of teachers, and a book dropped face-down on the ground. Amelia sidled over and picked up the book. It was a very junior reading book that she remembered from Form Two, and she began to leaf through it, recalling the bright pictures and the story, and all the big words that she'd

195

found so difficult then, but now seemed really easy.

'Amelia!' Amelia looked up, startled. Mrs Jacob was in front of her.

'Hasn't Mummy come yet?'

'No,' admitted Amelia. 'She's often late,' she added quickly.

'I know,' said Mrs Jacob, 'but not normally this late.' She looked hard at Amelia. 'She does know it's a half day today?' Amelia thought.

'Well, she knows it's the end of term,' she said eventually. 'She must know it's a half day.'

'Did you tell her?' persisted Mrs Jacob.

'No,' said Amelia in surprise, 'but she must know! It's always a half day on the last day of term.'

Mrs Jacob sighed.

'Perhaps', she said, 'she's forgotten. Just this once.'

Amelia stared at Mrs Jacob and felt a sudden angry hurt. Mrs Jacob must be right, her mother had forgotten to come and pick her up. She'd *forgotten* about her. No-one else's mother forgot about them.

A voice interrupted them both. It was Mrs Russet, Anna's mother, coming over from the other side of the playground.

'Is there a problem?' she said. She addressed Amelia in a sugary voice. 'Has Mummy forgotten all about you?' Amelia shrugged and went pink. Mrs Russet came closer. She was a very large lady, with curly hair; Amelia had sometimes seen her in church, doing readings in a loud voice with lots of flapping arms.

'I'll go and phone her,' said Mrs Jacob. She looked at Amelia and smiled reassuringly. 'Will she be at home, do you think?'

'She's probably at Forest Lodge,' said Amelia. 'She's always at Forest Lodge,' she added, gloomily, as Mrs Jacob hurried off.

'Is she?' Mrs Russet's eyes bored beadily into Amelia's face. 'Does she leave you all alone?'

'Well,' began Amelia, meaning to explain how Mary always came and looked after her. But a sudden resentment at her mother took over.

'Yes, she does,' she said sorrowfully. 'She leaves me all alone. All she cares about is Katie.'

Mrs Russet's mouth tightened and she folded her arms.

'Well, Amelia,' she said. 'What about coming home with us? If Mummy's too busy to remember about you?'

'Yes, go on,' said Anna. 'You can see my guinea-pig.'

'And then we can have some nice lunch,' said Mrs Russet cosily, 'and you can tell me *all* about it.'

Louise had spent much of the day in Linningford, trying to catch up with the minutiae of daily life. Since the accident, she realized, she hadn't paid a single household bill. Food shopping had been reduced to buying a few tins whenever she had a spare moment; most basic household items had run out or broken and not been replaced. And tomorrow was the start of Amelia's school holidays. She wanted the house to be in some kind of order before then. So the night before, she had sat down with a pencil and begun a list, starting modestly with light-bulbs; pay gas bill; first-class stamps. By the time the catalogue was finished, it was running onto a fourth sheet, and she was staring at it in amazed despair. But she had decided that, if it were at all possible, she would get everything done before she picked up Amelia from school.

Somewhere in her mind she had once been aware that on the last day of term, school finished at lunchtime. But this fact was submerged as she battled with a pair of heavy carrier bags through the morning throng, and found herself thinking, I'm never going to get everything done by three-thirty. As the day progressed she began to move more quickly; imbuing each transaction with a sense of urgency; pitting herself against crowds

197

of people, overheated lifts and surly shop assistants. She abandoned all thought of taking the toaster for repair, in favour of finding a special present for Amelia. She decided, hastily crossing it off the list, that plant food could wait for another day – but they really did need new tooth-brushes.

She arrived at the school on the dot of quarter to four, with a red face and a full car and a colouring book for Amelia waiting on the front seat. And then, as she opened the door and got out to an uncharacteristic silence, the truth hit her, and she leaned weakly against the car, her heart thudding and a light-headed amazement pervading her body. How could she have been so stupid? How could she have forgotten that school finished at lunchtime today?

For a moment or two she couldn't move, so astonished was she at her lapse of memory. It almost seemed a feat of achievement to have forgotten something so important. Then, as her astonishment began to abate, she felt a sudden guilty pang, all the stronger for being delayed. Where was Amelia? What had happened to her, if nobody had arrived to collect her?

Stupidly, Louise began to run towards the playground. Of course she wouldn't be there. The teachers wouldn't have left her. Louise imagined kind steady Mrs Jacob, Amelia's teacher, and her heart began to quail. What on earth would Mrs Jacob think of her? And all the other teachers? Would they put a black mark against her name?

And where, thought Louise again, arriving in the deserted playground, looking hopelessly around; where the hell was Amelia?

'If we win in the court,' said Amelia, sitting back comfortably on Mrs Russet's cushioned garden swing and accepting another chocolate biscuit, 'we're going to get half a million pounds.' She looked at Mrs Russet for a reaction and bit into the biscuit. Mrs Russet gave a satisfactory gasp.

'Half a million pounds,' repeated Amelia. 'We'll be half-millionaires.'

Anna, crouched down in front of the guinea-pig pen on the other side of the garden, called, 'Come *on*, Amelia. Come and see Nutmeg.'

But Amelia ignored her and looked at Mrs Russet. Mrs Russet was being very kind to her, Amelia thought. She'd given her a lovely lunch, full of treats, and now it was teatime already, and more treats. And all Amelia had to do was keep talking about the accident. Mrs Russet seemed very interested in it.

Now she looked at Amelia with huge brown eyes, and said, 'That seems an awful lot of money for a little girl like you to be talking about.'

'I know,' said Amelia simply.

'Did Mummy tell you about it?' Amelia flushed slightly.

'No,' she said, 'I just sort of heard it. Mummy and Cassian were talking about it one time.' She bit into her biscuit again. It was delicious, all chocolatey and filled with sweetened cream. The sort of biscuit they never had at home.

'The accident was all Mr and Mrs Delaney's fault,' Amelia added, with her mouth full. 'Cassian told me.' She licked her chocolatey fingers and looked at Mrs Russet. 'I'm not allowed to speak to Mrs Delaney any more,' she continued indistinctly, 'even though she gave me a Barbie doll. I like Mrs Delaney,' she added, 'but Cassian says she's neg-lent.' She said the word cautiously and looked up for approval, but Mrs Russet was gazing at her silently, waiting for her to continue. Amelia gave an inward sigh. She was running out of things to say.

'I hate the boring old court case,' she said eventually. 'That's all they talk about: Katie and the court case.' She eyed Mrs Russet surreptitiously and added pitifully, 'No-one cares abut me any more.'

She was hoping that Mrs Russet would offer her another biscuit, but instead Mrs Russet grabbed her hand.

'I've never heard anything so terrible,' she said. 'That you should feel so abandoned!' She looked at Amelia and blinked a few times. 'Does Mummy know you feel like this?'

'Well,' began Amelia, 'not . . .'

'Doesn't have time to listen, I expect,' said Mrs Russet, nodding vigorously. 'Or doesn't want to listen. Too busy with her million-pound court case to bother about her children. It's immoral, that's what it is. She wasn't even at Forest Lodge today. Who *knows* what she's been doing . . .' She broke off and leaned closer to Amelia.

'That Cassian,' she said. 'Does he . . . visit the house very much?' Amelia took another biscuit without asking and tried to think. What counted as very much?

'Well . . . quite a lot,' she said at last. Mrs Russet nodded vigorously again. The collection of bead necklaces strung about her neck jangled, and a red glow began to spread over her face.

'And what about poor Daddy?' she said. Amelia stared back at Mrs Russet. How did Mrs Russet know so much about them?

'We see him every weekend,' she said, her voice starting to tremble.

'And is he in favour of this court case?' said Mrs Russet in a suddenly fierce voice. 'Or does he think, as I do, that God moves in mysterious ways?' She looked at Amelia sternly. 'Everything happens for a reason,' she said, 'and every sinner receives his punishment.' She brought her face suddenly close to Amelia's. 'Would your sister's accident have happened if your mother hadn't been so distracted, thinking about her lover? Would it have happened if she'd been a decent responsible mother?' She spat the words out and Amelia shrank back in her seat. She didn't know what to say.

'Look,' called Anna, from the other side of the garden. 'Amelia's mummy's car is here.'

Amelia had never seen her mother so angry. She barely waited until they'd got into the car before she screamed, in a voice which made Amelia give a terrified jump, 'What did you say to that woman?'

Amelia stared back at her mother with a white face.

'Nothing,' she said in a shaking voice. 'Nothing really. Just things she asked me.'

'And what did she ask you?' said Louise bitterly. 'I know,' she added, before Amelia could reply. 'Is your mother a good Christian or an irresponsible harlot who brought this accident on herself?'

Amelia peered at Louise in terror.

'I don't know,' she muttered.

'She said she's going to testify against us!' shouted Louise. 'She's going to offer herself as a character witness, and give evidence in court that I don't look after my children properly!' Louise turned briefly towards Amelia.

'How do you think that makes me feel?'

Amelia gazed back in silence. She didn't really understand what had happened. One minute Mrs Russet had been all friendly, then she'd suddenly changed and started saying horrible things. And she'd had a huge row with Mummy, and now Mummy was furious, and it all seemed to be Amelia's fault. Suddenly Amelia gave a little sob. Louise turned to look at her, and the angry lines in her forehead softened.

'Oh, Amelia, darling,' she said. 'I'm sorry. It's not your fault.' She gave a small strange laugh, and changed gear roughly. 'It's my fault, just like she said. If I'd remembered to pick you up, this would never have happened.'

'It's not your fault,' said Amelia fiercely. 'I hate Mrs Russet,' she added. 'I wish she'd just go away.' Louise sighed.

'So do I,' she said, 'but somehow I think that's a bit unlikely.'

When they got home, Frances Mold was waiting on the doorstep. She looked worried and stepped forward as soon as the car stopped. Louise looked at her with a curious, not particularly friendly expression. She knew Frances was a close friend of Meredith Delaney. No doubt she was firmly in the Delaneys' camp.

'I've just had Gillian Russet on the phone,' said Frances, as Louise got out of the car. 'I'm afraid she was . . . a little worked up.' Her eyes moved briefly to Amelia and back to Louise.

'Amelia,' said Louise, handing her the door key, 'let yourself in, and then go and play in the garden.' As Amelia clattered off, Louise turned towards Frances with frank bitterness in her face.

'Don't tell me,' she said, 'you think she's right. You think I brought Katie's accident on myself as a punishment.' Frances's face didn't flicker.

'Of course not,' she said steadily. 'I'm afraid Gillian tends to get things out of proportion,' she added. 'Alan's had to speak to her before about this sort of thing.'

'Really?' said Louise sharply. 'And is he going to speak to her this time?'

'Of course,' said Frances simply. She sighed. 'Actually, I think he'll get quite angry with her.' She ran a weary hand over her face. 'Gillian has a lot to learn about compassion, but she's actually very well-meaning in many respects.' Frances looked at Louise earnestly. 'I hope you can manage to forgive her.'

Louise leaned back against the car. She felt suddenly very weak.

'That woman has no idea,' she said unsteadily, 'no idea what this has been like for us.'

'I know she hasn't,' agreed Frances. 'None of us has.' She came over and leaned back next to Louise.

'I feel I haven't been as supportive as I should.' She looked at Louise. 'I was wondering, when Katie comes home, whether I could help you with her. Perhaps I could come and read with her? Would that be helpful?'

Louise looked at Frances's earnest ugly face and felt almost tearful.

'I'm sure that would be a great help,' she said. 'Thank you.' Then, before she could stop it, her old defensive anger flooded to the front of her mind, and she added in a sharp voice, 'What will Meredith think? I thought you were a great friend of hers?'

'I am,' agreed Frances, 'but Meredith will, I'm sure, simply be glad that I can help.' She looked steadily at Louise. 'We all want to help, really. Unfortunately the Delaneys have been legally advised . . .'

'To stay away from us?'

Frances nodded slightly.

'I suppose you think', said Louise, her voice harsh and defensive, 'that we're evil people, taking Hugh and Ursula to court.'

'Not at all,' said Frances mildly. 'I have every faith in British justice. If you do have a case, then I'm sure the system will work.'

Louise stared at Frances, unaccountably dissatisfied by this answer. Then she shrugged. 'Well, Katie's coming home in a week or so,' she said.

'That's marvellous!' said Frances. 'I'll look out some easy reading books.' She looked anxiously at Louise. 'She is reading, isn't she?'

'Oh, yes,' said Louise, suddenly breaking into a smile. 'She's done so well! The programme at Forest Lodge is just wonderful. You'd almost never know . . .'

She broke off suddenly, as though struck by something, and frowned.

'Well, I'll be in touch,' said Frances. She looked seriously at Louise. 'And I'm sorry about Gillian Russet. I hope very much that Alan will be able to persuade her that testifying against you is not, as she seems to think, her duty. But I'm afraid she's not constrained to do what he advises; she's her own person.' She spread her hands helplessly.

'Well, thanks for trying, anyway,' said Louise. 'Thank you . . .' She swallowed. 'Thank you for everything.'

Meredith was not as glad as Frances had predicted. She glared at Frances as she handed her a glass of sherry, and said, reproachfully, 'You're supposed to be on our side.'

'Meredith,' remonstrated Frances. 'I'll pretend you didn't really say that.'

'Well, for Pete's sake, Frances,' said Meredith, 'this is taking good behaviour a bit far, isn't it? You'll be testifying against us in court, next.'

'Meredith!' said Frances, suddenly angry, 'I can't believe you're so obsessed by this case that you can't feel compassion for an injured child.'

Meredith stared at Frances, chastened.

'I know,' she muttered eventually, 'I'm sorry. I think it's really good of you to help out like that.' She took a sip of vodka. 'And I even think you're right about this nut-case woman,' she added. 'If she offers to besmirch Louise's character in court for us, we'll say, no thanks.'

'I think that would be wise,' said Frances.

'Even though', Meredith's eyes began to gleam, 'it would be great to have her up there on the stand. Wouldn't it? I mean, she's practically saying Louise threw Katie off the diving-board herself!'

'She's completely overreacted to the situation,' said Frances. 'I'm sure she'll calm down eventually.'

'That's what I keep saying,' put in Ursula, surprisingly, from her corner chair. 'I'm sure everyone will calm down eventually and this silly case will all blow over.'

Frances glanced at Meredith, who raised her eyebrows and shrugged her shoulders.

'I hope you're right, Ursula,' said Frances pleasantly, 'but, you know, I'd say there's a fair chance it might not blow over. You really should be prepared for that.'

Ursula, who was bent once more over her tapestry, looked up. She opened her mouth to speak, then closed it again. She had to admit, in her own mind, that her conciliatory letter to Louise had not been as effective as she had hoped. Louise had returned the bundle of banknotes almost immediately, accompanied by a short note which thanked Ursula politely for her kind wishes and added that she couldn't possibly accept so much money.

But Ursula had not given up. The bundle of money still sat, untouched, in her dressing-table, together with another, unfinished letter. She was absolutely sure that if only she could express herself properly; if only she could find exactly the right words, then all this unpleasantness could be overcome . . .

Ursula's thoughts were interrupted by Meredith.

'You know,' she was saying to Frances, 'what gets me is walking through the village and seeing everyone's faces, and knowing they've been talking about it.' She gestured dramatically with her arm. 'Seeing their gleaming eyes, and their hands rubbing together, waiting for our downfall. They just can't wait.'

'Rubbish,' said Frances. She grinned at Meredith. 'You're just getting paranoid.'

'It's true,' insisted Meredith. 'All the sympathy's on Katie's side. They think we must be child murderers or something. And what they really want is for the courts to make a huge award to the Kembers. A kind of lottery award. A couple of million pounds would do the trick. So they can all gasp to each other, and wonder what they would do if *they* won two million. Then, of course, when they realize it's us who's got to pay it, a few will start feeling sorry for us, but it'll be too late by then. Far, far too late.' She tossed her hair melodramatically.

'Meredith!' Frances was laughing. 'I'm sure no-one thinks like that.'

'Don't be too sure,' said Meredith darkly. 'You don't know how low people sink when the vicar's wife isn't around to keep them in line.'

She grinned wickedly at Frances, who blushed very slightly and said, 'Nonsense!'

Ursula, whose attention had drifted away during Meredith's little speech, put down her tapestry and stood up.

'I'm going to pick some raspberries for supper,' she said.

'I'll come out in a minute,' said Meredith. 'Have another drink, Frances.'

Frances hesitated, then she held out her glass.

'I think I need it,' she said cheerfully. 'After listening to nonsensical tirades from you *and* Gillian Russet in one evening . . .' She looked at Meredith and gave a little giggle.

'Actually,' she said, as Ursula closed the door, 'I was thinking, as I listened to Gillian shouting down the phone, that if any court heard such a dreadful diatribe against Louise, they would probably immediately find in Louise's favour. Just out of sympathy.'

Meredith grinned.

'I guess no witness is better than a lousy witness.' She lowered her voice. 'Mind you, what about poor old Ursula? If she has to testify as a witness, we're done for. Witless, more like.' She began to shake with giggles. 'She'll say something like . . . she always thought the swimming-pool was dangerous for children.'

'Don't!' said Frances, trying not to laugh. Suddenly Meredith stopped giggling.

'Oh Jeez. Why am I laughing about it?' She leaned back and closed her eyes. 'The worst thing is how long everything is taking. I mean, they haven't even filed their claim against us yet. This whole case could take years, and meanwhile we can't make any plans. Oh, no, better not do that; we might go bankrupt next year. What kind of life is that?' She took a swig of vodka, emptying her glass, and roughly put it down on a side-table, with a little crash.

Frances took a sip of sherry and looked seriously at Meredith.

'Why is it taking so long?'

Meredith shrugged. 'Alexis says there's been some delay on the other side. Apparently these things always take ages; lawyers are never in a hurry.' She ran a hand through her hair and winced as it was caught up in a tangle. 'It's fine for them,' she said in a bitter voice. 'They're not even paying their own fucking legal fees. Nothing to lose.'

'And you . . .'

'Alexis is being very generous,' said Meredith in a carefully flat voice, 'but he has to eat. He can't do it all for nothing.' She picked up her glass and got up to pour another drink, ignoring Frances's quizzical look.

When she sat down again, she seemed to be pondering whether to say something. Frances waited. Eventually Meredith said, in a low casual voice, 'What is it with Alexis, Frances? I really like him, you know.' She swallowed. 'I always thought he and I might . . . you know, get together.' She fingered the soft fabric of the sofa. 'And he's round here often enough – I'm sure he wants to make a move on me, but nothing ever happens.'

Meredith paused. She could feel Frances drawing breath, and hurriedly carried on, 'So I was wondering,' she said in a rush, 'do you think it would be a good idea to make a pass? Or do you think that would frighten him off?'

Meredith looked up. The expression on Frances's face scared her.

'What?' she said. 'What is it?'

'Don't you know?' said Frances. She exhaled sharply. 'I can't believe you don't know.'

'Know? Know what?' Meredith's heart began to thud. 'What should I know?'

'Oh, Meredith,' said Frances sadly. She took hold of Meredith's hand. 'Alexis is having an affair.' She paused and squeezed Meredith's cold hand tighter. 'He's having an affair . . . with little Daisy Phillips.'

Chapter Fifteen

Alexis lay entwined with Daisy on the floor of her sitting-room, while around them pounded and swirled a Sibelius symphony. He had just brought Daisy to a shuddering orgasm, and was now watching her face with almost unbearable tenderness, as her contorted features softened, her eyes slowly opened, and she gave him a shy embarrassed smile.

He stared at her silently, running his eyes over her flushed face; breathing in her scent; feeling the haunting, pulsating, powerful music coursing through the air and into his body. He felt as though each sense and every emotion was being tested to breaking-point. Daisy gave a little sigh and snuggled closer, so that her body fitted neatly into his. She smiled up at Alexis and he looked back; unable to express himself; unable to do anything except put out a trembling finger and gently push back a strand of her hair.

'I always . . .' began Daisy in a soft voice against his chest. She stopped. Alexis ran an encouraging hand down her back, around her waist, and began to tickle her tummy. She giggled.

'What do you always?' he said tenderly.

'I always think . . .' Daisy blushed. 'I think . . . will it really happen again? You know . . . will I . . .' She broke off and blushed even harder. 'Each time, it's so lovely, I can't believe it'll ever happen again.'

Alexis stopped tickling Daisy's tummy and kissed her neck. Daisy gave a little gasp.

'I don't mean', she added hurriedly, 'that I don't think

you . . . I mean, I know you're really . . .' She broke off and looked at him with worried eyes, as though afraid she might have given offence. Alexis threw back his head and laughed.

'Daisy, my darling, it's all right. You're allowed to doubt my technique if you like.' Daisy gave a little jump.

'But I don't,' she said anxiously. 'I didn't mean . . .'

'It's all right,' said Alexis. 'I know what you meant.' Daisy stared at him doubtfully for a moment, then smiled and closed her eyes.

Alexis stared at the roughly plastered, oak-beamed ceiling. The symphony had reached its inexorable climax; triumphant horns and strings pounded loudly around him. And inside, Alexis felt a soaring triumph to match. But it was a triumph dulled by a strange, chastening humility. He had felt humble ever since, a few weeks ago, they had made love for the first time – and for Daisy, it had transpired, the first time ever.

He still remembered the shock – of panic, guilt, and a sneaking relief – as he'd discovered that he was the first. He'd been sliding a cautious hand up between her legs, hastily shaking off his own trousers at the same time, trying desperately to judge her expression, ready at any moment to retreat if necessary. And, to pave the way slightly, he had murmured against her neck, 'It must seem strange for you – doing this with someone so much older.'

And she'd looked at him with dark aroused eyes, and said in a soft husky voice, 'It's strange anyway . . . the first time. It wouldn't really matter who it was with.'

Somehow the possibility that Daisy was a virgin had never before occurred to Alexis. He had always thought of her simply as . . . very young, unthinkably young. But a virgin, too? Wasn't that taking things too far? For a few moments he froze, and it came to him that he must immediately call a halt to the whole affair; that the idea of seducing a young, vulnerable, teenage virgin was disgusting, risky and morally unforgivable.

But a glimpse of Daisy's unsheathed breasts in front of him, of her quivering lips and her warm pink cheeks, distracted him from his principles. Furiously he reminded himself that she was eighteen; that she could make her own decisions; that he had not, by any means, forced himself on her. And when she gently put up one hand to caress his chest, Alexis's resolve had crumbled, his desire took over, and there was no turning back.

That first time had been painful, funny, unbearably moving. Painful for Daisy, funny for both of them, unbearably moving for Alexis. He'd left her in the early hours of the morning and driven home, staggered into the bathroom, and stared at himself in the mirror, in a kind of silent, elated, horrified amazement.

Since then the amazement had never quite gone away. Alexis sometimes found himself staring at Daisy, as though he were a stranger – taking in, as he had that day at the swimming-pool, her pale beautiful face, her hesitant manner, and her doubtful smile – and felt as though he had no right to be so close to her; as though he'd somehow tricked his way into a position of intimacy and would, any day now, be discovered, exposed, rejected.

And then he would begin, rather bleakly, to consider once again the huge chasm between their ages. Deliberately torturing himself, he would look first at her smooth face, and then at his own lined forehead; at her luxuriant locks and then at his own thinning greying hair. Her eyes were large and bright; his were small, hooded and weary-looking. He was old and jaded; she was fresh and new. A walnut and a peach.

Daisy shifted slightly and Alexis found his arms closing protectively around her.

'What,' she began softly, still with her eyes closed. 'What are we going to have for supper?'

* * *

Alexis had been staggered to discover Daisy's lack of culinary knowledge. He was used to women his own age, experienced cooks, who would tease him about his limited bachelor's kitchen, allow him to chop an onion or two, but basically take over the cooking for the duration of their relationship. This, despite the fact that he was not at all a bad cook. He generally favoured straightforward food that didn't take long to prepare: fillet steaks – charred on the outside, pink in the middle; grilled fish, basted with olive oil and lime juice; lamb chops, sprinkled with garlic and rosemary; roasted vegetables; interesting salads.

Daisy's repertoire, as far as he could make out, extended only as far as dried pasta combined with bottled pesto sauce – and maybe a can of tuna thrown in. She seemed to live on this diet, together with bowls of Shreddies, chocolate digestives, and the occasional pink grapefruit. The first time he'd cooked supper for her, she had astounded him by saying, in a casual way, 'Oh, *that's* what garlic looks like.' Alexis stared at her, almost lost for words.

'You're not serious? You've never seen garlic before?'

'Oh, yes, of course I have,' said Daisy quickly. 'Strings of garlic. But I've never seen what they look like inside.' She took in Alexis's expression and added earnestly, 'But I do love it. I love garlic bread.' She thought. 'Actually, there might be some garlic bread in the freezer.'

'Daisy,' Alexis had said, beginning to laugh, 'there's a little bit more to garlic than pre-packed frozen garlic bread.'

Now, watching Daisy as she inexpertly sliced a red pepper, Alexis said, 'Haven't you ever done any cooking?' Daisy looked up and pushed back the sleeves of her pale cotton kimono.

'Well, not really,' she said. 'At school . . . well, you don't really cook at school. And then on holiday we

212

didn't really cook either, and at home . . .' She screwed up her face. 'I suppose we must cook a bit at home,' she said eventually, 'but not very much. My parents often go out for supper, and when my brothers were at home they just used to phone up for pizzas and things like that. And if Mummy has a dinner party she gets in caterers . . .' She tailed off and looked down at the chopping board. 'I've done the pepper,' she said. 'What shall I do now?'

Alexis stared at her, feeling a sudden anger at these parents who blithely left Daisy alone in the dubious care of two brothers and a pizza delivery firm. A thought struck him.

'Didn't you have cookery lessons at school?'

'Oh, yes,' said Daisy. 'I made a swiss roll, but it broke when I tried to roll it up. And then I was given extra piano lessons instead, and I didn't have cookery any more.' She looked at Alexis anxiously. 'And I can't remember how to make the swiss roll.'

Alexis laughed.

'Well, that's a relief,' he said. 'Swiss roll is one of my least favourite things.' He opened the fridge, took out a bottle of Chardonnay, and briskly uncorked it. 'Anyway,' he said, 'school isn't where you should learn how to cook.'

'Where should you learn?' said Daisy.

'In your own kitchen, of course. You should learn to cook by cooking for people you really like,' said Alexis. 'Family, friends, lovers. That's how I learned. Not by making swiss roll in a classroom.'

He handed a glass of wine to Daisy, who stared into the bottom of it for a minute or two. When she looked up, her cheeks were burning red.

'Who did you . . .' she began hesitantly. 'Did you ever . . . have you been . . .' She broke off and looked away. For a few moments Alexis stared at her in puzzlement. Then his expression changed.

213

'Are you trying to ask me if I've ever been married?' he said gently. Daisy's head didn't move.

'The answer's no, I've never been married,' said Alexis carefully. He sat down on a kitchen chair. 'I had a long-term relationship with a woman I met through the law,' he said slowly. 'She was the same age as me and very ambitious. I asked her to marry me, but she didn't want to; she wanted to concentrate on her career.'

He stopped and took a slug of wine.

'Wh-what happened?' asked Daisy timidly.

'She left me after twelve years and married another man,' said Alexis. A sudden bleak expression came over his face. 'They've just had their second baby,' he said quietly.

Daisy stared at him in horror. She didn't know what to say.

'That's awful,' she whispered.

'It was pretty bad at the time,' said Alexis, 'but that's a while ago now; years, in fact. I've completely recovered.' He grinned at Daisy and took another huge gulp of wine.

Daisy gazed at him silently, unconvinced.

'Oh, Daisy,' said Alexis, 'don't look so upset.'

'I'm not,' protested Daisy. 'I'm just . . .' She broke off and looked at the floor.

'Talking about the past is never a good idea,' said Alexis easily. 'Now, why don't you go and play the piano? You said you needed to practise,' he reminded her.

'Oh, yes,' said Daisy. 'I do.' She looked at Alexis. 'But what about the supper?'

'I'll manage,' said Alexis, glancing at the ragged slices of red pepper on Daisy's chopping board and trying not to smile. 'I'll finish off and then come and listen.'

When she had gone, he worked quickly, assembling a fragrant chicken casserole, popping it into the oven and putting on a pan of rice. Then, refilling his glass, he went through into the sitting-room.

Daisy was practising the Brahms concerto which she was due to perform soon with the Linningford Symphony Orchestra. She was playing through the second movement, and had reached a passage of thundering chords which Alexis recognized. In the weeks that he'd heard her practising them, the chords had become louder, faster and more assured. Now she was hitting the keys of the piano with a confident power which staggered him.

As he watched, her hands pounded furiously up and down the keyboard, filling the room with blazing sound, until suddenly her fingers tripped up on the sleeve of her kimono. Impatiently, she pushed the sleeve up and began again. The music got louder and more impassioned. All of a sudden her fingers tripped on the kimono sleeve again; this time, without pausing, she shrugged off the kimono altogether. The two empty cotton sleeves dropped down to the floor behind her, and seemingly without missing a beat, Daisy kept playing. Her bare arms moved with even more vitality; her fingers thundered out the tune of the concerto; and her clouds of dark hair rose and fell around her naked shoulders. And Alexis watched her playing, oblivious of him; oblivious of anything else, and thought that in his whole life, he had never felt such overwhelming happiness as he did now.

Chapter Sixteen

Cassian was feeling very pleased at the way things were progressing. Louise's case seemed more promising every day; evidence was mounting up nicely, and the senior partner at the Linningford office had personally praised him, in a large meeting, for having spotted the litigious possibilities of the situation so quickly. This had been followed by some light-hearted joshing about Louise and her father, Lord Page, which Cassian had taken in good spirit. The chaps were obviously impressed, both by his work and by his connections.

And on the strength of all this, he'd persuaded some of the London boys to come down and get involved with the case. Just to make sure he wasn't forgotten about, back in the London office. That very day, Desmond Pickering and Karl Foster, both personal injury experts, were in Linningford for a meeting, and Cassian had persuaded them to come along afterwards to Melbrook and meet up with himself, Louise and – unfortunately but unavoidably – Barnaby. They were going to discuss the case for an hour or two, then Barnaby was going to leave, and Louise would cook the rest of them dinner. The conversation would turn to politics. Louise would impress Desmond and Karl with inside stories of the former Cabinet. Cassian would glow in reflected glory. And the result would surely be that next time a partnership was on offer, his name would be remembered.

So far so good. Cassian's one slight lingering annoyance was that he hadn't yet managed to meet Lord Page. Meeting Lord Page, and becoming friendly with him, was crucial to Cassian's political game plan. To grind up to Parliament through a series of dreary local government posts was one thing, but if he had the patronage of a senior statesman, Cassian reasoned, he would naturally find himself on a quicker and more successful route into politics. What easier way to impress a selection committee and inveigle himself into the right crowd, than by appearing as Lord Page's heir apparent?

And now that he was fully-fledged as Louise's lover; now that he was spending whole nights in her bed; now that he was actually involved in a case which Lord Page was funding, he felt entitled to a meeting with the great man. But she had not suggested it and, until now, he had felt that it would be too crude to mention it himself. Now he was not so sure.

A thrill ran through him as he imagined developing a friendship with Lord Page; with a peer of the realm. In spite of himself, he had a sudden brief memory of his grandmother, attired in lurid pink, drinking sweet tea from a silver jubilee mug. Despite the Italian accent still lingering under her whining Macclesfield vowels, she had always been devoted to the British royal family, and, by extension, all members of the titled classes. She would have been overwhelmed if he had told her about Lord Page.

But Cassian didn't communicate with his grandmother any more, nor with his parents, nor with his two stupid sisters. He had not been back to Macclesfield once since leaving for his first term at Oxford; and over the years since then, he had reinvented his background to such an extent that he now almost genuinely believed he came from some kind of Italian aristocratic stock.

He looked at Louise. The Honourable Louise.

'Darling,' he began pleasantly. Louise looked up from the paper banner she was making and flushed. She was still unused to sharing a breakfast table with Cassian, let alone hearing endearments over the toast.

'Yes?'

'I was just wondering how your father was.' Cassian looked earnestly at Louise. 'You mentioned a while ago that he wasn't well.'

'Oh,' said Louise vaguely. 'Well, he's much better now. He's got a private nurse who looks after him, so there's nothing to worry about.'

'You can't have seen him for a bit,' said Cassian lightly.

'No,' said Louise. She put down her marker pen and sighed. 'I did mean to go over when he wasn't well, but I just couldn't bear to take the time out from seeing Katie. But maybe now we can all go over there together.' She grinned at Cassian. 'Isn't it exciting!'

'What?' For a split second, Cassian looked blank. 'Oh, yes,' he added hastily. 'Tremendously exciting!' He glanced down at the banner which Louise was now decorating with flowers. 'WELCOME HOME KATIE,' it said, in bold multi-coloured letters.

'And are you keeping your father informed about the case?' persisted Cassian. 'Does he know how hard we're fighting?' That ought to earn him a few Brownie points in the old man's books, he thought complacently to himself.

'Oh, erm, yes. I told him all about it.' Louise flushed slightly and looked down. She could not tell Cassian that her father refused to take any interest in the details of the litigation, despite the fact that he was paying for it.

'Bloody lawyers!' he'd yelled, as soon as she'd begun to explain it. 'Can't stand the chaps. Just send along the bills and I'll settle them, but don't expect me to listen to their bloody claptrap! And don't start trusting the fellows, whatever you do!' Then, before she could gather her wits enough to interrupt, he'd told her at great length about his old chum, Dick Foxton, who was a marvellous lawyer, full of good sense, and why on earth hadn't Louise gone to old Dickie instead of these dreadful city chaps?

'The thing is,' Cassian was saying, 'it would be great to meet him.'

'Oh. Yes, I suppose it would,' said Louise. She smiled. 'Yes, that would be nice. Well, maybe in a couple of weeks' time. When Katie's got used to being at home.' As she said the words, a wide smile stretched involuntarily across her face. Cassian looked at her glowing expression, and realized that now was not the time to pursue a meeting with Lord Page.

Katie had improved so much over the last couple of weeks that her home-coming had been brought forward substantially. Today she was leaving Forest Lodge for good. She was due to arrive home at lunchtime, and Louise had spent some time creating a special celebration lunch. Bunches of blown-up balloons were bouncing around the kitchen, waiting to be put up, and Amelia was in her bedroom, busily making a welcome-home card. The air in the house was one of festive anticipation.

Cassian found it all rather irritating. He had long ago earmarked today as the date for the meeting with Desmond and Karl. They were important busy men; it was a huge honour, a momentous occasion. Louise should have been spending the day preparing a sophisticated dinner and witty anecdotes, not blowing up balloons and making banners.

And when he'd gently reminded her about the meeting, she'd been insultingly cavalier. First she'd casually suggested postponing it. Postponing it! As if Desmond and Karl didn't have bursting, fully booked diaries! As if this meeting hadn't been nearly impossible to arrange in the first place! Gently but firmly, feeling a frustrated impatience, Cassian had impressed upon her the important nature of this event; the prestige of working with Desmond and Karl; the absolute necessity of meeting them that evening. Whereupon Louise had shrugged and said, 'Oh, OK then.' No thanks for Cassian's efforts; no humble acknowledgement of the honour being bestowed upon her. It was almost degrading.

Now he looked firmly at Louise and took a sip of coffee.

'We'll have to make sure that Amelia and Katie are in bed before the meeting starts,' he said. 'We don't want them getting in the way.'

'Amelia won't go to bed at six o'clock!' objected Louise, giving a little laugh. 'I'll make sure she plays quietly in her room, and then she can go to bed at eight as usual. But I expect Katie will have an early night.'

'Well, we don't want any disturbances,' said Cassian. 'Perhaps Barnaby could go and supervise Amelia while we're having the meeting.'

'But he needs to be at the meeting!'

'Well, then maybe you could ask Mary Tracey to come and sit with Amelia.'

'What, and bring little Luke? He makes more noise than either of them!' Louise put down the pink marker she was using to draw flowers, and smiled at Cassian. 'Don't worry,' she said, 'I'm sure the girls will have had such an exciting day they'll go straight to sleep.'

Cassian looked sternly at Louise and wondered whether it was worth trying once again to convince her of the importance of this meeting. But as he was formulating the right phrases in his mind; as he was trying to adopt a severe, meaningful expression, the doorbell rang. Louise threw down the banner and hurried to the door; a moment later the unmistakable heavy tread of Barnaby could be heard in the hall.

As he entered the kitchen, Barnaby was saying gruffly to Louise, 'I got a bit upset by it. Hi, Cassian,' he added.

'Hello, Barnaby,' said Cassian politely. 'What upset you?' Some tedious agricultural catastrophe, no doubt.

'I just passed Hugh in the street,' said Barnaby uncomfortably. 'He looked absolutely awful. Really haggard and miserable.'

'Did you speak to him?' said Cassian sharply.

'No,' said Barnaby, looking downwards miserably. 'When he saw me coming, he . . . he crossed over onto the other side of the street.'

'Oh, well then,' said Cassian. 'It doesn't matter then.'

'It does matter!' exclaimed Barnaby. 'He looked appalling! I had no idea . . .'

'Oh, Barnaby, honestly,' said Louise. 'He was probably just having a bad day. Come on.' Her voice softened slightly. 'You're the one who's always saying that Katie should be our number one priority and nobody else matters. Don't get all worried about Hugh! Think about Katie!'

'I know,' said Barnaby slowly. 'You're right.' He looked at Louise's cheerful face and smiled cautiously. 'Tell you what,' he said, glancing around, 'I'll get going on the balloons.'

They arrived back from Forest Lodge just after one o'clock. The first thing Katie saw as the car pulled up was the old brown wooden gate. She peered at it through the car window, and felt, vaguely, that she'd seen it before.

'Welcome home!' said her mother, turning round and smiling brightly at her. 'You're home again!' Katie smiled because her mother was smiling, but inside she felt confused. She'd heard lots about home in the last few days, but she wasn't sure she remembered properly what it was.

Since the accident, there were lots of things that she didn't remember properly, and there were some things that she thought she remembered but weren't true. A couple of weeks ago, she'd been convinced that she had lived at Forest Lodge when she was a tiny baby; she could remember her father living there, and her mother, and Amelia, too. But Mummy had said that it wasn't true and she must have dreamed it.

'Come on, then,' said her father. 'Let's get you out of the car.' He leaned over and unbuckled Katie's seat-belt, then got out of the car and opened her door. Slowly, cautiously, Katie got out.

In front of her was a familiar house. Katie peered at it, then looked uncertainly at her father.

'Do you remember?' he was saying. He was smiling at her with his big wide smile. Everybody was smiling. Katie looked at the house again and felt a strange tweaking in her head. As she stared, she had a fleeting dreamlike memory of being inside the house, once, long ago. But the vision evaporated almost immediately, and suddenly she wasn't sure whether she'd ever seen the house before in her life. She felt cold and rather scared, and looked up at her father.

'When are we going back to Forest Lodge?' she said carefully. Sometimes, if she spoke too quickly, no-one could understand her. But Debbie, who came to see her every morning, had practised speaking slowly and steadily with her, and now she hardly ever rushed her words.

'We're not going back to Forest Lodge, Katkin,' her father said happily. 'You're coming back here for good!'

Katie felt a cold nervous fear creeping through her. She didn't want to stay at this strange-familiar house. She wanted her own bed and all her friends, and Mummy and Daddy to come and see her every day. She looked down at her shoes; smart new shoes that had been bought especially for today. Her face grew hot and for a moment she thought she might start to cry.

Then, suddenly, the front door opened. Amelia came running out, shouting, 'Welcome home!' Katie looked past her and saw the wooden floor and pale blue walls of the hall. As she did so, she felt more tweakings in her head. Gradually a cosy feeling began to spread through her; memories and pictures began to fill her head, and above all, a comforting weighty certainty. She knew this house; it was home.

'Let's play French skipping!' said Amelia, running up to Katie and giving her a hug. 'I missed you!'

Katie stood silently for a minute, her face blank and her mind painfully working. Then suddenly her face lit up and she gave a roar of delight. She ran down the path and into the house. Amelia followed right behind her and Louise and Barnaby hastened after them. They found Katie joyfully running from one room to another, stroking the sofa and the curtains and the kitchen stools. Amelia tried to stop her, but Katie shrugged her off with another roar.

'Leave her,' said Louise quietly. 'She's just so pleased to be home.'

By twenty to six the house had quietened down slightly, Barnaby had gone home to get changed for the meeting, and Katie had been persuaded into bed.

'Thank God for routine,' said Louise, descending the stairs and grinning at Cassian. 'That was the great thing about Forest Lodge. Bedtime was exactly the same, every day.'

'Yes, I'm sure,' said Cassian, who wasn't listening. He was peering out of the hall window, watching for Desmond and Karl.

'I hope they aren't lost,' he muttered.

'I'm sure they're fine,' said Louise cheerfully. 'Let's have a drink.'

As they went into the kitchen Louise felt her spirits lifting and a strange joyful lightness pervading her body. She felt as though she might float away with happiness. Katie was home, back in her old bed. Life was getting back to normal, and normal life had never looked so attractive.

223

'It's the relief which is so wonderful,' she said slowly, opening the fridge and getting out a bottle of wine. 'It's this amazing sensation of relief. I feel as though I've had a terrible headache for the last few months and it's finally going. My whole body feels happy.'

She poured out two glasses, watching the light reflected in the pale amber liquid, anticipating the taste, feeling an unbearable pleasure in being a simple unconcerned mother, able to drink a glass of wine while her children slept peacefully upstairs. Just like any other mother.

Then the doorbell rang, and Louise felt a predictable spasm of panic tear through her. Ever since Katie had started to improve; ever since things had started to look up, Louise had found herself experiencing flurries of nervous panic several times every day; almost as though her mind wasn't going to let her get away with it that easily. Every wave of panic was accompanied by a sensation of guilt and followed, like a stern reminder, by a painful recollection of the deep dragging despair of those first few weeks.

'I wonder who that is,' she said in an almost shaky voice, but Cassian had already leaped up to answer the door.

'Hello, Barnaby,' Louise heard him say in undisguised disappointment. 'Oh!' His voice was suddenly alert. 'Is that Karl and Desmond parking over there? Excellent. Why don't you go on through, Barnaby, and I'll wait for them.'

Louise had opened a beer for Barnaby by the time he reached the kitchen. He grinned shyly at her.

'Katie in bed?'

'Yes,' said Louise. She smiled back at Barnaby. 'That was a wonderful home-coming. I'm so glad you took the afternoon off.' Barnaby flushed slightly.

'It was good fun,' he said gruffly.

'Here we are!' They both looked up at Cassian's voice.

'Louise, this is Desmond Pickering and Karl Foster, from our London office. Desmond, Karl, allow me to introduce Louise Kember.'

Louise stood up. Behind Cassian in the hall were standing two extremely smart men. Both wore expensive-looking suits with button-down shirts and silk ties. Desmond's tie was covered in a repeating pattern of horseshoes, while Karl's was wittily decorated with little winged pigs. The two men smiled at Louise with identical smiles, and she had a sudden terrible desire to giggle.

'And this is Barnaby,' added Cassian, in kind but patronizing tones, as though Barnaby were the dog or the budgie.

'Hello!' said Barnaby, giving the two men his wide smile. Louise saw the younger man, Karl, running his eyes over Barnaby's suit, in what looked like mirthful amazement, and she felt a brief flicker of indignation. But there was no time for her to say anything because Cassian was ushering them all into the sitting-room, where he had laid out pads of paper and pencils and glasses of wine.

'So,' said the older man, Desmond, when they had all sat down. He looked at Louise. 'The facts of this case, as I understand them, are that your daughter was injured in a swimming-pool accident, and you would like to sue the owners of the swimming-pool. Is that it?'

Louise glanced at Cassian, and then, hesitantly, nodded. Desmond smiled kindly at her. Now that the two London lawyers were closer, Louise could see that they weren't quite the identical twins she had first perceived. Karl had fresh boyish looks, plumped out with a serene gloss of confidence. Desmond, meanwhile, had a long, intelligent, strangely ugly face. He looked older and wearier than Karl, but wore his confidence more easily, as though it were deeply and permanently ingrained in him.

'The first thing I always say to potential litigants', he was saying now, 'is that the law is a strange, rather unpredictable beast. However strong a case you have, you must be prepared for the chance of failure. You must also be prepared for a long hard fight.' He took a sip of wine. 'But I'm sure Cassian has said all this to you already,' he added, smiling at Cassian.

'Oh, yes,' began Louise. But Barnaby's voice cut across hers.

'Not to me, he hasn't,' he said. He gazed at Desmond with huge brown eyes. 'Are you trying to say we're going to lose?' Desmond exchanged the briefest of glances with Karl.

'Of course not,' he said warmly to Barnaby. 'I say these things to everybody. It's just a general warning.' He gave Barnaby his kind smile. 'You must realize that in a case such as this, nothing can be certain.'

'I thought you said . . .' began Barnaby, in a voice that was too loud for the little sitting-room. He coughed and started again, lowering his voice. 'I thought you said it was definite?' He looked at Cassian. 'I thought the letter from Ursula clinched it?'

Cassian looked at Barnaby in annoyance.

'Well, of course it's not definite!' he snapped. 'If the thing were completely and utterly definite, we wouldn't have to bother to go to court, would we? It'd just be "Advance to Go. Collect two hundred pounds". Or half a million, in our case.'

Karl gave a little snigger, but Desmond was looking concernedly at Barnaby.

'You seem to have been given the wrong impression,' he said. 'Nothing is certain until the judgment is given. That applies to all cases.'

'Or until you settle,' put in Karl, who had taken out a tiny calculator and was squinting at it.

'Yes indeed,' said Desmond irritably. 'But we won't get on to the issue of settling just yet. Do you understand . . .' He frowned. 'Sorry, it's . . .'

'Barnaby,' said Barnaby. He took a slug of beer and frowned. 'Yes, I understand. Sorry, I just got a bit rattled.' He shrugged. 'Going on about how we might fail. It just . . . I don't know. It worried me.'

'Of course it did,' said Desmond kindly.

'Of course it did,' echoed Karl, looking up from his calculator. They smiled in smooth unison at Barnaby.

'Shall we get on?' said Cassian, with ill-disguised impatience. He handed Karl and Desmond each a pile of photocopied sheets of paper. 'This is the case as it stands. Have a look.'

As the two men studied the papers in front of them, Cassian tried to impart his irritated impatience to Louise, but she was giving Barnaby a sympathetic smile. There was silence in the room, apart from the rustling of the sheets of paper.

'Where's the evidence from the diving-board expert?' said Desmond suddenly.

'Still waiting for it,' said Cassian. Desmond gave a grunt and turned the sheet.

Louise began to feel inexplicably nervous, as though she were on trial herself.

'Hmm,' said Desmond, when he had got to the bottom of the pile. 'There's a lot to work with here. Well done, Cassian.' Louise turned and beamed at Cassian, who tried to prevent a smile from spreading across his face. 'You've got some nice eye-witness evidence. I take it the diving-board expert will come up with the goods?' Cassian's face clouded.

'I don't know,' he admitted. 'He wouldn't say anything on the spot.'

'Well, I'm sure there are more where he came from,' said Desmond. 'If we need them.' He put the papers down and leaned easily back in his chair. 'A couple of things worry me, though,' he said. 'The first I think we can deal with quite easily.'

'What is it?' said Cassian quickly.

'The piece of evidence from the woman who said the children were running around and shouting before the accident.' Desmond shook his head at Cassian. 'I don't like that. Implies carelessness on the child's part.'

'But she's the same one who emphasized the fact that there wasn't a supervisor present,' Cassian said hurriedly. 'It's a useful bit of evidence, and I'm sure she'll be fine in court.'

Desmond frowned.

'Not good enough, Cassian,' he said. Cassian flushed. 'We need to anticipate the fact that the other side will claim contributory negligence.'

'Contributory negligence?' said Barnaby. 'What the hell's that?'

'That's when the plaintiff is found to have contributed to the accident, through his or her own carelessness or negligence,' reeled off Karl, who had begun tapping at his calculator again.

'But surely a child . . .' began Louise.

'Doesn't matter,' said Karl, without looking up. 'I'm thinking of cases like Davis v Leemings. And Brakespear v Smith.'

Louise and Barnaby exchanged glances.

'What happened in Brakespear v Smith?' Louise asked meekly.

'A ten-year-old girl was found seventy-five per cent to blame for being run over,' said Karl smoothly. 'Ran out into the road without looking.'

'Oh my God!' exclaimed Louise. 'That's awful! But Katie wouldn't . . .'

'In Davis v Leemings,' continued Karl inexorably, 'a twelve-year-old boy's damages were reduced by two-thirds because he ignored a warning sign. In Phillips v Fanshawe County Council . . .'

'Thank you, Karl,' interrupted Desmond testily. 'I think we get the picture.'

Louise was looking horrified.

'Surely no-one would try to say that Katie was to blame for her own accident,' she said in a rather shaky voice.

'I'm afraid they will,' said Desmond. 'If they've got anything about them, they'll certainly try. So we'll have to defuse their attack.' He looked at Louise. 'Does your daughter have a swimming teacher?'

'Yes,' said Louise, falteringly. 'But I just can't believe . . .' Desmond's smooth voice rode over hers.

'Right. Then we get the teacher to testify that Katie was a careful responsible pupil.'

'What if she wasn't?' said Karl impassively. Louise gave an indignant gasp.

'What do you mean?' shouted Barnaby. 'Are you saying . . .' Desmond ignored both of them.

'Doesn't matter. The teacher will testify that she was.' He paused. 'Think about it. You're the teacher. Are you going to admit that one of your pupils wasn't taught how to behave at a swimming-pool? No chance.'

Karl grinned admiringly down at his calculator.

'Good one,' he said and resumed tapping.

'But Katie was always careful!' exclaimed Louise. 'I mean, high-spirited, yes, but . . .'

'Yes, I'm sure she was,' said Desmond smoothly. 'Absolutely.' He smiled briefly at Louise, then looked down at his papers. 'Anyway, that's the first problem dealt with; the second is not so easy.' He looked at Cassian. 'These medical reports seem to imply a remarkably good recovery.'

'I know,' said Barnaby joyfully. 'Isn't it marvellous? She suddenly made great strides; she even came home early!' He stopped and looked helplessly at Louise. No-one was listening to him; Desmond's attention was still with Cassian.

'I thought this was a case of severe brain injury,' he said.

'It is!' said Cassian defensively. 'It was!' He looked down at his papers. 'Coma, brain clot, the works.'

'So what happened?' Cassian shrugged slightly.

'I don't know,' he said flatly, 'she just got better.' Suddenly he felt Louise's eyes burning into him. 'Which, of course, is wonderful news,' he added quickly.

'Wonderful for the child,' said Desmond; 'not so wonderful for the case. I'm not at all sure about five hundred thousand.' He glanced at Karl. 'You're the expert, Karl. What do you think?'

'I agree,' said Karl, finally looking up. 'We need a lot more than this to get anything like five hundred grand. We need – I don't know – psychiatric problems, maybe put in a bigger loss of earnings factor . . .' He broke off and looked at Louise. 'Was she particularly talented at anything?' Louise looked helplessly at Barnaby.

'She was talented at everything,' he said stoutly.

'Anything in particular?' pressed Karl. He looked at the others. 'You know Norrie Forbes? He had a great little case the other day. Young chap's hands crushed in a train door. Turns out he's a budding javelin thrower. Norrie had an Olympic selector in to rave about his chances. Won the case, of course. Fucking huge award.' He grinned. 'Anyway, the punch-line is, it turns out the chap was bored with javelin throwing. Apparently wants to go into computers, which he can do anyway.'

Cassian laughed and Desmond gave a wry grin. Louise caught Barnaby's eye. He had the same astounded look on his face that she could feel on hers.

'Don't you think . . .' she began, but she was interrupted by the door opening. It was Katie, clad in pyjamas and wearing a sleepy expression.

'Hello, Katie!' said Louise cheerfully. 'We've just been talking about you. Now, let's go back to bed.' Katie looked silently around the room, at the men in suits and the pieces of paper and glasses of wine. Then, suddenly she gave a huge grin.

'I'll play too!' she said in a loud clumsy voice.

'Not now,' said Louise and got up. Katie darted past her and ran into the centre of the room.

'Come on, Katkin,' said Barnaby. 'I'll read you a story.'

'No!' shouted Katie. She suddenly smiled again and, without pausing, began to take off her pyjama top.

'Katie!' exclaimed Louise. She glanced around apologetically. 'Sorry about this,' she said. 'It's one of the side-effects of the injury. They call it a loss of inhibition. We call it showing off.' Katie threw the pyjama top on the floor, and before she could start on her pyjama bottoms, both Louise and Barnaby hastily rushed forward. Barnaby got to her first.

'Now then!' he said, scooping Katie into his arms. 'Let's count the steps to the door!' He took a step. 'One!'

'One!' repeated Katie obediently. Clearly this was an old game. Louise picked up the pyjama top and handed it to Barnaby.

'I think you might want this,' she said, grinning ruefully at him.

'Thanks!' said Barnaby, grinning back. 'Two!' he added, and took another step.

'Two!' echoed Katie.

'Good girl!' said Louise. She looked at Barnaby. 'Do you want me to take over?'

'No, it's OK,' said Barnaby. 'I won't be too long. Three!'

'Three!'

'Well done!' As Barnaby shut the sitting-room door behind him, the sound of Katie's guffaw could be heard from the hall. Cassian sighed and leaned back in his chair.

'Well, she seems a lovely child,' said Desmond politely.

'She's wonderful,' said Louise, with shining eyes. 'She's still got a real sense of humour and she never gives up, however hard things seem.'

231

'She seems perfectly normal to me,' said Karl flatly. 'Is she really brain damaged?'

'Well,' said Louise steadily, 'part of her brain was damaged in the accident, yes; so some of her brain functions were impaired. But the point of rehab is that it tries to help other parts of the brain take over those functions. It's amazing, really, just how adaptable the human brain can be.' She flushed with pleasure. 'And Katie's responded very well to treatment so far. I mean, there's still a long road ahead, but it's been an absolute miracle . . .'

'She's still very disturbed, though,' said Cassian hastily. 'I mean, you saw her. She's lost all sense of how to behave; she laughs at things which aren't funny; she takes her clothes off at the wrong time . . . I mean, as far as her personality goes, the accident was a catastrophe.'

'Personality disorders,' said Karl interestedly. 'I love 'em. We had a great case, couple of years ago, where a woman was hit on the head and became a complete nympho. But the husband didn't want a nympho, he wanted his old frigid wife back. It was classic!' He looked at Desmond. 'You must remember that one. Brooks v Murkoff.' He began to tap again.

'Well, I think we can go a long way with personality disorder here,' said Cassian confidently. 'Since her accident, Katie's noisy, uncontrollable, impossible to live with . . . basically a complete walking disaster.'

'No she's not!' Louise's voice rose indignantly. 'She's fine! She's lovely!' Cassian sighed impatiently.

'Louise, she's not fine and she's not lovely,' he snapped. 'She's brain damaged! I mean, why the hell do you think we're suing?' Louise looked from one lawyer to another.

'Because of Katie's accident,' she said, in a voice which trembled slightly. 'Because of all the pain and suffering she went through. Because . . .'

'Pain and suffering!' Cassian's voice was dismissive.

'That's peanuts! We need long-term effects; we need psychiatric problems; we need loss of amenities of life; and we need you to testify.'

'What, and say my daughter's a complete walking disaster?'

'Yes!'

'Well, I won't! She isn't!' Louise's voice rose in distress through the house. There was a pause, then the sound of Barnaby running down the stairs. Desmond and Karl exchanged glances. Then the sitting-room door burst open and Barnaby appeared.

'What's wrong?' he demanded. Louise drew an indignant breath to speak, but before she could answer, from outside came the sudden loud wailing sound of an ambulance siren. Louise visibly jumped, and went pale. She clutched the arm of her chair and shut her eyes.

'Louise!' cried Cassian theatrically. 'Are you all right?' He leaped up and rushed to Louise, who put a trembling hand to her head.

'I'm fine,' she said in a faltering voice. 'Sirens still make me feel jumpy. It's stupid, really.' She grimaced. 'I wonder which poor person that was for.'

'Don't worry about that now,' soothed Cassian. 'Just lean back and take it easy.'

'Try to relax,' suggested Desmond.

'Absolutely,' said Karl cheerfully. 'How about some hot sweet tea? Or brandy? Or . . .'

Barnaby's hoarse voice interrupted him.

'What was all the fuss about?' he asked bluntly. 'I came down because I heard some shouting.'

'Nothing for you to worry about,' said Cassian at once. 'Just a small misunderstanding. I suggest, Barnaby, that we talk about it later. Now, I'm going to get Louise a glass of water.'

He got up and pushed past Barnaby, who opened his mouth, then closed it again. There was no point trying to argue with these fellows, he thought gloomily.

'In the circumstances,' said Desmond, 'perhaps we might leave it there for the moment.' He shuffled his papers and snapped shut his briefcase.

'Right,' said Barnaby reluctantly. 'Well, I'll be off, I suppose.'

'Good idea,' said Cassian, returning with a glass full of water.

'Bye, Barnaby,' said Louise. She smiled at him shakily. 'Thanks for coming.'

Barnaby said nothing. He felt irrationally angry, with Cassian, with himself, with Louise, with everyone. As he opened the front door, he heard the voice of that smarmy git, Desmond, saying in low engaging tones, 'You know, Louise, I've always been a terrific fan of your father.'

Barnaby closed the front door with a savage bang, feeling unsettled by the evening. As he stepped into the fragrant evening air, he said to himself, as he always did, 'I'm doing this for Katie. It'll be worth it for Katie.' But suddenly even that didn't seem certain any more; nothing seemed certain. Filled with doubts and fears and misgivings, Barnaby made his lonely way home.

Alexis and Daisy were curled up together in Alexis's generous double bed when the telephone rang.

'Damn,' said Alexis. 'Who the hell can that be?'

'Go on,' said Daisy, nudging him with her toes. 'It might be important.'

'Wrong number, more likely,' said Alexis, snuggling back down.

'Go on,' persisted Daisy, 'or I'll really embarrass you by answering it myself.'

Alexis gave her a strange unsmiling look.

'That wouldn't embarrass me at all,' he said. 'If you knew . . .'

'Go on!' said Daisy, pushing him hard with her toes

and giving a little giggle. 'Serves you right for not having a phone in your bedroom.'

'All right.' Alexis haphazardly wrapped his dressing-gown around him and pattered, barefoot, down the stairs. Daisy heard him cursing as he stubbed his toe and giggled. She couldn't hear him speaking because he was too far away, so she leaned back and looked at the ceiling and thought about the fingering in the third movement of the Brahms.

When Alexis reappeared at the door of the bedroom, she turned to him with a bright smile, saying, 'I think I've worked it . . .' But when she saw his expression, she tailed off. She had never seen Alexis look so shaken.

'Wh-what's happened?' she stammered. She felt an old familiar nervousness run through her body. Could it be anything she'd done? Had she upset him, somehow?

'What's wrong?' she tried again. Alexis blinked at her, and tried to smile.

'That was Meredith,' he began.

'Meredith Delaney? Is she OK?' Daisy peered at Alexis worriedly.

'She's fine,' said Alexis shakily. 'Fine.'

'Then what . . .'

'It's Hugh. He's had a heart attack.'

Chapter Seventeen

Hugh had been put in a private room on the cardiology ward. When Alexis arrived he was lying quite still in bed, his head resting on three plump pillows, his arm attached to some kind of drip. His eyes were closed and his face was pale and he was dressed in a white hospital gown which made him look disarmed and vulnerable. By the window stood Meredith, her shoulders hunched, her face downcast, and by Hugh's bed sat Ursula, looking small and frail and confused, like a little grey child.

Meredith was the first to look up.

'Hi there,' she said. Her voice sounded scorched and cracked. 'Thanks for coming.' Alexis met her eyes and then glanced at Hugh.

'Is he asleep?' he said gently. Meredith nodded.

'I think so.' She looked at Ursula.

'I'll take Alexis to get some coffee,' she said. 'You want some?' Ursula looked at her with blank frightened eyes.

'No thank you, dear,' she whispered eventually. 'Not just at the moment.'

As Meredith picked up her bag and shrugged on a jacket, Alexis looked around the silent cocooned room. He surveyed the low ceiling and smooth pale walls; he took in the plastic pitcher of water and blank television screen. The air was heavy and overwarm, and the whole atmosphere was one of oppression. And in the middle of all of it lay Hugh, still and pale and defenceless. Alexis could hardly bear to look at him.

Outside the room, Meredith gasped and sank down on a bench.

'You don't really want coffee, do you?' she asked, wrinkling her brow. Alexis shook his head. 'It's just so hard to talk about it with Ursula there,' continued Meredith, rubbing a hand over her face. 'I don't want to frighten her.' She paused and added in a low voice, 'I'm real grateful that you came. It was . . . it was good of you.'

Alexis looked carefully at her.

'What . . . What's the situation? Have they told you anything?' Meredith glanced down. For a few moments she was silent, then she looked up at Alexis with hot searing eyes.

'Basically, Hugh had a heart attack', she said slowly, in a voice which was tense with emotion, 'because he was stressed out. Because all day, all night, he does nothing except worry.' She paused and ran a thin hand through her hair. 'Because all he can think about is this *fucking* court case.'

She exhaled slowly and reached in her pocket for a cigarette. Alexis stared at her for a moment, then realized he was also holding his breath. He emptied his lungs in a gusty sigh, and watched, almost mesmerized, as Meredith flicked on the flame of her lighter.

'They're killing him,' she said suddenly, dragging deeply on her cigarette. 'They're fucking *killing* him!'

Alexis snapped back to attention.

'Are you sure . . .' he began cautiously, then broke off, as Meredith gave him a suspicious glare. He took a breath and tried again. 'Have the doctors actually *said* it was stress?'

'More or less,' said Meredith. She took a puff on her cigarette and hunched her shoulders miserably.

'Did they mention any other factors?' said Alexis in reasonable tones. Meredith scowled at him.

'Well, of course they did.'

'What, exactly? Too much alcohol?'

237

'Oh, Jesus! Why are you trying to shift the blame?' Meredith stood up angrily and her green eyes glittered at Alexis. 'You know why Hugh had this heart attack. It wasn't alcohol. It wasn't too many rare steaks. It was Louise and Barnaby fucking Kember and their stupid fucking court case.'

'Meredith, you don't know that . . .'

'Are you saying the case has got nothing to do with it?' Alexis stared at Meredith silently for a moment, then he sighed.

'Well . . . no,' he said slowly, 'I suppose not.' There was a short pause. Meredith stubbed out her cigarette, pulled out her cigarette packet, then changed her mind and put it away again.

'But I don't think', said Alexis suddenly, 'that the court case can be the only factor.' Meredith opened her mouth to protest and Alexis raised a hand. 'Think about it, Meredith,' he said firmly. 'Think about Hugh's lifestyle. He runs his own business; he drinks a lot – well, I mean, he's a wine-importer, for God's sake. And then . . . he's had a lot of strain in recent years. You all have.' Alexis broke off and looked at Meredith, to see how she was reacting. Her face was blank. 'I don't think', he continued, 'that blaming Louise and Barnaby for this is really going to help Hugh – and I don't think it's completely fair, either.'

'For Christ's sake!' shouted Meredith suddenly. 'Stop being so fucking British!' Her voice bounced off the walls of the little corridor and Alexis's head jerked up in surprise. 'I know what you're saying,' continued Meredith in shaky tones, taking out another cigarette and lighting it with trembling fingers. 'I know it's un-reasonable to blame the Kembers for this. I know there are other factors. I know that blaming them won't help Hugh get better.' She took a deep drag on her cigarette. 'But I don't fucking care, all right?' Her voice rose higher, and Alexis stared back at her, transfixed. 'I *want*

238

to blame them,' she cried, 'and I *do* blame them. I don't give a shit about seeing both sides of the story. I love Hugh, and he's had a heart attack, and it's all their fault! I'll never forgive them. And if you weren't so fucking uptight and reasonable, you'd never forgive them either.'

Alexis stared at Meredith. His heart was pounding with astonishment and, despite himself, a kind of awed admiration. His thoughts flickered between Hugh – blameless honest Hugh, lying in his silent hospital room – and Meredith. Impassioned, unreasonable, warm-hearted, red-blooded Meredith, battling on Hugh's behalf. In comparison, Alexis suddenly felt old and rather colourless.

'You're right,' he said abruptly.

'What?' Meredith gave an exaggerated double take, and the glimmer of a smile appeared on her face. 'I'm right? Don't I get a ticking off? Don't I get a lecture on "forgive and forget"?'

Alexis shrugged. His face felt dry and his reactions slow.

'I don't know,' he said. 'Maybe I am too reasonable, too uptight. Maybe we need more . . . more warriors, like you.' Meredith laughed.

'Hardly a warrior. I picketed against the Gulf War.'

'Exactly.' Alexis looked at her with serious eyes. 'I've never picketed against anything. You make me feel as though I've been sitting on the fence all my life. I wish . . .' He spread his hands helplessly. 'I wish I had a bit of your fire.'

'But I'm sure you have,' said Meredith quietly. 'Underneath it all . . .' She broke off and, for a moment, Alexis simply stared at her. His eyes ran over her strong intelligent face; her green eyes, still bright with excitement; her high forehead, tanned and faintly lined; her sensitive witty mouth. Her eyes met his, and Alexis found himself caught in her gaze.

Suddenly he realized he was holding his breath.

But then, breaking the spell, Meredith stood up. Alexis felt a slight surprising shock of disappointment.

'I ought to go back,' she said matter-of-factly. 'Hugh might wake up any moment.'

'Of course,' said Alexis. 'I'll come too.' He gave a heavy sigh and stood up. 'God, this is a bloody awful affair.' Meredith glanced at him.

'I know it is,' she said. 'That's what I've been saying all along.'

The next morning was dull and sunless, with a flat white sky and the feel of autumn in the air. Barnaby was walking slowly towards the village shop, when Sylvia Seddon-Wilson stopped her car and called him over.

'Barnaby!' she exclaimed. 'It's terrible news, isn't it?' Her eyes scanned his face greedily for a reaction, and when his expression turned only to puzzlement, a faint fleeting look of glee passed over her face. 'Oh dear,' she said, in tones that didn't quite hide her triumph at being the first to impart the news. 'I take it that you haven't heard?'

'Heard what?'

'About Hugh Delaney having a heart attack!' She paused dramatically, but immediately her attention was distracted as a car noisily overtook her, hooting as it did so. 'Shut up!' she yelled angrily after it. 'Bloody nerve, these people have got! Anyway,' she resumed chattily. 'Isn't it awful?'

She looked sidelong at Barnaby through the car window.

'Barnaby!' she exclaimed. 'Barnaby, are you all right?'

Cassian was saying goodbye to Desmond on the steps of the Linningford office. While Karl had taken the first train back to London, Desmond had spent the morning in further meetings and discussions with the

Linningford partners. The whole office had been made aware that a big shot from London was visiting, and the atmosphere that morning had been one of slight suppressed tension. Cassian, meanwhile, had sat smugly at his desk, glowing in the knowledge that everyone was well aware that Desmond had stayed with him the night before, and that they were working together on what everyone was now calling the Lord Page case.

Now he shook hands warmly with Desmond, wondering how many people could see the pair of them from their windows.

'It was very good of you and Karl to meet with the Kembers,' he said smoothly. 'And I think we're really well on course now with the case.'

'I hope so, Cassian,' said Desmond. He gave Cassian a quizzical look. 'I was talking about it with Karl this morning, and we both had to agree, it's not the strongest case in the world. You'll be doing very well to get half a million in damages. Very well indeed.' He smiled kindly at Cassian, who felt a slight splinter of alarm in the base of his spine.

'I'm quite confident,' he said firmly. 'I've taken on board the points you made, and they'll be dealt with.'

'And you're quite sure the parents will go through with it?' Desmond put down his briefcase and felt in his pocket for his car keys. 'Both Karl and I felt that they were . . . a little unprepared; that they might be reluctant to testify fully and convincingly on the damage done to their daughter . . .' He raised his eyebrows.

'They'll be fine,' replied Cassian quickly. 'They just need a bit of time to get into it.'

'Yes,' said Desmond. 'Time.' He narrowed his eyes slightly. 'Things seem to have moved extraordinarily rapidly in this case, Cassian. You didn't put any pressure on the Kembers, did you? You didn't hurry them at all?'

'No!' exclaimed Cassian at once. 'Of course not. They were just anxious to get things going. For their daughter's sake,' he added.

'Hmm,' said Desmond, 'I'm glad to hear it. Well, I'll be following events with interest, and I'll be very impressed if we succeed.' He walked towards his car, then turned back. 'As I'm sure you're aware,' he said, 'this case could provide some good publicity for us. Acting successfully for the granddaughter of Lord Page can't do us any harm.' He opened his car door. 'Some time,' he added, 'when you're in London, perhaps we could have dinner together at my club. Perhaps we could even ask Lord Page to come along.' He smiled at Cassian. 'So long, Cassian.'

As Cassian watched Desmond driving off smoothly, he felt a confusing mixture of emotions. His initial sensation of triumphant exhilaration slowly dwindled into a curious down-hearted feeling. Did Desmond and Karl really think his case was weak? A sudden unwelcome vision popped into Cassian's mind, of Desmond and Karl, gently laughing together at him. He scowled. He'd show them. He'd fucking well win this case; that would wipe the patronizing smile off Desmond's face.

Suddenly there was a noise behind him, and Cassian's secretary, Elaine, appeared at the top of the steps, carrying her handbag.

'I thought I'd go for lunch,' she said. 'If that's OK.'

'Fine,' said Cassian absently.

'Has he gone, then?' said Elaine. 'That guy from London?'

'Yes, he has,' said Cassian. Elaine looked around and lowered her voice.

'Has he offered you a flashy job in London?' she said. 'That's what everyone's saying.' She lowered her voice further. 'They're all dead impressed.'

At her words, Cassian felt an expanding sensation of

pride. The heavy feeling around his heart released itself and vanished. It was paranoid, he told himself, to imagine that Desmond's final smile had been anything but encouraging.

'Well . . . you never know,' he said impressively. 'I'm afraid I can't really talk about it.'

'Gosh,' said Elaine. She shifted her handbag strap on her shoulder and looked hopefully at Cassian for further scraps of information. When it was clear he wasn't going to say anything more, she sighed. 'Oh well,' she said. 'Shall I get you a sandwich while I'm out?'

'No thanks,' said Cassian. He wondered briefly whether to say, Lunch is for wimps, then decided against it. 'I think today I'll have lunch with Louise,' he said instead.

Barnaby didn't know what to do with himself. When Sylvia Seddon-Wilson had driven off, he stood quite still in the middle of the road, oblivious of passing cars, incapable of moving. His face was blank and his mouth was dry and a heavy pain had anchored itself in his stomach. An old woman passed by with her little dog, and he flinched, unable to meet her eye, or even move out of the way. He felt numb with shock; numb to the tiny flames of panic darting round the edges of his frozen mind; numb even to the incipient stirrings of a heavy looming guilt.

He had to find out more, he suddenly said to himself. He had to find out what had happened. He had to find out how Hugh was. His friend, Hugh, his old friend. The thought made him want to sit down on the pavement and bury his face in his hands, but instead, Barnaby took a deep desperate breath, and found himself beginning to walk. Without thinking, his steps began to take him in the direction of the Delaneys' house. He had to find out how Hugh was, he thought desperately. He had to find out . . .

And then, like a slap, he remembered. He stopped still again. What was he thinking of, going to the Delaneys' house? What was he thinking of? With a shudder he imagined Meredith shrieking at him, as she had at Louise. He imagined Ursula's distraught face. Maybe even Hugh himself, discharged from hospital. He would look up, with an ill grey face . . . Maybe the sight of Barnaby would bring on another attack . . .

'Oh God,' said Barnaby aloud, in a hoarse desperate voice. He looked around him at the empty street, then took a few uncertain steps back towards the shop. But as he thought of the eager curious face of Mrs Potter; the gossip; the voices dying down as he entered, his steps slowed down and once more he stopped still. He felt marooned and alone and suddenly desperate to see a friendly face.

And then, suddenly, it came to him. Without pausing, he retraced his steps and walked towards the village shop. He passed it without going in, took the next turning on the right, and went down the hill, towards the church.

Frances Mold and Daisy had just finished their usual morning cup of tea when the figure of Barnaby appeared on the vicarage path. Frances waved at him cheerily through the drawing-room window and mouthed, 'The door's open!' Then she turned back to Daisy.

'You know Barnaby, don't you, Daisy?'

'Sort of,' said Daisy shyly. 'I mean, I know who he is, but I've never spoken to him. I've never bumped into him or anything.'

'No,' said Frances thoughtfully, 'I don't suppose you have. None of us have seen much of the Kembers this summer. Understandably.'

There was a sound from the door and Barnaby appeared, pale-faced and breathing heavily. When he saw Daisy he gave a visible start.

'Oh,' he said in a gruff voice. 'Hello.' Daisy's eyes slid anxiously towards Frances, and she put her teacup down with a hand which trembled slightly.

'Hello,' she said breathlessly, 'I'm Daisy.' She smiled nervously at Barnaby, who made a visible unsuccessful attempt to smile back.

'Well,' said Daisy hurriedly, 'I think I'll go now, shall I?' She scrabbled under her chair for her bag, knocking against a little side-table with her foot as she did so.

'Daisy,' said Frances, 'there's no hurry. Why don't you have another cup of tea?'

Daisy looked up, her face red from exertion. She eyed Barnaby's distraught face and swallowed.

'Actually,' she said, 'I've really got to go. Thank you for the lovely tea and everything.' She paused by the door. 'And you'll come round and listen to the Brahms, before I perform it?'

'Of course I will,' said Frances warmly. 'Bye, Daisy. It was lovely to see you.'

When Daisy had disappeared up the path, Frances turned to Barnaby.

'You frightened her away,' she said in gently reproachful tones. Barnaby's gaze didn't move.

'I've just heard about Hugh,' he said. Frances's expression changed.

'Oh, yes,' she said soberly. 'Meredith phoned me this morning.' She looked up in sudden alarm. 'Nothing's happened since then, has it?'

'He had a heart attack,' said Barnaby hoarsely. 'He could have died.' Frances sighed.

'Sit down, Barnaby,' she said, 'let me pour you some tea.' She swirled the pot round and winced as she poured out a dark-brown stream of liquid. 'It's very strong,' she said, 'but then, perhaps that's just what you need.' She waited until he had begun to drink before she spoke again.

'As I understand it,' she said, 'Hugh's attack was

245

only very small. Of course it was frightening for them all, but I think he's on the mend now. Meredith was actually sounding quite cheerful this morning.' She looked at Barnaby. 'I think he was very lucky,' she said gently.

'I saw him a few days ago,' said Barnaby abruptly. 'In the street. He looked terrible, but I had no idea.'

'I don't think anyone had,' said Frances.

'He looked grey and old and sort of crushed,' said Barnaby. 'And . . . and he wouldn't meet my eye. He moved away across the street . . .' He broke off.

'Well now,' said Frances comfortingly. 'I wouldn't . . .'

'We used to be friends,' interrupted Barnaby bleakly. 'We used to go drinking together. We used to do each other favours.' He took a sip of the dark-brown tea. 'What sort of favour have I done for him now?' Barnaby's huge dark eyes looked up at Frances. 'What have I done to him?' he whispered. There was a pause. Frances looked at Barnaby with gentle compassion.

'Don't torture yourself, Barnaby,' she said. 'Remember, you've only been doing what you thought was right.'

'Right?' said Barnaby fiercely. 'Is it right to put your friend in hospital? To nearly kill him?' Frances looked at Barnaby carefully.

'Is that what you think you've done?' she said.

'Yes! Oh, I don't know.' Barnaby pushed a hand through his rumpled hair. 'I suppose it could have been anything, couldn't it? I mean, lots of people Hugh's age have heart attacks.'

'Certainly they do,' agreed Frances. Barnaby stared at her, unconvinced.

'We used to be such good friends,' he said heavily.

'I know,' said Frances. 'Perhaps you will be again.' Barnaby shook his head.

'It's too late for that,' he said.

'Maybe,' said Frances, 'maybe not.'

There was a pause. Frances took a sip of tea and waited.

'All summer', said Barnaby suddenly, 'my whole life has been Katie, and her treatment, and the case. That's all I've thought about. As though nothing else matters.'

'And now?'

'Now,' said Barnaby slowly, 'now I'm starting to remember that other people exist, too.'

Louise and Katie had spent an enjoyable morning in Katie's old classroom, with her old teacher, Mrs Tully, and a woman called Jennifer Douglas, who was in charge of reintroducing Forest Lodge children back into normal school life.

'I think', she had said at the end of the session, 'that Katie can start back straight away, if she likes. Mornings only, to begin with, and lots of rest when she needs it, but we want her to feel part of normal school life from the word go.' She looked at Mrs Tully. 'Staying down a year,' she said, 'being in a class with younger children; that won't make her feel stigmatized?' Mrs Tully frowned.

'I think it's unlikely,' she said. 'I'll be on the lookout for any kind of teasing, of course, but, you know, she won't be the first child to stay down a year, and on the whole the children here are very kind and accepting. They know Katie had an accident; they know she may need some extra help.' She smiled at Louise. 'They're all very fond of Katie. We all are.'

A sound from outside attracted their attention. Katie, who had been sent out to play, was joyfully screaming, as she careered around the playground on a plastic tricycle from the kindergarten. Louise gave a small grimace and looked at Mrs Tully.

'She isn't the same Katie,' she said bluntly. 'You don't quite realize . . . She may cause havoc to begin with.'

'Well, we're used to havoc,' said Mrs Tully cheerfully.

She looked at Jennifer Douglas. 'As long as she gets lots of rest . . .'

'Yes,' said Jennifer Douglas. 'The more tired she gets, the more attention-seeking she'll be. I like your idea of a little bed permanently set up for her.' She sighed. 'Not all schools are quite so accommodating.' She had looked at Louise. 'You know, you're very lucky.'

Now, eating lunch in the kitchen with Cassian and the girls, watching Katie carefully slicing her half apple into smaller pieces, watching Cassian clowning with Amelia and making her giggle, those words returned to Louise. She leaned back in her chair and felt a warm glowing sensation of relaxation spread through her body, until she wanted to wriggle with pleasure. Happiness, she supposed it was.

Cassian looked up at her and smiled.

'Desmond was very pleased with the case,' he said.

'Oh, good,' said Louise.

She smiled brightly back at Cassian, but underneath she could feel a shadow falling gently over her glow. Somewhere, somehow, she had lost enthusiasm for the case; for talking about it, or thinking about it, or even reminding herself of its existence. After Barnaby had left the night before, she had sat for a while, listening to the chat of the three lawyers over her head, telling herself firmly that she had overreacted, that she was irrational, that it would all be worth it in the end. But whatever she told herself, she could not get rid of a dismaying vision in her mind – a vision of herself having to declare in court, in public, that Katie was . . . what was the phrase? A walking disaster. Her darling little daughter a disaster. A trial to live with. A nightmare. How could she do it? How would she explain herself? – to Katie, to Amelia, to all their friends, to Mrs Tully? No point in thinking they wouldn't find out. No point thinking Katie wouldn't catch on to what was happening. No point thinking it wouldn't affect her morale; perhaps even her recovery. But there was nothing she could do about it now. It was too late to back out; she was powerless. Teams of important people were working on the case; everyone but her was committed to it. Everyone but her seemed to think that to go to court was an obvious rational course of events. And, of course, there was always the money at the end . . .

'I think we're really on course for victory,' continued Cassian. 'And I have to tell you, the boys at the office are pretty impressed. If we're successful, it could really help my career.'

'Oh, good,' said Louise again. She pictured Cassian's career in her mind: a long, abstract, glittering thing, disappearing into the distance – and now, it seemed, dependent on the case succeeding. The case was no longer, she realized wearily, just a court case; somehow it had become the foundation for Cassian's career, for their own relationship, for their future together. Her entire life seemed to be tied up in it; there was no way of escape.

'If things go well, it could mean a move to London,' said Cassian. He grinned at Katie. 'How would you like to live in London?'

'I've been to London,' said Amelia self-importantly. 'I saw Big Ben.'

'London?' said Louise. She gave a short little laugh. 'Why London? I thought you were based in Linningford.' Cassian grinned.

'Everyone has at least one stint in the provinces; to test their loyalty. But, I mean, I'm hardly going to stay here for ever, am I?'

'Oh,' said Louise. 'No. I suppose not.' Cassian's eyes met hers.

'London,' he said seductively. 'Shops and galleries and theatres and interesting people all around . . .'

'Maybe,' said Louise. She briskly began to gather the

plates together, as though to change the subject. Cassian regarded her for a few seconds, then looked at his watch.

'I've got to go,' he said regretfully. He looked at Katie. 'Although I hate to leave my favourite client.'

'See you this evening?' said Louise.

'Of course,' said Cassian. 'We can talk some more then.' He gave her a kiss, then blew kisses to each of the girls. They giggled and blew kisses back, more and more, until Katie blew one so energetically that she knocked over her glass of water, and Cassian raised his eyebrows comically and left.

When he had gone Louise sent the children out into the garden and started to clear up. But after dispiritedly mopping up the water on the floor, her energy seemed to evaporate, and for a while she simply stood still, staring out of the window, allowing her thoughts to patter lightly in and out of her head.

What she really wanted, she suddenly thought, was a holiday. She wanted a holiday. She wanted to lie down on a hot sandy beach and close her eyes, and listen to the sounds of people laughing and talking . . . and even swimming.

She paused in her thoughts. Swimming. Could she really consider going swimming? To test herself, she deliberately imagined Katie and Amelia paddling in the shallows, splashing each other, even swimming further out to sea. She conjured up image after image, waiting for the wave of terrible panic to overwhelm her, but it didn't come; she was safe.

'Swimming,' she said out loud. 'We could go swimming. We could all go swimming.'

'Mummy!' A shrill voice from outside interrupted her thoughts. It was Amelia. 'Can we have a chair for French skipping?'

'No,' Louise called back cheerfully. She put down the mop and walked straight past the pile of washing-up waiting to be done. 'You can't have a chair, but you can have me instead.'

As Barnaby came out of the vicarage he bumped into Sylvia Seddon-Wilson.

'Barnaby!' she exclaimed. 'I knew there was something I'd meant to ask you. It's my charity barbecue next week. In aid of Save the Children. Will you come?'

'Oh,' said Barnaby discouragingly, 'I'm not sure.'

'Oh, go on,' wheedled Sylvia. 'You need a nice evening out. It's only five pounds each, and that includes all the food, plus entertainment.'

'What's the entertainment?' asked Barnaby, in spite of himself. Sylvia's brow wrinkled.

'I'm not sure yet,' she said, 'but it'll be jolly good, whatever it is.' She paused. 'I don't expect any of the Delaneys to come,' she added brightly. 'What with Hugh in hospital and everything, so there's no need to worry about that.'

'I wasn't worried about that,' retorted Barnaby gruffly. He looked down, avoiding Sylvia's piercing gaze.

'No?' she said in disbelieving tones. 'Oh, good.' There was a slight pause. 'Then you'll come?' said Sylvia. 'It's next Friday.'

'Oh, OK,' said Barnaby, 'I'll come.'

'Marvellous,' said Sylvia, moving off down the path towards the vicarage. 'You can have some fun and forget all about that gruesome court case.'

When Barnaby arrived at Larch Tree Cottage, Sylvia's words were still in his mind. He knocked on the door, and when there was no answer, went round to the garden. Katie and Amelia were sitting on the grass, listening to Louise tell them a story. They all looked up when they saw Barnaby.

'Daddy!' squealed Katie, and leaped up to greet him.

'I've got some news,' said Barnaby, looking at Louise.

'I don't know if you've heard it. It's about Hugh. Perhaps', he glanced at the girls, 'we should go inside.'

After he'd told her, Louise sat completely still for a while, staring blankly out of the window, allowing her thoughts to settle.

'It could have been anything that caused it,' she said suddenly. 'Couldn't it?' She met Barnaby's gaze, urging him to convince her.

'Oh, yes,' he said, a little too late. 'It could have been anything, I'm sure.'

'I mean,' said Louise energetically, 'loads of people have heart attacks, don't they? I mean . . .' She broke off and looked at Barnaby. 'I feel awful,' she said more soberly. 'I had no idea . . .'

'I don't think anybody had,' said Barnaby.

'This bloody case . . .' said Louise, then she stopped. There was no point having another row with Barnaby about the court case. He would never understand her misgivings. He would just start telling her again how important it was to put Katie first, and how she had to stop being so irrational . . . 'I mean,' she continued weakly, 'it's completely taken over our lives.'

Barnaby looked at Louise. He supposed she was talking about her life and Cassian's life, not his life. He didn't count any more. A dull familiar pain began to gnaw at his chest. Somehow, while Katie had been in hospital and Forest Lodge, it had almost seemed as though he and Louise were, in some sense, back together again. They had been united as Katie's parents, like a proper family. But now, suddenly, he could see that as Katie got better and better, and as Louise and Cassian built up a life together, he would once again find himself being pushed onto the sidelines. He would be marginalized. Forgotten about.

He looked at Louise; she was waiting for him to reply. What were they talking about? Oh yes, the case; the gruesome court case. Barnaby suddenly felt sick of the case, sick of the whole thing. It was the court case which had turned Louise and Cassian into a couple. It was the court case which had given Hugh a heart attack. What else would happen before it was over? Was it really worth it? Was it really worth . . .

'Barnaby?'

Barnaby stared miserably at Louise and thought how scathing she would be if she knew what he was thinking.

'Well,' he said automatically, 'once they've issued the writ, things ought to start moving. And . . . and it'll be worth it in the end. For Katie.' Louise looked at him silently for a minute.

'Yes,' she repeated. 'It'll be worth it for Katie.'

And they looked blankly at each other, in a dull dissatisfying silence.

Chapter Eighteen

Alexis stood in Daisy's sitting-room, waiting for her to come downstairs. In less than two hours she was due to perform Brahms's second Piano Concerto in Linningford Abbey, and Alexis had never felt quite so nervous about anything in his whole life.

He stood staring out of the window, clenching his fists inside his pockets, imagining the gradual assembling of people that was to take place that night; that perhaps was already starting to take place. The orchestra gathering together; the audience filing slowly into the abbey; the expectant faces; the anticipation; the tension.

And then he imagined Daisy walking out, alone, into the middle of all that, into the bright lights and the attention. Daisy, who blushed if she caught the eye of a stranger in the street, who apologized as she let others through doors first, who shrank from public scrutiny like a shy deer. His quiet timid Daisy. He couldn't begin to imagine her surviving such an ordeal, yet that was what she was about to go through, and that was what was making him clench his fists, and disguise his nerves with a heavy frown.

There was a sound from the stairs and Alexis looked round. Coming into the room was Daisy. She was wearing a long navy-blue taffeta dress, with a narrow waist and a full rustling skirt. Her skin looked pale and milky against the deep blue and her dark hair fell like an inky cloud down her back.

'Hi,' she said shyly. 'Do I . . . do I look all right?'

Alexis stared back at her in foolish silence. He had never seen Daisy looking so beautiful, or so sophisticated.

'You look . . .' he began. He stopped. His eyes had landed on her hands, clad in a pair of red woollen fingerless gloves. Daisy followed his gaze.

'Oh yes,' she said, and giggled, 'I mustn't forget to take them off, must I?' She frowned and wriggled her fingers.

'I'll just do a bit more warming up,' she said, and abruptly sat down at the piano. A series of exercises, by now familiar to Alexis, immediately filled the little room. Alexis sat down and waited. He had something to give her, something which he should have whipped out of his pocket as soon as she entered the room, but her appearance had taken him by surprise. She looked suddenly poised as well as graceful; elegant as well as beautiful. She looked, he supposed, grown-up.

Eventually Daisy came to a stop. She paused, played a few random passages from the concerto, then got up and closed the piano lid firmly.

'That's enough,' she said. She rubbed her hands together briskly, and looked at Alexis. 'Shall we go?'

'In a minute,' said Alexis. He felt in his pocket. 'I've got something for you.' Daisy watched with huge eyes as he took a leather box out and handed it to her.

She opened it awkwardly and pulled out a gold necklace; a thin sinuous chain which trailed over her fingers and gleamed in the early evening light.

'It's beautiful,' said Daisy softly. 'I can wear it tonight, can't I?' She gave a sudden childish smile of delight. 'I can wear it tonight and it'll bring me luck! Oh, thank you!' She came close to Alexis and stood, beaming at him, rustling slightly in her taffeta dress. 'Thank you,' she said again, and kissed him gently. 'I love it.'

'And I love you,' Alexis found himself saying. Something which he'd never said to her before. 'I love you, Daisy.'

There was a short beating silence. Daisy's cheeks filled with a dark pink colour and she looked down. Alexis stood perfectly still and waited. Eventually, slowly, Daisy's eyes rose to meet his.

'And I . . .' Her old stammer had returned, and Alexis cursed himself. What kind of pressure was he putting her under? Tonight, of all nights. Bloody thoughtless idiot.

'And I l-love you, too.' She gave a little surprised gasp, and Alexis suddenly pulled her close to him, feeling the shiny fabric of her dress slipping against his shirt, smelling her rosy scent.

'You're going to be wonderful tonight,' he said fiercely. 'You're going to be just wonderful. And I'm going to be so proud of you . . .' He broke off. Daisy was panting slightly. He released her and looked at his watch.

'OK then,' he said more normally. 'Enough talk. Let's go.'

Louise was getting ready for Sylvia Seddon-Wilson's barbecue. It had taken a lot of persuading to make her agree to go to it, particularly when she discovered that Cassian was going to be away in London that night, discussing the final draft of the writ and statement of claims with Karl and Desmond. To her surprise, however, it had been Cassian who was most keen that she should go.

'You mustn't turn into a recluse!' he'd said, when she told him about it. 'I don't think you've been out since the accident, have you?'

'Of course I have,' retorted Louise.

'When?'

Louise stared at him and cast her mind back over the summer. What had she done in all those long summer evenings? All she could remember was sitting in hospital with Katie, or driving back from Forest Lodge, or slumping with exhaustion onto the sofa.

'Well, OK,' she said, 'maybe I haven't been much of a socialite. But to be honest, I don't really feel like seeing people at the moment.'

'Exactly,' exclaimed Cassian. 'That's what you've got to fight against. You've got to get back to your old sparkly self.' He grinned at her. 'Think of it as a dry run for next week.'

Louise grimaced. Cassian had arranged for them all to spend next week – the week before the girls' school term began – in London. A friend's nanny was going to look after the girls, while Louise and Cassian were going to spend the time doing nothing, as far as she could make out, but having lunch with people, or drinks, or dinner and the theatre. The busier their schedule became, the more pleased Cassian seemed and the lower Louise's heart sank.

'Why don't you buy a new dress?' Cassian was now saying.

'Oh, I don't know,' said Louise irritably. 'Anyway,' she suddenly added, 'I can't go. What about the girls?'

'Barnaby can have them.'

'He's going to the barbecue.'

'Oh.' Cassian frowned. 'OK then, get them to spend the night with a friend. Children still do that, don't they? They'd probably love it.'

And so it had all been fixed up. Katie and Amelia had been dispatched, with squeals of delight and plans of midnight feasts, to the house of Emily Fairly, a friend of Amelia's with a sensible mother. Cassian had driven off to London, promising to return the next morning with the writ, and Louise had been left alone to put on her party dress and brush her hair and try to pretend that she was looking forward to the evening.

She looked in the mirror and pulled a face. She looked, she thought, terrible. Her blond hair appeared lifeless; her skin was dull; and the turquoise cotton dress that had fitted so well last summer now hung, sack-like, off her frame.

Quickly she brushed a glowing bronze powder onto her cheeks, sprayed her hair with tiny shiny droplets, and painted her lips coral pink. She stared at herself. Now the surface was a little glossier, a little brighter, but underneath, she was still the same. She screwed up her face, then grinned energetically at herself, but above the grin, two dull defeated eyes peered back at her. Something's all wrong, she thought suddenly. Something's all wrong with me, but I don't know what it is.

By seven-thirty the abbey was nicely full of people and the orchestra was assembled. Alexis, who had chosen a seat as near the front as he dared, stared round at all the people who had gathered together to hear this concert – to hear Daisy – and felt a strange awed amazement, punctuated only by terrible pounding nerves. Daisy wasn't on until the second half; somehow he would have to sit calmly through some dreary piece of Mozart, clap and smile at the end, stretch his legs in the interval, all the while feeling this unbearable petrifying tension.

'Alexis!' At the sound of his name he jumped, as though expecting bad news, but it was Frances Mold, standing in the aisle at the end of his row and smiling cheerfully. 'I got here a bit late,' she continued, 'so I'm at the back. I just thought I'd come and say hello. It's exciting, isn't it?'

'I'm absolutely terrified,' admitted Alexis. Frances laughed merrily.

'She'll be fine!' she exclaimed. 'Look, I'd better go. See you in the interval?'

'Can't you sit up here, near the front?' said Alexis. 'What about those seats in the front row?'

'They're reserved,' said Frances. 'Never mind! The sound will be just as good at the back.' And she hurried off. Alexis looked crossly at the empty row of reserved seats. Who was it, he thought angrily, that hadn't even bothered to take advantage of their privileged position; hadn't even bothered to turn up?

During the first half he found out. The first piece – a nondescript little overture about which he hadn't even bothered to consult his programme – was over, and the applause from the audience had begun, when suddenly there was the sound of footsteps from the back of the abbey. Looking round, Alexis saw a smartly dressed couple hurrying up the aisle. Behind them, moving more slowly, was a twenty-something young man, dressed in ripped jeans and a crumpled T-shirt.

'Come *on*, Alistair,' Alexis heard the woman exclaim as she passed his row. 'We're late enough as it is!'

A jolt of recognition went through Alexis. Alistair – he knew that name. Of course – this must be Daisy's brother; the one who seemed to spend all his time travelling round the world, and those two must be her parents. This was Daisy's family.

He stared at them in surreptitious fascination as they sat down; these people about whom he knew so much, but had never met. He watched as Daisy's father sat down, stretched out his legs, and opened his programme with a shaking-out movement as though it were the *Daily Telegraph*. He watched as Daisy's mother began to take off her smart cream jacket, realized there was nowhere to put it, and shrugged it back on again. He watched as Daisy's brother sank easily into his chair and began to drum aimlessly on his denim-clad thigh.

As he watched, he began to feel an uncomfortable guilt at observing these strange-familiar people while they sat, completely unaware of him. At the same time, he felt a warm, overflowing friendliness towards them. Here was the most important part of Daisy's life to date, sitting a few feet away from him. Here were her roots;

her background; her formative influences. He stared at each of them in turn, looking for Daisy's features, searching for her expressions and mannerisms.

Suddenly the young man, Alistair, became aware he was being watched. He turned round, caught Alexis's eye, gave a puzzled frown, then turned back again. Alexis quickly looked away. Ridiculously, his heart began to beat more quickly, and for the first time, he began to wonder what he must look like to them.

Louise arrived at Sylvia Seddon-Wilson's house to find the garden full of people, music playing, and the smell of barbecuing meat filling the air. She paused at the gate, tossed back her hair, and tried to summon a feeling of cheery self-confidence, but the sight of the party in front of her filled her with an unaccountable sensation of sick anxiety.

She took a deep breath and swallowed, and tried to force herself to move forward, but her legs were tense and pinioned to the ground. She bit her lips, and looked around desperately for a friendly face to focus on, a kindred spirit whom she could quietly approach; but the bright faces in front of her all seemed to be those of threatening strangers.

'Come on,' she said aloud, 'stop being so stupid.' With a huge effort, she took a couple of steps forward and put her hand on the gate. Then suddenly, through a chance separation of the throng, she saw Barnaby. He was sitting on a low wall munching a chicken leg, talking animatedly to some woman she didn't recognize. And the sight of him – smarter than usual in a creamy pale shirt, but still instantly, almost joltingly familiar – filled her with a warm feeling of confidence. The crowd suddenly seemed benevolent. As she looked again, some of the apparent strangers metamorphosed into people she recognized; friends, even.

Without waiting for her fears to return, Louise strode

forward into the garden, struggling through the crowd towards the low wall. When she got there Barnaby had vanished, and for a moment she felt a resurging panic, but suddenly she heard his voice from behind.

'Louise!' He was holding a plastic cup in one hand and the remains of his chicken leg in the other. 'Haven't you got a drink?' he said. 'Let me get you one.' And to Louise's dismay, he began to move off.

'Barnaby!' she said. 'Can I come too?' she added more softly. 'I don't . . .' She shrugged. 'I'm a bit nervous about standing here all on my own.' For a moment Barnaby stared at her in puzzlement. Then, gradually, his face softened in understanding.

'Sure,' he said, 'we'll go together.'

As they walked, Louise cast around for something to say. She had spoken to Barnaby about nothing over the last few months except Katie and the case. It would have been easy to slip into the same well-worn grooves of conversation; begin with some comment on Katie's progress or what Cassian had said about the writ, but she didn't want to. She wanted to talk about something else; something different; something new. Surreptitiously she eyed Barnaby. What she would really have liked to ask was how come he'd bought himself a new shirt, but something made her hesitate. Did she still have the right to ask that kind of thing?

'Do you like my shirt?' said Barnaby suddenly. 'It's new.'

'I know,' said Louise. 'It's very nice.'

'I suddenly felt like wearing something new tonight,' he said. 'I don't know why. So I bought a new shirt.' He spoke proudly. 'It was easy.' Louise grinned.

'You look very good in it.'

'Really? Do I?' Barnaby turned to face her and she felt herself blushing slightly.

'Yes,' she said firmly, 'you do.' She sighed. 'I wish I'd bought something new. I feel so grotty.'

'You don't look it.' Louise gave a short laugh.

'Oh, come on,' she said. 'Yes, I do. I look dreadful.' Barnaby looked carefully at her.

'You look a bit tired,' he said.

'Exactly,' said Louise. 'I look tired and washed out and about forty-five years old.'

There was a pause, then Barnaby said, 'Rubbish.' Louise grinned.

'Nice try, Barnaby.'

They had reached the drinks table, and Louise watched as Barnaby poured her a plastic cup full of white wine.

'Cassian's taking us all to London next week,' she said, and noticed with a slight obscure satisfaction that Barnaby's hand wavered.

'London? Why?'

'To have some fun; to meet people and see things and go shopping . . .'

'Oh.' Barnaby handed her drink to her. 'Just your kind of thing.'

'Yes,' said Louise, 'I suppose so.' She took a sip of wine. Then she looked up and met Barnaby's face. He looked so gloomy that she said, without thinking, 'Actually, I'm dreading it.'

'Dreading it?' Louise gave a huge sigh.

'I don't know what's wrong with me. I just don't really feel like seeing people. I feel like hiding at home for the rest of my life.'

'Maybe it's just a reaction,' said Barnaby uncertainly.

'Maybe,' said Louise. She took another sip of wine. 'I just feel so tense all the time,' she continued suddenly, 'and depressed. As though I've got a big black cloud hanging over me. I just can't be all happy and lively and sparkly, like . . .' She broke off and shrugged. 'I suppose it's partly the case.'

'Yes,' said Barnaby slowly. 'The case.'

They looked at each other. Louise waited for Barnaby

to say, 'It'll all be worth it for Katie.' But he said nothing and took a sip of wine.

'Sometimes I think . . .' he began slowly. Louise stared at him.

'What?'

'I think . . .' But before he could continue they were interrupted by the unmistakable, penetrating voice of Sylvia Seddon-Wilson.

'Louise!' she cried gaily. 'I didn't see you arrive. So thrilled you could make it!'

They both looked up to see Sylvia bearing down on them. She was dressed in bright fuchsia pink and waving a book of tickets at them. 'Have you gone in for the raffle?'

'Not yet,' said Barnaby, feeling in his pocket for some change.

Sylvia looked at Louise.

'No Cassian?'

'No,' said Louise, 'he's in London. Working on the writ.' As she finished speaking, she was unable to prevent herself from glancing at Barnaby. He looked up and met her eyes.

'Oh dear,' said Sylvia, 'what a shame. Still, Barnaby's looking after you, is he?'

'Yes,' said Louise. 'Barnaby's looking after me.'

As the audience assembled back in its seats for the second half of the concert, Alexis sat perfectly still, trying to breathe normally and relax the muscles of his legs. But every time it occurred to him that, within minutes, Daisy would walk out to the grand piano gleaming darkly in front of him and begin her performance, his knees shot up again and his stomach flipped over and he felt an urge to swivel his chair round so that he was facing the other way.

To calm himself, he looked once again at the biography of Daisy in the programme, at the glamorous studio photograph and the long list of her awards and achievements. It was an impressive catalogue. She had won this prize and that prize; she had studied with this famous teacher and at that prestigious summer school. Alexis frowned. He could relate none of this to Daisy – a giggling girl who had never even seen the inside of a garlic clove.

Suddenly there was the rippling sound of applause breaking out. Alexis looked up, his stomach clenched. There in front of him was Daisy, walking to the front of the orchestra with the conductor, smiling, bowing, taking her seat at the piano. The conductor went to his stand, ponderously opened his score, and looked around at the faces of the orchestra. He looked down at Daisy, who smiled back. She placed her hands on the keyboard, and Alexis closed his eyes; he couldn't bear it.

Dimly he heard the first haunting notes of the concerto, played by a solo horn. He clenched his fists and felt his whole body tremble with tension. And then, as though from a great distance, he heard the first rising chords of the piano. Chords which he had heard on Daisy's piano, in isolation, many times, but until now, had never really made sense. Chords which Daisy had played to him in jeans, in her dressing-gown, in the morning and in the afternoon, and late at night. She'd mocked herself, telling him what a dreadful temptation it was to always start practising right at the beginning of a piece, assuring him he must know the start of the concerto off by heart by now.

What she'd forgotten was that while she could see and hear in her mind the part of the orchestra: the strings, the brass, the woodwind, Alexis – who had no musical training; who had, he now told himself, no imagination at all – had always been unable to flesh out Daisy's simple chords into the rich round orchestral sound that was now creeping through the abbey. He had never even begun to imagine this achingly beautiful, rising, flying music.

The orchestra made way for a solo virtuosic passage, and Alexis opened his eyes; this was familiar to him. The sound of the solo piano rang out into the air of the abbey as Daisy's fingers moved swiftly, expertly over the keys. Everybody was watching as she played: the audience, the orchestra, the conductor. Then, suddenly, the conductor turned back to his stand, brought down his arms, and with a pounding exuberance, brought the orchestra in. Alexis caught his breath. This music was half battle, half love affair, and Daisy was playing her part in each with a confident ease that he could never have imagined she possessed.

As the concerto thundered along, he watched her face, mesmerized. She was almost playing a game with the orchestra, smiling as their themes coincided, frowning as the music became more urgent and impassioned. His gaze ran slowly over the rest of her. Everything was elegantly in its place: her blue dress flowed faultlessly down to the ground; her hair shone glossily in the lights; her milky white arms looked suddenly strong and sure and invulnerable. This Daisy was someone he hardly recognized.

He sat still, gazing ahead, as the first movement gave way to the second; as the music grew urgent and desperate, as the crashing chords of Daisy's part echoed triumphantly around the abbey. Between the movements no-one moved. Everyone was, like him, staring agog at Daisy.

And then, as the third movement began, and the slow pearly piano melody began to rise slowly into the air, Alexis leaned back and closed his eyes. Into his mind came a memory of Daisy as he'd first seen her: tall, slender and gawky, tiptoeing her way through the Delaneys' garden, dipping her toe into the water, starting and blushing and biting her lip. He could barely reconcile that shy creature with the girl – the woman – performing in front of him now.

He frowned and shook his head slightly, as though to work it out. Then, as the music rose higher and higher, he suddenly realized that this was the first time he'd ever seen Daisy in a context apart from his own; in an environment other than that of the two of them, together in his house, or her house, or the village. They had spent the summer wrapped in one another's arms, ignoring everyone else, creating their own world. And in that world, he had built up a picture of Daisy in which she was isolated from the rest of her life – her parents, her friends, her life as a musician, all the other things which mattered to her.

Now, slowly, it came to him that his isolated summer-image of Daisy was as incomplete without the rest of her life as were the rising piano chords without the accompanying orchestra. She was not simply his beautiful, shy, stuttering girl. She was a pianist, a performer, a shining glittering talent.

She was, he suddenly thought, beyond him.

He leaned back in his seat and let the music soar over his head, and told himself several times how proud and amazed and happy he was; how thrilled he was to see Daisy looking so strong and confident; how pleased he was that finally he was hearing her perform. But underneath all the happy phrases, lurking in a distant corner of his heart which he rarely looked at, Alexis could feel, in spite of himself, the beginnings of a strange sad foreboding.

When Sylvia had finally left them, Louise looked at Barnaby.

'Perhaps,' she began, then stopped awkwardly.

'What?' Barnaby's eyes met hers.

'Perhaps, some time, we could have a talk. About things. Just the two of us.' Louise bit her lip. 'You know, about Katie and everything. Without anyone else there . . .' She tailed off, feeling foolish. But Barnaby nodded.

'I'd like that,' he said, and put his drink down on a stone bird-bath. 'What about now?'

'Now?' said Louise. 'But what about the barbecue?' Barnaby shrugged.

'I'm stuffed,' he said, 'I've already eaten about six chicken drumsticks.' Louise laughed.

'That wasn't what I meant,' she said. 'I meant, you know, talking to people and everything. It seems a shame leaving so early . . .' A thought suddenly struck her. 'What about your lovely new shirt?'

'It'll be just as lovely', said Barnaby, 'sitting over a glass of wine with you.' He took her drink out of her hand and put it down, next to his. 'C'mon, Lou, let's go.'

Chapter Nineteen

As the concerto galloped towards its conclusion and Daisy's final chords thundered into the air, Alexis sank back into his seat, feeling suddenly drained. There was an infinitesimal pause as the sound echoed round the abbey, then, all around him, the applause began; loud, steady, serious applause, that erupted into a roar as Daisy rose, beaming, to her feet.

Alexis gazed at her, at her glowing cheeks, and sparkling eyes, and at the gleam of gold around her neck. She bowed, once, twice, then allowed the conductor to lead her off. The applause continued as loud as ever.

Alexis noticed Daisy's mother, in between claps, consulting her watch. She said something to her husband, who nodded and said something back. And then both their heads turned to the front once more, as Daisy reappeared in front of the orchestra. A lady in a black dress appeared from nowhere and presented Daisy with a huge bouquet of flowers, and the man sitting next to Alexis gave a throaty cheer. When she heard the sound, Daisy's head swivelled towards Alexis and she gave him an embarrassed smile.

Immediately Daisy's mother turned and scanned the crowd suspiciously. Alexis looked down and studiously gazed at his hands; his old, wrinkled, un-talented hands. The sight of them filled him with a sudden depression.

Eventually the applause died away. Daisy walked off for the last time and the orchestra began to stand up and leave. Around Alexis, people began gathering their things together, waving to friends, suggesting a quick drink. Alexis sat perfectly still. He could see Daisy's parents heading towards the side of the abbey, obviously in search of Daisy. The natural thing would have been to get up, introduce himself, and join them, but the thought of greeting Daisy's parents, explaining who he was, watching their concealed expressions of shock and dismay . . . Alexis shuddered.

It seemed to him now that he and Daisy had spent the summer living in a bubble. A sheltered guarded world, cut off from public scrutiny, cut off from the rest of their lives, in which the only things which had mattered had been themselves. And now the bubble was about to burst.

'Alexis!' He looked up. It was Frances Mold again. She was flushed, and there was a huge smile on her face. 'Oh, Alexis! Wasn't she fantastic!'

'Wonderful!' said Alexis warmly. 'It was a brilliant performance.'

'Terribly moving, I thought,' said Frances, wrinkling her brow expressively. 'That slow movement. And such assured playing for someone so young. I mean, she's still just a child, really! She's amazing!'

'Amazing,' said Alexis quietly. His face felt numb.

'The thing is,' said Frances sorrowfully, 'I've got to dash, I'm afraid. I promised Sylvia I'd go to her silly barbecue. Tell Daisy I thought it was wonderful and I'll phone her in the morning, will you?'

'Of course,' said Alexis. 'She'll be thrilled that you came.'

'The whole village should have come,' retorted Frances. 'They're such Philistines, preferring a barbecue to this! I think we're the only ones here, aren't we?'

'I think so,' said Alexis. 'The Delaneys were going to come, but what with Hugh coming out of hospital today . . .'

'Yes,' said Frances, 'I suppose so. Anyway, I must go. Tell Daisy well done, won't you? Bye.' And she strode off back down the aisle, clopping in her sensible sandals on the ancient worn-down stones.

Alexis watched her go, and told himself firmly that now he *had* to go and see Daisy; he had a message to give her; it would be unforgivable not to deliver it. Slowly, creakily, he rose from his seat and shuffled past the row of empty chairs into the aisle. And then, even more slowly, he began to make his way, like a condemned man, towards the side of the abbey, towards Daisy and her family.

As he neared the vestry, he heard the sound of animated voices. He paused outside the door.

'I've no idea where she gets it from,' a woman's voice was saying. 'Not me, certainly.' She laughed gaily.

'Well, it was really quite a staggering performance,' said a man's voice. 'I bet the Academy can't wait to get its hands on you.'

'Well, I don't really know about that.' Daisy's gentle voice floated hesitantly through the door of the vestry, and Alexis felt a gnawing yearning pain in his chest. That was his Daisy.

He put his eye to the crack of the vestry door. In front of him, standing in an admiring circle round Daisy, were her parents, the conductor, the lady who had given her flowers, and another woman whom Alexis didn't recognize. Over in the corner, leafing abstractly through an old copy of *Church Times*, was Daisy's brother.

'Anyway,' Daisy's mother was saying, 'unfortunately we have to go back to London tonight.' Daisy looked up.

'I thought we were all going out to supper?' she said. 'With Alexis.' She frowned. 'I must find Alexis.'

'Yes,' said her father, 'where is this famous Alexis? We'd like to meet him.'

'I don't know,' said Daisy. 'I expect he's waiting somewhere.' The conductor grinned.

'Boyfriend?' he asked in perky tones.

'Sort of,' said Daisy shyly.

'You should have told us,' said the conductor, winking at her. 'We would have got him to present the flowers to you, wouldn't we, Maureen?'

'Oh, yes,' exclaimed the lady in the black dress. 'That would have been really romantic! To have a handsome young man, instead of an old crone like me!'

'Nonsense!' said the conductor gallantly. 'You did the job beautifully.'

Alexis moved away from the vestry door, leaned weakly back against the stone wall and closed his eyes. The gnawing pain in his chest grew stronger. What he wanted to do was rush into the vestry, take Daisy in his arms, cover her with kisses, and ignoring everyone else, tell her how proud he was of her, how beautiful she was and how much he loved her. But when he imagined pushing the vestry door open and seeing all those faces turning enquiringly towards him, a paralysing dread came upon him. He took a deep breath and stared up into the lofty roof of the abbey, willing himself courage, trying to summon up some confidence.

And then, suddenly, he heard Daisy's voice, raised in distress.

'But you can't go yet,' she was saying. 'You haven't met Alexis.'

'Well, darling, that's hardly our fault, is it? If he's gone home . . .' Daisy's mother's voice was crisp and efficient, and made Alexis wince just to hear it.

'He hasn't! He wouldn't just go home like that.'

'Well, then, where is he?'

'I don't know where he is.'

Daisy sounded desolate, and Alexis had a sudden vision of her standing, like a forgotten child, with a drooping lip and her flowers dragging sadly on the floor. He simply couldn't bear it. With a sudden burst

271

of passion, he strode forward and pushed open the vestry door.

'Hello,' he said in a slightly trembling voice. 'I'm sorry I took so long, my darling.' He smiled tenderly at Daisy, then held out his hand to her mother. 'How do you do,' he said, forcing himself to meet her gaze. 'You may have heard about me. I'm Alexis Faraday.'

Louise and Barnaby were sitting in the garden of Larch Tree Cottage. Louise had poured out two glasses of wine and Barnaby had unfolded a couple of garden chairs. He now sat on one of them, cradling his drink in his huge hand, leaning forward and frowning. Louise clenched her own glass and said nothing. They had walked back here from Sylvia's party almost in silence, and all the while there had grown inside her a strange, almost heady tension.

Now the tension was even stronger. She didn't dare to speak; inside her was an unarticulated obscure conviction that this moment was an important one; that to speak might ruin it – and her chances – for ever. Her chances of what? She didn't know. Neither did she know why this moment should be so important, nor why her heart started beating painfully every time Barnaby raised his head as though to speak. She felt as though she didn't know anything any more.

'I've been thinking,' said Barnaby abruptly, in a gruff earnest voice.

Louise jumped and stared down at her drink. Please, she found herself thinking. *Please*. And suddenly she realized what was wrong with her. I know what I want him to say, she thought, trying to keep her breathing steady. And I'm terrified that he won't say it, and if he doesn't say it, then neither can I.

'About the case,' continued Barnaby. 'You'll probably think I'm crazy,' he added. Louise's heart gave another little leap, and she gazed at him, holding her breath, half willing him to continue, half dreading what his words might be.

'But you know,' he said, 'sometimes I start to have my doubts.' He paused. Louise exhaled slowly. 'Serious doubts,' he added, gazing at her intently, trying to judge her reaction. Louise stared back at him, not daring to move a muscle of her face, not daring to risk throwing him off course before he'd even begun. 'I know I've always said it'll be worth it in the end,' he said in a defensive apologetic voice. 'But now . . . I'm not sure.' He frowned deeply. 'Hugh's heart attack really put things into perspective for me.'

'Wh-what are you saying, exactly?' said Louise. Her voice was trembling, and she took a deep shuddering breath. Barnaby leaned back in his chair.

'Last night', he said slowly, 'I was getting really depressed. I sat there, thinking about Hugh, who's in hospital, and Katie, who's out of hospital and doing fine, and the case, and all that money, and everything seemed all wrong, but there didn't seem to be any way out. I was going round and round in circles and feeling more and more miserable.' He paused and took a slug of wine. 'And then', he said, 'it suddenly occurred to me. We're *choosing* to go to court, we don't have to. No-one's forcing us. And . . .' He paused and looked uncertainly at Louise.

'What?' prompted Louise, falteringly.

'And, if we wanted to, we could . . .' He stopped, then continued in a rush. 'We could just call the whole thing off.'

There was a long shocked silence. Louise stared at Barnaby. She could feel her face turning pink and her breaths coming in short sharp gasps.

'I know,' exclaimed Barnaby, 'I'm crazy. You don't have to agree with me.'

'But I do!' cried Louise suddenly, her voice ringing through the garden. 'I do agree with you!'

To her astonishment a tear began to roll down her cheeks, and she gave a sudden involuntary sob. Barnaby stared at her in alarm.

'I'm the same as you! I don't want to go to court any more!' she wailed. 'I just want to get back to normal life. I just can't stand it hanging over us all the time . . .' She tailed off and broke down into shuddering sobs.

'Lou!' said Barnaby. He sounded shaken. 'Lou, are you all right?'

'Don't worry,' she spluttered, 'I'm fine. It's just . . .' She looked up at him through teary blue eyes. 'It's just . . . I don't know . . . the relief . . .' And she broke down again.

For a few minutes she sat with her head buried in her hands, rocking slightly in her chair, weeping uncontrollably. She was oblivious of anything except the hot redness in front of her eyes and her panting breaths and the wetness which coursed through her fingers. But gradually, as her sobs began to die down, she began to feel a gentle lifting in her body. The strains and tensions which seemed to have been building up inside her for months, very slowly started to ebb away. She felt her shoulders begin to loosen and her neck begin to relax and her taut constrained brow gently begin to expand. And inside her mind she began to be aware of a gradual lightening, an easing, a slipping away of the shadowy, looming, permanent edifice that had been part of her every thought and dream since the whole thing had started.

'It was just there all the time!' she suddenly wailed. 'It spoiled everything. All we could think about was the case! Oh God, Barnaby! What were we doing? We were mad!'

Barnaby's head jerked up.

'Do you mean . . .' he said hesitantly, studying Louise's wet, red, tear-streaked face. 'Do you mean you definitely want to call it off? I mean . . . I mean, a minute ago you were all in favour of it. You can't have changed your mind that quickly.'

Louise took a couple of slow shuddering breaths and rubbed her cheeks. Then she looked up at Barnaby.

'I haven't changed my mind,' she said. 'I've just opened it up and looked at what's really inside.' She paused. 'If you hadn't said anything, then, yes, I would have gone along with the case, but only because I didn't see any other option. I felt trapped. I just sort of assumed we had to go to court, whether we wanted to or not.' She gave a shaky laugh. 'As though it wasn't up to us all along. And now . . .' She pushed her hair off her wet face. 'Now I feel as if we were mad to keep going with the idea for so long.'

'But what about . . .' Barnaby shrugged helplessly. 'Oh, I don't know . . . the money?'

'The money,' said Louise flatly. 'No amount of money would make me go into a witness box and tell the world that Katie's a walking disaster.'

'What?'

'That's what they said, those lawyers. They said', Louise's voice trembled, 'she wasn't injured enough. They said we'd have to play up the personality changes; make her sound like a monster; unbearable to live with.'

'Bastards!' Barnaby stared at Louise.

'Either that or forget about half a million,' said Louise. She looked down. 'And anyway,' she added softly, 'what do we really want with half a million pounds of Hughs' and Ursula's money?'

There was a long pause.

'We don't,' said Barnaby.

'No,' said Louise, 'we don't. We don't want any of it. I can't even bear to think about it any more. I suddenly feel . . .' She ran her fingers shakily through her hair. 'I feel liberated. As though I've got rid of a disease that was poisoning me and making me sick.'

'That's a bit how I feel, too,' said Barnaby.

Louise smiled tremulously at him. For a few moments they looked at each other silently in the still garden air. Then Barnaby took a deep breath and said, 'What about Cassian?'

For a moment Louise stared at him, as though she didn't know who he was talking about.

'Cassian,' she echoed weakly. 'Oh, God. I don't know.' She took a sip of wine and winced. 'He'll be furious; he'll be absolutely furious.' Suddenly she gave a strange, almost hysterical little giggle. 'He'll go completely mad,' she said and giggled again. 'He'll probably explode.'

Barnaby stared at her. He opened his mouth to speak, then shut it again.

'I don't know how I'll tell him,' said Louise. Barnaby licked his lips nervously.

'Do you think . . .' he began. 'Do you think he'll try and make you change your mind?'

'Never,' said Louise determinedly. 'Let him try.' She sighed and sipped at her wine. 'The trouble with Cassian', she said in an almost conversational tone, 'is that he takes everything so bloody seriously. I don't think he even knows what a sense of humour is.'

Barnaby stared at Louise, unable to reply.

'All he thinks about', continued Louise, 'is his career, and his political prospects, and winning this stupid case. He wants to move to London, you know.' She looked up at Barnaby. 'He wants us to move there with him; the girls, too.'

Barnaby felt a jolting pang in his chest.

'To London?' he said weakly.

'Yes,' said Louise airily. 'That's what he says.'

'And . . .' Barnaby swallowed. 'Are you going to go?'

Louise put her drink down and looked straight at him.

'Barnaby,' she said gently, 'do you really think there's any future for me and Cassian now?'

Barnaby stared back at her for a moment, then he

looked down and shrugged. He felt unhappily confused. Louise drew breath to speak again, but she was interrupted by the sound of the telephone ringing.

'Oh, God,' said Louise. 'That might be about the girls. Hang on a minute.'

She hurried into the house and Barnaby leaned back heavily in his chair, trying to make some sense of this conversation; trying not to let himself draw the wrong conclusion; trying not to allow the insidious, corrupting, unstoppable emotion of hope to take root in his chest.

As Louise came back again he was frowning hard, and he looked up to speak. But she spoke first.

'It was . . .' Her voice was trembling slightly, and Barnaby felt a sudden thumping panic. He stared anxiously at her. Had something happened to the girls? To Katie?

'It was Cassian,' said Louise. 'His meeting was cancelled.'

The fearful beating in Barnaby's chest began to subside and he gave a small sigh of relief. Louise licked her dry lips.

'I told him we were calling off the case,' she said. 'I thought it would be easier that way. I thought he was miles away.' She gave a strange giggle. 'But he was calling from his car. He's going to be here in about five minutes.'

Daisy and Alexis stood at the corner of the square of grass in front of Linningford Abbey and waved. On the other side of the Crescent a gleaming red BMW signalled, then smoothly turned and disappeared through the narrow stone gateway. Daisy dropped her arm and sighed.

'I'm so glad you've met my parents,' she said happily. 'I think they really liked you.'

Alexis looked down at her innocent face and recalled,

in spite of himself, the expressions of suspicion and incredulity which had greeted him in the vestry. The mistrustful probing questions from Daisy's mother; the alarmed frown on her father's forehead; the looks of surprise from the others. All covered in a civilized veneer of friendly politeness.

The only one who had completely failed to conceal his hilarious astonishment had been Daisy's brother. He had stared agog at Alexis, then at Daisy, then back at Alexis. Then he'd sidled up to Daisy and said in a penetrating whisper, 'This your fella, then?' Daisy had blushed and smiled. 'Isn't he a bit past it?' continued her brother cheerfully, and Daisy had blushed even harder, and her mother had hastily asked Alexis, in a loud distracting voice, a question about his work.

Now Alexis smiled at Daisy and said, 'I hope they did. They certainly seemed very nice people.'

'Oh, yes,' said Daisy vaguely. 'Yes, they are.'

'They were talking about the Academy,' continued Alexis. 'You didn't tell me you'd won a scholarship there.'

'Oh,' Daisy shrugged, 'it wasn't anything much.'

'That's not what your parents seem to think, nor that conductor chap.' Alexis looked seriously at her. 'You know, Daisy,' he said, 'you have something very precious. I don't think I realized before today quite how precious it was. And how important it is that you make as much of it as you possibly can.'

He walked a few steps, sat down on the grass, still warm from the day's sun, and patted the ground next to him. Daisy sank down in a dark billowing cloud of taffeta, and nestled up to him.

'Today was lovely,' she murmured. 'Doing the concert, and seeing my parents, and them meeting you and everything.' She looked up at Alexis. 'This has been such a perfect summer.'

'I know it has,' said Alexis softly. 'Perfect.' He paused

278

and ran a hand through his hair. Daisy nestled closer.

'But, you know,' continued Alexis slowly, 'the summer's nearly at an end. And then you're going to move to London and start your new life at the Academy, and things might . . .' he swallowed, 'might be a little different.'

'What do you mean?' Daisy turned her head to look at him, wide-eyed. 'What do you mean, different? Do you mean us?'

'In a way,' said Alexis. He put up a hand and cradled her chin.

'Your life is just beginning,' he said gently, 'and it's going to be a very exciting life. You must make the most of it.'

'I know,' said Daisy. She stared at him. 'But we'll still be the same, won't we? I mean, I'll come down every weekend, and we'll still see each other nearly as much as we do now, that's what we said.'

'I know that's what we said,' agreed Alexis, 'and of course we will see each other, but . . .' He broke off.

'But what?' Daisy sat up, suddenly agitated. 'Wh-what's wrong?' In her distress she began to stumble over her words, and Alexis felt his heart squeeze painfully.

'Nothing's wrong,' he said. 'It's just . . .' He broke off and briefly closed his eyes. What was he doing? What the hell was he doing? Why was he torturing himself and Daisy like this?

'D-don't . . . don't you want to go out with me any more?' said Daisy. Her lips were quivering and her eyelashes batted nervously. Alexis stared at her, almost unable to reply.

'Of course I want to,' he said at last, his voice thick with emotion. 'Daisy, I love you.'

'And I love you, too,' said Daisy in a trembling voice. Alexis looked away. He could hardly bear to say what he was about to.

'But sometimes,' he said, forcing himself to speak,

279

'sometimes just loving each other isn't enough.' Daisy drew breath, and he carried on quickly before she could speak. 'When you get to London, you're going to meet a lot of new people, all your own age, and you're going to have a lot of fun. And, I hope, you're going to work very hard at your music.' He paused. Daisy was silent.

'And all I wanted to say,' he continued, 'was that you mustn't come back down here every weekend. You must go out and have fun, and join in with all the others. And if,' he swallowed, 'if you happen to meet someone – a boy – who's a bit nearer your own age . . .'

'I won't!' said Daisy passionately. 'I wouldn't ever . . .'

'You might,' said Alexis gently, 'and if you do, you mustn't feel bad. You mustn't feel guilty.' He somehow managed to smile at her. 'We've had a perfect summer together, and nothing can ever change that, but now you're moving on.'

'I don't want to move on,' whispered Daisy. She bit her lip. 'I want to stay here with you. I wish I wasn't going.'

'I know you do,' said Alexis thickly. 'God, so do I.' He suddenly pulled her close to him and buried his face in her soft, white, scented neck.

'Let's not think about the future,' he murmured against her skin. 'Let's just enjoy the next two weeks. And then, when you move to London – well, we'll just see how it goes, shall we?'

'OK,' said Daisy in a shaking voice. She pushed him away slightly, and he saw, with a small shock, that her cheeks were stained with tears. 'I'll always love you, Alexis,' she said. 'It wouldn't matter if I was in London or here or . . . or on the moon. And I think,' she hesitated, 'I think you're wrong. I think that's all that counts. We love each other, and . . . and nothing else matters at all. That's what I think.'

Alexis stared back at her for a few trembling moments.

'I'm an old fool,' he said at last. Daisy gave a surprised giggle.

'No, you're not!' she said.

'I am,' said Alexis. 'I don't know what I've been thinking of. I should be wining and dining you, sweeping you off your feet. We should be celebrating! What are we doing, sitting here?'

He got to his feet, and held out his hands to Daisy. 'Now,' he said. 'You're the star, so you can choose. Red wine, white wine, or . . .'

'Champagne,' said Daisy, 'of course!'

'As much as we can drink,' said Alexis. He looked at her ruefully. 'Daisy, don't ever again listen to a word I say,' he said. 'Please.' Daisy giggled.

'OK,' she said, 'I won't.'

'Good,' said Alexis. 'Now, let's go and find some champagne worth drinking.'

Louise and Barnaby sat, in silence, in the kitchen of Larch Tree Cottage. They had neatly folded up the garden chairs, brought the wine inside, and sat down to wait. That was five minutes ago. Now every little sound from outside made them start and glance towards the door, then look sheepishly at each other and back down again.

Barnaby stared miserably into his glass of wine. He felt as though he had been on the brink of something outside, on the edge of a new understanding, a new beginning, even. If they'd just had a bit more time to talk . . . He glanced covertly at Louise and her words floated through his mind. 'Do you really think there's any future for me and Cassian?' Barnaby clenched his fist tightly. He felt like smashing it down on the table. What did she mean? Was she asking him a question? Was she trying to tell him something? Was she teasing him? He couldn't stand this roundabout talk.

Suddenly there was the sound of a key in the

lock. Louise jumped, and looked at Barnaby.

'I feel like hiding under the table,' she whispered. 'Don't you?'

But there was no time for Barnaby to reply, as into the kitchen strode Cassian. He looked office-smart, and swung his briefcase jauntily. To Barnaby's amazement, he was smiling.

'Hello,' he said. 'Hello there, Barnaby. Nice to see you.'

'Oh,' said Barnaby, taken aback. 'Yes.' Surprise made him sound gruff and ungracious, and he suddenly felt a bit unsure of things. Had Louise really made up her mind about the case? Why was Cassian looking so cheerful? What was going on? He watched as Cassian sat down and poured himself a glass of wine; he looked completely unperturbed. Barnaby glanced at Louise, who was looking down pensively. He couldn't tell what she might be thinking, and in spite of himself, his heart began to beat nervously.

'So, I gather', said Cassian smoothly, 'you've been having second thoughts about the case.' He spoke to Barnaby, as though Louise were not there, or didn't count. Or as though she didn't agree with Barnaby.

'Well,' said Barnaby, glancing at Louise, 'yes. We've decided we don't want to go any further with it.'

'I understand completely,' said Cassian kindly. 'It's a very daunting prospect, going to court, but don't worry, you'll be fine. So what I suggest is that you have a careful think and sleep on it, and don't rush into any decision yet.'

'Well,' began Barnaby doubtfully. He looked at Louise again; she wasn't saying anything. What was wrong? Had she changed her mind about the whole thing? He looked up at Cassian, who was politely waiting. Someone was going to have to say something. Barnaby frowned.

'The thing is, Cassian,' he said, 'I really think we've

made up our minds already.' He glanced at Louise and, when there was no response, ploughed on. 'We think the case is going to be too much of a strain, both on us and on Katie,' he said, 'and there's no guarantee of getting any money, and even if there were, the Delaneys . . .' He tailed off feebly.

'The Delaneys are your friends,' suggested Cassian.

'Well, yes,' said Barnaby, 'something like that.'

'Yes,' said Cassian. He didn't sound surprised. 'Well, as I say, have a good think, and I'm sure you'll come round to the idea again.' He smiled at Barnaby. 'You know, you owe it to Katie.'

'Don't say that!' Louise's voice interrupted him like a whiplash, and both men jumped. 'Don't you dare say anything at all about Katie,' she said in a fierce deliberate voice. 'You have no idea at all. This case isn't going to help her! It's going to label her as some kind of helpless head case! It's going to tell the world that her whole life has been ruined! What kind of help is that?'

'Louise,' said Cassian in soothing tones. 'I realize it's difficult to face up to Katie's needs . . .'

'I face up to them every day, thank you!' exclaimed Louise. 'I know exactly what her needs are. She needs a normal life and support and encouragement, not a bloody legal battle to screw her up!'

'Oh, right,' said Cassian in scathing tones, 'and I suppose all this comes free, does it? All this support and encouragement?'

'Most of it, yes!' said Louise. She folded her arms and looked straight at Cassian. 'Katie is not a victim any more,' she said. 'She's just fine. We've been incredibly lucky, and I think it's time for us to start appreciating that a bit more. All of us.'

'Well, great,' said Cassian sarcastically, 'that's a lovely romantic vision, but what happens, I wonder, when Katie grows up? And she realizes that she could have had half a million pounds, but her parents were too lily-livered to go to court? What are you going to say to her then?'

'For a start,' said Louise furiously, 'I think you should just stop talking about this famous half a million pounds. I'm not stupid, I saw the way those other lawyers were looking at each other. We would never get that much in court, never!'

'That's not . . .' began Cassian. But Louise interrupted him.

'And even if we did! Even if we did! What do we need it for?' She paused and glanced at Barnaby. He was gazing at her, mouth open in shock. She gave him a quick grin and looked back at Cassian. 'We're OK for money,' she said slowly. 'We're more than OK. And when my father eventually dies . . .' She swallowed awkwardly. 'Well, then we'll be even . . . even more OK. And for us to go to court and fleece Hugh and Ursula of all their life's earnings, just because Katie happened to be in their pool and not someone else's . . . well, it's immoral.' She took a sip of wine and both men eyed her warily. 'You can say what you like, Cassian,' she continued calmly, 'but we're not going ahead with this case. We should never have got into it in the first place.'

'Louise,' said Cassian smoothly, 'I can tell you're a bit upset.'

'Oh, shut up, Cassian!' shouted Louise exasperatedly. 'You can't tell anything! You can't tell when a case starts to look weak; you can't tell when someone really does change their mind.' She paused. 'You can't even tell right from wrong.' Cassian glared at her.

'This case is *not* weak!' he shouted. 'It's a very strong case, backed up by some of the finest legal minds in Britain, and if you pull out now, I can tell you, you'll be making a big mistake!'

'Fine!' cried Louise. 'Let us make a mistake. At least we'll be able to sleep at night!'

'And actually,' pointed out Barnaby in a low gruff

voice, 'we could always sue later on, if we wanted to. We've got up until Katie's eighteen.' Cassian shot him a look of pure loathing.

'How very clever of you, Barnaby,' he said in a voice which quivered with anger. 'Any more top legal tips from Farmer Giles?'

'Leave him alone!' shrieked Louise. 'God, you're a shit, Cassian.'

'Well, you're a fool!' retorted Cassian. 'You're both fools! This case could be a gold-mine!'

'We don't need a gold-mine!'

'Yes, well, I do!' Cassian suddenly yelled. 'I fucking well need this case to happen! Everyone knows about it; everyone's involved in it. I mean, the London office is helping to draw up the writ. The London office! Do you know what that means? Do you know how important that makes it? Do you know what a fucking *disaster* it'll be if I have to turn round and say, Oh, sorry, the clients have changed their minds?' He stopped, panting slightly; Louise and Barnaby exchanged astonished glances.

'I should have known,' he continued in slightly more controlled tones, 'you fucking well haven't got a clue, have you? Either of you. Bloody peasants.'

There was a thunderous rasping as Barnaby pushed the kitchen table forward by about three feet. His face was bright red and he was breathing heavily.

'That's enough!' he bellowed. 'That's enough! Now get out, and don't ever dare to talk to my wife like that again, or I'll kill you!' He stood up, a big rough giant. Cassian raised an eyebrow.

'Of course,' he said, 'now we move on to physical threats; the last bastion of the cerebrally challenged.'

'Shut up!' commanded Barnaby.

'Oh reall . . .' began Cassian, but he broke off into a yelp as Barnaby's huge hand grasped his shirt by the neck.

'Now,' said Barnaby, breathing heavily, 'either you go, or I throw you very hard against that door. And then I pick you up and throw you again.'

'Louise!' squawked Cassian. 'Tell him to stop! This is assault. I'm warning you,' he said furiously to Barnaby.

'Take me to court,' said Barnaby, throwing him back down into his chair. 'See if I care.'

Cassian smoothed his hair down with trembling hands and straightened his tie.

'Louise . . .' he began. But she cut him off with a raised hand.

'If I were you, Cassian,' she said gently, 'I'd go. Now.' Her mouth twisted into an unwilling grin. 'You don't know what these peasants are like when they get really angry.'

Cassian stood up. He looked from Louise to Barnaby and back to Louise again; his face white; his features distorted with anger.

'You'll be hearing from me,' he said curtly and picked up his briefcase.

'Goodbye, Cassian,' said Louise.

'Oh, fuck off,' said Cassian.

Louise and Barnaby listened as he walked furiously out of the house, slammed the door, and started up his car. Then, as the sound died away, they looked at each other.

'Well,' said Louise, 'I wonder if he got the message.'

Chapter Twenty

The next morning Meredith woke at seven o'clock. She looked at the clock on her bedside table, cursed, and flopped back onto her pillows. The night before she had taken a herbal sleeping draught, to give herself the chance of a good night's rest. But now, although her body felt heavy and sluggish, her mind was racing, as alert as ever. Impossible to go back to sleep. She turned over angrily, and tried to remember a Buddhist chant she had successfully used before in moments of anxiety. But even as the words formed in her mind, she was remembering, with a pang, Hugh's pale face and frail form as they'd led him out of the hospital the evening before.

Before leaving, she'd spoken with Hugh's consultant, trying desperately – irrationally – to get a promise out of him that this wasn't going to happen again. But instead of giving her the blank reassurances she craved, the consultant had taken the moment as an opportunity to explain to her exactly what changes Hugh must make to his lifestyle, exactly what state his arteries were in, and exactly what all the family could do to help. He'd pressed on her a cheerful educational poster depicting food groups in bold cartoon characters, and suggested that she put it up on the fridge. She'd stared back at him, wondering how he could be so obtuse. It's not the fucking food! she'd wanted to shout. It's the fucking court case!

They'd had a cautious evening at home, trying to act normally. Ursula had carefully prepared supper out of a recipe book given to her at the hospital, and they had all exclaimed with forced cheerfulness over the poached salmon without hollandaise sauce and raspberries sprinkled with orange juice instead of cream. Hugh had automatically reached for a bottle of wine, then stopped, hand still outstretched. And Meredith had wanted to weep. Not because of the wine, or the hollandaise sauce, but because, behind the jollity, behind the united pretence that they all suddenly felt like drinking lemon squash instead, loomed an unspoken fear, an unforgettable, permanent shadow.

Abruptly, she pushed back the covers and got out of bed. From behind the curtain were peeping tiny dazzling rays of light; the promise of another bright day. She pushed up her window and breathed in the fresh air; still summery, still mild, but with a hint of autumnal bite. Meredith didn't know whether this made her feel sad or relieved.

'What a fucking awful summer,' she said aloud. She leaned out and squinted down at the silent, dewy, glistening grass. She took a few deep breaths, closed her eyes and felt the breeze on her face, and suddenly the heavy torpor seemed to leave her legs. She turned back into the room and began quickly to get dressed. Before breakfast; before the beginning of the day and the return to real life, she would go for a walk. A long, fresh, cleansing walk.

At half-past eight the phone in Louise's bedroom rang. She picked up the receiver, listened for a few seconds, then said, firmly, 'I don't think so, Cassian. I think we both know it's a bit late for that.'

She listened for a few more moments, then, with deliberate care, she replaced the receiver. She lay back and stretched luxuriously.

'That's the first time I've ever done that,' she said. 'Cut

someone off mid-flow. I have to say, it's a wonderful feeling.'

'What did he want?' said Barnaby sleepily.

'My body,' said Louise.

There was a rumpling sound from next to her, and Barnaby's head appeared from under the duvet, tousled and still half asleep.

'Are you serious?' he said.

'No,' she said, in regretful tones, 'I don't think so. He was just generally grovelling. I think he was hoping we'd changed our minds about the case.'

Barnaby regarded her for a moment, then flopped heavily back down onto his pillow with a thump that made the whole mattress quiver.

'I don't understand you,' he said. 'I thought you were in love with him.'

'I know,' said Louise. 'I thought I was, too.' She sighed. 'I realized something was wrong when we started talking about calling off the case. I found myself thinking that it would probably mean the end for me and Cassian, and instead of feeling upset, I felt . . . relieved, more than anything else.' She shrugged. 'I don't really understand it.'

'Well, it doesn't matter,' said Barnaby contentedly. 'What matters is that we're back together again.'

'Are we?' said Louise sharply.

'Aren't we?' Barnaby sat up abruptly and looked at Louise with a puzzled frown. 'I mean, after last night, and . . . and everything . . .' He gestured vaguely around.

'I know,' said Louise patiently. She sighed. 'Look, Barnaby, I'm not saying we can't get back together, but you mustn't think that just because Cassian's out of the picture, everything's suddenly rosy. We had problems way before he came on the scene.' She pushed back her hair and pulled her knees up under the duvet. 'The thing you've got to get straight', she said deliberately, 'is that I wasn't having an affair with Cassian behind your

289

back. I wasn't. I used to go and see him, yes. But we used to talk, that was all.' In spite of herself, she could feel a note of resentment creeping into her voice. 'When I tried to tell you, you wouldn't listen. You just listened to your own suspicions and the village gossip.'

'Well, you shouldn't even have been talking to him,' said Barnaby gruffly. 'The creep.'

'Barnaby!' exclaimed Louise angrily. 'You still don't get it! I'm allowed to see and talk to whoever I like, whether they're a creep or not. God, if you still don't understand that . . .'

'I do,' said Barnaby hastily. 'I do understand it.'

'Do you?' said Louise.

There was silence in the little room.

'I think', said Louise eventually, 'that it would be a good idea for me to take the girls to London next week as planned. We'll go on our own, and have a good holiday, and then we'll come back and . . .' She looked at Barnaby. 'And then we can talk.'

'Yes,' said Barnaby seriously. 'Good idea.'

'I really need to get away,' said Louise, 'and I think the girls could do with a change of scene too.'

'Yes,' said Barnaby again. 'Good idea.' There was a pause. 'Louise?'

Louise raised her eyes. Barnaby was looking yearningly at her.

'I don't suppose I could come with you?' he said. 'To London?'

'Oh, Barnaby,' said Louise. She began to laugh. 'But you hate London.'

'I know I do,' said Barnaby, 'but I'd like it if I went with you. I could take the girls to the zoo, and show them Big Ben, while you go shopping in Harrods. It'd be great. What do you think?' He looked at her eagerly, a huge entreating smile on his face. Louise couldn't help smiling back.

'Maybe,' she said at last. 'Maybe.'

Meredith walked quickly, feeling the morning air filling her lungs and a pink tingling glow spread over her cheeks. The roads were empty of cars this early on a Saturday morning; most people seemed to still be in bed.

Without really noticing, she headed towards the church. The graveyard was silent and the headstones damp with an early morning moisture. She sat down on the single wooden bench, closed her eyes and tilted her face towards the gradually warming sun. She waited for a calming relief to spread through her body; for the natural power of the sun's rays to channel her energies in a positive direction; for her mind to achieve a balanced position of acceptance. But when, a few minutes later, she opened her eyes again, nothing was different. Unless she concentrated very hard, she could not rid her mind of all her background whining worries – about Hugh, about Ursula, about the case, and shrieking loudly above the rest, her bitter, fruitless, constant feeling of anger.

Her mind flicked to Simon, and away again. She had been thinking of Simon more and more over the last few weeks; on the night of Hugh's heart attack she had dreamed a long and happy dream about him, and had awoken to the realization that he was dead with a shock that almost reduced her to tears. But in her waking moments she was well used to fielding emotions about Simon. Now, in an automatic reaction, she got to her feet and thrust her hands in her pockets. It was way past nine o'clock; time to head home.

'Of course', said Louise, 'the first thing we must do is tell Hugh and Ursula.'

Barnaby stopped in the middle of buttoning up his shirt and stared at her.

'My God,' he said, 'I hadn't even thought of that; I

291

hadn't even thought what it'll mean to them.' He looked down sheepishly. 'All I've been thinking about is us.'

'Yes, well,' said Louise, 'that's important too.' She gave him a little smile. 'But I think we ought to tell them as soon as possible, don't you? We ought to go round there this morning.'

'Or phone them, maybe?'

'No,' said Louise decisively. 'We've got to tell them face to face. They deserve it.'

'OK,' said Barnaby. He looked at his watch. 'Let's go round there straight away,' he said enthusiastically.

'Now? Before breakfast?'

'Why not?' said Barnaby. 'Good news can't wait for breakfast.'

'What if they're not up yet?'

'They will be,' said Barnaby confidently, 'and if they aren't, we'll wait.'

'Well . . . all right then,' said Louise. 'All right. Just let me get dressed.'

She reached behind her neck to fasten her dress and frowned, as she missed the button.

'I'll do it,' said Barnaby at once. 'Let me.' He bounded over, seized the fabric from out of her hand, and attempted to fasten it.

'Damn,' he said, breathing heavily, and grasping the fabric harder with his huge hands. 'It's tiny.'

Louise automatically opened her mouth to say, Oh, for heaven's sake, Barnaby, give it here, I'll do it. Then, thinking again, she closed it, and found herself gazing silently, with a fondness bordering on love, at his serious frowning reflection in the mirror.

On the way home, Meredith took a different route from the way she'd come. She was walking briskly along, her mind full of abstract floating thoughts, and just beginning to feel hungry, when something ahead of her made her stop in her tracks, take a sharp inward breath, and clench her fists inside her pockets.

There, unmistakably, in front of her, was Alexis's car – smooth, green, and parked at a skewed angle to the road, carelessly, as though its owner had been thinking of other things as he parked it.

Before she could stop them, Meredith's eyes moved from the car to the wrought-iron gate swinging casually open nearby, to the charming orchard garden and, only a few yards away, the front door of a pretty little cottage, stout and thick and shut tight against the rest of the world.

Daisy Phillips's cottage. Behind that cosy front door, in some bloody cosy little bed, Alexis lay with Daisy Phillips, with a dumb teenager young enough to be his daughter.

Meredith didn't quite understand her own reaction to this affair. When Frances had first told her about it, she'd been astounded at her own nonchalant attitude. 'Damn!' she'd said carelessly, swigging back her vodka. 'Looks like I missed the boat.' And ever since then she'd tried to maintain a semblance of cool indifference. She even thought she'd managed to fool herself. But now, seeing Alexis's car parked so casually, so, so . . . *familiarly*, outside Daisy's cottage – as though that was where it belonged – Meredith began to feel a raw hot feeling of hurt rising through her. Her cool, calm, sophisticated veneer felt as though it were being melted in patches, and her breaths began to come more quickly. Why did he choose Daisy? she found herself thinking, like an aggrieved five-year-old. Why didn't he choose me? She felt suddenly exposed, vulnerable and, un-characteristically, close to bursting into tears.

'I've had enough,' she muttered aloud, walking past Alexis's car, looking away and trying to ignore the painful pangs below her ribs. 'I've just about had enough.'

As she entered the drive of Devenish House, her stride

293

slowed down. She felt a sudden dread of seeing Hugh and Ursula; of having to summon up a smile and a cheery greeting. She took a few deep breaths and tried to focus her thoughts on something positive, but her mind batted relentlessly between disturbing images of Hugh, Alexis and Simon. Emotions surfaced in uneven, uncontrollable waves; there was no room for anything else.

She couldn't face Hugh and Ursula while she was in this state; couldn't face seeing anybody. For a while she stood completely still on the gravel of the drive, trying not to panic, trying to work out what to do, where to go. The friendly face of Frances Mold flashed through her mind, and for a moment she considered taking refuge in the unquestioning vicarage. Then she remembered that it was Saturday morning. Frances would be in church, busy with the flower ladies.

An unfamiliar, unwelcome feeling of loneliness began to spread through her. Where was her self-sufficiency? she asked herself furiously. Where was her independence? Where was her sense of humour? She bit her lip and pushed her hand through her hair, and wondered whether she should simply turn round and go for another long walk. And then the answer came to her: she would go to her studio and paint. She would paint until she had worked out of her system the anxiety, the hurt, the grief. She would channel the destructive feelings pounding round her body into something positive. She would make use of the moment.

Quickly she headed for the back of the house and towards her studio, then she remembered she didn't have the keys on her. An uncharacteristic white-hot annoyance flashed through her body.

'Fuck,' she said aloud, and quietly opened the conservatory door. She would quickly get them from her bedroom and hope that no-one heard her.

But as she moved silently through the conservatory, she heard voices from the hall. She paused, mid-stride, and wondered whether to back out again, into the garden, but that would leave her stranded. So, taking a deep breath, she pushed unwillingly forward into the hall.

What she saw made her stop still and draw in breath sharply. There, by the door, talking to Ursula, were Barnaby and Louise Kember.

Meredith felt herself recoil slightly and her heart begin to beat more quickly, in anticipation of a confrontation. She glanced quickly at Ursula, but Ursula looked unperturbed. She was standing near the stairs, dressed in her pretty blue and white dressing-gown, actually smiling up at Barnaby. As Meredith came in, she turned and beamed at her.

'Meredith, dear,' she said. 'I'm so glad you're back! The Kembers have come here with some wonderful news.'

Meredith stared blankly at Ursula. Dimly she registered that Louise and Barnaby were holding hands.

'They're calling off the case,' said Ursula. 'They've decided not to go to court after all. Isn't that marvellous?'

Louise smiled hesitantly at Meredith, who looked back numbly. Her throat felt constricted; she was unable to speak.

'We suddenly realized that we just couldn't go through with it,' said Louise, in a rush. 'For . . . for several reasons. We're pulling out completely. And we just wanted to say how sorry we are, for all the trouble it's caused, and everything. I hope you can forgive us.'

She smiled again at Meredith.

'Well, dear, isn't that lovely?' said Ursula, beaming at Meredith. 'Hugh will be so pleased.'

Meredith stared back at her with a white, taut face. All the emotions that had been pounding separately

295

through her body seemed to be coming together in one huge rolling tidal wave of anger.

'Lovely?' she managed to whisper. 'You're saying this is lovely?'

She stared at Ursula's smiling face for a few seconds, trying desperately to keep on top of it, trying to keep her head. But then, suddenly, the wave broke, and through her body surged a terrifying fury which she couldn't begin to control.

'You've ruined our lives!' she screamed, rounding on Louise and Barnaby like a killer tigress. 'You've ruined our lives, and you have the nerve to come here, like Mr and Mrs fucking Happy Couple, and expect to be forgiven! Well, it's too late! You should have thought of that before you decided to take everything away from us. You should have thought of that before you gave Hugh a heart attack!'

She swooped on Louise, so that their two faces were only inches apart.

'I will *never* forgive you', she said savagely, 'for what you did to Hugh. Do you think you can take that away by saying sorry? Do you?' Her voice rose to a scream. 'Because if you do, you're wrong. Our lives will never be the same again, and it's your fault! It's your . . . your greed which did it all. You don't ever deserve to be forgiven. Ever!'

Louise took a step backwards. Her face was white and trembling and there were unshed tears in her eyes.

'Meredith!' said Ursula in an almost sharp voice. 'You don't know what you're saying, dear.'

'Don't defend them, Ursula!' shrieked Meredith. 'Don't let them get away with it that easily!'

'It's not easy!' cried Louise suddenly. 'OK, we made a mistake, and we're sorry, but we haven't had it easy!'

'We'll do anything we can to make up,' said Barnaby gruffly. 'We'll pay your legal fees, and we'll visit Hugh . . .'

'We don't want your fucking money, and we don't want you in this house!' Meredith's voice lashed across the hall.

'Meredith!' said Ursula. 'You really mustn't talk like this! I'm sorry,' she said quietly to Louise. 'She was very upset by Hugh . . .'

'Don't apologize for me!' yelled Meredith. And suddenly, to everyone's horror, she burst into huge, pent-up, shuddering sobs. Barnaby caught Louise's eye. She looked aghast.

'Don't apologize for me!' Meredith shouted again, furiously wiping her eyes. 'If I'm embarrassing you, Ursula, then I'll go, but I'm not going to forgive them. Not now, not ever.'

And abruptly, without looking any of them in the face, she turned, and half walked, half ran up the stairs. As she rounded the corner of the landing, she gave another huge sob.

Barnaby relaxed his grip on Louise's hand. He looked shaken.

'I'm so sorry,' he began in a low trembling voice. Ursula looked up at him.

'Yes,' she said simply. 'Yes, so am I.'

'I didn't realize', he said, 'how destructive this case was. I didn't realize how much damage we were causing.' He gazed entreatingly at Ursula. 'I just don't know what we can do to make up,' he muttered in a hopeless voice. 'I just don't know. I just wish we could start again. I just wish . . .'

He broke off, and there was a long miserable pause.

'We ought to go,' said Barnaby eventually, 'we've disturbed your morning enough.' He took Louise's hand. 'We'll be in touch.'

'No, don't go yet,' said Ursula. She drew her dressing-gown more closely around her and looked thoughtfully at them both. 'We all need some fresh air, I think. Let's go outside.'

* * *

The morning air felt clean and pure as they stepped out of the warm dank conservatory. As they walked, Barnaby took several deep breaths, then glanced at Louise; she still looked pale and shocked, and seemed unable to return his tentative smile. Through his head rang Meredith's bitter screams, and he winced. Then his eyes swivelled over to Ursula; her face was collected, composed, almost serene.

Suddenly, with a shock, Barnaby realized where she was heading.

'Here we are,' said Ursula softly. Louise and Barnaby looked at each other. In front of them, glistening bright blue in the pale sunshine, was the swimming-pool.

They watched numbly as Ursula sat down by the water's edge, and obediently did the same when she gestured to the ground next to her. Louise stared ahead blankly, shrinking at first from the gleaming silent pool, from the memories and the horror and the danger. But the water had a strange compelling power. After a few minutes, without quite meaning to, she found herself slipping off her shoes and, one by one, very slowly, lowering her feet into the pool. The clean chilling water rose gradually up her calves until her legs were knee-deep; vague mushroomy limbs floating in the blueness.

'I always knew', said Ursula in a soft, almost dreamy voice, 'that you would decide against going to court in the end. I knew it. I tried to tell them,' she smiled at Louise, 'but no-one would listen to me.'

'We didn't know ourselves until last night,' said Louise.

'I knew it,' repeated Ursula gently. She lowered a hand into the water and trailed it along the shiny surface. 'I knew you would come round, eventually.' She looked at Louise with a faintly complacent expression.

'It was my letter, wasn't it?'

'What?' said Louise, startled.

'My letter,' said Ursula happily. 'I was so sure that when you read it – when you understood – you would change your mind.' She beamed at Louise. 'Wasn't I right?'

Louise looked at Ursula's innocent face. Into her mind came a vision of pale mauve paper covered in foolish, incriminating, loopy writing, now filed away as evidence in one of Cassian's files. She bit her lip.

'Well,' she said eventually, not looking at Barnaby, 'I suppose it did help, yes. In a way.'

'I knew it would,' said Ursula. She sighed contentedly and smiled at Louise. 'And you were never really in love with that young man, were you?'

Louise glanced at Barnaby. She felt herself turn pink.

'Well,' she said, 'no, not really.'

'There,' said Ursula in a satisfied voice, 'I knew that, too.'

Louise leaned back on her elbows, closed her eyes, and felt the water lapping gently, soothingly, against her legs. They floated aimlessly, weightlessly, in the cool supporting depths; she felt almost as though she might float off with them. Without thinking, she said, 'I must take the girls swimming.'

She broke off abruptly. A tiny tension ran through the silence like a silvery thread.

'Before the end of the summer,' she carried on bravely. 'Just so that . . .' She paused uncertainly. 'So that they don't . . .' She tailed away and bit her lip. A breeze rustled the leaves in the trees nearby and she felt goose bumps rising on her bare arms.

'I think', said Ursula at last, 'that's a very good idea.' There was a pause, then she added in hopeful, hesitant tones, 'Is it true . . . is it really true that Katie is going back to school?'

'Yes,' said Louise eventually. 'Yes, it is. She's going

to start off part-time and see how she does. She's . . . she's much better.'

'Oh, I'm so glad,' said Ursula in a voice that trembled slightly. 'I'm so, so glad. We all hoped and prayed so much . . .'

For a long while nobody said anything. Then Barnaby asked in a hoarse voice, 'How's Hugh?'

'He's much better, too,' said Ursula. 'Much better.' She smiled at Barnaby. 'Everything's much better now.'

Louise's lips quivered and she began to cry softly. Tears streamed like warm raindrops down her face.

'I'm so sorry,' she said hopelessly. 'I don't know what else to say to you. I'm so sorry.'

'Don't,' said Ursula gently. 'Don't cry . . . and don't be sorry.' She reached over and put a warm papery hand on Louise's. 'Be glad,' she said. 'Be glad that the worst is over now. For all of us, the worst is over.'

Louise gave a huge shuddering sigh, and gratefully clasped Ursula's hand. She looked up at Barnaby and gave him a hesitant, tearful smile. And the three of them sat together in a gentle silence, staring ahead, watching the deep blue water glinting in the sunshine.

THE END

THE TENNIS PARTY

For my parents,
David and Patricia Townley

I would like to thank Araminta Whitley,
Sally Gaminara and Diane Pearson,
and above all,
Henry Wickham

Chapter One

It was the sort of warm, scented evening that Caroline Chance associated with holidays in Greece; with glasses of ouzo and flirtatious waiters and the feel of cool cotton against burnt shoulders. Except that the sweet smell wafting through the air was not olive groves, but freshly mown English grass. And the sound in the distance was not the sea, but Georgina's riding instructor, intoning – always with the same monotonous inflection – 'Trot *on*. Trot *on*.'

Caroline grimaced and resumed painting her toe-nails. She didn't object to her daughter's passion for riding – but neither did she comprehend it. The moment they had moved to Bindon from Seymour Road, Georgina had started clamouring for a pony. And, of course, Patrick had insisted she should be given one.

In fact, Caroline had grown quite fond of the first pony. It was a sweet little thing, with a shaggy mane and a docile manner. Caroline had sometimes gone to look at it when no-one was about and had taken to feeding it Ferrero Rocher chocolates. But this latest creature was a monster – a huge great black thing that looked quite wild. At eleven, Georgina was tall and strong, but Caroline couldn't understand how she could even get onto the thing, let alone ride it and go over jumps.

She finished painting her right foot and took a slug of white wine. Her left foot was dry, and she lifted it up to admire the pearly colour in the evening light. She was sitting on the wide terrace outside the main drawing-room of the house. The White House had been built – rather stupidly, Caroline felt, given the

9

English climate – as a suntrap. The stark white walls reflected the sun into the central courtyard, and the main rooms faced south. A vine bearing rather bitter grapes had been persuaded to creep along the wall above Caroline's head; and several exotic plants were brought out of the greenhouse every summer to adorn the terrace. But it was still bloody freezing England. There wasn't much they could do about that.

Today, though, she had to concede, had been about as perfect as it could get. Translucent blue sky; scorching sun; not a gust of wind. She had spent most of the day getting ready for tomorrow, but luckily the tasks she had allotted herself – arranging flowers, preparing vegetables, waxing her legs – were the sort of thing that could be done outside. The main dishes – vegetable terrine for lunch; seafood tartlets for dinner – had arrived from the caterers that morning, and Mrs Finch had already decanted them onto serving plates. She had raised an eyebrow – *couldn't you even bring yourself to cook for eight people?* – but Caroline was used to Mrs Finch's upwardly mobile eyebrows and ignored them. For Christ's sake, she thought, pouring herself another glass of wine, what was the point of having money and not spending it?

The riding lesson was over and Georgina came bounding across the lawn, long blond rivers of recently plaited hair streaming down her back.

'Mummy,' she called, 'Dawn said my rising trot was more controlled than it's ever been! She said if I ride like that in the East Silchester gymkhana ...' She looked impressively at Caroline. Then what? thought Caroline. Then you'll win? Then you'd better give up? She had no idea whether a rising trot was supposed to be controlled or utterly abandoned. '*And* my jumping's getting better,' added Georgina.

'Oh good, darling,' said Caroline. Her voice was husky, roughened by cigarettes and, lately, a bottle of white wine nearly every evening.

'Nail varnish,' said Georgina. 'Can I put some on?'

'Not on those filthy nails,' said Caroline. 'You need a bath.'

'Can I when I've had my bath?'

'Maybe. If I have time.'

'I want bright pink.'

'I haven't got any bright pink,' said Caroline, wrinkling her nose. 'You can have this pretty pale pink or red.'

'Red, urggh.' Georgina pulled a face. Then she jumped up onto the terrace and swung on the back of Caroline's beechwood chair. 'Who's coming tomorrow?'

'You know who's coming,' said Caroline, carefully applying a second coat to her left foot.

'Nicola's coming, isn't she?'

'Mmm.'

'Is she better yet?'

'Getting better.'

'Shall I take her riding? Is she allowed?'

'You'll have to ask Annie. I don't see why not. But make sure you take Toby, too.'

'He's too little to go on Arabia.'

'All right, then, he can watch.'

'Can I be in the tennis tournament?'

'No.'

'Can I wear my tennis skirt?'

'If you want to.'

'Can I be ballgirl?'

'You can if you want,' said Caroline, 'but you'll get bored.'

'No I won't,' said Georgina. 'I know how to do it. You roll the balls along the line and then you hold them up and throw them to the people playing. Poppy Wharton's cousin was a ballgirl in Wimbledon, and she saw Navratilova. I can serve overhead, too.'

She threw up an imaginary ball and took a swipe at it, bumping into Caroline's chair as she did so. The nail varnish brush smudged.

11

'Fuck,' said Caroline without rancour.

'No-one's going to see your feet, anyway,' said Georgina. 'Will you put some on my fingers?'

'After your bath. You need clean nails. Yours are all horsy.' But Georgina had lost interest and was doing a handspring on the lawn. Caroline, who had once trained as a gymnast herself, looked up. They didn't teach them to finish off properly any more, she thought; to land neatly and present to the judges with a pretty smile. At Georgina's boarding-school, no-one took gymnastics seriously. They did it to strengthen the girls for more important pursuits – netball, lacrosse, and always the horses. None of them seemed interested in competitions, show routines, shiny leotards and ribbons – the stuff of which Caroline's childhood had been made.

Patrick Chance, walking up to the house from the tennis court, saw his beautiful, agile daughter turning cartwheels against the setting sun, and stopped for a moment, taking in her effortless grace, her vitality and energy. Was every father as sentimental as he? He found it difficult, talking to other parents, to emulate their easy nonchalance. Whereas they shrugged off their children's achievements, he could not resist cataloguing Georgina's; could never resist breaking off in conversation to point out that his daughter had just gone into the ring, yes, competing in the under four-teens, even though she was only just eleven. When the other parents nodded, smiling, and turned back to their chatter, his heart would beat with suppressed rage and incomprehension. But look at her! he always wanted to cry. Just look at her! She plays the piano, too, he would say, desperate to win back their attention. Coming on very well, her teacher says. We thought we might try her on the flute.

Caroline, he noticed, had turned her attention back to her nail polish. It still pained him that she didn't

12

share his fervent appreciation of Georgina – and refused to join in when he began to eulogize about her, even when they were together on their own. Particularly because, to be fair, there was a lot more in Georgina that Caroline could claim as her own than he could. Mother and daughter shared their blond hair, their athletic frames, their tendency to burst into raucous laughter. But perhaps that was why Caroline was so blasé about Georgina. She was used to beauty, physical accomplishment and popularity. Whereas Patrick, short, stumpy and short-sighted, was not.

He continued walking towards the house and Georgina started walking towards him in a crab.

'Hello, Daddy,' she panted, and collapsed on the ground.

'Hello, kitten,' he said. 'Good riding lesson?'

'Brilliant.' He looked up at Caroline.

'Everything under control for tomorrow?'

'The food's on the plates, if that's what you mean,' said Caroline. 'And Mrs Finch went over the bedrooms this morning.'

'Who's next door to me?' demanded Georgina.

'The little Mobyn twins and that nanny girl. What's her name?'

'Martina I think,' said Patrick. 'She's German. Or Austrian, or something.' Georgina wrinkled her nose.

'Why couldn't it be Nicola and Toby?'

'Ask Daddy,' said Caroline acerbically. 'He insisted that Charles and Cressida go in the big spare room, so the twins have to go in the one next to you. Cressida', she enunciated the word with deliberate care, 'likes having them near by.'

'Why couldn't they all go down the passage?' suggested Georgina. 'And Annie and Stephen go in the big spare room and Nicola and Toby next to me?'

'Daddy wants Charles and Cressida to have the big room,' said Caroline, 'because they're very rich, and he doesn't want them to sneer at us.' Patrick flushed.

'Now that's not true at all. I just thought it would be nice for them to have that room. Since they haven't been here before.'

'They probably never will be here, either,' said Caroline briskly. 'What's the betting they phone and cancel tomorrow morning?'

'They can't do that,' said Patrick, too quickly, he realized.

Caroline raised suspicious eyes. 'Why the hell not? That's what they usually do. How long have we been here? Nearly three years. And they've always been too busy to make it to anything.'

'Cressida is a shithead,' said Georgina. Caroline gave a cackle of laughter. Patrick stared at Georgina.

'Where on earth did you learn language like that?'

'Don't be so boring,' said Caroline. 'Why do you think Cressida's a shithead, sweetie? You hardly know her.'

'I liked Ella,' said Georgina mulishly.

'You can't possibly remember Ella,' said Caroline.

'I do,' said Georgina. 'She was really nice, she used to sing me songs. And Charles used to play the guitar.' Patrick looked admiringly at her.

'What a memory! You must have been only about six then.'

'I liked Seymour Road,' said Georgina simply. 'I wish we still lived there.' Caroline gave another cackle of laughter.

'There you are, Patrick, so much for the country life!' Her blue eyes held his mockingly for a moment, and he stared back with an impotent rage. Her eyes seemed to reflect his own failures and worries back at him, reminding him in a tacit instant of the disappointments and disillusionments of the last thirteen years.

'I must go and draw up the chart for tomorrow,' he said abruptly. For Georgina's sake more than his own he walked onto the terrace and kissed his wife on the mouth. She tasted, as she had done when he

14

first kissed her behind one of the stands at the *Daily Telegraph* personal finance exhibition, of lipstick, cigarettes and alcohol.

'I'll be eighth seed if you like,' she said, when his head came up again. 'I don't rate myself very highly at tennis.'

'It's doubles,' he said, irritation rising.

'Mixed doubles,' said Georgina, who was once again in a crab position. 'I could play with Toby, and Nicola could play with one of the twins. And the other twin could play with the nanny. How about that, Daddy?'

But he had gone.

As Patrick entered his study, he felt rather deflated. Caroline's last dig about the country life had touched an unexpected sore spot. Life at Bindon had not turned out quite as he had wanted, and he, too, often felt a secret nostalgia for the days at Seymour Road. He had decided that they should move into the country really for Georgina's sake. All the smart little girls that he met at her school seemed to live in villages, in old rectories and farmhouses, with dogs and horses and sheep. None of them lived in red-brick villas in the suburbs of Silchester.

So they had sold 24 Seymour Road, moved to Bindon and bought Georgina a pony. Here, Patrick had felt, they would move into a new level of existence. His mind had been filled, in the few weeks before the move, with images of large houses with sweeping drives, aristocratic girls leading horses out of loose boxes, croquet on the lawn, young boys called Henry and Hugo for Georgina to grow up with.

But Bindon wasn't like that. Hardly any of the families living in the village were what Patrick thought of as 'county'. Many had moved to Bindon out of Silchester, or even London, attracted by the quick rail link to Waterloo. They made Patrick shudder, with

15

their whining London voices, so different from Georgina's clipped schoolgirl tones. Besides, they tended to keep to themselves, relying for their social life on parties of friends down from London – and, when those dried up, often moving back to London themselves. The previous owners of The White House had sold to move back to Battersea, bored with a village life that they hadn't even tried.

For there was a village community of sorts in Bindon. Patrick and Caroline attended church every other Sunday, patronized the village fête, and were on amiable terms with the farmer whose land bordered their own. They knew the old lady whose family had once owned the manor house – and who now lived in a nearby cottage. They knew the fluttery pair of sisters whose brother had been the vicar of Bindon before he died. They knew the rather eccentric Taylors, who had lived in Bindon for generations – and probably married each other for generations, Caroline liked to add. But nowhere had Patrick found the smart, sociable, double-barrelled, Country Life families for which he was looking.

The trouble with Silchester, he had heard another parent at Georgina's school saying, was that it had turned into another London suburb – full of bloody commuters. Patrick, who himself commuted to London, was not offended by this remark. He knew he wasn't the proper thing – neither was Caroline. But Georgina could and would be, if only she could mix with the right people. He was now looking seriously at moving further into the country – Dorset, Wiltshire, Somerset, perhaps. He had visions of a big Georgian house; perhaps ten or twenty acres. If this year went well, perhaps they could start looking.

If this year went well.

Patrick's eye fell on his desk; on the paperwork he'd prepared for tomorrow. He would ask Charles casually into the study after lunch. No hassle, just an agreeable

16

piece of business between friends. Besides, hassling wasn't Patrick's style. Never had been. Even when he'd been a cold-call salesman, he'd always retreated gracefully at the first sign of annoyance, playing it cool and courteous. Always courteous. Sometimes they were intrigued; sometimes he even found the punters phoning *him* back. When he sensed he'd got their interest, he would sometimes switch on the intimate, enthusiastic, I'm-doing-this-for-you-as-a-friend routine. But not if they were sophisticated investors – or, most tricky of all, thought they were sophisticated. Then it would be the smooth, I'm-not-going-to-insult-your-intelligence approach. Selling's all about judging the client, he thought. There's a way into anyone's pocket.

He sat down, put the folder marked 'Charles' to one side, and began carefully drawing out the chart for the tournament. But a doubt kept swimming around in his mind. Charles and Cressida had always managed to cancel when they'd been invited to Bindon before – an ill child; a recalcitrant nanny; once, less believably, two cars that wouldn't start. And although he'd got Charles' absolute assurance that they would be attending the party tomorrow, the very thought that they might somehow pull out caused distress signals to go shooting down Patrick's spine. If they didn't meet tomorrow, there would probably be no chance of seeing Charles for several months.

He sat back in his chair, staring blindly at the bookcase. Was it worth phoning Charles and Cressida to check that they were coming? He rehearsed the call in his mind. A relaxed, unpressured tone of voice – 'Charles, old boy, don't tell us you're going to blow us out again. Caroline will never forgive you.' Or, if he got Cressida, some domestic query that would please her – 'Just checking that the twins aren't allergic to goose-down quilts.' He reached for his Filofax and dialled the number, fingers trembling slightly.

'Allo?'

Shit. The German nanny. But perhaps Charles was there.

'Hello there, could I speak to Mr Mobyn?'

'He isn't here, I am sorry, is there a message please?'

Fuck.

'It's Patrick Chance here, just checking that you're all coming to the tennis party tomorrow?'

'Tennis party.' The girl sounded doubtful. Patrick held his breath. 'Yes, I think we leave here at ten o'clock.'

'Good, good.' Patrick tried not to sound too elated.

'What is the message please?'

'Oh, erm, no message,' said Patrick. 'Just checking you were all still coming.'

'Shall I ask Mr Mobyn to call you back?'

'Yes. Look, it really doesn't matter,' said Patrick. 'I'll see you all tomorrow, all right?'

'Is that the message?'

'Yes, all right.' Patrick gave in.

He replaced the receiver and closed his eyes. By this time tomorrow it should all be in the bag; signed, sealed and stamped. He picked up the folder and flicked through it a couple of times. But he was already completely familiar with its contents. He put it into his top drawer, closed and locked it. Then he spread out the sheet for the tournament chart and began to write the names of the four pairs across the top. Patrick and Caroline, he wrote. Stephen and Annie. Don and Valerie. Charles and Cressida.

Charles and Cressida Mobyn were attending a drinks party at the house of Sir Benjamin Sutcliffe, before a charity performance of the *Messiah* in Silchester Cathedral. They mingled, holding glasses of Kir Royale, with the most eminent residents of Silchester – many of whom lived, like they did, in the Cathedral Close – together with a sprinkling of celebrities from around the area and even a few from London. Sir

Benjamin's drawing-room was long and high ceil-inged, with enormous unshuttered windows looking directly onto the floodlit Cathedral, and most of the guests were turned unconsciously towards the view, looking up every so often as though to check it was still there.

Cressida was one of the few guests present with her back towards the Cathedral. Tall, elegant and queenly, she seemed oblivious of its towering presence; even though she was universally acknowledged as one of the most tireless campaigners for the West Tower Fund. Indeed, her name was listed on the back of tonight's concert programme as one of the hardwork-ing committee members who had made it all possible.

She was talking now to the well-loved radio pre-senter who would be making a speech at the beginning of the concert. The radio presenter was gesturing flamboyantly at the splendid sight of the Cathedral, and Cressida, looking slightly taken aback, turned to look at it. Almost immediately, she turned back and smiled politely at the presenter. She had, after all, seen the Cathedral nearly every day for the last four years. She did, after all, live opposite it.

Charles, watching her from the other side of the room, could follow her thoughts as easily as his own. After all this time, the combination of her blinkered mind, her rangy blond beauty and her wealth still acted on him like an aphrodisiac. When Cressida, at the breakfast table, looked up from the newspaper and asked in all innocence what they meant by pri-vatization – or what on earth was wrong with insider dealing – he invariably felt an immediate surge of sexual energy. When she opened letters from her portfolio managers, frowned in slight puzzlement, and threw them down beside her plate, he didn't know whether to laugh or cry. Contrary to popular belief, he hadn't married Cressida for her money. He had mar-ried her for her complete indifference to it.

19

The only child of a successful toy manufacturer, Cressida had been raised by her aristocratic mother to live on a stream of chequebooks, shop accounts and credit cards – all to be paid off by Daddy. Even now, she invariably carried little cash. Her portfolio of investments, managed by a blue-blooded investment management firm in London, kept a steady flow of income into her Coutts account, and it was now Charles, not Daddy, who undertook the monthly reckoning up of bills.

The portfolio had diminished rather sharply in size over the last three years. A large chunk had gone on the house in the Cathedral Close, and another on buying out Angus, his former business partner. Charles was now the sole proprietor of the Silchester Print Centre, part gallery, part shop, dealing in prints of all descriptions. When he, Angus and Ella had run the Centre together, it had been different. They had put on lots of exhibitions of new young artists; had held printing workshops; had sponsored an annual print competition at the local technical and arts college. Now, running it more or less on his own, and engrossed with Cressida and the twins, Charles found himself veering towards the safer, more predictable end of the market. Old prints of Silchester Cathedral; prints of watercolours by Sargent; even posters of Van Gogh's *Sunflowers*. He defended this path to himself on financial grounds: the figures weren't as good as they had been; it was time to stop throwing money around on experimental projects and consolidate. When a small voice in his brain pointed out that the figures had only got worse *after* he'd given up on all the experimental projects, he ignored it.

He didn't regret leaving Ella. Occasionally he felt momentary stirrings of nostalgia for their cosy existence together in Seymour Road. But that hadn't been real life. This, mingling with important people in an important house in the Close, was real life. Discussing schools for the twins, instructing Coutts to open bank accounts for them, was real life. Being asked, as he had been today, to be godfather to the Hon. Sebastian Fairfax – that was real life.

Homely, red-brick Seymour Road had simply been a preparation for the real world. He remembered it fondly and still held affection for it – but it was the same affection he felt for his childhood rocking-horse when he outgrew it. As for Ella, he hardly ever gave her a thought.

The lights were on at 18 Seymour Road when Stephen Fairweather pushed his bike through the gate and padlocked it to the fence. The overgrown front garden smelt of fresh evening air and honeysuckle; as he pushed open the front door, this was combined with the aroma of frying mushrooms.

Downstairs, in the cosy basement kitchen, Annie was making mushroom omelette while Nicola sat at the kitchen table, carefully colouring in a map of Africa. Stephen stood at the door watching her for a moment. His heart contracted as he saw her clenching the pen, controlling the movements of her arm as best she could and frowning with impatience when a sudden jerk sent the green colour shooting outside the black outline of the map.

Colouring was good for her co-ordination, Nicola's physiotherapist said. Anything which used the damaged right side of her body should be encouraged. So the kitchen table was permanently heaped with colouring-books, beanbags for throwing and catching, skipping-ropes, crayons, cutting-out scissors, spillikins, rubber rings, rubber balls, jigsaws. Next to her map of Africa, Stephen saw Nicola's holiday project folder. 'Africa is a continent, not a country,' he read. 'Zambia and Zimbabwe are in Africa. The weather is very hot and there is not very much water. Sometimes the people starve.' Nicola had just been starting to

21

learn to write when she had had the stroke. Now her writing was spidery, with ill-formed letters ground hard into the page. He could read frustration in every jagged line.

She looked up then, and her thick spectacles gleamed with pleasure.

'Hello, Daddy!' Annie looked up from the frying-pan.

'Stephen! I didn't hear you come in!' He crossed the kitchen, ruffling Nicola's hair on the way, and gave Annie a kiss. Her cheeks were bright red from the heat and her dark hair had curled into tendrils around her face. 'Did you have a good day?' she asked.

Stephen closed his eyes and briefly reviewed the last twelve hours. An early train journey into London; an hour's wait at the department to see his supervisor for fifteen minutes; a sandwich at the British Library while waiting for the documents he'd requested; a few hours' good work; a late appearance at a seminar he'd promised to attend; back onto the train and home . . . He opened his eyes again.

'Yes, not bad,' he said.

Stephen was scheduled to finish his Ph.D. the next summer. At the rate he was going, it might just be possible – but still the thought of marshalling his assorted notes, ideas and theories into a coherent, substantial thesis filled him with a blank dread. Information that had seemed solid enough when he put together his thesis proposal, arguments that had seemed weighty and convincing, now seemed to have become gossamer thin, floating out of the grasp of his mind whenever he attempted to formulate them in academic English or even find a place for them in his introduction.

At the department, at seminars, even at home with Annie, he remained outwardly confident, assuming with a worrying ease the veneer of someone who knows he is going to succeed. He never articulated his secret fear – that he simply wasn't up to the rigours of such an ambitious project; that he should have stayed as he was: a humble schoolmaster with no pretensions to changing the face of fourteenth-century musical history.

He opened the fridge and cracked open a beer.

'Did I say I had a good day?' he said humorously. 'I must be mad. Mark wasn't free to see me when he'd said he would be, my papers took forever to arrive, and I was coerced into going to the mad Bulgarian woman's seminar.' Nicola giggled.

'Is she really mad?'

'Barking,' said Stephen solemnly. 'She entertained us for an hour with her views on the music that is all around us in nature.'

'Birds singing,' suggested Nicola.

'If only,' said Stephen. 'No, she was talking about trees, and snails' shells, and other completely soundless creatures.'

'Definitely mad,' said Annie. Stephen took a swig of beer.

'And did you all have a good day?' He looked around. 'Is Toby in bed?' Annie grinned.

'Yes, we wore him out with a walk on the downs. We took a picnic up there. It's been such wonderful weather.'

'And then we got everyone's clothes ready for tomorrow,' said Nicola. Stephen looked puzzled.

'What's tomorrow?'

'The tennis party, of course,' said Nicola in tones of amazement. 'You must know about that!'

'He does know,' said Annie. 'He's just pretending he's forgotten.' Stephen shook his head.

'No, this time I didn't have to pretend. It really had gone straight out of my mind.'

'Good thing Mummy remembered,' said Nicola, 'all our things needed washing.' Stephen grimaced.

'I didn't know I had any "things".'

'Old white shorts and an aertex,' said Annie briskly. 'And your racquet's just about OK. A string's missing, but . . .'

'But someone with my talent doesn't need the equipment,' said Stephen. 'I know. What about you?'

'Well actually,' said Annie, blushing slightly, 'Caroline very kindly said I could borrow some of her things. I think she realized . . .' She tailed off and her dark eyes met Stephen's green ones. For a moment, he felt a flash of anger. He knew Caroline's sympathetic, slightly too-loud remarks; her appraising looks; her complete incomprehension as to why anyone would chuck in a perfectly good teaching job to do more *studying*, for Christ's sake. He would be aware of her no doubt kindly meant gesture all day. But to say any of that to Annie would be unforgivable.

'Very good of her,' he said lightly. 'Pity Patrick's such a fat bugger. Otherwise I could have swanned around in his Lacoste. Perhaps I will anyway.' And, hoisting his rucksack onto his back, he went out of the kitchen and up the stairs to put away his books.

Chapter Two

Caroline woke up the next morning to the sensation of Patrick's warm breath on her neck. Keeping her eyes closed, she registered first the fact that a brightness, which must be the morning sun, was penetrating her eyelids with a red glare. Then she became aware that Patrick's stubby fingers were roaming over her body, under her nightdress, stirring her unwillingly into a pleasurable wakefulness. Still she kept her eyes closed, mimicking sleep, or at least inertia.

Even when Patrick pushed his way into her, with the unmistakable enthusiasm of the early-morning fuck, she managed to keep her face impassive. She focused her attention on what she was going to wear that day, then forced herself to wonder whether she ought to pluck her eyebrows, until suddenly, with an involuntary cry, her concentration was overcome and she surrendered to pleasure.

When Patrick had exhausted himself he collapsed beside her. 'You enjoyed that,' he said in an accusing tone. Caroline ignored him. 'Didn't you?' he persisted. She shrugged.

'I suppose so.'

'So why did you pretend you didn't?' He raised himself on one elbow and looked at her. Caroline smiled lazily. Her fingers were tingling and she felt benevolent.

'I don't know,' she said. 'Probably to piss you off.'

They lay in silence for a few minutes, then Patrick heaved himself up, avoiding Caroline's eye. He wrapped an unnecessary towel around himself and disappeared reproachfully into the *en suite* bathroom.

Caroline, staring after him, couldn't quite summon the energy to call after him. Once upon a time she would have followed him into the shower; kissed and made up under the powerful blast.

But this morning she felt indolent and heavy limbed. She could barely bring herself to scrabble for her cigarette case, let alone leap up for a repeat session. She stared up at the white ceiling, at the white muslin curtains, translucent with morning sunshine, and wondered vaguely why she could no longer bring herself to respond to Patrick's lovemaking. She certainly wasn't frigid, and he certainly hadn't lost his touch. Perhaps it was just that she didn't want him to feel pleased with himself.

She sighed, reached for her lighter and, without moving from the pile of broderie anglaise pillows, lit up a menthol cigarette, inhaling deeply and blowing clouds of smoke up into the canopy of their dark, oak four-poster. She could hear the shower going; it wouldn't be long before he came back in, probably still with that wounded look. Well, today he would just have to remain wounded. He would soon cheer up. And he should count himself bloody lucky that they still occupied – even if not always in perfect harmony – the same bed. She could think of couples who had experimented with single beds and separate rooms – never to return to the cosy familiarity of a shared duvet.

But when Patrick came in again, hair slicked back and chest gleaming with droplets of water, he was actually whistling. Caroline peered at him suspiciously through the haze of smoke and waited for him to say that smoking in bed was a fire hazard, but he briskly threw open his wardrobe, pulled out pristine white socks, shirt and shorts, and began to get dressed.

'Why are you so bloody cheerful?' she demanded, as he tucked in his shirt. He ignored her, and began to comb his damp hair. Then he pulled open the curtains and thrust open the window. A breeze billowed the curtains, and Caroline, warmly cocooned in the duvet, scowled as the cool air hit her face.

'You should get up,' he said. 'It's going to be another scorcher.'

'What time is it?'

'Nine o'clock. We should get cracking. They'll probably all get here around ten-thirty, eleven. The Mobyns are leaving at ten.' He looked at himself in the mirror and made a few imaginary shots.

Those bloody Mobyns again, thought Caroline, and gave Patrick a distrustful look.

Stephen and Annie arrived in Bindon at exactly ten-thirty. The roads out of Silchester had, contrary to Stephen's predictions, proved remarkably clear, and even the children had chosen their ice-lollies at the service station with a brisk efficiency.

'I hope we're not too early,' said Annie, as the car pulled into the Tarmac drive of The White House. 'Are there any other cars here yet?' They all peered out of the windows. A sprinkler was playing on the semi-circular lawn in front of the house, swinging round to douse the immaculate shrubs bordering the drive; then swinging back to play on the central flower-bed. As it changed direction, a spray of drops landed on the car, and the children shrieked with laughter.

'There's a car,' said Nicola, pointing to the very shiny navy-blue Mercedes which was parked at a skewed angle in front of the house.

'That's Caroline's,' said Annie. 'We must be the first. Well, they did say to arrive between ten and eleven.'

'Can we go under the sprinklers?' said Nicola. Annie glanced at Stephen.

'I'm not really sure . . .'

'Why shouldn't they?' he said, in a slightly defensive voice. 'They won't do any harm.'

'OK then, but make sure . . .' Annie tailed off as

27

Nicola and Toby slithered out of the car. Toby ran cleanly towards the lawn, a little brown body in blue shorts and T-shirt. Nicola hurried along beside him, her right foot trailing slightly with an expedient awkwardness. She always forgot about using both feet when she was in a hurry. Once under the spray, they seemed unsure what to do; eventually they began to splash each other rather ineffectually.

Stephen sighed.

'This is what Nicola needs more of,' he said. 'Fresh air, exercise . . .' Annie bit back the retort that she already got plenty of exercise and looked sidelong at Stephen. He was frowning disconsolately; staring through the window at the impressive façade of The White House. He had been moody all morning; disparagingly plucking the threadbare strings of his racquet during breakfast, snapping at Toby when he knocked over the milk.

Annie was pretty sure the trouble was his work. He had stopped coming back from the library overflowing with ideas and enthusiasm; whenever she tried to question him about it he became defensive and cut her short with some sarcastic rejoinder. So different from the way he'd been when his research was just a hobby; when there was no pressure on him to produce anything tangible. She longed for him to open up to her and share his worries – but then she wasn't sure he'd even admitted them to himself.

'Here we go,' said Stephen. Annie looked up and followed his gaze. Emerging from round the side of the house, a portly figure in expensive-looking tennis gear, was Patrick.

'Perhaps we'd better get out of the car,' said Annie, trying to inject a note of humour into the atmosphere. Stephen gave a reluctant half-grin and opened the door.

Patrick had seen them and was waving his racquet at them with an expansive grin. He approached the car, calling something incomprehensible.

'Hello, Patrick!' called Annie.

'Is the car all right here?' said Stephen, as Patrick approached.

'Absolutely fine,' said Patrick. 'Unless . . .' They all involuntarily turned to look at it – a dusty old Vauxhall, with the paintwork scratched where Stephen had once backed it into a gate. 'Unless you want to put it under the trees,' he said. 'It'll get a bit hot in the sun.'

'Good thinking,' said Annie. Stephen got back into the car and began to manoeuvre it onto the patch of grass under the trees.

'Come and have a drink!' said Patrick, putting his arm round Annie's shoulders.

'Oh yes, I . . .' She turned towards the children, still capering on the lawn.

'They'll come when they're ready,' he said, following her thoughts. 'I know Caroline's looking forward to seeing you.'

'You're very persuasive,' said Annie, laughing. He felt warm through his shirt and he smelt of expensive aftershave. As they passed Caroline's car she trailed her fingers admiringly over its smooth surface.

'Isn't that lovely?' she said.

'It's a pretty little machine,' agreed Patrick. 'Bought it last year for Caroline's birthday.'

'Oh yes, I remember. Lucky thing!'

'Try telling her that. She's after something more racy now.'

'What, like a Porsche?' said Annie, impressed.

'Ssh! Don't mention the P-word. I'm trying to get her to stick with this one.' As they rounded the corner of the house, Annie gave a backward glance to the Mercedes, gleaming expensively in the sunshine.

'You must be doing well,' she said. Patrick shrugged.

'It hasn't been a bad couple of years. I've been keeping my end up somehow. Just going with the flow. You know how it is.'

29

'Not really,' said Annie, honestly. 'There isn't much of a flow in Seymour Road.' Patrick laughed.

'Don't knock Seymour Road! I have fond memories of that street.'

'Do you?'

'Don't look so surprised. In fact, Georgina was saying only yesterday how much she wished we still lived there.' He gave Annie a rueful look and she laughed.

'Typical children! Never grateful!'

'That's what I said.'

They came out at the back of the house, and Caroline looked up from the terrace, where she was pouring out drinks for two people Annie didn't recognize. She was looking very brown, thought Annie, looking down at her own pale legs with a slight twinge.

'Annie!' shouted Caroline. 'Just in time for some Pimm's!' She sploshed a rather dark amber liquid into a long glass held by the strange woman, who giggled affectedly.

'Now, now,' said the man. 'Can't have you getting tipsy before you play, Valerie.'

'Why the hell not?' enquired Caroline, filling the man's glass. Valerie giggled again.

'Hello all,' said Patrick. 'Annie, meet Don Roper and his daughter Valerie.'

'How do you do?' said Don, winking at Annie. He was a stocky, cheerful-looking man, with a rather large face and eager eyes.

'Hello!' carolled Valerie. She seemed slightly younger than Annie – perhaps around thirty – and had the same large face as her father, but to less pleasant effect. Her skin was pale and dead-looking and her hazel eyes had a rather flat sheen.

'What can I get you?' said Patrick, gesturing expansively to the glass drinks trolley.

'Pimm's would be lovely,' said Annie. 'But if I could have it a little weaker than that . . .' Caroline poured out nearly a glassful of the dark liquid and added a splash of lemonade.

'Have some mint,' she said, poking about in the top of the jug. 'And a couple of strawberries.'

Annie sat down on a steamer chair, took a sip of Pimm's and waited for the kick of alcohol to hit her stomach. The sun was hot on her face and she wished she had brought some sunglasses. Looking surreptitiously at the others' clothes, she realized she was certainly going to have to avail herself of Caroline's offer of an outfit. Valerie was nattily attired in Slazenger, while Don's shorts looked so crisp as to be almost uncomfortable. And Caroline was looking her usual glamorous self, in a pale-pink sleeveless tennis top and matching pleated skirt. Her thick, blond, highlighted hair was in a bouncy pony-tail and she was wearing a white towelling wristband on each arm.

Stephen came striding around the corner of the house, carrying Toby on his shoulders.

'Hi, everyone,' he said.

'What a sweet little boy!' cried Valerie.

'Have some Pimm's,' said Patrick. 'Have you met Don and Valerie?'

'How do you do?' said Stephen. 'I'm Stephen Fairweather.'

'And who's this?' said Valerie archly at Toby. Toby buried his face in his father's neck.

'Our son, Toby,' said Annie.

'What a gorgeous creature,' said Valerie. 'I do love children.'

Nicola followed round the corner, with a drenched T-shirt and gleaming spectacles. Her right leg dragged slightly as she went, and she was panting.

'The sprinkler's *brilliant*!' she said. 'It's better than going swimming.'

'You look as if you have been swimming!' said Caroline, smiling warmly at Nicola. 'Does Georgina

31

know you're here? She can't wait to see you.' Nicola flushed slightly with pleasure.

'I haven't seen her,' she said.

'She must be in her room,' said Caroline. 'Do you want to go and find her? Or do you want to cool down and have a Coke?'

'I think I'll go and find her,' said Nicola, looking with alarm at the smart chairs and strangers on the terrace.

'You know where her room is. Take Toby, too, if you like.'

'Yes, go on, Tobes,' said Stephen. 'Go and annoy the big ones.' He grinned at Nicola.

As Nicola hurried off, Toby in tow, Valerie turned to Annie with a mixture of horror and sympathy on her face.

'Oh dear, poor little girl,' she said. She had a high, rather flutey voice. 'It must be so difficult for you.'

'Not really,' said Annie.

'She must be a very loving creature,' continued Valerie. 'I read in an article that children with disabilities are often the most rewarding.'

Annie and Stephen glanced at each other.

'But your little boy,' she continued, 'he's quite normal, is he? I must say, he looks a charming child.'

Nicola proceeded timidly along the long, cool corridors of The White House, trying to remember which door was Georgina's. She kept a firm grip on Toby; Georgina's house was full of things, balanced on pedestals and shelves, which she recognized as both expensive and easily broken. She vaguely supposed that was why Caroline and Patrick hadn't had any more children after Georgina. Everyone knew Georgina was neat and tidy and never dropped things or ran into them; but if they'd had someone clumsy like her, or Toby, who never kept still . . . They passed a little table laden with Lladro china ornaments and she shuddered to think of them all lying broken on the floor; knocked off by a sweeping arm movement or one of Toby's tennis balls.

Eventually she thought she'd found the right door and knocked timidly.

'Come in!'

Georgina was sitting at her desk by the window, and she looked up, her face bright, as they entered.

'Brilliant! You're here!' she said. 'Why are you all wet?'

'We went under the sprinklers,' said Nicola, a little shamefacedly.

'I do that sometimes,' said Georgina, kindly. 'Do you want a drink of water?'

'Yes please,' said Nicola, watching mesmerized as Georgina went to a large transparent water dispenser in the corner of her room.

'Isn't it brilliant?' said Georgina. 'Mummy got it for me because I'm always coming out for drinks of water at night. The water in my bathroom is yuck.'

She returned to her desk and lifted up a sheet of paper covered with writing.

'I've got a plan sorted out for what we're going to do!'

'Can't we go and see Arabia?' said Nicola.

'Of course,' said Georgina. 'But we need something for this afternoon.' Nicola took a sip of water. It was cool, clean and delicious. She looked at Georgina and waited.

'I've decided we're going to do a play,' said Georgina. 'We can make one up. Isn't it a brilliant idea? We can rehearse today and do the performance tomorrow. We can have costumes and everything. What do you think?' Her bright blue eyes fixed on Nicola determinedly, and Nicola stared back with respect.

'All right,' she said. 'That sounds brilliant.'

*   *   *

Annie and Caroline, passing Georgina's door on the way to Caroline's bedroom, heard her issuing instructions in clear tones.

'Bossy little cow,' said Caroline, rolling her eyes. 'Thinks she's in some bloody Angela Brazil novel.'

'It's a shame they aren't outside, it's such nice weather,' said Annie.

'You're right!' exclaimed Caroline. 'I never think of things like that.' She pushed open Georgina's door. All three children looked up.

'You should all go outside,' said Caroline. 'You'll never get brown in here.'

Caroline's walk-in wardrobe was nearly the size of the boxroom at 18 Seymour Road. Annie watched, trying unsuccessfully to remain nonchalant as Caroline tossed tennis shirts, skirts, T-shirts and shorts onto the bed in a heap of sugary pastels. Some were plain, some discreetly trimmed, others a riot of abstract pattern. She surreptitiously eyed the logos, despising her heart for beating faster as she recognized not only well-known sporting labels – Ellesse, Tacchini, Lacoste – but also the more universally coveted insignias that no-one could be unaware of these days. Gucci. Yves Saint Laurent. Chanel. Her gaze fixed on a plain white T-shirt with two interlocking Cs. How much must that have cost?

'I don't know what kind of thing you like,' Caroline was saying. 'Try them all on, if you like.'

'I don't know where to start,' said Annie. 'I didn't know you were so keen on tennis.' Caroline looked surprised.

'I'm not, really. We go to the country club over at Henchley – and you need proper tennis stuff for that. Not only whites, thank God. I mean, you need a really good tan to be able to wear white.'

Annie, who had been about to pick out a white sleeveless tennis top, changed her mind.

'What do you think?' she said helplessly. Caroline looked at her consideringly, and Annie involuntarily glanced down at her legs – pale and short, though not flabby. Rather like the rest of her. She had the sort of English complexion which veered from deathly white to embarrassingly pink, and she tended to leave the rest of her body to its own devices.

'Apricot,' said Caroline decisively.

Stephen was onto his second glass of Pimm's. He stretched out his legs in the sunshine and wondered how he would ever summon up the energy to play tennis. Patrick had appeared with a large chart labelled 'The White House Tennis Tournament' and was busy explaining it to Don. Valerie was awkwardly picking out pieces of fruit from her drink and popping them into her mouth. Her hazel eyes met Stephen's and she giggled.

'Ooh!' she said. 'I really think . . .' She petered off, and gazed down into her drink again. There was a pause, during which Stephen gave an inward sigh. It would be too rude to ignore her.

'Do you live in the village?' he said conversationally. Valerie started, and looked up at him. Her forehead was moist, and a few strands of her shaggy brown hair had stuck to it.

'Ooh no!' she laughed, as though he had said something preposterous. 'No, I live in London. But Dad lives here, just along the road, and Patrick phoned him up and asked whether I'd be home this weekend.'

'Lucky that you were,' said Stephen.

'Not really lucky,' said Valerie. 'When Dad told me about the party, I took Friday off work to come down. I did a bit of shopping, too, spending all my salary at once!' She giggled loudly.

'So you came down specially?' Stephen was surprised.

'Well, I do enjoy the tennis, and meeting new people.

35

I play at a club in London, which is very good, and there are social events every so often, you know, discos and parties, karaoke evenings sometimes . . .' Stephen nodded in slight bemusement. 'But then, no-one talks very much at a disco,' she carried on, 'and I'm never quite sure what to wear.' She abruptly stopped speaking, and Stephen found himself quite floored for an answer.

Annie couldn't believe how attractive she felt wearing Caroline's apricot-coloured polo shirt and pleated skirt. She stared at her reflection in the mirror, and smelt the deliciously flowery scent which Caroline had insisted she try.

'And you must have a go with this moisturizer,' said Caroline. 'It stops wrinkles and helps you go brown quicker.' She brandished a silver pot at Annie. 'Put it on all over.'

'I should say no,' said Annie. 'That looks extremely expensive.'

'Forty quid,' said Caroline. 'But it's worth it. And Patrick earns enough.'

'He must be doing really well,' said Annie, temporarily closing off her conscience in order to smear forty-pound cream all over her legs.

'I think they all are at his company,' said Caroline. 'People are buying investment plans like there's no tomorrow. God knows how they can afford them. Especially at the moment. But his bonuses have been incredible.'

'What does he get bonuses for?' said Annie. 'Sorry, I'm incredibly ignorant.'

'They give him a target and if he reaches it he gets a sodding great bonus. All of this' – Caroline gestured vaguely out of the window – 'is from bonuses.' Annie began to apply the cream to her face.

'It's not fair!' she said. 'They should give teachers bonuses for getting kids through exams! Or give

36

Stephen a bonus for finishing his thesis.'

'They should bloody well give me a bonus for putting up with Patrick's moods,' retorted Caroline. 'If he thinks he's going to miss a target he gets really edgy. Drives me crackers.' She sighed, and picked up a tennis skirt still in its embossed cellophane wrapper. It was pale blue and white striped, with a gold logo in the corner.

'I'd forgotten all about this one,' she said, in surprise. 'I must wear it some time.'

When Annie and Caroline got outside again, they found Patrick anxiously looking at his watch.

'I wanted to kick off at eleven,' he complained, 'but the Mobyns aren't here yet.'

'So what?' said Caroline. 'You only need two couples at a time. We can easily start now.'

'But Charles and Cressida are supposed to be on first,' said Patrick. 'And besides, I wanted to explain the chart to everyone first.'

'For Christ's sake!' exclaimed Caroline. She picked up the chart and surveyed it. 'Here we are,' she said. 'Second match: us against Don and Valerie.' She rolled her eyes at Annie, who giggled. Patrick was staring at the chart.

'I suppose that would work,' he said grudgingly.

'Come on then!' said Don. 'Chop, chop, Valerie.' Valerie scrambled to her feet, grabbed for her racquet, and in doing so knocked over the open bottle of Pimm's.

'Ooh!' she shrieked. 'I'm so clumsy! Caroline, I'm so sorry. Oh, I've cut my hand! What a stupid thing to do!'

When the Pimm's had been mopped up and Valerie had disappeared upstairs with Caroline for a plaster, Stephen sidled over to Annie, who was surreptitiously admiring her reflection in the glass terrace doors.

'You look great!' he said. 'That's a wonderful colour on you.' Annie looked down to savour her new shiny self. Even her socks were little pieces of luxury – fluffy white towelling with apricot-coloured pompoms bobbing gaily over the backs of her plimsolls.

'It's quite nice, isn't it?' she said, trying unsuccessfully to affect nonchalance.

'You should ask Caroline where she buys that kind of thing,' said Stephen. 'Perhaps you could get some new tennis clothes for yourself.'

'At these prices? I don't think so!' Annie's eyes crinkled with amusement. 'If you only knew what this little crocodile costs!'

'Even so,' said Stephen robustly. 'You deserve a few nice things.'

'I've got plenty of nice things,' she retorted. 'A particularly lovely brown coat, for example.' Stephen's mouth twisted into a smile in spite of himself. The brown coat had been donated to Annie by his mother, a well-meaning lady who had spied it at a church bazaar and thought it just the thing for her busy daughter-in-law. It had orange stitching around the lapels, a virulent green lining, and, as Annie often observed, about twenty-five years' life still in it. It hung on the kitchen peg, so that Mrs Fairweather could see it when she came to babysit, and it never ventured out of the house.

'Perhaps we should sew a little green crocodile onto that,' said Stephen.

Caroline and Valerie came out onto the terrace, Valerie's left hand decorated with a plaster.

'Good thing it wasn't your right hand,' said Annie, watching her pick up her racquet.

'I don't know,' said Valerie doubtfully. 'The thing is, I've got a double-handed backhand.'

'It wasn't a deep cut,' said Caroline dismissively. 'Just a scratch. You'll be fine.'

Valerie made a few cautious swings with her racquet and winced slightly. 'I'll be OK,' she said.

'Perhaps we should be given a handicap,' said Don in a semi-jovial tone. 'A couple of points per set or something.' Patrick looked up and gave an uncertain laugh.

'That's getting a bit technical for me,' he said.

'It's not important,' said Don. 'It's just that if Valerie's at a disadvantage because of her hand . . .' The two men stared at each other, and Annie suddenly realized that Don was serious. She stared at Valerie's hand. The plaster was about an inch long. She couldn't possibly have hurt herself badly.

'Valerie,' she said, 'do you really think your tennis is going to be affected?' Valerie looked up with a pained expression.

'Oh no, I shouldn't think it'll really matter. I mean, if I try to avoid playing on my backhand . . .'

'Good,' said Caroline loudly, lighting a cigarette. 'Then you won't need a handicap, will you? Right, let's get started.' She swept Valerie off the terrace and down the grassy path to the tennis court, giving Don a contemptuous glance as she did so. The others followed meekly behind in silence. The path led down a slight incline to the tennis court, surrounded by hedges and with a lawned area for viewing. It was a grass court, in immaculate condition, and Annie stared with pleasure at the inviting soft greenness.

'Lovely!' she said. Patrick turned and smiled at her.

'Looking good, isn't it?'

'I've always said this is a fine court,' said Don surprisingly. 'You've heard about the American at Wimbledon? He asked the groundsman how to get a court into that condition. "It's very simple," said the groundsman. "You just roll it and water it, roll it and water it . . . for a hundred years." ' Don looked around with a pleased look. 'Nothing finer than a good English grass court. Although, of course, it's not a surface I'm used to. Too fast, you see.'

'We both usually play on all-weather courts,' put in Valerie. 'Grass is quite different.'

39

'So you'll have to excuse us while we accustomize,' said Don cheerfully to Caroline. 'You'll probably wipe the floor with us to begin with.'

'I expect we will,' agreed Caroline in a bored voice. Patrick shot her a look and gave a little laugh.

'I shouldn't think that's very likely,' he said. 'You sound very professional. I'm afraid we hardly ever get to play.'

'Aha!' said Don, with a knowing expression. 'It's always the ones who say they never play! Don't believe a word of it, Val!'

As he and Valerie went onto the court, and Annie and Stephen sat down on the bank to watch, Caroline beckoned to Patrick.

'Out of interest,' she said sweetly, 'why the fuck did we invite Don?' Patrick looked uncomfortable.

'He's not so bad really,' he said. 'I didn't realize he'd take it all so seriously. Besides,' he added defensively, 'Don's quite a good client of mine. It doesn't hurt to show a bit of goodwill.'

'Oh, for Christ's sake! I should have known it was something like that.' She looked sideways at Patrick. 'I suppose that's why you invited the Mobyns, wasn't it? Because they're good clients?' Patrick shrugged and looked away. 'This is supposed to be a party, Patrick. For our friends. Not some bloody corporate hospitality event.' She took a furious drag on her cigarette. Patrick glared at her.

'Just remember', he hissed, 'that it's people like Don who pay for all of this, for your new tennis racquet and your new hairdo and those poncey cigarettes. Not to mention the house, and the car, and the pony . . .' He broke off as Don came to the side of the court.

'Discussing tactics, are you?' he said in a jovial voice. 'Now remember, no playing on Valerie's injured hand.'

'Oh for Christ's sake,' muttered Caroline.

'Of course we won't,' said Patrick loudly. He

avoided Caroline's gaze. 'Right, come on, darling. Let's give them hell.' He grinned at Don who chuckled appreciatively. Caroline rolled her eyes and stubbed out her cigarette.

As the four began to knock up, it was soon obvious that Don and Valerie were serious players. Valerie was slogging the ball determinedly at Patrick, while Don was hitting cunningly sliced shots to Caroline. She swiped wildly at each spinning ball, then stared in distaste as it swerved away beyond her reach.

'These balls aren't bouncing properly,' she announced eventually. 'I'm sure that's not allowed.'

'It's called a spin shot,' said Patrick. 'It's perfectly legal.' Caroline gazed at him crossly.

'Well, it's fucking annoying.'

'It's the action of the racquet, you see,' put in Don. 'It's very simple.'

'Well, could you not do it, please?' said Caroline firmly. 'It really puts me off.'

Don and Valerie stared at her in amazement. Patrick smiled hastily at them.

'Caroline's sense of humour on court is something else,' he said. 'You mustn't take her seriously.'

Don and Valerie won the toss and chose to serve. Patrick waited, eyes narrowed, as Don bounced the ball twice, drew back his racquet with a contorted, looped action, and hit the ball smartly over the net. Patrick lunged for it and promptly sent it out.

'Bad luck, Patrick, good serve, Dad,' hooted Valerie. She was standing right up at the net, jumping up and down, clearly ready to blast to oblivion any shots that came her way.

'Patrick, that was complete crap,' said Caroline loudly. Annie, sitting on the bank, began to giggle.

'Look at Valerie's face,' she whispered to Stephen.

Valerie gazed in bemused horror at Caroline as she sauntered to the back of the court. She turned to exchange looks with Don, but he hadn't heard Caroline's comment and was preparing to serve again. He bounced the ball twice, tossed it up, and hit it elaborately to Caroline's forehand. Caroline drew back her racquet and slammed the ball straight at Valerie.

'Ouch!' cried Valerie, clutching her shoulder.

'Sorry, Valerie,' drawled Caroline. 'I was trying to pass you. Fifteen-all, I think that is.'

Stephen caught Annie's eye and snorted with laughter. 'This is priceless.' He got up, and took her empty glass. 'I'll get some more drinks. Tell me what happens while I'm away.' Annie nodded, then leant back on the grass, feeling pleasurably the cool blades of grass against her bare arms; closing her eyes and listening to the irregular sound of ball against racquet. Thwack, thwack, thwack. 'Out!' 'Fucking hell!' 'Thirty-fifteen.' Then silence, then thwack, thwack, thwack, again.

Annie felt calm, happy, slightly numbed from the alcohol, and almost perfectly content. She was suddenly reminded of summer afternoons at school, lying by the tennis courts, listening dreamily to the sound of the players, with nothing to worry about but prep and choir practice and what would be for supper. Although of course, she reminded herself sternly, some of those things had been far more worrying at the time than they sounded now. Double biology had blighted her week far more than any of the duties she had to carry out nowadays. But still, in retrospect, she thought, her life was easy then. It had order, proportion and a definite framework constructed by others. What would the school timetablers make of her life as it was at the moment? Inefficient, rushed and ill-proportioned? Or maybe hers didn't count any more. As a mother, perhaps her function was simply to make sure her children's lives were as ordered as her own had been.

As the thought of the children passed through her head, she experienced the customary irrational stab of fear that she always had when they weren't in front of her – that they were in danger, injured, killed, through her own irresponsible fault. But the dart of pain as her heart jumped was muffled; the sensation of fear slight. They were with Georgina, a sensible girl; Stephen was up at the house and would hear any screams of distress; she was feeling too indolent to get worked up. She felt her mind drift further and further away from consciousness. Should she make an effort to watch the game? Or should she allow herself to fall asleep?

She was woken what seemed like a moment later by Stephen placing an ice-cube on her forehead.

'Aah!' she screamed, and opened her eyes to see his upside-down laughing face above her. 'You rotter!'

'I think Valerie should be allowed to take that serve again,' came a voice from the court. She swivelled her head, to see Don gazing disapprovingly at her.

'This is quite an important point,' he added meaningfully.

'What's the score?' called Stephen cheerily.

'Three-all in the tie-break,' said Don, and turned back. 'Take two, Val.'

'I told you to watch and tell me what happened,' complained Stephen quietly as he sat down beside Annie. 'I've obviously missed all the excitement.'

'Well, what took you so long?' retorted Annie.

'It took me half an hour to find the kitchen,' said Stephen. 'And another half-hour to find the ice-cube dispenser. But I knew madam wouldn't like her Pimm's warm.'

'You were right there,' agreed Annie. She took several long gulps of the amber liquid.

'Mmm, lovely.'

'Good stuff, isn't it?' agreed Stephen. 'Now, tell me how a tie-break works.'

'Three-six,' called Don.

'Don and Valerie need one more point to win,' said Annie. 'Look, we must watch.'

Patrick was preparing to serve. The first went slamming into the net.

'Fault,' said Don and Valerie in unison.

Patrick threw up the second ball and sent it gently curving over the net, landing neatly in the service box.

'Foot-fault,' came Don's voice. Valerie, who had been running for the shot, stopped in her tracks.

'Was it?' she said breathlessly.

'Foot-fault?' said Caroline incredulously.

'I'm afraid so,' said Don. 'I saw it quite clearly. Your foot was over the line. If you're not happy about it, we could play the point again . . .' He raised his eyebrows at Valerie.

'No, no,' said Patrick, attempting a genial voice. 'I'm sure you're right. So that must be . . .'

'Our set,' said Valerie promptly. 'And match.'

'Well, what a thrilling end,' said Caroline, in sarcastic tones. Patrick glanced at her sharply.

'Was that really a foot-fault?' Annie asked Stephen quietly. He shrugged.

'Christ knows. I can't see from here.'

'I shouldn't think Don can see very clearly, either,' she said, catching his eye meaningfully. They both turned and looked at Don, shaking hands with a beaming face. He looked utterly satisfied with himself.

'Oh well,' said Stephen. 'If it's that important to him . . .'

'I suppose so,' said Annie. 'But it doesn't seem fair, somehow. You shouldn't just get things because they're important to you.'

'Shouldn't you?' said Stephen. 'I don't see why not.'

Annie thought for a moment, and opened her mouth to reply, but was stopped by the approach of Don and Patrick, striding up the grass bank.

'Well done,' she said in a hearty voice. 'What a close match.'

'Wasn't it just,' said Don. 'There were some good rallies there.'

'Especially the last one,' came Caroline's voice from behind. 'That was a corker.'

Annie looked down, and tried not to giggle.

'Who's on next?' she said hurriedly. 'Is it us?'

'You against Charles and Cressida,' said Patrick. 'When they arrive.'

'Tell you what,' said Annie to Stephen, 'let's go and get some practice in.'

She led Stephen down to the court and they began to knock up. The others watched for a few shots. Annie clearly played competent schoolgirl tennis – but Stephen could barely get the ball over the net.

'Sorry,' he kept saying. 'Damn. Sorry, could you get that?'

Caroline watched as Don's face relaxed at the sight. Nothing to worry about there, he was clearly thinking; he and Valerie would soon have that two off the court. Suddenly, Caroline detested him intensely.

'Darling, I'm going to go up to the house,' said Patrick softly, coming over to her. 'I've got a bit of business to look at – and I'll be there if the Mobyns arrive. All right?'

'I suppose so,' said Caroline, morosely lighting a cigarette. She couldn't think why she had looked forward to this fucking party.

'You played really well,' said Patrick, even more quietly.

'Tell that to your friend Don,' said Caroline, blowing smoke into Patrick's face. Patrick shrugged resignedly.

'I know,' he said. 'You don't have to tell me.'

Caroline watched his stumpy form disappear up the path with a mixture of dislike and resignation. She then turned her gaze to the tennis court. Stephen was preparing to serve. He threw the ball far too high, took back his old wooden racquet in an inexpert swing, and whacked it over the hedge.

'Blast,' he said. 'I'd better go and get that.'

Caroline closed her eyes. What a crew of men.

Bloody Patrick, odious Don, and Stephen, who, with his old shorts and stringy legs, was clearly a complete incompetent. She'd always thought he was a bit odd – and now, look at him, couldn't even play a decent game of tennis, let alone earn enough to buy his wife some proper clothes. She couldn't think how Annie managed to stay so happy, with that wimp around her the whole time. Then a picture of Patrick came into her mind – and she couldn't think how she stayed so fucking cheerful herself.

Chapter Three

Patrick was in his study when the Mobyns' Bentley pulled into the drive. He glanced out of the window when he heard the low, discreet hum of the engine, and gazed at the distinguished curves of the car with a mixture of envy, resentment and a thudding excitement. He saw the car pause, and glimpsed a blond head looking about as if uncertain of where to park. The natural reaction would have been for him to bang on the study window, shout a greeting and then hurry outside to welcome the family. But Patrick sat where he was. He wasn't ready yet to see Charles.

Caroline appeared around the corner of the house, carrying a tray of drinks. She shouted something to Charles, who promptly stopped the engine. The car door opened, and he got out, stretching his legs and looking about him appraisingly. Then the nanny, a dumpy girl of about nineteen, got out of the back. She heaved a large, squashy hold-all out onto the ground, and delved back inside the car for the twins – identical blond toddlers, who began walking off in different directions as soon as she put them down. Last to appear was Cressida. Long legs, immaculately clad in beige trousers; smooth, bobbed, pale-blond hair; a calm, unlined face. She greeted Caroline with a blank smile and kissed her dispassionately on each cheek.

Patrick couldn't help comparing the two women as they stood together talking. Both blue-eyed blondes, both in good shape, both wearing expensive clothes. But Caroline was just a bit browner than Cressida; her hair was a bit brighter, her make-up a bit stronger, her voice quite a lot louder. Next to Cressida's understated elegance, her blue eyeliner and gold bracelets seemed a bit much. She suddenly burst into loud laughter, and Patrick saw Cressida smile politely at her, a look of slight incomprehension on her face. Charles was looking up at her in amusement. What on earth had Caroline been saying? Suddenly Patrick felt a wave of fierce affection for his wife. They were made of the same stuff as each other – something stronger, coarser, more highly flavoured than the Cressidas of this world.

He looked down at the papers on his desk. His year's performance figures stared back up at him. He had done well by any standards. For Christ's sake, he had sold those bloody investment plans to practically anything that moved. His total was twenty per cent higher than last year. But, of course, that wasn't good enough for the bastards. He'd hit all his targets last year – so this year they'd moved the targets up. He pulled out the firm's bonus chart. The highest bonus figure – one hundred thousand pounds – glowed enticingly at the top of the sheet. But to get that he still had to do a lot of business. His year ended in a week's time and he was still eighty thousand pounds short. It was almost worth putting the eighty thousand into a plan himself, to make sure he reached his hundred thousand bonus. Except that he didn't have that kind of capital. And he would never buy any of the investment plans he sold.

What he needed was for somebody to make a quick lump-sum investment of eighty thousand within the next week. He glanced out of the window again. Charles was carrying one of the twins over to be kissed by Caroline. He was laughing and looked relaxed – as well he might be, thought Patrick. It was all a far cry now from the days in Seymour Road, when Charles and Ella had cooked spaghetti every night and gone backpacking round Europe when they could afford it. Then, it had been Patrick who had helped

Charles out, with a loan – admittedly relatively small – when Charles' print gallery had seemed about to fold. It had been Charles who had teased Patrick about money; had told him to relax, chill out, come round and smoke some grass with him and Ella.

And now he was driving a Bentley and wearing a navy-blue blazer. He didn't need anyone's help any more, least of all Patrick's. Cressida had paid the loan back in full as soon as she married Charles. Or perhaps it had even been before. She had clearly hated the idea of Charles being in debt to anyone. But as favours went, Patrick reckoned Charles still owed him one.

As Caroline led the way to the main guest room, Charles looked around, impressed by what he saw. Patrick had, of course, told them about his new house – but somehow Charles hadn't imagined anything so sumptuous. The whole place reminded him of early-Seventies James Bond films. Not at all in his or Cressida's style, of course – he could see her recoiling as they passed a fitted cocktail bar – but certainly luxurious and, he was sure, very expensive.

Although, of course, property out here was bound to be cheap compared to central Silchester, where they lived. And for a location like that of the house in which he and Cressida lived – right in the Cathedral Close, with a garden – well, anyone would have to pay a lot. Nevertheless, Charles began to feel a strange sensation of resentment as he passed along the cool corridors, glimpsing out of the window what looked suspiciously like a stable block in the distance. Since marrying Cressida, he had become accustomed to thinking of himself as the one who had made good; the one who was to be envied – and he had consciously avoided parading his luck in front of his old friends.

If he had ever given any thought to Patrick and his career, it was to marvel that he, Charles Mobyn, actually numbered a financial salesman among his

49

friends; friends that now included the most ac-
complished, prominent and socially important people
in the county. He knew Patrick made a lot of money –
of course he did – but he never thought of this, this
salesman's money as ever being transformed into anything that he, Charles, might covet. And yet, taking in
the obvious comfort of Patrick's and Caroline's life
here, Charles couldn't resist making a brief, disloyal
comparison with the house in the Cathedral Close –
Georgian and listed, undoubtedly, but also rather
gloomy, drafty and expensive to keep up.

The principal guest bedroom suite was a symphony
of pink, from the headboard of the bed – shaped like a
shell – to the tissues on the dressing table.

'I hope you've got everything you need,' said Caroline. 'If you want a Jacuzzi, just press the controls on
the wall.'

'Very kind,' murmured Cressida chillingly.

'Right,' said Caroline. 'Well, see you downstairs.'
The door closed, and Charles and Cressida looked at
each other. Cressida touched the bedcover gingerly.

'Satin,' she said. She felt underneath. 'Satin sheets,
too. Ghastly. I shan't be able to sleep.'

'I don't know,' said Charles. 'Satin sheets might be
rather fun. And a Jacuzzi!'

Cressida sighed and dropped her bag on the floor
with an air of forbearance. 'I'd better check that the
children are all right.'

'I'm sure they're fine,' began Charles, but she disappeared out of the room. He dumped his bag on
the bed and began to change swiftly into his tennis
clothes.

By the time Cressida returned he was ready.

'They've got cotton sheets, thank God,' she said.
'Decorated with My Little Pony, needless to say.'

'Priceless!' said Charles. 'I must go and have a look.
Is Martina all right?'

'She thinks it's all lovely,' said Cressida. 'She's got a

50

blue, shiny quilt edged with polyester lace.' Charles grinned. Martina, their nanny, had spent her childhood in a cosy little box outside Bonn, and had not taken well to life in the Mobyns' house. She had trailed around miserably all winter clad in leg warmers and fingerless gloves, and there had been a memorable scene once when she had got unsuspectingly into a bath full of icy cold water. It had transpired that in Germany – or at least Martina's Germany – the plumbing never went wrong.

'Oh yes,' Cressida added, brandishing a sheaf of letters at Charles. 'She picked up the post on the way out and forgot to give it to us.' Charles grimaced.

'I thought the idea of going away for the weekend was to get away from all of that.'

'This is hardly "away for the weekend",' said Cressida crushingly. 'It's not exactly like going down to the Blakes', is it?'

The Blakes lived in a mansion in Devon and were having a house party that weekend. Cressida had tried to persuade Charles to agree to chucking the tennis party and going to Devon instead, but he had proved immovable. They had almost had a serious row about it. Now he looked at her wearily.

'For God's sake, Cressida, we've been to the Blakes' house a million times. But we've never come here. These are my friends, you know.'

'I know they are,' said Cressida.

'It would be nice', continued Charles, 'if I could feel they were your friends too.'

'Well, I don't think that's very likely somehow,' said Cressida. He looked at her furiously.

'Why not? Why can't you at least try?'

'Oh Charles, honestly! What on earth have we got in common?'

'You've got me in common,' said Charles. 'Shouldn't that be enough?' He picked up his racquet. 'I'm going outside. It's too hot in here.'

Outside, in the corridor, he saw Martina and the twins emerging from their bedroom.

'Hello there!' he said cheerfully. 'Everything all right?'

'Everything is fine,' said Martina. 'This is a very nice house. So big, so beautiful . . .' She gestured admiringly.

'Well, yes, I suppose it is in its own way,' said Charles. 'All right, boys?' He looked down at the twins. 'Oh no!' They had sidled over to an alcove by the window. Ben was about to put a glass elephant in his mouth and James was tugging at a pale curtain with chocolate-covered fingers.

'Mrs Chance, she gave the boys chocolate biscuits,' said Martina apologetically, pulling James' hands away and wiping them with a tissue. 'I tried to tell her that Mrs Mobyn did not like it, but she wouldn't listen.'

'Don't worry,' said Charles, removing the elephant from Ben's grasp. Ben's face crumpled, and he held his hands up entreatingly to his father. 'No, Ben. It's dangerous. Let's get these horrors outside.'

'Mrs Chance said we should go and look at the horse,' said Martina doubtfully.

'Grand idea,' said Charles. 'Do you want to see a horse, Ben?' Ben made a grab for the elephant again.

'See the horsey?' said Charles encouragingly, putting the elephant carefully back on its display table and carrying Ben off down the corridor. 'See the horsey?'

'Horsey,' echoed Martina, picking up James. 'We go to see the horsey.'

'She's not a horsey,' said Georgina cuttingly. 'She's a pony.'

'Of course she is,' agreed Charles hurriedly. They had arrived at the paddock to find Georgina leading Arabia round the perimeter while Nicola sat astride, clutching the reins awkwardly and beaming with pleasure. Toby sat peacefully on the fence watching, a placid little boy with a sunny smile. When she saw them, Georgina turned round and brought Arabia up to the fence.

'Isn't she gorgeous!' she said proudly. She buried her face in the pony's mane. 'You're so beautiful!' she murmured.

'Georgina's teaching me to ride,' said Nicola. 'I can walk.'

'Very good!' applauded Charles. He held Ben up to see.

'Look, Ben! Look at the lovely hor . . . er pony!'

Martina was cowering behind, staring distrustfully at Arabia.

'Bring James nearer so he can see,' said Charles. He turned round. 'What's wrong, Martina? Don't you like horses?' Martina stepped forward nervously a pace or two, then retreated as Arabia threw up her head and whinnied. Ben looked up at Charles, his eyes huge with astonishment.

'Come on,' said Georgina impatiently. 'Let's go round again, and trot this time. You'd better put a hat on.'

Charles watched compassionately as Nicola fumbled with the chin strap of the hard hat. Her poor right hand struggled to keep up with the left, and she grunted several times in frustration as the webbing slipped out of its buckle. Georgina watched without expression, neither hurrying Nicola nor offering assistance. Martina gave an initial exclamation as she saw Nicola's jerky hand moving uncertainly up to her chin – but, after a look from Charles, kept quiet.

'Right,' said Georgina, when Nicola had eventually succeeded. 'Let's go.' She pulled gently on Arabia's reins, turned round, and began to walk around the paddock, gradually increasing her pace to a run.

'Hold on!' she shouted at Nicola. 'Go up and down when she starts trotting!'

It was an unexpectedly moving sight. Georgina's

hair streamed behind her in the sunlight as she jogged round the paddock; meanwhile, Nicola bounced up and down with a mixture of delight and terror on her face. Charles stole a look at the faces of the twins. They were both staring enraptured at the scene.

Eventually Georgina led Arabia back up to the fence.

'Do you want a go, Toby? You can't go on your own, but you could sit in front of me,' she said. Toby giggled and shook his head.

'I suppose these two are too small,' said Charles, gesturing to the twins.

'Yes, they are a bit,' said Georgina. 'They probably couldn't even sit on a pony without falling off.'

'I'd love them to learn to ride,' said Charles. 'Perhaps when they're a bit older.'

'You wouldn't need to buy two ponies,' said Georgina. 'If they stay the same size they could always share one.'

'Maybe,' said Charles. 'Ponies are very expensive creatures.'

'So what?' said Georgina disconcertingly. 'You must be able to afford it now you're so rich.'

As Cressida unpacked her clothes, carefully shaking out the creases as she had been taught at school, a frown furrowed her brow. Charles was angry with her for being rude about his friends – and perhaps she had been a bit blunt – but what was she supposed to say? Surely he could see that she could never become friendly with that jumped-up salesman and his tarty wife?

It did not occur to Cressida that her own father had been, in his own way, a salesman himself. Owners of large factories were not, in her mind, at all the same thing as vulgar men like Patrick, who, she noticed, hadn't even bothered to come and greet his guests. Besides, it was her mother, the aristocratic Antonia Astley, with whom Cressida identified most strongly.

Her mother had always avoided becoming friendly with the wives of her husband's colleagues. 'Think of yourself as a precious present,' she had once said to Cressida, 'not to be squandered on whoever happens across you first.' She had, of course, been talking about sex, Cressida now realized – but it was actually a useful principle for friendships in general.

The trouble was, people like the Chances had no idea of graduating slowly towards friendship – they seemed to treat every chance acquaintance as familiarly as they did each other. Cressida shrank from the kisses, jokes, references and banter which surrounded this kind of event. Caroline, in particular, was the kind of woman who would soon assume an intimacy which Cressida was far from sharing; who would quiz her on intimate subjects and then perhaps even refer to them in front of strangers. It was safer, Cressida thought, to keep one's distance right from the start, before things got out of hand.

She recalled a woman whom she'd met once on holiday, staying in a friend's apartment at Menton. The woman had been amiable enough as a beach companion; they had lent each other sun cream, magazines and books. But her conversation had gradually turned to areas which Cressida rarely discussed with anybody, let alone a stranger. She had become more and more persistent, first laughing at Cressida, then becoming offended, and calling Cressida a stuck-up cow. It had been even worse when it transpired that the woman was quite a friend of George Wallace, whose apartment Cressida was staying in.

She frowned uncomfortably at the memory and began to change into her tennis dress. She felt upset by Charles' determined affection for the Chances, and not just because they were not her sort of people. It was also because the Chances – together with just about everyone else here, probably – belonged to that time of Charles' life which Cressida preferred not to think about; the period before he had met her, when he had been living in Seymour Road with that woman (Cressida never articulated Ella's name, even in her thoughts). Of course, everyone could see now that she would have been all wrong for him. But Cressida still felt sometimes that the Seymour Road crowd thought it a shame that he'd left her. There had certainly been a bad atmosphere among them at the wedding.

They'd managed to avoid seeing any of them since then, apart from the odd chance meeting in Silchester – and Cressida had thought that would be the end of it. But then, after months of silence, the invitation had appeared from Patrick and Caroline, warmly pressing them to come and play tennis.

She finished buttoning up her tennis dress, carefully brushed her hair with her Mason Pearson brush and looked in the mirror. Her legs were carefully waxed, her hair well cut and her face discreetly made up. But it did not occur to Cressida to stare at herself gloatingly or try to imagine the appearance she would make on the court. She turned round briefly to check that her dress was straight at the back. Then she turned her attention to the letters still lying on the bed. Perhaps she should go through them. That would please Charles. He always complained that she never opened a letter unless she recognized the handwriting on the envelope.

But a shout from outside distracted her. She went to the window and saw Charles looking up. He was grinning broadly and looked as though he'd been running.

'Come on, Cress!' he shouted. 'It's lovely out here!' Cressida smiled in slight relief. He wasn't angry any more.

'All right!' she called. 'I'm coming!' And without giving the letters another thought, she hurried out of the room.

*   *   *

When they arrived at the tennis court, they found Annie and Stephen knocking up. Caroline was lying in a deck-chair, smoking a cigarette and applauding; Patrick was nowhere to be seen.

'We're a bit out of condition, I'm afraid,' said Stephen.

'Speak for yourself,' retorted Annie as they came off court. She kissed Charles. 'It's super to see you!' she said.

'Hello, Cressida,' said Stephen. 'How are you?'

'What a lovely name!' piped up Valerie. 'I don't think I've heard that one before. Is it from a book?' Cressida gave her a look of astonishment.

'Charles, Cressida,' said Stephen, hiding a smile, 'meet Don and Valerie Roper.'

'How do you do?' said Cressida.

'Don lives in our village,' called Caroline from the deck-chair, her voice husky with cigarette smoke. The thought seemed to tickle her, and she started laughing rather drunkenly.

'Pleased to meet you,' said Don, nodding at Charles.

'Don and Valerie have just thrashed us,' said Caroline. 'It was a thrilling match, ending on a foot-fault.'

'Ooh!' said Valerie, then blushed as everyone looked at her.

Caroline had swivelled round in her chair to look at Cressida.

'I love your dress,' she announced. 'Where did you get it?' Cressida forced herself to smile at Caroline.

'I had it made for me,' she said.

'I might have known,' said Caroline, in slightly mocking tones. 'There you are, Annie, you think I've got a good wardrobe, but I've never had anything made for me. I bet that cost a packet, didn't it?' Cressida's hand tightened round her racquet, and she laughed lightly.

'Go on, how much? Two hundred? Three hundred?'

'Really?' said Annie. 'Would it be that much?'

'Might be more,' said Caroline. 'Or might be less.

Depends if a designer makes it or your granny makes it!' she cackled with laughter again. 'Actually,' she added, 'I don't think I'd like to have my things made for me. I mean, the whole point of buying clothes is going and trying them on in the shop.' She smiled reminiscently. 'When I was young,' she said, 'I used to spend my entire Saturday going round Biba and Mary Quant, trying on clothes. It was great. You just stripped off what you were wearing and tried everything on in the shop. Once I walked right out of Biba wearing a brand-new outfit!'

'But that's shop lifting!' said Valerie, in a shocked voice.

'No it isn't,' said Caroline scathingly. 'I didn't mean to do it. I just forgot what I was wearing when I went in.'

Charles had turned to Annie. 'I've just seen Nicola trotting round the paddock on Georgina's pony. She was doing very well.'

'She's talked about nothing else for the last few days,' said Annie, smiling. 'She simply adores coming here. And Georgina's very good with her.'

'So I noticed,' said Charles. 'There's a lot to that young lady.'

'Are they still in the paddock?' asked Annie. 'I might go and have a look.'

Charles shook his head.

'They were just finishing,' he said. 'Georgina was beginning to organize them all into some game or other. Including our two,' he added to Cressida, 'and Martina, believe it or not. That's our nanny,' he explained. 'Georgina seems to have her well under control.'

'What on earth are they all doing?' said Annie. 'They're a bit of a mixed bag to be playing together.' Charles shrugged.

'I don't want to know. Let them get on with it.' He looked up and gave a smile of surprise. 'At last!

Patrick, where have you been?' He went forward and grasped Patrick warmly by the hand.

'I'm sorry I wasn't around when you arrived,' said Patrick. 'Ah, Cressida, there you are.' As he went to kiss her, his eyes fell on Caroline's grinning face and he looked away. 'Right, who's on next?'

'Annie and Stephen,' said Don. 'Against Charles and Cressida, as a matter of fact.'

'Splendid,' said Charles. 'Come on, Cress, let's go and warm up.'

The Mobyns made an elegant couple on court, both well-schooled in the strokes, agile and deft. Cressida began hitting some practice serves, and Don turned to Valerie.

'I can see we've some competition here,' he said. 'Look at the way her serve spins away from the forehand. You'll have to be careful with that.' Valerie was staring, awe-struck, at Cressida.

'She's really good,' she said.

'His serve is harder, but probably easier to return. More straightforward,' continued Don.

'She looks a bit like Princess Diana,' said Valerie. Stephen raised his eyebrows at Annie.

'Well, you never know,' he said conversationally. 'She might be related to her.'

'Ooh! really?' Valerie swung round.

'I don't think so,' said Annie firmly, glaring at Stephen. But he was not to be put off.

'Her mother was the Honourable something,' he said thoughtfully. 'Or was it Lady something? Very smart, anyway, I know that much. And I'm sure I've heard something about a royal connection.' He nodded wisely at Valerie, who was staring at him, agog.

'Well,' she said, 'I must say . . .'

'Valerie,' interrupted Don, 'watch the way Cressida guards the net. She'll be difficult to pass. Look, her eye never leaves the ball.'

Annie and Stephen joined the court and began to

knock up with Charles and Cressida. Both Charles and Cressida considerately modified their games slightly as they realized the standard of the Fairweathers. But even so, every second ball Stephen hit seemed to go in the net. Annie was slightly better, but as Charles gave her a few practice volleys, she turned and looked at Stephen in dismay.

'He hits it so hard!' she wailed. 'I'll never get any of these!'

'Don't worry,' said Stephen. 'It's the playing that counts.'

'Yes, but what if you can't play?'

Caroline was watching Cressida critically.

'She thinks she's in bloody Wimbledon or something,' she said disparagingly.

'Who, Annie?' said Patrick in mock surprise. 'I wouldn't have said so.'

'Very funny,' said Caroline. 'Just look at her,' she persisted, watching as Cressida neatly put away a backhand volley. 'Thinks she's a bloody pro.'

'She's got a nice technique,' said Patrick. 'We could all learn from her.' He looked around. 'Where's Georgina? She should watch a bit of this.'

'Christ knows,' said Caroline. 'She said she'd be ballgirl. That didn't last long.'

'The play's *The Three Little Pigs*,' said Georgina firmly. 'The reason is, we all know the story, and the little ones can be the pigs.' She looked at the twins. 'Can you be pigs?'

'The pigs are the most important people,' objected Nicola.

'No they're not,' said Georgina. 'The wolf is more important than the pigs.'

'Who's the wolf?'

'I am.'

Nicola felt a familiar crushing sense of disappointment come over her. It was to be the same here as it was everywhere. She looked down, nursing her bad hand, and remembered countless nativity plays, school concerts, speech days; endless conversations held over her head by people who thought she couldn't understand: *'That little Fairweather girl – we're going to have to put her at the back'*; *'Poor little thing, we'll have to take her out of the dancing'*; *'She really can't manage – can we find her something else to do?'*

'But the most important of all', continued Georgina, 'is the man who sells the straw and the twigs and the bricks to the three little pigs.'

'What?' Nicola was confused. She didn't even remember that there was a man. 'Is he in the Ladybird book?'

'I can't remember,' admitted Georgina. 'But he must have been there. They didn't just find the straw and things on the road, did they? And if they hadn't bought such stupid stuff to build their houses with, the wolf wouldn't have got them. Would he?' She looked impressively at Nicola.

'Except the bricks,' said Nicola, who had a logical mind.

'Except the bricks,' agreed Georgina.

Nicola was beginning to feel a faint ray of hope. But such rays were deceptive, she knew from experience. She put her head down again.

'Aren't you going to ask who's the man who sells the straw and twigs to the little pigs?' demanded Georgina.

'Who's the man who sells the straw?' mumbled Nicola. There was a silence, and she cautiously looked up. Georgina was grinning at her.

'You, stupid! It's you, of course!' Nicola started to smile, and instead broke into laughter; loud laughter, that emptied her lungs of breath and filled her face with colour. Instinctively, Georgina leaned over and gave her a hug. Martina, who had sat silently watching all of this, suddenly appeared overcome by emotion and looked away.

'Look at her,' said Georgina. 'She's crying. Soppy.' She began to giggle, and Nicola, strung up, began to join in almost hysterically. Toby, who had wandered off, came back and started laughing companionably with them, whereupon Martina harumphed crossly and got up.

'You can't go!' said Georgina. 'You've got to look after the twins.'

'Perhaps she should be in the play,' said Nicola reasonably. 'She could be mother pig.'

'All right,' said Georgina. 'Martina!' she called. 'Will you be a mother pig?'

Martina glared at Georgina, muttered something in German, picked up the twins and stalked off towards the house.

'I don't think she understood,' said Georgina, beginning to laugh. 'I think she thought I was *calling* her a mother pig.' The three children fell on their backs in the sun in fits of giggles.

'Mother pig!' gasped Nicola, fuelling fresh paroxysms of mirth.

When she couldn't laugh any more, she lay still, giving the odd gurgle, staring up at the sky and smelling the mixture of grass, earth, and the scent of Arabia on her clothes.

'I'm really glad we're staying the night,' she said lazily. 'I wish we lived here all the time.' Then she wished she hadn't said it. Georgina would think she was soppy. She stole a look at her. Georgina was lying flat on her back, staring straight up at the sky. Slowly she turned and looked at Nicola with fierce blue eyes.

'So do I,' she said.

Chapter Four

Lunch was served on the terrace. Mrs Finch, Caroline's daily, had appeared towards the end of the match and called uncompromisingly from the top of the path, 'Mrs Chance, I'm here.'

'Oh hello, Mrs Finch,' shouted Caroline, turning towards her and causing Cressida to lose concentration and hit her first serve in the net. 'Can you dole out the lunch? You know where it all is. And then perhaps tidy up a bit.' Cressida was waiting patiently to serve. 'Sorry about this,' called Caroline cheerfully. 'All right, Mrs Finch?'

'Yes, Mrs Chance.'

So this was Mrs Finch, thought Annie, glancing up from the court. Not the apple-cheeked retainer that Annie had imagined whenever Caroline had referred to her, but a thin, determined-looking woman in her mid-thirties, with dyed-red, curly hair. She had the local accent, but her voice was sharp and strident; she and Caroline had obviously failed to get a cosy employer-employee relationship going.

Annie watched Mrs Finch survey with disapproval the dishevelled scene of tennis racquets, bottles, ashtrays and glasses, then pick up her shopping bag and disappear up the path. Perhaps her family once owned the village, thought Annie romantically. Perhaps she can't bear to come back and clean the house where her grandfather was once lord. Then it occurred to her that The White House was only about ten years old. But maybe this had been the site of the manor.

'Annie!' Annie started as the ball went whizzing past her.

'Gosh, sorry,' she said, and giggled guiltily. 'I wasn't concentrating.'

'Game, set and match,' said Stephen.

'Oh no! Did I just lose us the match? How awful.'

'Six-one,' said Charles, approaching the net, hand outstretched. 'Thanks very much. Good game.'

'You are kind, Charles,' said Annie. 'I should think you were bored rigid.'

As she came off court, her mind returned to Mrs Finch.

'Valerie,' she said. 'Is there a manor house in the village? Or was there ever?'

'Ooh!' said Valerie. 'Didn't you know? Dad bought the old manor house. He's going to turn it into a hotel. It's ever so pretty.'

'Oh,' said Annie, disappointed.

'Are we changing for lunch?' asked Cressida.

'Christ, no,' said Caroline. 'Unless it's into a bikini. I wouldn't mind doing a bit of sunbathing.'

The players collapsed on the grass and Patrick began dispensing the drinks.

'I might have a go at the Pimm's,' said Valerie. 'This fruit cocktail's really delicious,' she added to Caroline. 'I can't think what you put in it.'

'Most refreshing,' agreed Don, who was reclining on the grass. 'And a very interesting flavour to it.' He smiled beatifically. Annie gave Valerie another glance. Her cheeks were pink and she seemed in very good spirits.

'Let me try it,' she said casually, taking a sip from Valerie's glass. 'Ahh, I see what you mean,' she said, catching Caroline's eye. Caroline snorted into her glass of Pimm's. 'Maybe you should stay with it if you're going to play again later.'

'Nonsense,' said Don jovially. 'This is a party, is it not? I always say, it's a mistake to take the sporting side of these events too seriously.'

'I hear you're going to open a hotel,' said Stephen conversationally to Don.

'That's right! I've found a super location here in Bindon. The old manor house, no less. Bound to be a winner. Although it still needs a lot of work done to it.' His face clouded over slightly. 'It's been an expensive business.'

'Were you in the hotel trade before?'

'Me? No! I trained as an accountant. Worked in the City for twenty years, then thought, Sod this, I'm going to do something I enjoy. Fine wines, good food, company all the year round – and a beautiful house. What could be better?'

'It sounds wonderful,' said Annie. 'When do you open?' Don drew in breath sharply.

'We were scheduled to open this autumn,' he said. 'Now it looks as though it'll be Christmas. There's still some building and decorating work to be done, and getting the brochures ready. Valerie's going to take care of that. Then all I need to do is find a good cook and a housekeeper – someone with a bit of class. You know what I mean.' He looked at Annie thoughtfully. 'In fact, if you hear of anyone – or any kind of hotel staff, come to that – I'd be grateful if you'd send 'em my way. Can't run the place all on my own!' Annie looked surprised, and glanced at Don's wedding-ringed hand.

'So Valerie's mother . . .'

'Passed away three years ago,' said Don abruptly. 'Breast cancer. Fifty-three, she was. She went to the doctor as soon as she found the lump, but it was already too late.'

'How terrible,' said Annie. 'I'm truly sorry.'

Don looked sharply at her. 'I hope you go for your scan every year, do you?'

'Well,' said Annie hesitantly.

'Could have saved Irene, a scan could. If she'd only gone for a check-up.'

'I'm not sure I qualify yet,' said Annie soothingly. 'But I will find out.'

'Pay for one if you have to,' insisted Don. 'That's

what I say to all the ladies I meet now. Get yourself scanned. You never know. I pay for Valerie to be scanned every year. I see it as a tribute, almost, to Irene.'

'How lovely,' said Annie awkwardly – then, aware that this didn't sound quite right, added, 'I mean, what a thoughtful gesture.'

They were interrupted by Caroline.

'Lunch is ready,' she said. 'And before you start saying how wonderful it is,' she added to Annie, 'I didn't cook it. The caterers did.'

Annie struggled to her feet, feeling the effect of a morning's drinking. The backs of her legs were covered in grass stains and the apricot tennis ensemble was looking rather rumpled. But I won't have to wash it, Mrs Finch will, she thought, and was amazed to discover how elated that made her feel.

The children were already on the terrace, piling their plates high with potato salad and crisps.

'What about some of this lovely vegetable terrine?' said Annie to Toby encouragingly. He wrinkled his nose and shook his head. 'Or some mushroom quiche?'

'Don't bother,' said Stephen idly. 'Let him eat what he wants. Potato salad and potato crisps. Obvious, really.'

Valerie was first to start filling her plate. She approached each dish with an exclamation of delight, and then loudly wondered what it was.

'Ooh! This looks like a swiss roll! But it must be savoury. How imaginative. I wonder what's in it. Is the green spinach?'

'Full of iron, spinach is,' observed Don. 'Ah, spring onions in the salad, I see. You know, they apparently reduce cholesterol. Worth knowing, that is. Worth repeating, too.' He chortled merrily. 'Get it? Worth repeating. Spring onions.'

Valerie suddenly hooted with laughter. 'Ooh Dad,

really!' She glanced at Cressida, standing at the other side of the terrace. 'What will people think?'

Cressida was not thinking of Don and his joke. She was wondering how early they could leave the next day without appearing rude. They would, presumably, attend church in the morning – and no doubt a large Sunday lunch would have been planned – but she didn't see why they shouldn't leave as soon as that was over. She would, however, have to broach the subject delicately with Charles. He seemed to be enjoying himself immensely, heaping food onto his plate in indiscriminate piles, and cheerily waving his glass in the air as he chatted to Caroline. She rarely saw him so abandoned. It was as if he was on holiday. But did that mean that everyday life with her was the equivalent of work? For a moment her mind teetered uneasily on the edge of the question, subconsciously aware that to answer it might be to come to some alarming, unwelcome conclusion. But even as she began to feel disturbed, her mind fluttered and lost grip of the problem, and her thoughts slid easily onto the more mundane reflection that Charles really should put a hat on in this sun.

Valerie came up to her, munching in an unattractive manner.

'You should have some lunch,' she said, 'it's delicious.'

'I will in a minute.'

'I suppose you're used to lovely food like this all the time,' continued Valerie. She gazed at Cressida admiringly. 'But you've got such a good figure. I expect you always just eat a little of everything, to be polite.' There was a pause, while Cressida tried to work out what this woman was talking about.

'I attend a lot of charity events,' she said eventually.

'Yes, you must do,' said Valerie. 'I suppose you've got loads of lovely ballgowns?' Cressida looked around for escape.

'If you'll excuse me, I think I'll go and get myself some lunch,' she said, giving Valerie a taut smile.

'That's all right,' said Valerie brightly. 'I could do with some seconds myself.'

After lunch, no-one seemed inclined to move. Everyone lolled on chairs or on the grass, except for Cressida, who was sitting bolt upright, unable to escape Valerie's fawning commentary. Patrick looked around. Now may be the moment. He sauntered casually across to Charles, who was lying back with his eyes closed.

'Remember that collection of prints I started,' he remarked. 'Well, I've been adding to it.' Charles opened one eye.

'Really? What have you bought?' Patrick laughed.

'Now you've caught me. I can't even remember who they're by. They're both modern, though. Cost me a fair bit, too.'

'Where did you get them?' Charles' attention was now fully engaged. 'You could have come to us.'

'I know,' said Patrick. 'But these were impulse buys. In London.' Charles scowled.

'I expect you were robbed.'

'Probably. In fact, I was hoping you'd come and give them a look. Tell me just how much I was ripped off.'

'Now?'

'Why not? While everyone's asleep.' He surveyed the dozy scene. 'I don't know how we're going to get anyone back on the tennis court this afternoon.'

Charles reluctantly got to his feet.

'OK, let's come and see the damage. Although I really wish you'd contain your impulses until you're in the Print Centre. Then you can be as impulsive as you like.'

'I'll remember that,' said Patrick, 'next time I'm feeling in the mood.'

Patrick's study was cool and tranquil, and for a few

68

minutes the men blinked, trying to focus in the dim light. Charles sank into a leather sofa.

'This is a nice room,' he said. He looked around. 'I bet you haven't read all those books.'

'No, but I'm intending to,' said Patrick. 'Actually, Caroline bought a lot of these. Because they look nice, I think.' Charles shrugged.

'And why not? The book as a visual art-form. I think it has potential. Why should we bother to read what's inside?' He reclined further into the squashy leather. 'So, show me these prints.'

'Here you are.' Patrick placed two small, unframed prints on his lap. Charles sat up and, with a practised eye, looked carefully at each, turning them over, scrutinizing the signature, examining the texture of the paper.

'Actually,' he said eventually, 'I think these are rather nice. Where did you get them?'

'Mocasins. Bond Street.' Charles sighed.

'Of course. My word, Patrick, you must be doing all right for yourself if you can afford to impulse buy there.'

Patrick shrugged. 'It's the right time to be investing. I realize it, my clients realize it. I mean, if I'm doing well, you should see how they're doing. If I had the money to invest properly in some of the ventures I know about . . . Well, let's just say I wouldn't be buying little prints; I'd be onto the big stuff by now.'

Charles was still examining the prints, and Patrick judged it best not to interrupt him.

'One of my clients', he said, 'invested ten thousand pounds five years ago. Emerging markets, he went into. Now he's sitting on a hundred thousand.'

'Really?' murmured Charles absently.

'He said to me, "If I'd known that would happen, I would have invested ten times as much. I'd be a millionaire!"' Patrick laughed reminiscently. 'I said to him, "How do you think I feel? I did know that would

69

happen – but I hadn't got anything to invest!"' He paused. 'And it's true. Those of us who know what's a sure winner can't take advantage of it – meanwhile, all the people who could afford to put their money in don't know about it!' He laughed gently. 'It's a crazy world.' Charles raised an eyebrow.

'Come on, Patrick, you must have a few thou lying around to invest.'

'I wish,' said Patrick. 'Look around. House, cars, pony. None of it comes cheap. But I can tell you, if I had the cash, I know exactly where I'd put it.' He stopped. 'Cigar?'

'Thanks.'

Patrick took his time snipping the cigars, picking up the onyx lighter, taking a few puffs, before continuing.

'There's an investment fund', he said confidingly, 'which is going to blow all the others out of the water. No-one knows about it yet. I'm not even telling all my clients. We've had a policy decision only to tell a few. Our most loyal customers. We're telling them now, while they can get in at a low price. It's a bit like a reward for staying with us over the years. And I can tell you, every single person we've told has snapped it up. We're almost oversubscribed.' Again he laughed gently. 'One man took all his money out of every single investment he held with us and put it all straight into the new fund. It caused a real headache, I can tell you! The administration was a nightmare.' He took a puff on his cigar. 'Not bad, these, are they?' Charles eyed him thoughtfully.

'I take it', he said, 'that you're going to tell me why this fund is so marvellous. It would seem a bit cruel to lead me on so far, and then shut the door in my face.'

'Well,' Patrick seemed doubtful, 'I'm not really supposed to be telling anybody except our existing clients. But, since you were so good as to tell me I wasn't ripped off with those prints,' he laughed, 'I owe you one.' He took a breath. 'Where do I start? I suppose you're familiar with the idea of investing in international equities?'

'Stocks and shares,' said Charles.

'Right,' said Patrick. 'And are you familiar with the idea of investing in futures and options? That's to say, promising to buy shares in the future, at a certain price?' Charles shrugged.

'I dimly remember being told something about it once. What's that got to do with it?'

'Well,' said Patrick, 'this fund invests half in stocks, calculates which way the price is going to go, and then uses the other half to work the market with futures and options.' Charles shook his head.

'You've lost me. I was never any good at maths.'

'That's a shame. If you knew a bit more about it, you'd see the potential. If you're interested, I've got some graphs somewhere that explain how it works.'

Charles looked alarmed. 'I don't think so.' He looked at his watch. 'Shouldn't we be getting back?'

'Of course, that's not our only fund,' interrupted Patrick smoothly, 'although it's the most exciting. We've got some that are safe as houses – boring as bricks, we call them. It really depends what kind of attitude the investor has got to risk. I mean, take yourself. What kind of approach have you got to risk?'

'I don't really know,' said Charles, diverted briefly. 'It's quite an interesting question, isn't it? What is one's attitude to risk?' He puffed on his cigar. 'I mean, I suppose leaving Ella and marrying Cressida was quite a risk. But at the time it seemed the obvious thing to do.'

'Exactly,' said Patrick. 'That's the kind of problem our fund managers deal with all the time. Investing in a certain stock may seem the obvious thing to do – but sometimes you'll get far better results by doing the unobvious.'

Charles wasn't listening.

'I sometimes wonder what it was about Cressida that

attracted me,' he said slowly. 'And I think it was that she was so different from Ella.' He pushed his hands through his hair, and stared ahead with a sudden bleak expression. 'Ella and I had been having problems – well, you know that. Most of it was over the gallery. I mean, it was so stupid, things we used to fight about. She used to get completely irrational in arguments, and that would drive me mad.' He winced at the memory. 'She's so passionate, Ella, and she believes in things so strongly, that she can't understand anyone who doesn't agree with her – or, even worse, doesn't really care. She used to accuse me of being too apathetic, of sitting on the fence. She really used to lay into me. And then one day, during all of that, I met Cressida. She was like an antidote to all the shouting and screaming. I mean, Cressida never even raises her voice.'

'She's a very elegant lady,' agreed Patrick. He left a decent interval of silence before saying, 'Now, I wonder what her attitude to risk is? In investment, I mean. Because—'

'Look, Patrick,' interrupted Charles in an exasperated voice, 'can't you see? I'm not interested. I'm sure you've got wonderful investment plans and there are all sorts of opportunities just dying to be exploited. But, if you don't mind, could you find someone else to do the exploiting? Our portfolio is managed by a very reputable company in London, and I'm afraid we haven't got any spare capital to put into any of your plans.' He looked at Patrick kindly. 'It's nothing personal. No hard feelings.'

Patrick stared at Charles through a haze of black and red. It wasn't possible that he had completely failed; that he hadn't even mustered ten or twenty thousand's worth of business. He thought of the hundreds of thousands that Charles must, *must* have under his control now, and his heart began to thump hard at the thought of his failing to garner any of it. The blind anger he felt towards Charles, still sitting there smiling at him, was tempered by the pragmatic realization that he must keep things on a pleasant basis. If it had been anyone else he would have launched into a more aggressive selling routine. But Charles wouldn't react well to that. And there was always the chance he might be interested in the future.

But underneath it all, Patrick knew that he had muffed it, probably for ever. Charles regarded him with an air of superiority that was hard to cut through; probably later he and Cressida would laugh about the way their oikish host had tried to flog them a dodgy investment plan. The thought drove out all pragmatism from Patrick's mind. Charles was looking fidgety; soon he would get up and go and the chance would be lost for ever.

'So who is it that manages your investments?' Patrick found himself saying. (What was he doing? Rule one: never refer to your opponents.) Charles gave him an amused look.

'As a matter of fact, it's Fountains. You know, the private bank.' Patrick summoned up a casually concerned look.

'Really? They're still taking on clients for portfolio management? I'm surprised.' (Rule two: never *ever* be derogatory about your opponents.) 'I heard they'd been going through a rough patch.'

'Really?' Charles regarded him with slight amusement. 'Well, I can assure you, Patrick, they've served us very well, and Cressida's family for the last fifty years. And that family certainly knows how to look after its money.' He made as if to get up. Patrick stared at him desperately, unable to stop him, but knowing that once he was outside the study door, all would be lost.

Suddenly his attention was caught by a small figure crossing the lawn outside the study window. It was Georgina, looking flushed and happy and hot, clutching a pile of straw and laughing something to Nicola,

73

who followed. The sight of his beautiful daughter, who was the reason behind his efforts and yet was so entirely oblivious of them, sent waves of panic coursing through Patrick's body, as he observed Charles drawing his feet up, getting ready to make his departure.

'Just listen to what I've got to say,' he blurted out. 'It won't take long. Then you can talk to Cressida and make up your minds together. No pressure.' Charles' smile faded, to be replaced by a look of distaste.

'Look, Patrick, I don't think I can put it more plainly. I'm not interested in buying anything from you. Our money is doing quite nicely where it is.' He hesitated, and then added, 'And to be frank, I think it's a bit much trying to do business with one of your guests. This is supposed to be a party, isn't it? Keep your charts for the office.'

Patrick felt burning humiliation cover his face and his chest heaved.

'You weren't so picky when it was you who needed money, were you?' he shouted. His voice came out much more loudly than he had intended, and Charles, who had been getting up, sat down again in surprise. 'You weren't so picky', said Patrick more quietly, 'when you needed that loan for your precious gallery, were you? Quite happy to come and talk business in my kitchen, you were then.'

'I know I was,' said Charles. 'I was very grateful and I still am. But that was entirely different.'

'No it wasn't,' said Patrick. 'One neighbour doing another a good turn. I had the money then and you needed it. Now you've got it, and I need it. I'm not even asking you to lend it to me. Just have a look at some of the investment plans I've got to offer.'

Charles sighed. 'Look, Patrick, I didn't realize you really needed the money. I mean,' he gestured around him, 'you hardly give the air of someone who's hard-up.' Patrick said nothing. 'If I did put some money into one of your funds,' said Charles, 'how much are we talking?'

Patrick didn't move for a second. His cigar had gone out; he carefully relit it. When it was going properly again he looked up at Charles.

'I would think around a hundred thousand? Perhaps eighty?'

'What?' Charles looked genuinely shocked. 'You must be mad, man. If that's the kind of money you need, you've got the wrong guy.' He paused, and thought. 'I could put around five thousand into a plan if that was any use to you. Perhaps seven or eight at a pinch.'

Patrick's face felt numb. Seven or eight thousand. And he was eighty thousand short of his target. It was hardly worth the ink. With an effort, he looked up at Charles and gave him a professional smile.

'I'll have a look through my fund details and put together a package which I think might suit you. How's that?'

'Fine.' Charles seemed relieved. He got to his feet. 'Coming back outside?'

Patrick shook his head. 'No, I'll just sort out a few things in here. See you later.'

They smiled at each other again and Charles left the room. Patrick went over to his desk and sat down heavily in his leather-bound swivel chair. The folder marked 'Charles' was still lying to hand in his top drawer. With a scowl he took it out and ripped it in two. Then, suddenly feeling drained, he slumped down on his desk and buried his head in his hands.

Chapter Five

Stephen, sitting alone on the grass with the remains of his raspberry pavlova, felt as if he had had too much. Too much food, too much drink, too much envy. As the day wore on, he was becoming more and more aware of how rich and successful everyone here was compared to him and Annie. Patrick and Caroline, Charles and Cressida; even Don, with his manor house hotel. They all had the air of comfort, if not wealth; they all had reached their goals. Whereas he hadn't even worked out what his goal was.

He abruptly stood up and shook the crumbs of meringue off his legs. Annie looked up drowsily. 'Just going for a little stroll,' he said. 'I won't be long.' She smiled and closed her eyes again. Caroline and Don seemed to be asleep; Valerie was chatting animatedly to Cressida. She paused and glanced up at him, and he hurried off before she asked him where he was going – or, even worse, suggested accompanying him. He was in no mood for talking.

He walked briskly and mindlessly to the far end of Patrick's grounds, beyond the tennis court, past the paddock, till he was at the fence which bordered the garden with a field full of sheep. Then he turned and surveyed the scene behind him. The White House was almost invisible behind the trees. There was no sign of anyone else. He was on his own.

Stephen sighed, and sank down onto the grass. He didn't want to see any of them, not even Annie. They all seemed to be mocking him; his failure to reach the same goals as them; his dusty old car, his scruffy old clothes, his indeterminate career path. Annie, too, though she didn't mean to, had slipped into the clothes of Caroline with consummate ease; over lunch they had giggled together like schoolgirls, and his last ally in this glossy, alien world seemed to have slipped away to the other side.

Where had he gone wrong? Until he left Cambridge, he had seemed one of the chosen ones – a bright, popular scholar who gained his first in history, took part in the university musical scene, acted, debated, even rowed for a term. 'A brilliant all-rounder' was how his final reference from his tutor described him, 'destined to go far'. He had left intending to become an academic. His M.Phil. had gone well, and he had begun research for a doctorate. In those days, he had still been the bright, intellectual success among his peers, who themselves were pursuing careers in advertising, accountancy, even retail management. Stephen, left behind in Cambridge, had felt sorry for them, having to settle for such tedious jobs. And that had been the sentiment among everyone at Cambridge. He could still remember his tutor gently mocking one of his friends, who had joined a well-known firm which made cooked meat.

But what the hell was wrong with cooked meat? That friend now figured frequently in the business pages of newspapers, as his company mounted takeover after takeover. The contemporary who had 'wasted himself' in advertising now had his own agency. He had recently been quoted in the paper as saying that he thought graduates weren't worth the space. 'Give me a sixteen year old any day,' he had said. 'I'm tired of these graduates who think they're God's gift because they can quote a bit of Plato.'

After four years of making notes, attending seminars, and tutoring the odd undergraduate, Stephen's doctorate had not taken shape. He was disillusioned, lonely and poor. And then he had met Annie. The burning desire to achieve knowledge, to be published, to make his mark in the academic world, had been succeeded by more mundane requirements. A house, a car, an income. The decision to take a teaching post in the comfortable city of Silchester had seemed an obvious one.

And for a while, he had seemed to be swimming with the rest of them. His income from teaching wasn't bad, a legacy from his father had bought them a house, they were able to afford a comfortable life. He had befriended a local history expert; had joined a local choir; all his needs had seemed to be fulfilled. It was only in the last couple of years that the canker had started. Seeing contemporaries' names in the lists of university appointments as well as on the finance pages. Realizing that he was destined to have neither the prestige of an academic career nor the financial rewards of a commercial one. For a few months he had been severely depressed. Was this mediocre, suburban life all he, who had been one of the brightest stars at Cambridge, was to aspire to?

It had been Annie who had proposed, then insisted, that he should go back to studying. He had carried on, sporadically, with his research since abandoning the doctorate; his notes still sat in their folders; his original ideas still had backbone to them. If he took a year's sabbatical, perhaps two, she suggested, they would be able to manage with their savings and her part-time work. It wasn't too late for him to achieve his ambition of becoming Dr Fairweather. Her enthusiasm had given him the impetus to submit a fresh proposal, find himself some funding, negotiate a sabbatical with his school, and begin his research all over again.

Stephen hunched his back over his knees. The familiar sinking feeling which he had whenever he thought of his thesis had gripped his stomach again. He couldn't, couldn't admit to Annie that his thesis wasn't going, let alone going well, that he was terrified of failure, that he had no-one to confide in. He gazed miserably at the ground. Had he made yet another mistake? Should he have stayed in teaching? Should he have decided to move into a more lucrative area? Taken accountancy exams? Don, bloody smug Don, with his moron daughter, seemed to have done all right out of accountancy. Why had everybody derided it at Cambridge? Patrick, who hadn't even been to university, was making a fortune; Charles might have been in financial straits once, but he was doing all right now. They were all moving onwards and upwards, to bigger and better things, while he and Annie were left behind.

His legs were beginning to feel stiff, and Stephen stood up. He would have to rejoin the party before people began wondering where he was. He began walking reluctantly back towards the house. His hair felt rumpled and he was sure his shirt must be covered in hay.

He walked past the tennis court, avoiding the terrace, and went round to the front of the house. He would go and tidy up before facing the others. As he entered the cool house, he saw Charles disappearing out of a side door at the end of the hall. He paused, and looked at himself in the hall mirror.

'Stephen! Didn't hear you come in!' Stephen turned in surprise. Patrick was standing at the door of his study.

'Thought I'd have a quick wash and brush up,' said Stephen. 'I'm sure I need it.' Patrick waved his hand dismissively.

'Come in and have a cigar. I'm not sure I had this brand last time you were here. I'd appreciate your judgement.'

'I'm hardly in a position to help you, since the only time I ever have a cigar is when I'm here,' said Stephen, more harshly than he had intended. Patrick gave him a surprised look.

'Come in anyway.'

'Sorry,' said Stephen, stepping into the long, dim room. 'I guess I've had too much sun.' Patrick clapped a hand on his shoulder.

'Come on, Stephen. We're friends. If you can't sound off to me, who can you sound off to?'

Stephen sank on to the leather sofa. The ashtray on the table to the side of the sofa was full.

'Have you been soliciting Charles' advice, too?'

'What?' Patrick looked taken-aback as he sat down. Stephen gestured to the ashtray.

'About your new cigars. I saw him going outside just now.' Patrick paused.

'Oh. Yes, I did ask him what he thought. But actually, I'm afraid to say we were talking business.'

'The gallery again? I would have thought he was OK for money by now.' Patrick smiled as if at a nice memory.

'No, not the gallery. Just a bit of an opportunity I was able to put his way. He should do quite nicely out of it.'

'Oh.' Stephen held up his cigar to the lighter. 'He's become quite a capitalist, old Charles, hasn't he? All a bit different from the Charles we used to know and love.'

Patrick shrugged. 'It's not really a question of being a capitalist. Anyone would take advantage of this opportunity if they knew about it. Did you see Charles' face?'

Stephen shook his head.

'Pity. I was wondering how wide his grin was.'

'Why?' said Stephen curiously. 'What's this fantastic opportunity?'

Patrick grimaced. 'It's very boring. And quite technical. You don't really want to hear it.'

'Why not?' Stephen looked up, nettled. 'How do you know I don't have a stash of cash, just waiting to invest?'

'I don't. Do you?'

'No.'

'Well then.' Patrick took a puff of his cigar and looked thoughtful. 'Although, of course, that's not quite true,' he said. 'You do have a stash of cash.'

'What?'

'It's not an obvious one, but it's there, if ever you need it.'

'What are you talking about?'

'Your house.'

'What, eighteen Seymour Road?'

'Must be worth a fair bit now.'

'I'm sure it is,' said Stephen. 'But you forget, we live there. If we sold it, we'd only have to buy another one.' He began to laugh. 'We're simple folk, Patrick. We don't have spare property hanging around to sell.'

'I know that. But you don't have to sell your house to get all its potential from it.' He looked directly at Stephen. 'You don't have a mortgage, do you?'

'Well, no,' said Stephen. 'We just about had enough from my father's legacy to buy it outright.'

'And that was, what, ten years ago? It'll have held its value since then, I'm sure.'

Stephen was silent, listening.

'My point is only this,' said Patrick. 'That, if you wanted to, say, if you needed the money, you could always take out a mortgage on your house.'

'That's a bit extreme,' said Stephen. 'I mean, it's one of the things I'm continually grateful for, that we don't have mortgage payments to worry about.'

'I know that,' said Patrick. 'I'm just telling you in case you ever need a large sum of money. Say, for an emergency.'

'Some emergency it would be!' said Stephen.

'Or, of course, if you thought you could make a bit of money out of it,' added Patrick. 'But I don't suppose that would really be your scene.'

'What wouldn't?' demanded Stephen.

'It's something that some of my friends in the City have been doing,' said Patrick. 'I'd do it myself, if I weren't mortgaged up to the hilt already. The idea is, you take out a mortgage on your house and invest the money yourself. Then, as long as you can beat the interest rate on your loan, you make a profit.' He chuckled. 'And let's just say that beating the interest rate hasn't been a problem.' He paused, and took a puff from his cigar. 'But these are all fairly high-powered people. They know where the opportunities are.'

'Is that what Charles is doing?' asked Stephen.

'More or less,' said Patrick. 'I can't really discuss it, I'm afraid – stupid really, considering we're all friends, but rules is rules.' He stood up. 'Anyway, you haven't told me what you think of the cigar.'

'The cigar's great,' said Stephen absently. He looked around the luxurious, book-lined room, took in the aroma of leather and expensive cigar smoke, let his mind range over the words being bandied about. Investment, profit, money. That was what real life was about these days; a life that, so far, he had taken no part in. When was the last time anyone had talked to him about making money? He was a mere teacher; an impoverished academic; forever on the outside of this fast, financial world. But that could change.

'Tell me,' he said cautiously. 'If, say, I took a mortgage out on my house and put the money into the same scheme that Charles is investing in – would I beat the interest rate? Would I make money?' Patrick began to chortle.

'Would he make money, he asks! You want to know if you'd make money? A client of mine put ten thousand pounds into a plan just like this one five years ago; now he's sitting on a hundred thousand. He said to me, "If I'd known that would happen, I would have invested ten times as much. I'd be a millionaire!"'

'Really? Only ten thousand?' Stephen sounded interested.

'But the point is', said Patrick, 'that he should have put in ten times that much. He'd never have had to work again. In your case', he looked at Stephen, 'I'd recommend at least eighty thousand. That must be about, what, a third of your house's value?' Stephen shrugged.

'You tell me.'

'Our house sold for two hundred and twenty thousand. And prices will have come up again by at least another twenty since then. If you, for argument's sake, invested eighty thousand, it would only be a third of your available capital. Really, you'd still be underinvested – but, then you probably want to play safe.' He looked at Stephen. 'Tell you what,' he said, 'I've got some charts in here. Just so you can see the sort of thing I'm talking about. And while we're at it, what about a brandy?'

Stephen leant back into the leather and took a puff of cigar. He suddenly felt buoyant and sophisticated. Charles was not the only one who could do business with Patrick. He watched pleasurably as Patrick poured out two generous glasses of brandy, and then sat up intelligently as he approached, bearing a series of colourful-looking graphs. Stephen took a sip of brandy.

'Fire away,' he said. 'I'm all ears.'

Cressida was clutching her glass harder and harder as Valerie's hooting, fluting voice poured a mixture of inane observations and sycophantic questions into her ears. Caroline and Annie were chatting quietly to each other with a cosy intimacy that was impossible to join; Stephen had gone for a walk; Charles had disappeared off somewhere with Patrick; and Don had popped home to feed the dog. There was no escape.

'I do love your ring,' said Valerie. 'Is it a real diamond?' Cressida nodded, feeling a sudden, alien desire to shout, 'No, it's out of a cracker!'

'I thought it must be,' said Valerie. She glanced down at her own pudgy, white hands. 'I've never bothered with rings,' she said.

I'm not surprised, thought Cressida, eyeing Valerie's slug-like fingers with distaste.

'I don't suppose . . . would you mind if I tried it on?' continued Valerie in a rush, looking at Cressida with suddenly eager eyes. She thrust a finger out and Cressida shuddered.

'Actually,' she said, 'I must go and find Charles.' She got up, stiff from the morning's tennis.

Valerie looked down disappointedly. Caroline, glancing up, saw Cressida making her escape and called, 'What do you want to see Charles for? You must see him enough every day!' She smirked at Cressida, who gazed at her in cold fury.

'There was something I wanted to mention to him,' she said offputtingly. 'If you'll excuse me.'

As she passed through the terrace doors into the house, she heard Caroline sniggering, and then Valerie's voice calling, 'Cressida! Charles is out here! He's walking towards the paddock! Cressida!'

Cressida ignored them. She went quickly through the hall, suddenly desperate to get up to their bedroom for some peace. Voices were coming from behind one of the doors; she recognized them as Patrick's and Stephen's. But her tennis shoes were silent on the carpet and she was soon safely behind the door of the spare room. She sank onto the bed, grimacing as her skin slipped against the satin.

She looked at her watch. It was only three o'clock. Another twenty-four hours to go at least. It was simply too much. But she had promised Charles she would try to make an effort. He wouldn't be very impressed if he heard how she'd skulked away inside, ignoring his friends. She would have to say she had come inside for a reason. To finish unpacking – her eyes fell on Charles' half-empty suitcase – and deal with the letters. Of course.

She went into the bathroom – rather nicely done, she grudgingly admitted to herself – and splashed her face with cold water. Then, feeling restored, she went back into the bedroom to tackle the rest of the unpacking. She left the letters until last, until she'd put away every one of Charles' shirts, socks, pieces of shaving equipment and cuff-links. Then, with a sigh, she sat down at the pink-frilled, kidney-shaped dressing table in the corner of the room and began to slit open the envelopes. .

She left the crisp, white, London-postmarked one till last, even though it was addressed to her rather than to Charles or both of them. It was bound to be some boring notice to shareholders, or a statement of account that she would immediately pass onto Charles. As she opened it, her mind was still on the dress bill that the last envelope had contained (was it for the cream suit or the cocktail dress? Charles would be bound to ask her), and for a few moments she didn't register the words before her.

Then, gradually, they began to impinge upon her consciousness; one by one arresting her attention; bouncing off her brain and mixing themselves up in her mind so that, with a sudden exclamation, half of impatience, half of panic, she closed her eyes, opened them, and forced herself to read the letter, slowly from the beginning.

When she had finished reading it for the first time she thought she might be sick. With customary self-control, she folded the letter, slid it carefully back into its envelope, and put it with the others. She sat completely still for a moment, staring blankly at her reflection in the mirror, reminding herself that she was a complete ignoramus when it came to financial affairs. No doubt it was all a mistake.

But before she could even finish articulating the thought, her hands had grabbed the envelope again and ripped it open, and she was gazing at the sheet of paper once more, her hands unable to hold it still, her heart thumping, her eyes flickering from the heading at the top of the paper down to the signature and up again, focusing first with disbelief, then with terror, at the figure, in pounds sterling, glaring in black and white in the middle of the page.

She closed her eyes for a moment, swaying in her chair, and emptied her mind. Then she opened her eyes again. The letter was still in her hand; the figure in the centre of the page still glared blackly at her, seeming to increase in size until it filled the whole of her view and she could see nothing else. With a sudden smart of humiliation, she clutched her stomach and rushed into the bathroom.

When she emerged again, her legs felt shaky. She looked at herself in the mirror and was shocked to see that her face was white, her lips were dry, her whole face seemed to have crumpled. She longed to lie down, curl up and bury her head in her knees. She sank to the floor of the bedroom and sat still for a few seconds. But she was self-conscious and could not relax. This was a stranger's house – what if someone came in and saw her behaving oddly? Then a more alarming thought occurred to her. The letter still lay on the dressing table, for anyone to see. With a sudden dart of panic, she looked around for somewhere to store it until she could show it to Charles. At the thought of Charles, another spasm hit her stomach, and she half-crawled, half-ran into the bathroom.

Coming out again, her first priority was to remove the letter from the dressing table. She looked feebly around the room for somewhere to put it. Was Caroline the sort to employ a maid to turn down the beds? One could never be sure of the limit to the excesses of that sort of parvenue. Eventually, she slipped it into the lining of her beauty case. Then, paranoically, she immediately imagined Caroline coming in to borrow some make-up, fiddling with the case, saying loudly, 'You've got something stuck in here,' pulling it out, reading it, gazing up in horror . . .

But that really was a foolish, hysterical way to think. With the letter safely out of sight, Cressida began to feel better. She slapped her cheeks, combed her hair, and sprayed some scent behind her ears. She rubbed some lipsalve vigorously into her lips and took a few deep breaths, as she had been taught in elocution lessons when she was eleven.

But when she went to the door of the room, she found that her nerve was failing her. Twice she reached for the door handle, paused with her hand on the knob, physically unable to leave the safety of her temporary haven. On the other side of the door were people, reality, Charles, the children. This side of the door there was only herself, the pink satin bed and the letter – which, stuffed into her vanity case, didn't really exist yet. Not while she hadn't told anyone about it.

She looked at her watch. Half-past three. Earlier she had been desperate for time to move on; now she wished it could stay still. She would have to tell Charles tonight, in bed, where there was no chance of anyone hearing. Until then, for a few hours, perhaps she could pretend nothing had happened. But she would have to display her usual confidence. She would have to put on a good show. Summoning up unknown reserves of determination, Cressida grasped the door handle firmly and strode out into the corridor and, staring ahead blankly, unthinkingly, her mind deliberately dead, she made her way out into the garden.

Chapter Six

Caroline and Annie had taken a jug of Pimm's down to the tennis court. There Georgina was teaching Nicola to play tennis while Toby sat happily in the umpire's chair. Nicola grasped the lightweight racquet awkwardly, and swung ineffectually at each ball that Georgina threw, only occasionally making contact. But Georgina continued patiently to make cheerful, encouraging comments.

'She's incredible, your daughter,' said Annie quietly.

'I could say the same thing to you,' said Caroline. 'Nicola's made so much progress. You must be thrilled to bits. I mean, did you ever think she'd be able to play tennis?'

'Well,' said Annie, 'we never gave up hope. But I have to admit, there were times when I couldn't see her leading a normal life.' She gazed silently ahead for a moment. 'She's got so much willpower,' she continued, 'she's so absolutely determined to succeed, it makes one feel quite weak in comparison. She's got more tenacity than both of us put together.'

'And she's bright, too, isn't she?' said Caroline.

'Oh yes,' Annie flushed with pleasure. 'I think in other circumstances she might have been labelled gifted. But it would seem a bit ironic, under the circumstances.'

They both involuntarily looked at Nicola's skewed foot, her clenching, uncoordinated arm, her glowing face.

'Poor little sod,' said Caroline. 'How does the school treat her?'

'Oh, very well, considering,' said Annie slightly

defensively. 'It must be difficult for them. She's so bright, and so enthusiastic to learn, but then when she has to write it all down, of course, she's much slower than all the others. She gets very frustrated with herself. And then,' she added, slightly bitterly, 'some of the teachers seem to think that nothing can be any good unless it's written out neatly.'

'Doesn't sound great to me,' said Caroline. 'No offence.' Annie shrugged.

'What can you do? They're overstretched, they're busy, they haven't got time for a child who doesn't conform. I do all I can to help Nicola at home, but . . . How's Georgina getting on?' she added abruptly.

'Oh, great guns,' said Caroline. 'Reckons she's going to be head of junior house next term, whatever the hell that means. I think she's getting in a bit of practice on poor old Nicola. She's getting far too bossy.'

'Oh, I wouldn't worry about Nicola,' said Annie laughing. 'She loves it. She simply gobbles up all those boarding-school books – pretty trashy stuff, really. And to meet someone who actually does all those things – you know, trunks and tuck boxes and dormitories – is utter bliss.'

'Well, tell her she can come and pack Georgina's trunk any time,' said Caroline, 'since I'm the one who always ends up doing it.'

'Oh, but that's the mother's job,' said Annie, grinning at Caroline, 'and she's supposed to hide a little surprise under one's nightie. That's what my mother always did.'

'Then she was a mug,' said Caroline. 'As soon as Georgina's in the senior school she's doing her own trunk, or it doesn't get done. Anyway, she's much better than me at that kind of thing. I can't understand how she turned out so bloody efficient.' They both looked at Georgina, busily picking up tennis balls.

'So she's going to stay on at St Catherine's?' said Annie. Caroline shrugged. 'We had a bit of a look round other senior schools, but there didn't seem any point moving her. It's a lovely school, she can take her pony there, the staff seem OK – a bit snotty maybe, but, you know, all right basically. And she knows the place.'

'It is a lovely school,' agreed Annie. 'I remember visiting it once, when Nicola was tiny.'

'Really?' Caroline looked surprised.

'We always meant to send her to a private school', said Annie, 'when she was eight or so. We thought that would give us time to get the fees together. Toby, too.' She shrugged. 'Things didn't work out quite as we planned. First the stroke – then Stephen going back to his doctorate.'

'How much longer does he have with that thing? He's been doing it for bloody ages.' Annie shrugged.

'Depends how it goes. Another year, perhaps two.'

'Christ, I don't know how you put up with it. I couldn't. I mean, no job, no money – I'd go crazy.'

'Well, he still teaches a bit,' said Annie, 'and I do proofreading when I have the time. It's not so bad, really. And with no mortgage on the house and no school fees – you know, we can keep our outgoings quite low.' Caroline shuddered.

'Rather you than me. Can't you persuade Stephen to get a job again, give up this degree?'

'It's what he wants to do,' said Annie firmly.

There was a noise behind them and they both looked round. Cressida had come down the path to the tennis court and stood, watching the girls playing tennis. As they turned, she seemed to wobble slightly. Her face was drained of blood and her smile appeared artificial.

'Hello, Cressida,' said Annie cautiously. She hesitated, and then added, 'Are you all right? I mean, do you feel OK?'

'You look terrible,' said Caroline, bluntly. 'Must be too much sun. Here, sit down.' She drew up a chair and patted it invitingly. 'Have some Pimm's. Or do you want something stronger?'

'If you've had too much sun, perhaps you shouldn't have any alcohol,' said Annie.

'Is it the sun?' Caroline peered closely at Cressida's face. 'Hang on a minute. Do you feel sick? Is there any chance you could be . . . ?' Cressida gazed at her uncomprehendingly. 'You know, pregnant,' said Caroline impatiently. 'Are you? Tell me quick before I pour out all this lovely booze and you say you can't drink it.' Cressida exhaled sharply.

'Don't worry,' she said slowly, 'I can drink all I like.'

'Attagirl,' said Caroline approvingly. She gave Cressida an appraising look as she poured out the drink. 'There, now you relax and take it easy,' she said. 'I always thought playing tennis was a bad idea. Why not just have people round for the weekend? That's what I wanted to know. But Patrick insisted on this stupid tournament and now the whole thing seems to have turned into bloody Wimbledon.'

'That's hardly fair,' protested Annie. 'We've only had two matches. And I like playing tennis. What about you, Cressida?' she said, turning to Cressida in a friendly manner. 'You're really good. You must enjoy it.'

'What?' said Cressida, looking up distractedly. 'Sorry, I didn't hear you.'

'It doesn't matter,' said Annie, glancing at Caroline.

'Hello, you lot, all sitting around doing nothing?' It was Patrick, beaming and jovial and smelling of cigars. Behind him was Stephen, looking defiantly pleased with himself.

'Have you two been gorging yourselves on cigars?' asked Annie, shooting a teasing look at Stephen.

'Cigars and brandy,' said Patrick, briskly rubbing his hands. 'Just the job before a game of tennis.'

'I don't know how you can!' exclaimed Annie. 'I feel zonked enough as it is.'

'Ah well, you women don't have the stamina, that's what it is,' said Patrick. 'Isn't that right, Stephen?'

'I wouldn't like to say,' said Stephen, grinning back at Patrick. He seemed in buoyant spirits, thought Annie. Perhaps she should stock up on brandy and cigars at home.

'Now, we must get back to business,' said Patrick. 'Where's the chart?'

Caroline groaned loudly.

'Here we are,' he said. 'It's Cressida and Charles against Don and Valerie.'

'Well, we haven't got Don, we haven't got Valerie and we haven't got Charles,' said Caroline. 'We're doing well.'

'Who hasn't got Charles?' Charles emerged around the corner, carrying one of the twins. Behind him followed Martina, carrying the other twin, and Valerie.

'We've just been to look at your lovely horse,' began Valerie. 'I must say, he's a beautiful creature.'

'It's a she,' said Caroline. 'Where's your dad? You're supposed to be playing.' Valerie looked worried.

'I think he went home to feed the dog. Perhaps he got held up.'

'The thing is,' said Caroline, glancing wickedly at Annie, 'if he doesn't make it back we'll have to treat the match as if you lost, by default. We'll have to score you both nil. Unless you want to play Charles and Cressida on your own?'

Valerie's eyes darted nervously up the path. 'I'm sure he won't be long. Shall I give him a ring?'

'Why not?' said Caroline kindly. 'You know where the phone is.' Valerie disappeared up the path and Annie erupted into giggles.

'What did you say that for?' said Patrick. 'There's no hurry.'

'So what? Serve Don right for being such a git.'

Charles went over to Cressida, kissed her lightly and perched on the arm of her chair.

'I heard you were trying to find me,' he said. 'Was it something important?'

'Oh, no,' stammered Cressida.

'You know,' he continued, 'I really think it would be a good idea to get the boys a pony when they're old enough. We could move to a bigger place with a bit of land, perhaps. Have you seen Georgina's pony?'

Cressida shook her head numbly. Charles' eyes shone with enthusiasm.

'It's a very nice animal,' he said. 'And Georgina's not at all a bad rider. I can see her eventing in a few years' time. I'd really love the boys to be able to do the same one day.'

'Eventers are expensive,' said Cressida in a dry, scratchy voice. She stared at her hands, and forced her thoughts away from the bedroom with the pink satin cover and the vanity case and the letter.

'Well, yes,' said Charles, surprised, 'but then so are a lot of things. Anyway, it's just a thought.' He leapt up and picked up his racquet.

'Right!' he shouted at Georgina and Nicola, still on the tennis court. 'Who's going to give me a game?'

'Hello, beautiful.' Stephen came over and wrapped his arms round Annie from behind. 'Doesn't she look fantastic in that gear?' he said to Caroline.

'Marvellous,' said Caroline.

'I've been telling her to ask you where you bought it,' said Stephen. 'I think my wife deserves a new tennis outfit or two, don't you?' Annie turned round to face Stephen.

'You've been drinking too much brandy,' she said, laughing, but slightly puzzled. She peered at his eyes. They were very bright and didn't meet hers properly but darted quickly about. If he had been one of the children, she would probably have called him over-excited and told him to go to bed. But why was Stephen suddenly in this manic mood?

Stephen was aware of Annie looking puzzledly at him, but he ignored her gaze. He was feeling confident, alive and invigorated. He watched Charles racing about the tennis court, clowning with the children – and didn't feel the customary stab of envy. He looked genially around at his expensively clad friends, noting their gold watches and smart racquets, for once without a pang of jealousy. He was now up among them. He was as able as Charles, Don or any of them, to make high-powered deals over fat cigars; to talk of his investments, to wink knowingly at Patrick when he talked of stocks, shares and portfolios.

Signing that piece of paper had given Stephen the biggest rush of adrenalin he could remember having since discovering he'd got a first at Cambridge. Patrick had produced a beautiful Cross fountain pen and invited him to sit at his desk. He'd watched benignly as Stephen ran his eyes down the small print – looking for what? Stephen hadn't really been sure – and suggested Stephen took it away with him to think about. But Stephen had made a dismissive, rather debonair gesture.

'Think about what, Patrick?' he'd said. 'Whether I want to be rich or poor? I reckon I've thought about that enough already.' Patrick had chuckled appreciatively and poured out yet another brandy. Stephen had taken one, final look at the paperwork and then signed briskly, coolly, matter-of-factly; as though he were used to making that kind of transaction on a regular basis.

Stephen tightened his grasp around Annie as his mind skated over the exact figure he'd signed away to Patrick. Patrick had assured him that it would all be covered easily by a part-mortgage on their house, and that he would be able to fix it up as soon as he got to the office on Monday. And of course, as Patrick had explained, there was no point thinking about it in the context of everyday amounts of money. Making a serious investment was quite a different business from, say, paying the gas bill, or even buying a car. Patrick had certainly looked unconcerned at the amount

Stephen was entrusting to him. He was obviously used to sums as big as, if not bigger than, this one.

The feeling of power which Stephen had suddenly felt, dealing in such a large amount of money, was irresistible. He was suddenly reminded of a stag party to which he had once been invited by a Cambridge friend whose father was in the hotel business. They'd stayed, six of them, all expenses paid, at a big London five-star hotel over the weekend. By the end of the stay, the delight of signing large bar bills, choosing steak à la carte and drinking the mini bar dry had gone to Stephen's head. He'd lingered in the hotel shop after they'd all checked out, fingering cashmere jerseys and silver-plated tankards appraisingly, desperate to pro-long his role in the world of the rich. The exorbitant prices had begun to appear reasonable to him, detached as they were from the reality of his student grant and weekly budget. He'd even eventually gone so far as to buy a ridiculously expensive leather wallet, embossed with the name of the hotel, signing the cheque without flinching; even wondering aloud whether he ought not to have the key fob as well. And now he was experiencing the same heady sensation. He caught Patrick's eye and grinned.

'That's a fine brandy you keep,' he said jovially. Patrick's eyes twinkled.

'Well now, you'll have to sample my other favourite after dinner,' he replied in a genial tone.

'Looking forward to it!'

Patrick smiled again at Stephen, and then turned away. His sensation of sheer delight at having snared his last, his most crucial deal, was proving difficult to control. He stared down at his hands, unable to stop a beam creeping over his face. One hundred thousand pounds bonus. One hundred thousand pounds! He clenched the back of the chair in front of him, and took a deep breath. It had been almost impossible to stay calm as he had slowly manoeuvred Stephen into signing away exactly the right sum of money. It had been pure artistry, the way he had paced his pitch, balancing nonchalance with enthusiasm, keeping the warmth in his voice, the credibility in his smile, not pushing, but inviting. When it had come to the actual signature, he had almost lost his cool. Seeing Stephen poised, pen in hand, over the documents, scanning the page, looking as if he might hesitate, the desire to force his pen down on to the page and *make* him sign had grown frighteningly strong. But somehow he had managed to remain outwardly sanguine, resting his fingers lightly on the back of Stephen's chair with a tense patience, keeping his voice smooth.

And finally it had happened. Stephen had signed away eighty thousand pounds of his money. Patrick didn't allow himself to consider whether this was a safe move for Stephen. He had explained what the fund was; he had allowed Stephen to make up his own mind – it was Stephen's decision, not his. And eighty thousand wasn't so much, really. Not compared with the amount of business Patrick had already done that year. He remembered with a quiver of delight his performance charts, waiting in his desk drawer for the final figures. He would be top salesman again that year. And would be well rewarded. Patrick gazed at Georgina, playing tennis beautifully and giggling hysterically as Charles pretended to miss all her shots, and he felt a surge of triumph. Now they could afford a new house, a new pony – anything his daughter wanted, she could have.

His eye fell on Charles and he felt a twinge of anger that he had not been able to close the deal with him. Fucking tight git. But then, Charles was always there for the future. Whereas Stephen . . . Patrick shook his head. Stephen was about the least likely person he could imagine having as a client. It had never even occurred to him to pitch at Stephen. But a good salesman should be able to sell to anyone. And he had excelled himself that afternoon. It had been a model exercise in salesmanship. Suddenly he felt too keyed up to stand still, and he wandered over to Caroline. He ran his hands over her hips, and nuzzled her neck.

'You're gorgeous, you know that?' he whispered. 'Fucking gorgeous.'

Caroline eyed Patrick suspiciously. First this morning's good mood, now this. What was he up to? She had not failed to notice him invite Charles into his study. What had been his reason? To look at those prints he'd bought a couple of weeks ago. She'd been surprised when he'd shown them to her. Weird, modern efforts – not his kind of thing at all. It really wouldn't surprise her to learn that he'd bought the prints especially to have an excuse to ask Charles into his study. And Charles had gone along trustingly. But it didn't fool her. Had Patrick tried to sell some sort of plan to Charles? And had he succeeded? She glanced up at Patrick's face. He had an expression of suppressed glee; his mouth was twitching into a smile and his eyes were bright. He must have sold Charles something. No wonder he was in such a good mood. No wonder he had plied poor old Stephen with brandy so generously. It must have been a big deal. Caroline looked consideringly at Charles, romping on the tennis court. He seemed in a good mood as well. She inwardly shrugged. Good luck to them. And now Patrick had achieved his aim of extracting money out of Charles, perhaps they wouldn't have to invite them over again. She could certainly do without Cressida's bloody miserable face about the place.

Eventually Don turned up, rather flustered, and was ushered onto the tennis court by a smirking Caroline. Valerie followed him, looking rather anxious, and finally Cressida got up and made her way silently onto the court. Her face was still pale, and she fingered her racquet in a desultory way. But Don's face lit up as he saw her and realized that he and Valerie were to play against Charles and Cressida.

'Here's a real challenge, Val!' he exclaimed. He turned and grinned perkily at Annie and Stephen. 'This'll be a nightmare! Wake me up when it's all over!'

Annie smiled back encouragingly.

'Fucking prat,' murmured Stephen.

Georgina and Nicola, usurped from the tennis court, flopped down, panting, on the grass.

'You're very good at tennis,' said Annie to Georgina.

'I'm all right,' she replied conversationally. 'I'm in special coaching at school. But I'm not in the house team. You see, about ten people in each house have special coaching if they're good enough, but only six are in the team. And a reserve.' Patrick raised his eyebrows at Caroline.

'You didn't tell me Georgina was having special coaching for tennis.'

'That's because I didn't know,' said Caroline unconcernedly.

'Sweetie,' Patrick addressed Georgina, 'why don't you tell us things?' Georgina shrugged.

'I do tell you things.'

'You didn't tell us about that.'

'I forgot.' Georgina abruptly leapt up. 'Time for another rehearsal. Martina, bring the twins.' She looked around and called in a stentorian voice, 'Toby! Come on!'

'What are you rehearsing?' said Annie.

'A play,' said Georgina, discouragingly. 'You'll see it tomorrow. Toby!'

'He's stuck in the umpire's chair,' said Nicola. 'Someone'll have to get him out.' But already Martina had put down the twin she was carrying and hurried over to release Toby from his perch.

'She's certainly got them all organized,' said Stephen admiringly, as the troop of children left the tennis court. 'Even the nanny.'

'She'll overdo it one of these days,' said Caroline. 'Not everyone likes being bossed about.'

'She doesn't boss people,' objected Patrick at once. 'She just gets what she wants. That's the way you've got to be.' Caroline rolled her eyes at Annie and said nothing. She turned her gaze to the tennis court.

'Bloody hell,' she said after a few moments. 'What the fuck's wrong with Cressida?'

The four on court had begun to knock up. Don was sending a series of swift, low balls to Cressida, who seemed barely able to return them.

'Sorry,' she kept saying, as another went into the net.

'Saving it till the match,' quipped Don. 'I know that trick!' He beamed at Cressida, who returned a weak smile. They tossed for sides; Don and Valerie won. As they walked to the back of the court, Don began to mutter to Valerie an audible series of instructions and warnings about Cressida's and Charles' play.

'Guard the net; she's got a nasty sliced forehand, might take you on the hop; don't try to lob him unless it's over the backhand. Is he steady at the net?' he suddenly demanded.

'Well, quite steady,' stammered Valerie.

'Mmm. Well, don't play to either of them at the net. Off you go, now. It's me to serve, remember?'

Valerie scuttled to the net and Don prepared to serve to Cressida. She stood, apathetically watching his mannered action, and lunged dispiritedly when the ball came spinning into her service box.

'Bad luck, darling,' said Charles. Don shook his head and clicked his tongue.

'You had that one,' he said to Cressida. 'Don't know what happened there.'

Charles returned the next serve straight to Valerie, who put it away with a vicious volley.

'Good girl,' said Don. 'Nice approach, that was, well away from the body.' He prepared to serve to Cressida

99

again. The first serve went out, and he stood stock still for a minute or two, as though meditating on the horror of such a mistake. Then, shaking his head slowly, he took a second ball from his pocket and served again. His second serve was a looped shot which landed just the other side of the net and bounced surprisingly high. Cressida, who had begun to run forward, was taken unawares, and hit the ball wide. It veered towards Valerie, who made an exaggerated jump aside to avoid it, and landed well outside the tramlines.

'Forty-love,' called Valerie.

'Sorry,' said Cressida to Charles. 'I can't think what's wrong with me.'

'Watch the ball,' piped up Don. 'That's always the answer. If things are going badly, don't think about anything but the ball.'

'Yes,' said Cressida shortly. Don served again, Charles returned the ball to him, and he sent an easy shot to Cressida. She volleyed it straight into the net.

'You're just not watching the ball,' said Don complacently. 'That's all it is. Isn't that right, Valerie?'

'Well,' said Valerie uncertainly. She looked at Cressida's face, drawn and tense. 'Maybe.'

Cressida's misery seemed to be getting deeper and deeper. Sitting quietly by the side of the tennis court, watching Charles clowning with the children, it had abated slightly, and she had, for a few blissful minutes, forgotten about the letter. But now she could think of nothing else. And everyone seemed to be watching her. Don, with his comments; Valerie, with her cow eyes; even Charles, thinking he was encouraging her by turning round and making faces behind Don's back. Caroline and Annie, too, were probably staring at her, wondering why she was playing so poorly.

She stared blindly at the tennis net, trying to rationalize her feelings. The letter could be a mistake – was probably a mistake. Charles would soon sort it out. He would sort it out. She repeated it to herself, trying to sooth herself into a state of calm. But a pounding background worry would not let her spirits rest. What if it wasn't a mistake? What if they had to pay? Where would they find the money? Cressida had successfully managed to close her ears to most of the financial information that had passed her way during the last ten or so years since her mother had died. She had only a hazy idea of her fortune; an even hazier one of where it had been invested. But she knew that most of it had dwindled away since her marriage. Was there still enough there? She screwed up her mind, trying to remember what her last account from the portfolio managers had said.

'Darling?' Charles was looking quizzically at her. 'We're changing ends.'

Cressida flushed and her head jerked up. Everyone was staring at her. Of course. They had lost the first game. Charles was already on the other side of the court; Don and Valerie were hovering at the net, looking at her in polite surprise. They were all waiting for her. Any minute now, someone would ask her if she was feeling all right. Caroline was so insensitive, she would probably shout out something awful, like, was it Cressida's period and did she want some Feminax. Or they might guess that something was wrong, and show a horrible, over-familiar sympathy.

The thought of exposing herself – her vulnerabilities – to these awful people, stiffened Cressida's resolve. She simply had to pull herself together. She gave a chilly smile, and quickly walked round to the other side of the court.

'Sorry,' she murmured to Charles. 'I was miles away.' She narrowed her eyes. She would just have to concentrate. Turning towards the net, she focused her attention on a particular corner of netting. 'Concentrate,' she muttered to herself. 'Concentrate.' She tried to blank everything else out of her mind.

'One-love down,' said Charles cheerfully. 'Looks like I'm going to have to pull something pretty special out of the bag. Eh, Cress?' He served to Don; a straight-forward unpretentious shot. Don returned the ball straight to Cressida, obviously expecting her to miss. But she stuck her racquet out, almost in a reflex action, and whipped the ball away.

'Great shot!' shouted Charles in delight.

'Well played,' said Don tetchily.

'Wow!' said Annie. 'That's more like it.'

The next game passed quickly. Cressida's mind, black with misery, had blocked out everything but returning the ball. She was unaware of the score; un-aware of the looks of amazement as she sent one after another top-spin forehand rocketing into the far corner of the court.

'Cressida, darling, your serve.' She looked up, startled, to see Charles smiling affectionately at her. 'You're playing incredibly.'

Cressida felt as though she might burst into uncon-trollable sobs. Instead, she picked up two balls and prepared to serve. She threw the first ball high, far too high, and hit a serve which ballooned right out of the court.

'Mummy!'

Cressida ignored Georgina's high-pitched cry and threw the ball up again. It went behind her.

'Have another,' said Charles.

'Mummy, look who's here!'

This time Georgina's excited shriek was too compel-ling to ignore. Cressida, Charles, Caroline, everyone, looked round.

Standing next to Georgina, barely taller than her, was a smiling girl with a glowing, tanned face. She was dressed in an Indian-cotton dress of bright turquoise, and her golden-brown hair was tied up in a scarf of the same colour. The dress, sleeveless and low cut, showed off a pair of full breasts, tanned as far as the eye could see to the same colour as her face, and the rest of her body was similarly voluptuous – rounded shoulders, dimpled arms, a slightly curved belly visible through the thin cotton of her dress. A gold chain round her neck glinted in the afternoon sunlight; her feet were shod in brown leather sandals and she carried a large leather bag. Her deep-brown eyes quickly surveyed the scene, and she murmured something to Georgina, who laughed slightly and then looked nervously at her mother. The entire party stood looking at the girl for a minute or two in silence. Then Stephen spoke.

'Jesus Christ,' he said. 'It's Ella.'

Chapter Seven

'I'm so terribly sorry,' said Ella. She and Caroline had
gone inside and were walking up the stairs. 'I just
assumed Georgina was, well, you know . . .'

'Telling the truth?' supplied Caroline. 'Fair enough,
why shouldn't you?'

'She was very convincing,' said Ella. 'I really thought
she'd asked you. I mean, otherwise I'd never have
come. Maybe she'd forgotten about the party?' she
added suddenly.

'No chance,' said Caroline. 'She's known about it for
weeks. When did you say you phoned?'

'Oh, four or five weeks ago,' said Ella. 'I was still in
Italy. I asked her if it was OK to come over, and she
said she'd go and ask you. She was away from the
phone for a few minutes, then she came back and said
you were in the bath but you'd said it was fine. I mean,
I didn't see any reason not to believe her. I suppose I
should have called again, to check it was still all right
to come, but you know what it's like . . .' She grinned
guiltily. 'Have I ruined the delicate balance of your
gathering?'

'I'd say you've ruined Charles' delicate balance all
right,' said Caroline, smirking. 'Not to mention his
charming wife's. Did you see her face?' Ella shook her
head.

'I have to say, I avoided looking at either of them.'
Caroline glanced swiftly at her.

'Are you OK about it? I mean, seeing them?'

'Yes, I am,' Ella said slowly. 'I'm fine. It's been long
enough now, and there have been others since Charles.

I don't want him back or anything. But even so . . . I look at her, and I think . . .'

'You think, You rich cow,' said Caroline. Ella laughed.

'Something like that.'

'That's what we all think.'

Caroline halted in front of a door. 'Since it was Georgina's idea to tell you it was all right to come,' she said, 'I think the least she can do is donate you her room.'

'Oh no,' protested Ella. 'I can go anywhere. I've got a sleeping-bag . . .'

'Rubbish,' said Caroline. She opened the door. Georgina's bedroom was large, light and spotlessly tidy. The window, the dressing-table mirror and the water dispenser all glinted in the late-afternoon sun; the books and pencils on the desk were neatly arranged; a single china horse and a lamp stood on the white bedside cabinet.

'Very nice,' said Ella. Caroline shrugged.

'I'm sorry we can't come up with another spare room. You would have thought this house was big enough.'

'How many bedrooms has it got?' said Ella, dumping her bag on the sheepskin rug in the middle of the floor.

'Six, altogether. But they're all taken.' Ella was peering round the bathroom door.

'Lucky Georgina. This is really nice.' She sat on the bed. 'Makes a change from sleeping-mats and mice running up and down my legs all night.' Caroline gave her a horrified look.

'Is that what it was like?'

'Not all the time.' Ella laughed at Caroline's expression. 'It was pretty sordid in India and bits of South America – but I've been back in Europe for the last four months. Still, nothing as luxurious as this.' Caroline shook her head.

105

'I don't know how you did it,' she said. 'Three weeks is enough for me, however nice the place is. Didn't you get homesick?'

'A little. After the first two months I got really miserable and I thought about chucking it in and flying home. But I got through that pretty quickly. It was really basic things that were getting me down – like no hot water and the food. I got quite ill at one point. But, you know, I got used to it. And the whole experience was so wonderful . . .' Her eyes were shining.

'Mad woman,' said Caroline. 'Well look, welcome back.'

'Thank you,' said Ella. 'And apologies again.'

'It's my bloody daughter who should be apologizing to you,' said Caroline. 'I honestly don't think it ever occurred to her that you might not *want* to see Charles.'

'Oh, I don't know,' said Ella. 'I'm actually quite looking forward to talking to him now. He looked so completely amazed.' She looked down at herself. 'Is it all right if I have a bath straight away?'

'Oh, sure, go ahead,' said Caroline. She pushed open the door of the bathroom. 'We have the water hot all the time, so use as much as you want. I'll go and get you a towel.'

When she returned, Ella was standing unselfconsciously naked, brushing out her honey-brown hair while hot water thundered into the bath. Her creamy-brown body was curved and dimpled, and with each stroke of the hairbrush her full breasts rose and fell.

'Here you are,' said Caroline, holding out a pair of huge white towels. 'What a wonderful tan.'

'Actually I got this on the beach in Greece,' said Ella, who was engrossed in teasing out a knot in her hair. 'I was with a bunch of nudists – or, at least, nude sunbathers. It was very eye opening.' She looked up seriously, caught Caroline's lascivious eye, and they both dissolved into giggles.

'That's not what I meant!' protested Ella eventually, still snorting with laughter.

'Then it was a Freudian what's-it,' said Caroline. 'You can't be getting enough sex.'

'Well, actually,' said Ella mysteriously, 'that's where you're wrong.' She winked at Caroline and took the towels.

'Why? Who? What's been happening?' demanded Caroline.

'I'll tell you later,' said Ella, 'maybe.' And she disappeared into the bathroom.

Outside, the tennis match was nearing its conclusion. Cressida, gripping her racquet tightly, was not allowing her concentration to slip. She didn't dare think about where she was, or with whom she was playing. Her eyes were fixed on the ball; her shots had sharpened up; and she was playing to win. The harder she concentrated on the game, the less easy it was to think about the disconcerting arrival of Ella; or about the letter waiting for Charles upstairs; or even about the grim prospect of a whole evening with these awful people. She skimmed a winning forehand past Valerie at the net, collected up the balls, and walked swiftly to the other end of the court to serve.

Charles paused at the net to exchange a pleasantry or two with Don. But Don was looking ruffled.

'She's playing well, your wife,' he said.

'Isn't she?' Charles shot a puzzled glance at Cressida, who was bouncing the ball up and down and staring fixedly at the ground.

'Wonderful concentration,' said Don. 'You see, Val,' he addressed his daughter, 'if you concentrated a bit harder, you wouldn't keep making all those mistakes.' Val looked down, and scuffed her shoe with her racquet.

'Well,' said Charles quickly. 'I make that five-four.'

'Now come on, Val,' said Don sharply, as they walked off. 'We really need to win this game.'

As soon as they were in their positions, Cressida served; a long, hard, textbook-style serve. Valerie returned the ball rather hesitantly to Charles, who lunged at the ball and mishit it. It skimmed the top of the net and fell neatly into the tramlines. Valerie pounded forward, but the grass was soft and it barely bounced.

'Sorry about that,' called Charles cheerfully. 'It could have gone either way.'

'Five-love,' called Don. Charles repressed his start of annoyance. He was becoming unreasonably irritated with Don's familiar, clubby tennis terms. 'Five-love'; 'van-in'; 'one more please'; 'that was just away'. Why not say the ball was out?

'Fifteen-love,' he called back firmly. Not that Don would notice.

Cressida served again, a hard, fast, spinning shot which licked across the court to Don. Don drew back his racquet in his exaggerated style, and sent the ball up high over Charles' head.

'Out,' called Cressida shortly. 'Thirty-love.'

She served once more to Valerie, who sent it into the net.

'Forty-love.' Don was looking rattled as he prepared to receive Cressida's serve. It came hard again, to his backhand. He sent a rather weak shot to Charles, who drew back his racquet and sent a thundering shot into the corner of the court. Charles threw up his racquet with a whoop of delight.

'I'm afraid it was just long,' said Don quickly.

'Was it?' Charles looked surprised. 'OK then. Forty-fifteen.'

'But it wasn't out,' came a stern voice from above. 'It was in.' Everyone looked up. There was Georgina, sitting on the branch of a tree. 'I saw it,' she said. 'It was about two inches in.' Don looked disconcerted.

'What did you think?' he said, turning to Valerie. She turned bright red.

'Ooh,' she said. 'I didn't really see it. It was going too fast.' She giggled embarrassedly.

'It was in,' insisted Georgina. 'I've got a better view than you.'

'Oh well,' said Don, in a belated attempt at light-heartedness. 'I'm sure you're right. That's set and match, then. Congratulations.'

Cressida smiled feebly at Valerie and tried not to wince as she shook her clammy hand.

'Ooh, gosh, well done,' said Valerie, as they all walked off. 'I thought you'd probably beat us.'

'Now, that's a loser's attitude,' said Don. 'No-one gets anywhere by thinking they're going to lose. The first rule of winning is to believe you're capable of winning.'

'Oh, give us a break,' muttered Charles.

'What's the second rule?' asked Georgina.

'Aha,' said Don, twinkling at her.

'*I'm so glad you asked me that* . . .' whispered Stephen to Annie, who furiously bit her lip.

'The second rule', said Don, 'is to make others believe you're capable of winning.' He looked meaningfully around.

'But what if you're not?' said Georgina.

'Not what?' said Don.

'Not capable of winning?' said Georgina. 'Like, what if I thought I was really good at . . .' she thought for a bit, '. . . ice-skating. And I told everyone I was really good. But really I was rubbish.'

'Georgina,' interrupted Caroline, 'go and get your stuff out of your room and take it to Nicola's room. You'll be sleeping there tonight.'

'Brill!' said Georgina, deflected from her speech. 'In a sleeping-bag?'

'Yes,' said Caroline.

'Wicked!' said Georgina, slithering down the tree. 'Come on, Nick.'

'Don't just go charging in,' warned Caroline. 'Ella's having a bath.'

'Is Ella having my room?'

'Yes,' said Caroline. 'I think it's the least you can do, don't you?' Georgina blushed slightly under Caroline's piercing look.

'I suppose so,' she said, shifting from one foot to the other.

'Well, go on then,' said Caroline. 'And knock first.'

'It's all right,' said Georgina. 'I've seen Ella without any clothes on before. She won't mind.'

There was a short silence as she and Nicola ran off, during which the image of Ella without any clothes on hung unavoidably in everyone's minds.

'Right,' said Caroline briskly. 'I think I'm going to get changed. We'll be having dinner around eight, with drinks beforehand.'

'Very civilized,' said Stephen. 'What about the kids?'

'I've sorted that out. They'll have theirs earlier on, in the kitchen. Mrs Finch is organizing it.'

'Bliss,' said Annie. 'I think I'll just lie here for a few months or so.'

'I'm afraid not,' said Patrick. 'You're on again, against us.'

'No!' groaned Annie.

'Patrick!' said Caroline. 'I've got to get changed! Can't we leave it till tomorrow?'

'Hear, hear!' said Stephen.

'Well, I suppose so,' said Patrick grudgingly. 'But we must play it. Otherwise we won't know who's in the final.'

'We will,' said Annie. 'Promise.'

'We'll be off home then, to change,' said Don. 'Drinks around seven-thirty, Caroline?'

'Whatever you like,' said Caroline dismissively.

'Yes, seven-thirty,' said Patrick, smiling at Don.

Caroline wandered slowly up to her bedroom. Passing the room where Georgina had moved to, she heard sounds of rumpus, and wondered briefly whether to

110

intervene. But she really couldn't be bothered. And she had more important things to think about. The first was the sudden appearance of Ella. Although, of course, she disapproved of Georgina's lying, a part of her, she realized, rejoiced at the discomfort of Charles and Cressida. This was a meeting which probably would not have happened otherwise. And it would serve Charles right to see what he had turned down.

Ella was looking utterly radiant – and had obviously had an incredible trip. So glamorous, thought Caroline, to go whizzing off round the world like that. Although perhaps it sounded better than it really was. Caroline's own idea of a holiday was being shipped, with no effort on her own part, from front door to airport to hotel to beach. But Charles had always liked those hippy, student holidays with backpacks and no tour rep – and would probably love to go round the world like that. Caroline made a note to herself to ask Ella loudly about her travels at dinner – and watch Charles' face. She smiled to herself as she turned on the taps and watched the water gushing into her bath-tub.

'Having a bath?' It was Patrick, bustling cheerfully into the room. 'Going to be long?'

'Yes,' said Caroline uncompromisingly.

'OK then. I'll read the paper. Give me a shout when you've finished.' He opened the balcony door and went to sit outside. Caroline watched him distrustfully, then quickly stripped, leaving her clothes on the floor, and got into the hot, scented, foamy water. She opened her mouth to call to him, and then realized that she would be overheard.

'Patrick, come here,' she shouted. 'Patrick!'

'What?' He appeared at the bathroom door.

'I want to talk to you. Close the door.'

'What about?' He stood and let his eyes run over her body in the foamy bath water. She ignored him.

'About Charles. No,' she held up a hand, 'let me

111

finish. I know what you were up to today. You tank him up, disappear off to the study on some pathetic pretext and then all of a sudden, I can just see it, you haul out the brochures and sell him some completely unsuitable product just for your bloody commission.'

'Now wait a moment,' said Patrick, raising his voice.

'Sssh!' hissed Caroline. 'Do you want everyone to hear?'

'Now wait a moment,' he repeated more quietly. 'You can stop talking about *my* bloody commission. It pays for your food, your clothes . . .'

'OK, OK,' she said impatiently, 'but I'm not completely hung up about it like you are. Anyway,' she held up her hand again before he could interrupt, 'the point is, why do you have to do business in the house? It's bad enough entertaining people like Don because they're *good clients*,' her voice mocked the phrase, 'but when you invite Charles Mobyn here just in order to sell him some crappy policy . . . it's really naff.' Her blue eyes regarded him with disdain.

'And how', he said, 'do you know I sold anything to Charles?'

'Oh, it's obvious,' snapped Caroline. 'You disappear off with him; the next thing you're in a really good mood, doling out brandy and cigars like there's no tomorrow. Either you sold some whacking great plan to Charles or else you've got a coke habit I don't know about.' Patrick gave a small smile. He peered into the steamy mirror, licked his finger and smoothed his eyebrows.

'Or else', he said casually, 'I sold some whacking great plan to someone else.'

'What?' Caroline stared at him in surprise. 'Who? Cressida?' Patrick continued smiling pleasurably at his reflection. 'Don?' she said.

'I sold the plan', he said slowly, 'which will take my bonus this year up to . . . go on, have a guess how much.'

'Don. It must have been Don. He didn't go off to feed his dog at all, did he? He went off to be conned by you.'

'One hundred thousand pounds,' said Patrick, relishing the sound of the words. 'That's not salary, that's bonus. One hundred thousand pounds of lovely bonus.'

'But Don's strapped for cash. He's in real trouble, Valerie told me. He can't have invested that much.' Patrick broke off from his pleasant reverie and looked at her in surprise.

'It wasn't Don. What made you think it was him?'

'Well who the fuck was it then?' Patrick smiled at her.

'Stephen, of course.'

Annie was trying to make conversation with Mrs Finch in the kitchen. The children, including a resentful Martina, were assembled round the table, munching fish cakes, cheesy baked potatoes and salad. Georgina had insisted on grinding piles of fresh black pepper on to everyone's potato, with the result that Toby had found his too hot to eat and had had to have the topping scraped off. Annie suspected that Nicola was finding hers a bit too hot as well, but was valiantly refusing to say anything in front of Georgina. She was breathing rather heavily as she put each forkful in her mouth, and was gulping lots of water. The Mobyn twins, meanwhile, had each been given a mound of grated cheese, which was now all over the table, the floor, their hair and stuck between their fingers. Martina gave each of them a perfunctory wipe every so often, but otherwise seemed content to leave them to their own devices and stare moodily into space.

Mrs Finch was sitting on a kitchen stool, smoking a cigarette. Having discovered that Annie was willing to give a hand with administering the children's supper, she had relinquished all responsibility, and was now comfortably regaling Annie with the failings of the village shop.

'Went in there the other day, when I'd forgotten to get a sweet for our evening meal. There wasn't nothing I could buy! I just had to walk straight out again.'

'What were you looking for?' said Annie absently, as she poured out glasses of Ribena.

'Well ... I don't know,' said Mrs Finch consideringly. 'A nice chocolate mousse, maybe. Or crème caramel. Those ones that come in little glass pots, they're nice, now. Or a frozen gâteau. But you have to go to Safeway for those.'

'Are we having chocolate mousse?' said Georgina suddenly.

'You're having ice-cream,' said Mrs Finch. 'Raspberry ripple.'

'Yummy!' said Nicola. Mrs Finch regarded her fondly.

'Poor little pet,' she said. 'It's a shame.'

'We were thinking of taking the children to church tomorrow,' said Annie hurriedly. 'Do you know what time the service is?' Mrs Finch wrinkled her nose.

'Can't say I do. I see them walking up there sometimes on a Sunday, you know, but I can't say I've ever noticed what time it was.'

'So the congregation isn't very big?'

'Oh, I don't know about that. It's a pretty church; people come to it from other villages. I'd say they get a fair crowd. I was married in that church, you know,' she added surprisingly.

'How lovely,' said Annie enthusiastically. Mrs Finch stubbed out her lipstick-stained cigarette end, and nodded.

'Fifteen years ago, that was. Reception at the Horse and Groom in Moreton St Mary. We went on a package to Ibiza for the honeymoon. First time I'd been abroad. You wouldn't believe it now, would you?'

'Well, no,' said Annie.

114

'We've been abroad every year since then. Spain, Portugal, the Canaries, you name it. This year, we went to the Gambia. Took the kids, you know, proper family holiday. They loved it, of course. Lee, that's our eldest, learnt how to water-ski. He's got a real knack. We're thinking about Florida next year. Disneyworld.'

'Gosh,' said Annie.

'You fond of holidays abroad?'

'Well,' said Annie honestly, 'I do love going abroad, but we haven't been away for a while. It's a bit difficult.' Mrs Finch nodded wisely.

'I suppose what with the kiddy and all . . .' Her eyes fell on Nicola, awkwardly spreading butter onto a piece of bread.

'It's not that,' said Annie hastily. 'More the money, really.' She laughed.

'Finished!' announced Georgina. 'Shall I get the ice-cream?' Mrs Finch nodded, and lit another cigarette. Georgina disappeared out of the kitchen and Annie put her dirty plate in the dishwasher. Mrs Finch didn't move.

'Can't decide between Florida and California,' she said musingly, as Annie returned to her seat. She took a long drag on her cigarette. 'Maybe we should do both.'

Patrick couldn't understand why Caroline was so angry.

'Oh very funny,' she had said, lifting up a foamy leg to admire it. 'Come on, who? It's Charles, isn't it?'

'No it's not. I told you. Stephen.'

'Oh right, yes, Stephen's really got that kind of money.' Her tone was confidently sarcastic, and Patrick, who usually glossed over the details of his business transactions when he talked to Caroline, felt nettled.

'He has if he takes a mortgage out on his house.' He gave her a triumphant look. 'Which he has done, more or less.'

'What?' Caroline's leg stopped moving and she turned disbelieving eyes on him.

'It's very easy to set up,' said Patrick. 'I mean, if you think about it, he's underborrowed at the moment. Not using his potential.'

'You've conned him into taking out a mortgage?' Patrick looked uncomfortable.

'There's no need to put it like that.'

'How much?'

'Does it matter? It's well within his means.'

'What means? He hasn't got a job, or had you forgotten? How much?'

'I think he'd probably want that information to remain confidential,' said Patrick smoothly.

'Fucking hell, Patrick!' Caroline got out of the bath with a great swoosh of water and stood in front of him, dripping and furious. 'How much?'

'Only eighty thousand, for Christ's sake! Stop getting so worked up. His house must be worth at least three times that.'

'He's borrowing eighty thousand to invest?' Caroline put her hand to her head. 'And what's he putting it in?'

'Is it really relevant? You wouldn't understand even if I told you.'

'Like hell I wouldn't! It's not that Sigma fund, is it?' Patrick started.

'How do you know about that?'

'I'm not completely stupid,' she said scathingly. 'I know what you're up to. I know all about the fucking Sigma fund and your fucking bonuses. Jesus Christ! How could you do it?'

'I really don't see what the problem is.'

'Yes you fucking do. Don't pretend you don't. It's obvious. Annie and Stephen can't possibly afford to pay that kind of mortgage. They'll struggle for a bit and then they'll come to you in about a year's time and ask for their money back. And how much will you give

116

them? Or rather, how much will you cream off in fees? Ten thousand? Twenty thousand?'

'There won't be any question of that,' said Patrick huffily. 'Annie and Stephen can well afford a small mortgage like that. And the fund should do extremely well over the long term.'

'Patrick, they haven't got any fucking income.' Caroline's eyes blazed at Patrick. 'What good is the long term?' Patrick looked at her for a second.

'Calm down,' he said irritatingly, and walked into the bedroom, out onto the balcony.

Caroline stared after him in rage for a minute or two. Then she roused herself to action. She dried herself briskly and slapped on body moisturizer, thinking furiously. Patrick really had sunk to new depths. He'd always been an unprincipled salesman – that had been something that had attracted her to him in the first place. He and his friends, in their flashy suits, with their oversmooth voices and eager darting eyes, had tickled her fancy, had made her laugh. And at the beginning, Patrick had treated her a bit like a favoured client – deferential murmurs, respectful remarks, but all the time that tacit undercurrent: *we both know what we're here for, don't we?* Except that she wasn't there to buy financial services.

She gazed at herself in the mirror, remembering herself, the busty promo girl with the blond hair and the big smile. No wonder Patrick had fallen for her. In fact, he'd been incredibly cool about the whole thing, considering how desperate he was to have her – although she'd only found that out later. Half the time it had been her worrying that he'd gone off her. Incredible, really.

And what a bastard he'd turned out to be.

'You bastard,' she said to the mirror. She smiled. Despite her protestations, the thought of Patrick once again as an unprincipled salesman faintly excited her.

She conjured up an image of Patrick fifteen years

ago: determined, pugnacious, cocky. Young and virile; forthright and thrusting. They'd met when they were both working at a personal finance show in London. She'd been on some other firm's stand, handing out leaflets for a champagne draw. On the fourth day, she rigged the draw so Patrick won the champagne, and they spent the afternoon getting steadily drunk. Then he'd pulled her behind the stand and kissed her. She could still remember the shock waves that had gone through her drunken mind. Was she really kissing this short, ugly person? And becoming excited by it? He'd pulled up her company promotional T-shirt, groaned at the sight of her breasts, pushed aside the lace of her bra and fastened his lips to her nipple. She'd almost cried out in ecstasy. Then he'd pulled himself away.

'Gotta go,' he'd said. 'Clients out there. Gotta get them.' And she'd stared after him with swollen, tingling lips that ached to be kissed by him again.

Caroline stared at her lips in the mirror. They were still full, still kissable. Her breasts were still firm; her skin still soft and smooth. And Patrick was still a bastard. They might both be fifteen years older now, but really they were no different from the way they'd been then. This realization cheered her. But at the same time, she was angry with Patrick. Little as she thought of Stephen, he was still a friend, and Annie more so. Caroline was in fact, she realized, very fond of Annie. And Nicola. The idea of them falling into financial trouble, worrying over the bills, quarrelling about money, upset her. An image came into her mind, of Stephen hunched over the kitchen table, sobbing, of Annie comforting him, of Nicola appearing at the door, wide eyed and worried.

Patrick came in from the balcony and caught her eye in the mirror. He looked guarded and suspicious.

'You're a real bastard,' said Caroline. 'A real heel.' Patrick opened his mouth to speak and then closed it again. 'And poor old Annie and Stephen have no idea.

They trust you completely, did you know that? They deserve to be put right.' Patrick's frown deepened, and he strode towards the bathroom. But Caroline got up and stood in his way. 'They need a good friend to tell them what you're really like,' she said.

'You're not going to say anything,' said Patrick. 'You know which side your bread is buttered. You lose me clients, I lose money, we both end up poor.'

'Hardly poor,' scoffed Caroline.

'If no-one wants to buy financial services from me, then yes, poor,' retorted Patrick. 'It doesn't take much to ruin a reputation. Remember what happened to Graham Witherspoon? Excuse me.'

Caroline stared after him angrily. Half of her wanted to warn Stephen and Annie to cancel the deal, for their own sakes. But Patrick was right. One disillusioned customer – however good a friend – was enough to spread the word and lose customers. In fact, being a friend made it worse. Graham Witherspoon had been a colleague of Patrick's. He'd been a top salesman until once he'd drunkenly told a dinner party full of friends and clients that his products were rip-offs. After that he'd barely sold a thing, and soon after that he'd been fired. Should she risk that happening to Patrick?

Frowning slightly, she walked into her wardrobe. She hadn't yet given a thought to what she was going to wear. Absently, she pulled out cream satin knickers and bra, a buttercup linen shift dress, matching suede pumps from Italy. She put them all down on the bed and took out her jewellery box. Gold knot earrings and her diamond solitaire ring. She wasn't going to have that cow Cressida out-jewelling her. To be on the safe side, she added a diamond bracelet. She sprayed herself all over with scent and then dressed, admiring her brown shoulders against the yellow; pointing her foot and rotating it prettily.

She looked in the mirror. Simple but chic. Too simple? She imagined the impression she would make against the cream leather sofa in the living-room, holding a champagne glass, laughing at a joke. Her eyes landed on the gold earrings. Too dull. She ripped them out and searched for her diamond studs. They sparkled in her ears, and she smiled at her reflection. One could never have too many diamonds. Was that a famous saying? Or had she made it up?

She pondered on it as she walked down to the living-room, admiring herself in every shiny surface that she passed. She surveyed the empty living-room with satisfaction, poured herself a glass of champagne and sat down on the sofa. The plight of the Fairweathers had, for the moment, quite vanished from her mind.

Chapter Eight

Cressida shifted uncomfortably, took another sip of champagne and gazed out of the window at the sun setting over the glowing fields. She felt marooned and rather miserable. The leather sofa she was sitting on was soft and very squashy, and having sunk into it, she didn't think she would be able to get out of it without an effort. Charles, who had been sitting next to her, had sprung up to examine an antique cricket bat which Patrick was showing to Stephen, and so far no-one had taken his place. Caroline and Annie were giggling at the far side of the drawing-room, lingering at the built-in bar while Caroline poured out a glass of champagne.

Caroline's raucous laugh rang out through the room, and Cressida flinched. She couldn't bear Caroline's rowdy spirits at the best of times; least of all now, with the worry of that letter still in her mind, and still unshared. She hadn't been able to find a suitable moment to take it out and show it to Charles; first of all she'd felt too nervous to bring the subject up, and then Martina had appeared with the twins, wanting to know if they could use the Jacuzzi in their bathroom. Charles had suggested this, it transpired, and he spent the rest of the time before dinner romping in the bathroom with the twins, covering the floor in bubbles, and thoroughly over-exciting them.

In the end, Cressida had retreated to a bathroom that she'd found at the end of the corridor, which no-one else seemed to be using. She'd gone through her usual routine mechanically, using the same make-up that she'd been taught to apply at the Lucie Clayton grooming school fifteen years ago and had never digressed from since. She had brushed out her hair, sprayed on scent and smiled bravely at herself in the mirror. But now she felt cold inside her dress, and her smile stopped at her lips. Hadn't she once read somewhere that babies learnt to smile as a defence mechanism? That was all her smile was tonight – a defence, to stop people looking too closely, or saying 'Cheer up', in that dreadfully hearty way.

Her mind kept veering between optimism and despair. Of course, the letter must be a mistake. As soon as she told Charles about it, he would reassure her, point out the error, put his arms round her and say fondly, 'You really haven't got a clue about money, have you?' It would be like the time she decided to pay some bills herself for once, and ended up paying them all twice. That had happened just after they'd been married, and Charles had been so amused. He actually seemed to like it when she made blunders and didn't understand things. And just as she thought she'd got something sorted out in her mind, she would try to make an intelligent comment and he would burst out laughing at her. She was always one step behind. So, of course, this letter must be another mix-up. There would be something she hadn't thought of, or didn't know about, that would explain it all. They would both be laughing about it tomorrow.

So why did the thought of it make her feel sick, and anxiously swirl the drink round in her glass? She recalled the sum of money mentioned and shuddered. She was rich, of course she was. But was she that rich any more? Could she stand such a demand for money? She willed herself to remember what Mr Stanlake, her portfolio manager, had said at their last meeting. She could remember his thin-lipped smile; his clean, cool handshake; the view from his window and even the face of his well-groomed secretary who always brought them coffee. But what had been said? How much was left of her assets? She fingered the fabric of her dress. Perhaps she could find out what her financial situation was before telling Charles about the letter. It would take time, but then, this house didn't seem the right place to tell him. Especially not now. Not now that girl – woman, whatever she was – had arrived.

Right from the start, Charles had always been unwilling to talk about Ella, and Cressida certainly hadn't wanted to rake up his past. She knew hardly anything about Ella, apart from the fact that Charles had lived with her for at least five years in that house in Seymour Road. In fact, before this afternoon, Cressida had never even known what Ella looked like. Somehow she'd been surprised when she saw her. She had imagined her slightly fatter, slightly less . . . she searched for a word in her mind . . . exotic looking.

She was jolted out of her thoughts by a sudden burst of laughter from Caroline and Annie. Caroline was brandishing a bottle of Malibu.

'Annie, you haven't lived if you haven't tried this,' she shrieked. 'It's great stuff!' Annie's cheeks were flushed and her eyes were bright.

'But I've still got some champagne,' she protested, as Caroline began pouring it out.

'So what?' Caroline looked around wickedly and then put the bottle of Malibu to her lips.

'I once did a promotion for Malibu,' she said, wiping her mouth. 'Or was it Pina Colada? We all wore grass skirts and loads of fake tan. Really orangey stuff. I got it all over the sheets when I went to bed that night.' She paused. 'But then, if I remember rightly, they weren't my sheets, so I didn't give a shit.' She broke into bubbling laughter again.

Patrick had gone to fetch more of his cricket memorabilia, and as he entered, his eyes swivelled distrustfully in the direction of Caroline's laughter. Then they fell on Cressida, sitting alone on the sofa.

She immediately flashed him a bright, rather desperate smile, and willed him to rejoin the men. She intuitively felt that Patrick was the sort of man who would realize that something was wrong and wheedle it all out of her with no effort at all. He looked at her half-empty glass and called to Caroline.

'Sweetheart, some more champagne over here, I think.' He smiled at Cressida, and she smiled back, even harder.

'Lovely view, isn't it?' she said, gesturing out of the window. Her eyes fell on the fields and she strove for something further to say. 'Lovely colours,' she added eventually. Patrick nodded.

'We do get a superb sunset here,' he said. 'I've taken some marvellous photographs. I'll show you later.'

'That would be lovely,' said Cressida feebly. There was a silence, in which Patrick's eyes seemed to penetrate hers. Her lips trembled; she looked down, and was aware of a pink tinge spreading over her cheeks.

'Cressida,' began Patrick, and moved a step closer. Cressida stared fixedly at her knees, unsure why she was blushing.

Then, to her relief, the door opened, and Don and Valerie came in.

'Hello!' hooted Valerie. 'Are we late?'

'No, no,' said Patrick genially. He moved to kiss her cheek, and she ducked awkwardly towards him, so that they collided with some force. As his head rose, Patrick's eye met Cressida's with the briefest of flickers, and she found herself grinning down into her champagne glass, feeling ridiculously warmed. When she looked up, she saw Patrick shaking Don's hand with a perfectly straight face and Valerie waving at her as though they were separated by several miles.

'Ooh! I do love your dress,' said Valerie. 'It's just like mine!'

This, Cressida realized, gazing at Valerie in slight horror, was not far from the truth. Both of them were in simple, tailored, navy-blue dresses. If Cressida's was in exquisitely cut linen and Valerie's in ill-fitting polyester, Valerie certainly couldn't tell the difference.

'I do love the classic look,' exclaimed Valerie complacently, sitting down beside Cressida. Her white hand shot out and fingered the fabric of Cressida's dress; Cressida suddenly and irrationally felt sick.

'Yours is lovely,' Valerie said. 'Where did you get it?'

'London,' murmured Cressida.

'Me too,' said Valerie. 'In the sales. Actually, it's not quite the right size, but it was such a bargain!'

'Drink, Valerie?' said Patrick genially. 'Champagne?'

'Ooh, lovely!' said Valerie. She settled back next to Cressida. Her legs, dead white apart from a strip of pink sunburn down the front of each, were covered in the minute red dots of skin which has been recently shaved and a plaster was flapping at the heel of her navy-blue patent-leather shoe.

Cressida glanced surreptitiously over at Caroline, who was now opening another bottle of champagne. She was a vision of yellow, with her buttercup dress, golden skin and bright blond hair, shining under the spotlights of the bar. She had too much make-up on, in Cressida's opinion, and was being her usual vulgar outrageous self, but at least she looked vivacious with it. And Annie, in her richly patterned Indian sarong dress, looked flushed, happy and animated. She had caught the sun on her cheeks, and had twisted her hair up into a knot. Cressida had never seen her look so attractive.

Looking down at her navy-blue lap, and at Valerie's, Cressida suddenly felt as if she were back at school – and she and Valerie were the misfits of the form. Her dress – beautiful and expensive though it was – seemed both dowdy and over-smart at the same time. And she was the only woman in the room wearing tights, she noticed. She took a miserable sip of champagne. Everything about her seemed wrong. Yet she had worn exactly the same outfit a few weeks ago – to drinks with the Marchants – and felt entirely at ease.

Patrick had made his way over to the bar. Caroline was sitting alone on a bar stool, sipping a huge cocktail with her eyes closed.

'Sweetness,' he said, 'people are waiting for drinks.'

'Here you are.' Caroline eyed him balefully and gave him the open bottle. 'You can take this round.' Patrick gave her an annoyed look.

'I meant', he said, 'you could go round and talk to a few people.'

'I'm talking to Annie,' said Caroline obstinately. 'She's just gone to the loo. She'll be back in a moment.'

'Well, you can't talk to her all evening,' said Patrick, in an attempt at jocularity. 'We do have other friends.'

'Friends!' mocked Caroline. She swivelled round on the bar stool and raised contemptuous blue eyes to Patrick's. 'Are you Annie's friend? Are you Stephen's friend? Well, if you are, Christ help your enemies.'

Patrick shifted uncomfortably. 'I hardly think this is the place,' he whispered.

'Exactly,' replied Caroline in a grudgingly low voice. 'Neither is it the place to rip off people who trust you. Like they do. Like they did, perhaps I should say.' Patrick peered at her with mounting anxiety.

'Caroline!' he hissed. 'You bloody better not have said anything to Annie.'

'Or what?' Caroline's smile challenged him.

'Hello, Patrick!' Annie's cheerful voice hailed them and Patrick smiled uneasily.

'You're looking lovely tonight,' he said.

'I'm feeling wonderful,' said Annie cheerfully. 'It's been a really super day! I can't tell you how much we've both enjoyed it. And the children have been in heaven.' She turned to Caroline, smiling. 'Nicola worships Georgina even more than she did before. She's insisted on calling their bedroom the dormy. And I think Georgina's going to do her lights-out, go-to-sleep, head-prefect bit for them later on.'

'My God,' said Caroline. 'We really have raised a little Hitler.' Patrick frowned, and opened his mouth to protest, but then changed his mind.

'Dinner soon, do you think, sweetheart?' he said.

'We're still waiting for Ella,' pointed out Caroline. Patrick's frown deepened.

'Oh yes,' he said shortly. 'Well, I'll go and take some more champagne round.'

'I'm sure she won't be long,' said Annie soothingly.

Charles was ignoring Cressida's pleading looks from the sofa. She was stuck next to the dreadful Valerie – and for that he couldn't help feeling sorry for her – but there was something in him tonight that couldn't bear to sit tamely down with his wife. He felt an unspecified anticipation; a slight exhilaration; a mood of gaiety and energy. It was probably, he thought to himself, the combination of outdoor exercise, sunlight and champagne. He didn't allow himself to wonder why this mood had only overtaken him after the surprise appearance made by Ella. He was used, after four years of marriage, to swiftly diverting his thoughts whenever they turned in the direction of Ella; remembering only the bad times; most of the time blocking her memory completely from his mind.

Stephen seemed in good spirits too, he noticed; more sure of himself than he had been that morning. He and Don were still poring over old photographs, programmes, score sheets, cricket balls, even a couple of old cricket pads. Patrick's collection of cricket memorabilia was clearly fascinating them. Charles found it boring. The cricket bat had been interesting to look at, both aesthetically and as an historical artefact – but endless lists and photographs of bygone players were really not his thing. And yet he still hovered by them, studiously avoiding Cressida's wan face. He was in far too good a mood to have to go and sit beside his miserable-looking wife.

Cressida's spirits had plummeted even further. Her position on the sofa was uncomfortable and she could feel that her dress was rucked up; but to stand up and shake herself out would draw attention to herself – and at that moment, she didn't feel as if she could bear anyone's eyes on her. Her glass was warm from the clutch of her fingers; her stockinged legs were uncomfortably slippery against the leather of the sofa; and Valerie's shrill voice was unending.

She had regaled Cressida for the last fifteen minutes with unsavoury pieces of gossip from the London office where she worked. She related each story in a detached, almost innocent voice, that displayed her complete ignorance of how these affairs might utterly destroy a marriage; ruin a relationship of trust; shatter a family. To Valerie, it was all fair game for entertainment.

'And then you'll never guess what,' she was saying. 'Michelle – that's his secretary – went and called his wife by the wrong name. She nearly died!' Valerie paused, and looked with bright eyes at Cressida, waiting, without much hope, for a response. Cressida was evidently a disappointment as a gossip partner. 'But that wasn't when she guessed,' she continued. 'The wife, I mean. It was about two months later. And it was such a stupid mistake. She saw his expenses list – and one of them was for a double hotel room. He just didn't think on his feet. I mean, he could have come up with a story or something, but he just told her everything. Next thing, he was off sick for a week.'

Cressida was beginning to feel sick herself. She had never heard such a sordid catalogue of misdemeanours. She felt like weeping for the wife's sake. For all the wives' sakes.

'Are you OK?' said Valerie, becoming aware of Cressida's downturned face.

'I'm fine,' said Cressida shakily. 'I'm just a bit tired.'

'I know what, I'll get you a drink of water,' said

Valerie, suddenly self-important, casting herself as Cressida's aide. 'I'll get you a nice glass of Perrier, shall I?'

'That would be lovely,' said Cressida. 'And perhaps I'll go outside on the terrace.'

'Get some fresh air, good idea,' said Valerie. She placed her clammy hand on Cressida's arm. 'You probably had too much sun today.' Cressida fought off the desire to retch.

As Valerie made off to the bar, Cressida struggled to her feet. Her dress was, as she had thought, rucked up at the back, and the linen had become rather creased. Not only that, but a spare button or something inside the dress seemed to have been caught on her tights. She fiddled uncomfortably at the spot. The only solution was to go to the bathroom and see what was wrong. She put her drink down and made for the door. But it opened before she could get there. A husky, coppery voice cried, 'Sorry I'm so late!' and Ella made her entrance.

She was wearing a dress made from layers of floating chiffon in palest yellow, cinnamon and burnt orange. Around her neck was a long string of amber beads, on which was strung a large, ornate silver cross. Her cheeks were radiantly glowing and her hair tied up in a silk, coffee-coloured scarf. Her deep-brown eyes surveyed the room, and she smiled first of all at Patrick, who was dispensing champagne to Stephen.

'I'm terrible,' she said apologetically. 'Once I get into a hot bath I just can't get out. Am I shockingly late?'

'No, no, don't be silly,' said Patrick. 'Come in and have a drink.' He led Ella in, until she was suddenly directly in front of Cressida. Cressida hastily stood up straight, stopped fiddling with her frock, and flashed her bright smile.

'Hello,' said Ella. 'We didn't really get a chance to meet this afternoon. I'm Ella Harte.'

'Yes, how do you do,' said Cressida in a colourless voice. She felt like a shadow beside this voluptuous, glowing figure. 'I am Cressida Mobyn.' She saw Ella flinch very slightly before taking her outstretched hand.

'It's funny,' said Ella, looking round at Charles and Stephen, who were watching in uncomfortable fascination. 'I somehow hadn't taken in the fact that you'd be called Mobyn. I associate the name Mobyn, you see, with Charles.'

Her hand was warm, and as she moved closer, Cressida was aware of a pulsing, foreign scent. There was a split second of silence before Cressida spoke.

'Well,' she said brightly. 'It was strange for me just after we were married. Having a different name. But I'm quite used to it now. I sign cheques without thinking.' She smiled again. Ella looked at her for a few moments without speaking, and then smiled slowly herself.

'I should think you do,' she said. 'Cressida Mobyn.' She rolled her tongue round the name. 'Well, I'm glad we've met.' Cressida tried not to look surprised.

'Oh, so am I,' she lied, in complete incomprehension.

Caroline, roused at last to hostess-like behaviour, had hurried over to where Ella and Cressida were standing. Now she chipped in.

'Come and get a drink, Ella,' she said, leading her away from Cressida.

Cressida watched them go with an unfamiliar feeling of resentment. Ella was plainly a member of the favoured group. She wondered whether to go to the bathroom and straighten her dress. It might look as though she was offended by Ella being there. Which naturally, she thought briskly to herself, she wasn't.

'Hello, darling,' said Charles, coming up to her with a rather unnatural smile. 'I see you've been talking to Ella. I'm glad you two have met at last.' Cressida stared at Charles in renewed incomprehension. Why would anyone be glad that she'd met Ella? She couldn't see any benefit in it at all.

As Stephen went into dinner, he felt agreeably content. He was relaxed and glowing after the day's tennis; his appetite was sharpened by the sight of the plates of delicately arranged smoked salmon on the table, and he still had a lingering sense of exhilaration at the deal he'd done with Patrick. He glanced at the others, following him in to the dining-room. They all looked sophisticated and cosmopolitan – even Annie. An image of their usual homely family suppers flashed through his mind. Annie always looked pretty, he thought loyally, even when she was hot and bothered over the stove, or coping with Nicola in a frustrated mood. But tonight her face was alive and excited, and she seemed to be laughing a lot. That was Caroline's influence, of course. He'd forgotten quite how determined that woman was to have a good time.

'Hello.' A voice at his elbow caused him to turn round. It was Ella, her dimpled face creased in a smile. 'I haven't said hello to you properly yet,' she continued. Stephen bent to kiss her cheek, which was smooth, glowing and smelling faintly of coconut.

'You're looking very well,' he said, aware that he was dealing in clichés. But how else was he to talk? 'Travelling certainly agrees with you . . .'

'. . . or something,' she finished, laughing. Her brown eyes searched his face. 'And you? Are you happy?' Stephen shrugged casually. He remembered now that Ella had always stood just a little closer than other people; asked slightly more penetrating questions; had always pursued a difficult line of enquiry where others would meekly have said 'oh, I see' and changed the subject.

'I'm fine,' he said easily. He smiled at her; his new, confident smile.

'I told Caroline I wanted to sit next to you,' said Ella. 'I want to hear all about your thesis. I'm so thrilled that you're doing it at last.' She darted to the table, peering at the name places.

'Here we are,' she called. 'We're over here,' Stephen joined her slowly, his confident air seeming to slip away slightly with every step. He had almost forgotten about his thesis. He had cast himself, this afternoon, as a leisured, moneyed deal-maker, enjoying some tennis among friends. He had almost convinced himself that this comfortable and luxurious house, not the grubby libraries and teaching rooms of the university, was his natural environment. Was he now to be forced to go over in his mind his failed attempt at scholarship; to recall the unwieldy, uncertain mass of dubious information and half-baked arguments that haunted and mocked him in his dreams? He flinched at the memory of it. Look at Patrick over there. He seemed to be doing all right, and he'd never been near a university in his life. Let alone given up a relatively well-paid job late in life in the vain pursuit of some sort of academic recognition. Wasn't this easy, leisured life what he really aspired to? He sank uneasily into a plushy, upholstered dining chair and smiled jovially at Valerie, who was sitting on his other side. But Ella was tugging at his sleeve.

'Now,' she said, shaking out her napkin, squeezing lemon over her salmon and looking seriously at him through her lashes. 'I really want to know. How's your research going?'

As Mrs Finch cleared away the plates from the first course, Charles looked over at Stephen and Ella again. What were they finding so much to talk about? Stephen was gesturing animatedly; Ella was nodding enthusiastically. She was leaning forward towards Stephen, clasping her hands, unwittingly pushing up her breasts until a full, golden-brown cleavage was on show. Or was it unwittingly? Charles looked away, and then looked back again.

'But that's amazing!' Ella's husky voice travelled across the table to him. 'Absolutely fascinating.' Charles could bear it no longer.

'What's fascinating, Ella?' he asked in a hearty voice. The whole table stopped talking and looked at him. He ignored Cressida's pale, questioning face, Caroline's raised eyebrows, Patrick's smirk, and ploughed on. 'Sorry, I couldn't help overhearing that something was fascinating. I was just wondering what it was.'

Ella raised her eyes, slightly contemptuous, slightly amused, to his.

'We were talking about Stephen's thesis,' she said. 'It's so interesting. But you must know all about it, I suppose. I'm hearing it all for the first time.' Charles looked at Stephen. Everyone was waiting for an answer.

'Of course,' he said eventually. 'Your thesis. Terribly interesting.'

'Do you think so, Charles?' said Stephen, grinning at him in mock-surprise, knowing full well that Charles couldn't give a damn about his thesis. Charles forced himself not to glare at Stephen. He suddenly felt an irrational hatred for him, sitting next to Ella, breathing in her scent, touching her bare arms, sharing her jokes. But it was Charles that Ella was now looking at, twisting her amber beads thoughtfully round her fingers. He had to say something.

'Oh yes,' he said. 'Seventeenth-century stuff, wasn't it?'

'Fourteenth,' said Ella. 'You're not telling me they were writing mystery plays in the seventeenth century?'

'Mystery plays?' said Charles in surprise. 'Since when has your thesis been on mystery plays, Stephen?'

'Since my original proposal was turned down,' said Stephen, grinning. 'Only about two years ago.'

'I haven't kept up,' said Charles apologetically. To his surprise he did feel genuinely ashamed. He had a sudden flashback to cosy suppers in the Fairweathers' basement kitchen. He remembered Stephen outlining his latest piece of research; eyes lit up with the thrill of discovery; gesticulating with a piece of garlic bread or a pasta-laden fork; pausing in his rhetoric only to swallow a mouthful of food or wine; then looking up to see Annie and Charles giggling at him. And Ella, of course. She had always been there.

'I think the idea of our own local mystery play is wonderful,' said Ella. 'The Silchester Mystery Play. We should organize for it to be put on. In the Cathedral.'

'We could do it for charity,' said Cressida suddenly. She had been following the exchange with very little enthusiasm. She had no idea what a mystery play was and no interest in Stephen's thesis. She did not trust Ella; she couldn't think why Charles was insisting on talking to her, and she was longing for bed. But an instinctive desire to win back Charles' attention, coupled with her belief that it was one's duty to contribute to general conversation, forced her valiantly to speak. Having spoken, she sank gratefully back into her chair.

But Ella had fixed her attention on Cressida.

'What a wonderful idea,' she said, in an intense voice. 'Could you organize something like that?'

'Well,' said Cressida faintly, 'I'm on several charity committees. In Silchester, you know.'

'It's perfect,' said Ella. 'You can stage a show in the Cathedral. Get professional actors. It'll be a marvellous occasion.' She beamed at Stephen. 'And wouldn't it help your research? To see it actually performed?'

'Well, yes,' said Stephen. 'I suppose it would.'

'Of course it would,' said Ella. 'You must let me know when it happens. I'll come back especially to see it.'

'Back?' said Charles in spite of himself. 'Back from where?' Ella gave him a curious look.

'Oh,' she said. 'Didn't I tell you? I'm starting a job. In Italy.'

'Ooh, how lovely!' exclaimed Valerie. 'Imagine working in Italy!'

'What are you going to do?' said Annie.

'I'm going to be assistant,' said Ella, 'to someone called Maud Vennings. She lives in Italy most of the time.'

There was a slightly stunned silence. Ella grinned at Caroline, who shrugged back. Ella had told Caroline about her new job earlier in the evening – but since Caroline had never heard of Maud Vennings, the announcement had not made much impact. Now Annie was the first to speak.

'Maud Vennings? The painter?'

'Yes, the painter,' said Ella, delicately spearing a piece of seafood tartlet and eating it thoughtfully. The others gazed at her in awe.

'We saw a programme about her, didn't we, Val?' said Don. 'On the telly. Isn't she a real eccentric? Lives all by herself in some huge castle?'

'Yes, I suppose you could call her eccentric,' said Ella. 'She used to live all by herself. But now I'm going to be living with her. And we won't be on our own. We're starting up a series of residential workshops. Painting, food, wine, walking . . . that kind of thing.'

'A package holiday, you mean,' said Charles, unable to keep a sneer out of his voice. He was experiencing a feeling perilously close to jealousy.

'Not really,' said Ella, giving a secretive smile. 'It will only be open to painters of talent. Graduates of the art colleges, that kind of thing. We might branch into music, as well. Maud knows a lot of musicians. And they'll be guests of hers. It's not a business. But she still needs someone to organize it all.'

There was another pause, as everyone took in the implications of this.

'I suppose', said Don eventually, 'she's absolutely loaded.'

'Her paintings sell for hundreds of thousands of pounds, don't they?' said Valerie eagerly. 'Those nude girls. I've a postcard of one of them on my wall at work.'

'I've got a poster in the kitchen,' said Annie.

'I went to see an exhibition of hers in London once,' volunteered Cressida. 'I think it was for Save the Children.' Charles shot her an angry look.

'So, do tell us, Ella,' he said, unable to contain his incensed curiosity, 'how on earth did this come about?'

'Well, it was quite simple,' said Ella. 'I wrote to her and said I was coming to Italy and would it be possible to visit her. I thought I might try to interview her or something. I don't really know what made me do it. But she said yes. So I went to see her, and she invited me to stay for dinner, and that was it, really.'

'She said yes, just because you wrote her a letter?' Charles' outrage was transparent.

'It was quite a long letter,' said Ella, consideringly. 'I told her about myself, and my life, and why I was coming to Italy . . .' She broke off and smiled at Charles. 'I think she thought it all sounded rather interesting. And we got on really well, right from the start. She told me the other day that as soon as she saw me, she knew she wanted me to live with her.'

Valerie's eyes widened.

'It said on the programme that she might be a bit of a . . . you know.' She broke off. 'Lesbian,' she whispered.

'Did it?' said Ella. She paused, fork halfway to mouth. 'Well, you never know,' she said. 'Perhaps she is.'

Coffee had been served, Don and Valerie were making signs of departure, and the others were still sitting in the drawing-room. The doors to the terrace were still open, and the sweet smell of night air mingled with the lingering aroma of coffee. Annie dreamily swirled a cognac round in her glass. It had been such a lovely day. Her muscles ached agreeably, her skin was warm with sunburn, and her stomach replete with food. She was also, she realized, quite drunk.

'See you tomorrow!' Don's grinning face interrupted her reverie.

'Sorry? Oh, yes, see you then,' said Annie.

'We'll be along to watch your match,' he said. 'Bright and early.' Annie clutched her head.

'But I'll feel dreadful tomorrow!' she cried.

'Drink a glass of water for each alcoholic drink you've consumed,' advised Don cheerily. 'That's my advice.' Annie felt a sudden, uncharacteristic urge to throw her glass at him. She deliberately took a large gulp of cognac, looked up, and spluttered as she saw Caroline grimacing at Don behind his back.

'I'm such a child!' she wailed, when Don was out of the door. 'I've regressed thirty years.' She looked accusingly at Caroline. 'It's all your fault,' she said. 'I was a sane human being before today.'

'No you weren't,' retorted Caroline. 'Remember apple bobbing at that Hallowe'en party? That got really out of hand.' She and Annie collapsed into giggles at the memory.

'I got completely soaked,' said Annie.

'We all did,' said Caroline.

'And Nicola kept saying, "No, Mummy, like this,"' called out Stephen, who was watching Annie in amusement.

'Poor old Nicola,' said Annie, fondly wiping her eyes. 'I don't think she'd ever seen me drunk before.'

'She was good at apple bobbing,' said Caroline.

'She still is,' said Annie robustly.

'Sweet Nicola,' said Caroline. 'She's a darling child.'

'Oh Nicola!' chimed in Ella, from the sofa. 'I love her to pieces!'

Ella had commandeered two thirds of the sofa and

was reclining comfortably, shoes kicked off, head thrown back. The remaining part of the sofa was, as yet, unclaimed. Stephen was sitting near by on the floor; Annie and Caroline were by the fireplace; Cressida was sitting on her own, on a low leather pouffe. Charles was the only one not sitting down; he paced about the room like a big cat, unable to keep his eyes from swivelling towards Ella every time she spoke or moved.

She was again pursuing the subject of the Silchester Mystery Play.

'Really, Stephen, you must put it on,' she insisted, sitting up and hugging her feet through the gauzy layers of her dress.

'I'll think about it,' said Stephen, smiling at her.

'Don't just think about it! Do it!'

'It may not be as simple as all that,' he said. 'These things take a lot of time, a lot of preparation, a lot of money. A serious amount of money, if you want it done well. Where am I to find that?' Ella shrugged.

'You can always find money if you really want it.'

Charles had been listening to this exchange. Now he came over and, with deliberate casualness, sat down on the bit of the sofa not occupied by Ella. She looked at him silently. There were only inches between them; her feet were almost brushing against his trousers.

'If you wanted some money,' he said, looking not at Stephen but at Ella, 'we could always put some up. The Print Centre. It's just the sort of project we should be involved with.' Ella's eyes held his insolently.

'How much?' she said challengingly. Charles' breathing quickened slightly.

'Five, ten thousand, maybe?' he said. Ella didn't move. 'Fifteen?' his voice cracked.

'Fifteen thousand pounds?' Stephen exclaimed. His voice rang through the room. 'My word, Charles, that's very generous!'

Cressida, who had been staring, unheeding, at the

carpet, looked up. Were they talking about money? Was Charles promising fifteen thousand pounds to someone? The memory of the letter flooded into her mind; a pang of alarm shot through her body. She had to speak. 'Sorry, Charles,' she said awkwardly, flinching as everyone turned to look at her, 'what were you saying?'

'It's all right,' said Charles, 'it's just Print Centre business. Nothing for you to worry about.' He turned away. In a slight haze, Cressida took in the fact that he was sitting on the sofa with Ella. And yet when she had been sitting on the sofa earlier on, he had insisted on standing up. It was like a bad dream. And worst of all was the untold secret of the letter.

'What sort of business?' she persisted. Charles gave her an annoyed look.

'A sponsorship deal. We're going to back the Silchester Mystery Play. You can help to organize it.'

'Oh,' said Cressida. Waves of panic went through her. She had to tell Charles. Before he promised any more money. She had to talk to him.

Shakily she stood up, and flashed a smile around the room.

'I think I'll go to bed actually,' she said. She smiled hard at Charles. 'Are you coming, darling?' Charles gave her a surprised, rather irritated look. He glanced at his watch.

'It's not midnight yet,' he said. 'Do you want to go so soon?'

'Yes, I think so,' said Cressida, staring at him with what she hoped was a meaningful expression. 'It's been a long day.'

'Well, I think I'll stay up a while longer,' said Charles. 'See you later.' Cressida stood still for a few seconds, trying not to appear desperate.

'You won't be too long, will you?' she said eventually. She was aware of how awful she must appear to everyone. They would all laugh at her when she was gone but she couldn't bear another hour going by without having told Charles about the letter.

'No, I won't be too long,' replied Charles evenly. 'Good night.' He turned back to Ella, leaving Cressida stranded in the middle of the room. She began to back uncertainly towards the door.

'Good night, Cressida,' said Patrick kindly. 'I hope you sleep well. If you want anything, just shout.'

'Good night,' chorused the others.

'Don't worry,' said Caroline, smirking. 'We won't keep Charles up much longer.' Cressida flashed a smile at her, and hurried out through the door, tears stinging her eyes. They were all laughing at her. And Charles despised her for trying to rush him off to bed.

She went hurriedly through the hall and up the stairs, wondering if it was too late to run herself a hot bath. She walked briskly along the pale corridor, which seemed much longer now than it had been during the day. But when she reached the door of the boys' bedroom she paused. She had been preoccupied that evening, and had said good night to them in a rush. Now she carefully pushed open the door and looked into the moonlit room. Two little blond heads glinted on their pillows; Martina was gently snoring in the corner and the floor was carpeted in toys. She moved in a few steps, longing to pick up her babies and hold them tight against her chest, to feel their puny heartbeats and let their soft breathing soothe her. But a sense of discipline stopped her from doing anything so silly. The boys needed their sleep; she would disturb Martina; what would people think if they saw her? She stood a few seconds more, then reluctantly tiptoed out of the room and made her lonely way to her own bedroom.

There was a general atmosphere of hilarity in the drawing-room once Cressida had left. Patrick went round and filled everyone's drinks; Caroline put a compact disc on the hi-fi. Soon, the rhythms of South American dance music were pulsing through the room. Charles leant back on the sofa and let the sound wash over him. Ella was tapping her foot and softly swaying. Then Caroline got up and began to dance. Her trained dancer's limbs were still supple; her sense of rhythm faultless. Her hips gyrated; her hands gently skimmed her pelvis and thighs.

'Very good,' applauded Ella. 'That's just how they do it.'

'Did you learn any dancing when you were in South America?' asked Annie, watching Caroline in admiration. Ella shrugged.

'A little.'

'Oh, go on!' Annie's eyes were bright, like a child. 'Show us.' Ella smiled, and uncoiled herself from the sofa.

'I need a partner. Caroline?' Caroline held out her hands to Ella, as if for ballroom dancing.

'Closer than that,' said Ella. 'Much closer.' She pulled Caroline towards her, grasped her firmly and began to move her feet, gyrating her hips back and forth. Caroline followed her movements hesitantly and Stephen, moving quietly to the hi-fi controls, turned up the volume of the pulsating music. Nobody spoke. The two women's bodies moved around slowly as if joined by the hips; Caroline's face intense with concentration, Ella's stern and distant. Charles wondered with a sudden fierce pang of jealousy whom she was thinking about. He was beginning to feel unbearably aroused by the sight of Ella and Caroline; looking at the faces of the other men, he suspected he was not the only one.

The atmosphere was broken when the song ended, and Caroline collapsed onto a chair in fits of laughter.

'Take me to South America,' she cried dramatically. 'If that's how the men dance, I want to go there!'

'It's how the women dance, too,' said Ella quietly. But everyone was looking at Patrick, who had stood up

141

and begun to sway his hips in imitation.

'I don't think so, Patrick,' said Stephen comically. 'Better leave it to your wife.'

Patrick sat back down, adopting a disgruntled air, and Ella returned to her place on the sofa. The mood of hysteria seemed to have vanished.

'I'll make some more coffee, shall I?' volunteered Annie.

'I'll show you where everything is,' said Caroline.

Out in the kitchen, Caroline sat down on a chair.

'Actually,' she said, 'I'm not sure I know where everything is. Christ knows where Mrs Finch puts the coffee.' Annie giggled.

'You live in a different world,' she said, opening and closing cupboard doors. 'Not knowing where the coffee is in your own kitchen!'

'Well, I usually leave it out on the side,' said Caroline. 'But that silly cow always puts it away. Try that cupboard. No, that one.' Annie put the kettle on, put coffee in the pot, then came and sat down beside Caroline.

'It's been such a lovely day,' she said. 'I can't thank you enough.' Caroline smiled.

'We should get together more often,' she said. 'I really miss all of you, being stuck here in this village.'

'But it's so lovely here!' exclaimed Annie, surprised. 'Especially for the children. Nicola's had such a wonderful day. Well, we all have, really.' She glanced at the door. 'I think it's done Stephen some good, too,' she added in a low voice. 'I didn't actually realize he and Patrick were such good friends. But they've been chatting away all day.' She beamed at Caroline, but Caroline had a slight frown on her face. She seemed to be thinking.

'When does Stephen finish his thesis again?' she said abruptly.

'In a year or two,' said Annie, looking slightly surprised.

'And what happens after that? Jobwise.' Annie shrugged.

'He'd really like to go into higher education. Perhaps a junior teaching post at one of the universities, or a research fellowship.'

'And do those pay well?' Annie grinned.

'No, they don't. But it won't be for ever. He'll move up to better things.'

'And meanwhile . . . ?'

'Meanwhile, we manage.' Annie looked honestly at Caroline. 'We're very lucky, compared to some. No-one goes into academia to be rich.' She glanced up. 'Look, the kettle's boiling.'

The drawing-room was quiet as Caroline and Annie came back in with the coffee. The music was soft again, no-one was talking, and the sound of the terrace door banging in the wind made them all jump. Caroline put down the tray, closed the terrace door and began to pour out the coffee. When everyone had a cup, she took a deep breath.

'We're all old friends here,' she said. 'We all know each other well enough to talk frankly. And now that it's just us six, there's something I want to say.' Everyone's heads rose interestedly. 'There's a . . .' Caroline paused, searching for the word, 'a particular matter I'd like to discuss. It actually only concerns Stephen and Annie – and Patrick and myself – but somehow I'd like everyone to hear it.' She paused, took a sip of coffee, and gave a defiant glance at Patrick. 'It's a financial matter,' she added. Patrick's heart started beating faster. He tried to give Caroline a silencing yet unobtrusive stare, but she was ignoring him. The stupid fucking bitch. What was she going to say? What was she going to tell them? I'm going to kill her, he thought. I'm going to fucking kill her.

Cressida had undressed as slowly as she could. She brushed her hair, removed her make-up, rubbed moisturizer into her face with upwards movements and applied eye cream. Eventually, when she was utterly ready for bed, when there was nothing else she could do, she looked at her watch. Half-past midnight. And Charles was still downstairs. The ominous phrase 'Don't wait up' floated through her mind. But tonight she had to wait up. She had to talk to Charles, urgently. She fingered the letter, which she had retrieved from her vanity case, and unfolded it. Then she folded it up again without reading it. She could remember what it said without looking. And Charles would soon explain it all to her.

She gazed at herself in the mirror. Her skin was taut with worry; her eyes anxious. Suddenly she missed her father. He had been a generous, comforting figure; mostly absent, but larger – and louder – than life when he was there. He had always been a welcome antidote to the peculiarly feminine air of worry that built up in the house when he went away. Her mother, who was prone to particularly feverish panic attacks, would pour out her woes as soon as he appeared through the door; he would listen apparently seriously to her worries, point out the flaws in them – and eventually have her laughing at herself. Cressida could remember his hearty guffaw; his huge, strong hands; his down-to-earth air which would cause her mother to cringe even as she was locked in his embrace.

But now he was dead, and her mother too. Cressida could feel the tears rising and took a deep breath. She no longer allowed herself to weep for either of them. She drank half a glass of water, switched off the light in the bathroom and went back into the bedroom. She paused by the side of the pink satin bed and made a few, rather inarticulate attempts at prayer. After a while, unsatisfied with herself, she stopped. She climbed into bed, shivering slightly, and sat up against the pillows, clutching the letter, waiting for Charles.

Patrick couldn't quite believe his ears. He stared incredulously at Caroline, who beamed gaily at him.

'We've discussed it fully, haven't we?' she said. 'Darling.' Patrick smiled feebly at Stephen and Annie. Stephen looked shell-shocked; Annie's eyes were shining.

'We couldn't let you,' said Stephen eventually.

'Rubbish,' said Caroline briskly. 'We've only got Georgina to pay for. We might easily have six sets of school fees to fork out every year. One extra won't make any difference. And it makes us mad to see Nicola's talents wasted at that school. She needs a better chance in life. Patrick thinks', she added, 'that Nicola should have riding lessons.' Patrick's head jerked in amazement. 'He thinks St Catherine's would do wonders for her confidence,' she added blithely.

'Didn't you say that, Patrick?' Patrick glared at her.

'Yes, yes,' he said. 'Wonders.' He turned to pour himself another brandy and caught the eye of Ella. She grinned at him, as if she knew exactly what was going through his mind.

'I think it's a lovely gesture,' she said. 'I'm sure Nicola would benefit from private education. It's very generous of you.'

'Very,' said Charles sardonically. 'Six years of boarding-school doesn't exactly come cheap.'

'Well, of course, we'd pay as soon as we could,' said Annie eagerly. 'We'd think of it as a loan.' She gave Patrick a wide smile. 'All my instincts and manners tell me we must refuse your offer; but when I think of Nicola, of how much it would mean to her . . . I don't think I can bring myself to.' Her eyes began to moisten. 'Look at me!' she exclaimed. 'I'm pathetic!'

'I don't know.' Stephen was still frowning. 'As Charles says, it is a lot of money.'

'It's all relative,' said Caroline. She flashed a wicked look at Patrick. 'I mean,' she said deliberately, 'think how much money Patrick deals in every day. What's a few years' school fees compared to that?' Watching in impotent fury, Patrick saw this idea taking root in Stephen's mind. Christ, Stephen was so fucking naïve. After today's performance in the study, he probably thought Patrick dealt in sums of eighty thousand every minute. And Caroline knew it.

Stephen raised doubtful eyes to Patrick, and Patrick forced himself to smile.

'Caroline's right,' he said, hardly able to believe he was saying it. 'We can easily afford it.' If we forget any idea of new cars, let alone a new house, he thought. And Caroline can fucking well get rid of her Barbados brochures.

'Good,' said Caroline. 'That's settled. I'm so pleased. We both are, aren't we, sweetheart?'

'Delighted,' said Patrick, and knocked back another brandy.

Chapter Nine

Nothing much more was said for a while. Annie, who had drunk more than anyone – including herself – had quite realized, began weeping quiet, unobtrusive tears of gratitude at Caroline's and Patrick's offer. Stephen smiled apologetically round the room and put his arm round her; the others sat blankly as if overcome by sudden torpor; staring silently down into their coffee grounds with numbed, drunk, late-night expressions. After a while, Caroline began to yawn rather ostentatiously. Stephen glanced at his watch and began to shift position; Patrick quietly collected the coffee cups and put them back on the tray.

Charles realized, with alarm, that the party was breaking up. Suddenly the idea of tamely going up to bed filled him with horror. After this evening, he felt alive and invigorated. He felt young again. Hearing about Ella's travels, about her friendship with Maud Vennings, talking about artists, even discussing Stephen's mystery play, had suddenly reminded him of what he used to be like. Christ, how his values, his interests, even his idea of a good time had changed since marriage. Or, really, since Cressida. When was the last time he had stayed up all night, or got stoned? When was the last time he had thrown himself headlong into an argument, debating the point for debating's sake – even if he agreed with his opponent? When was the last time he had spent a whole evening excitedly sketching out some new project for the Print Centre that was doomed to be a commercial failure?

He glanced down at his wrist, expensively cuffed in a Jermyn Street shirt, expensively adorned with a

147

Swiss watch. Of course, his life had changed. No-one could expect him to remain a bloody hippy all his life; to live off bread and sex and cheap drugs. And it wasn't just him. The world had changed. It was Stephen who was the oddity these days, still idealistic; still naïve; still poor. Charles' thoughts flickered complacently to the house in the Cathedral Close. It had cost a fucking fortune, that house.

His mind paused, and waited for the customary kick of pleasure that thinking about his new wealth generally brought him. But this time it hadn't worked. The feeling of excitement in his stomach had nothing to do with his wife and her worldly goods. He imagined her face, waiting for him upstairs; pale, insipid, stupid. Going up to bed was unthinkable.

He glanced at Ella, clutching her knees and gazing dreamily at nothing.

'I feel like a bit of a walk,' he said quietly. 'A breath of fresh air. Want to join me?' Ella regarded him consideringly.

'All right,' she said eventually, and smiled her secretive smile. 'You can show me the garden. Caroline,' she said, raising her voice, 'it's not too late to go walking in the garden, is it? We won't get bats in our hair?'

'Oh no,' said Caroline, 'I don't think so.' She looked puzzledly at Patrick, swaying very slightly. 'Bats?' she repeated. 'I don't think so.'

'Go ahead,' said Patrick, smiling at them over Caroline's head. 'Just leave the terrace door open and shut it firmly behind you when you come back.'

'Well, good night,' said Charles hurriedly, not wanting to look at their faces.

'See you all tomorrow,' said Ella. 'Sleep well.'

As Ella opened the terrace door, Charles felt a slight quailing. Perhaps it would be better to announce that he had changed his mind; that he was feeling tired; that he thought he would turn in after all. But before he could make up his mind to do this, he was out into the soft, black, anonymous night. He lingered on the terrace, breathing in the night air, looking at the dark forms of the garden. The fairy lights were still on and he felt as though he were playing a part in some old-fashioned film. Some enchanted evening ... A tune flickered through his mind.

'I thought you wanted to walk?' Ella was already halfway across the lawn.

'Oh, coming,' said Charles. As he hurried to join her, someone turned off the fairy lights from inside. The garden was plunged into darkness and Charles paused in his stride.

'Where are you?'

'Here.' Her voice travelled, low and husky, through the night air, and he walked blindly towards it, feeling for bumps in the grass with his feet, trying to adjust his eyes to the darkness.

'Here, silly.' He had walked past her. He turned back uncertainly and felt a warm hand seize his.

'You urban creature,' she mocked. 'You've forgotten how to use your eyes properly.' At the touch of her hand, a delicious tingle spread from Charles' neck, up past his ear and over his head. He followed her meekly towards the hedge, through the gate and into the field beyond. As they brushed past the hedge, a bird noisily flapped its way out; further down in the undergrowth there were more animal scufflings.

'In Africa,' said Ella, 'all the animals come together at night to drink. Even those that don't normally mix. It's a wonderful sight.'

'You went to Africa?' ventured Charles. He had never discussed Ella's travels with her, aware that she had gone off, initially, because of him; because of the break-up. At the time, she had not even told him that she was going; he had learned it from Angus, his old business partner, who had sided firmly with Ella.

'Yes, I did,' said Ella. They fell silent for a while.

Charles could not think of a single word or phrase that would not sound banal. He woefully tried to remember what he usually talked about. Memories of conversations with Cressida floated into his mind, but were entirely visual. He could not even recall the sound of Cressida's voice, let alone what she ever said, or what he said in return.

'The Ethiopians', said Ella thoughtfully, 'are the most wonderfully elegant race.' She paused. Charles felt foolish. Should he say something? 'It was one of the things that struck me most about the country,' continued Ella. She was striding forward with a regular pace, not looking at Charles, but talking as though to herself. 'All the people have very fine bones, and aristocratic features. The women are utterly beautiful. They wear these wonderful white robes, which go down to the ground and cover their heads, so they look as if they might be Arabic rather than African. And each robe has an embroidered border. Some are simple and plain, but others are very ornate. I was told they even use thread made from pure gold.'

As Ella talked, Charles listened, enchanted. He had forgotten her husky, dusky, coppery voice; had forgotten her power of telling a simple story so that it captivated her listeners. He walked silently in the dark, willing her to continue for ever. The further they walked from the house, the more he heard her voice, the later it got, the more alive he felt. An unspecified exhilaration ran through him as he considered the empty hours of the night which stretched out before them.

'And then we tried to eat a traditional Ethiopian dish called injera,' Ella was saying. 'It had the exact look, texture and taste of carpet underlay. In fact, maybe it was carpet underlay.' She gave a sudden gurgle of laughter. Charles suddenly felt fiercely jealous. Once, he had been the worldly-wise, experienced one. He had instructed Ella in the vagaries of modern art; had taught her how to eat semolina as a savoury dish; had introduced her to drugs and oral sex. But now she had leap-frogged ahead of him. She had seen, smelt, touched and tasted places he was never likely to see. She had mixed with the kind of people who would despise Charles, his wife, his car, his sailor-suited blond twins. She had met and been invited to live with Maud Vennings. This last, Charles could hardly bear to think about. If it hadn't been for him, Ella would probably never have heard of Maud Vennings.

'When do you go to Italy?' he said abruptly.

'I don't know yet,' said Ella. 'When I get tired of England, I suppose. I've been back a month, and already I'm getting itchy feet.'

'I never thought you were a natural traveller,' said Charles in a rather suspicious voice.

'No, neither did I,' said Ella mildly. 'I surprised myself by how much I enjoyed it. I was expecting to hate it.'

'Then why did you go?' The question was out before Charles could stop himself. Shit, he thought to himself.

There was a short silence. Then Ella spoke.

'Do you want to know why I went?' she said, in a light, toneless voice. 'Do you really want to know?' Charles was silent. 'I decided to go', she continued, 'when I bumped into you in the street, just after you'd moved out of the house and it was all over between us. It was in Silchester. I was coming out of the wool shop, thinking about something else completely, and there you were.'

'Well, I do live in Silchester,' said Charles, defensively.

'I still remember it so clearly,' said Ella, ignoring him. 'You sort of waved, and smiled, and you kissed me on both cheeks and pretended to be pleased to see me, and said I was looking well. But you didn't look me in the eye. And then you rushed off without

151

saying anything else. That was the first time I'd seen you since we broke up, and the way you acted, I could have been anyone.'

'Rubbish,' said Charles feebly.

'I didn't want you to take me in your arms and say it had all been a mistake. Well, perhaps I did want that. But if I couldn't have that, what I wanted most of all was to talk about it. To you. Not to well-meaning people who didn't understand.' She smiled. 'But you ran away, and pretended I didn't exist. And I couldn't bear that. So I decided to go away.'

They had come to the far side of the field, and she sank to the ground, her voluminous skirts ballooning darkly around her. Charles sat more gingerly, feeling in the blackness for thistles, nettles, suspicious patches of mud. He could see nothing of Ella but the glint of her eyes.

'I didn't mean to run away,' he said. 'I'm sorry.' He struggled for words. 'We should have talked.' He reached impulsively for her hand, brushing against her thigh in the darkness, suddenly wanting to feel her warm flesh against his. But she pulled her hand away.

'I was so alone,' said Ella, in her low, penetrating, merciless voice. 'You had the Print Centre, you had all your friends in Silchester, you had Cressida. I didn't. How do you think I felt?'

Charles desperately cast his mind back, trying to remember what he'd thought; how he'd felt. But it was all a blank. He couldn't even remember why he'd fallen for Cressida in the first place. He began to think he had never had any feelings at all.

'I was a callous bastard,' he murmured.

'Don't glamorize yourself,' said Ella. 'You were a typical male.' She threw her head back and her throat gleamed palely in the moonlight. Charles stared at her, disconcerted. She had grown up on her travels; she had new ideas, new ways of thinking, a new self-assurance. He wondered, with a stab of jealousy, who had put those new ideas into her mind. She moved slightly, and the moonlight shifted onto her breasts, glinting on the exposed curves; highlighting her shoulder where her dress had slipped down. Slowly, cautiously, he stretched out a hand and touched her shoulder. She didn't move. He drew his finger down, over the swell of her breast, then up to her neck and behind her ear. He began to caress her neck.

An owl hooted near by, and he jumped, startled. Suddenly it came to him that he was alone with Ella in the middle of a field in the middle of the night, and that they were about to make love. Then he wondered why he hadn't realized this sooner.

Patrick and Caroline walked up the stairs with Stephen and Annie in a state of jovial *bonhomie*. They embraced affectionately, then departed to their various rooms. But as soon as they were alone in their bedroom, Patrick rounded on Caroline with coldly furious eyes.

'Just what do you think you're playing at?' he demanded.

'What do you mean?' Caroline walked past him and sank heavily onto her dressing-table stool. She leaned forward and stared at her face in the mirror. Then she groaned.

'Oh God. I'm so fucking *old*.'

'Don't change the subject,' said Patrick sternly. 'You realize how much the fees to that place are?'

'What place?' said Caroline unconvincingly.

'Don't make me laugh,' said Patrick shortly. 'Well, all I can say is, it's your loss. Those fees are coming out of the money I spend on you. No Porsche, no Champneys, no Barbados.'

'I don't care!' hissed Caroline, suddenly swivelling on the stool to face him. 'I'm glad. I don't give a monkeys about Champneys. Or bloody Barbados. You only suggested going there because one of those snotty mothers at Georgina's school said she'd been there.'

She picked up a hairbrush and began to drag it angrily through her hair. 'I can see right through you, you know that, Patrick? You think ladies of leisure spend their whole time going to Champneys and Barbados, so you decide I've got to go, too. Bloody social climber. Well, perhaps I'd rather go on a package to Tenerife!'

'Don't be ridiculous,' said Patrick.

'What's wrong with Tenerife? What's wrong with a bit of real life for a change?'

'You're a fine one to talk about real life,' mocked Patrick. 'The phoniest PR bimbo of the lot, you were. Promoting this, promoting that, never an idea what any of the products were about, whether they were any good, just smile at the customer and take the money!'

'It was a job, Patrick,' said Caroline in a low, furious voice. 'And there's not a lot of those about for an out-of-work, unqualified dancer like I was.'

Patrick was silent for a moment, pulling out his cufflinks in abrupt gestures. When he spoke again it was on a different line of attack.

'Anyway,' he said truculently, 'if you don't like Georgina's school, why do you want to send Nicola there?'

'I do like the school,' said Caroline. 'I think it's a great school. I just don't get on with the other mums. Come on, Patrick, I'm not exactly Lady Holmes, am I?' Patrick twitched at the thought of Lady Holmes, the mother of one of Georgina's school friends. A smart, condescending woman who always managed to make him feel grubby and unpatrician. 'And you're not exactly lord of the manor,' continued Caroline brutally. 'Nothing like. So why try to be? Why not just admit you're a rich pleb?' Patrick flinched, and turned away.

'If I want to get on in life a bit,' he said, his voice stiff with embarrassed anger, 'it's for Georgina's sake.'

'Oh yes? Well, I reckon we've got on quite far enough, thank you. I know what you've been thinking. We should make a pile more money, sell up, move on somewhere else, pretend to be smarter than we are, make new friends. Well perhaps I like it here. Perhaps I've got friends here. Perhaps I don't want to be smart, and go hunting, or fishing, or whatever it is that lot do to get their kicks.'

Patrick turned to face Caroline, smiling in contempt.

'You've got friends? What, those scrounger Fairweathers? You're paying their bloody school fees; what are you going to do next, invite them to live here?'

'If I were you,' said Caroline, her voice quivering with anger, 'I wouldn't say one word about the Fairweathers. Not one word. Otherwise you might just find me popping along to their room and whispering a few things in their ears. Like the fact that their so-called friend has just conned them completely. Like the fact that they'll never be able to afford that mortgage. Like the fact that the Sigma fund has a high-risk rating. Like the fact that they're probably going to lose all their money.' Patrick stared at her in surprise. 'You think I know sod all, don't you, Patrick?' she said. 'Just a bimbo with a big smile? Well, I know more than you think. I know that you're someone who can't be trusted, for a start.' Patrick was silenced, watching her warily like a cornered mouse. Caroline got up and paced about restlessly, suddenly alive, her eyes glittering.

'I can't believe you,' she said, in a sudden outburst. 'You're completely immoral. And you actually have the nerve to complain about my offer to them. Christ, you con Stephen out of eighty grand, and you can't afford a few thousand a year for his kid?'

'It's not as simple as that,' began Patrick.

'What *is* it as simple as, then?' interrupted Caroline. 'As far as I can see, Stephen is still the loser.'

'Stephen will do very well from my advice,' said Patrick.

'Like hell he will. He stands to lose a fucking fortune. In fact, there's something else I want you to do as well as the fees.' She sat down on the bed and gave him a defiant look.

'What?'

'I want you to promise that if Stephen can't keep up his mortgage payments, you'll help him out. Just temporarily.'

'You're mad,' said Patrick.

'You owe it to them,' said Caroline. 'I want you to promise.'

'Bloody hell, I'll be supporting them for life!'

'Well then, tell Stephen you think you gave him the wrong advice. Cancel the deal.' Patrick looked at her.

'Do you know how much that deal was worth?'

'Do you know how much a friend is worth?' Caroline stared at him with bloodshot blue eyes.

'Oh, for fuck's sake!' shouted Patrick, suddenly losing his temper. 'Where's all this crap coming from? What's a friend worth? I'll tell you. Fuck all. When did any of our friends ever do anything for us? Never.'

'That's because we've never had any fucking friends!' Caroline shouted back. 'Never! Annie's my first proper friend, and I want to keep her!' To her dismay she felt a fat tear rolling down her cheek.

'What do you mean, we've never had any proper friends,' said Patrick, incensed. 'We've plenty of friends.'

'What, clients you mean?' cried Caroline. 'They're not friends. And neither are those awful people from your work. I can't stand them.'

'Well, what about the people in the village?'

'They're all horrible. I hate them.' Caroline was weeping bitterly now, hugging her knees and not bothering to wipe away the mascara that ran down her face. As Patrick watched her he was reminded of the way she'd wept when she discovered she couldn't have any more children after Georgina. It was one of the few times he'd seen her childlike and vulnerable. Most of the time she was either relentlessly cheerful or determinedly bad-tempered. Rarely did she let her guard down. Suddenly he was filled with a strong wave of compassion, mixed up inextricably with sexual desire. Caroline was sniffling now, refusing, as she always did, to blow her nose properly. He moved towards her uncertainly, sat down beside her on the bed and put his arm around her shoulders rather awkwardly.

'Of course I'll help them out,' he murmured. 'I didn't realize it meant so much to you.' Caroline buried her wet face in his poplin shoulder and sobbed with renewed vigour. Patrick rubbed her back gently, muttering the sort of soothing words he hadn't uttered since Georgina was about four. Both his wife and daughter were usually so self-possessed as to make him feel, if not unwanted, then certainly not needed. But here was Caroline, whimpering against his chest, looking to him for comfort, asking him to help her. Gently he brushed strands of golden hair out of her eyes and lifted her red, blotchy face till she was looking at him; silent now, but still shuddering with emotion. She opened her mouth to speak, but Patrick hastily leant forward and kissed her swollen lips. Let the picture continue in his mind; let his vision of Caroline as damsel, himself as saviour, last at least for a while. Let her not come out with some cutting or, even worse, unconcerned comment that would put him back in his place again; shatter the picture he was building up.

He kissed her firmly, kneading the tense muscles in the back of her neck; moving down to caress her breasts; swiftly and determinedly unzipping her yellow dress. She said nothing, but her breaths came quicker and shallower, and she gave one small sigh of pleasure as his lips found her nipple. Then, as though they couldn't stop themselves, her hands came creeping up beneath his shirt; running over his chest; undoing his buttons, one by one. Patrick's incredulity soon turned to exhilaration. Caroline was his again. It was something he'd thought would never happen. And if her price was having to shell out regularly to Annie and Stephen – well, perhaps it was worth it. After all, it was only money.

Charles lay, sated, unwilling to move, ever. His body was exhausted, his sexual urges satisfied; even his mind felt as though it had undergone a rigorous workout. He felt unable to hold a thought in his head or to formulate any kind of purpose; he doubted he could even string a sentence together. Various bits of his body were exposed to the night air, and there was now a faint breeze in the air. But although he could feel himself shivering and goose flesh rising, he lay motionless, unable to summon up the energy to cover himself up.

He had fucked Ella vigorously, brutally almost; pulling up the diaphanous layers of her skirt, pushing her down into the ground, burying his face in her creamy, pillowy, coconut-scented skin. He had roughly pulled off her string of amber beads when they got in his way, and ripped off his own shirt when it began to irritate him; and had swiftly come to an orgasm which tore through his body so intensely that he cried out with a voice he barely recognized.

Even now, little waves and stray sparks of pleasure were still alive in him. His skin was numb to the damp grass, the stones, the bump in the small of his back, in the same way that his mind was numb to the fact that he had just committed adultery. He was almost unaware of anything happening outside his own body; his senses were channelled inwards while his thoughts ran abstractly free.

But gradually, after a while, he became attuned once

more to the outside world. He became aware of Ella, lying peacefully a small distance away and, he suddenly realized, humming gently to herself. He became aware of the sight that the two of them must present. He became aware that he was lying nearly naked in the garden of a friend, with a woman who wasn't his wife. And she was humming. For some reason this last disconcerted him most of all.

With a huge effort, he raised himself on one elbow and looked over at her.

'You're humming,' he said.

'Yes,' agreed Ella, still lying flat on her back, staring up at the sky. She began to hum again. Charles didn't recognize the tune. He flopped back down and wondered what was going through her mind. Did she regret what had happened? Did she appreciate this was the first time he'd been unfaithful to his wife? Did she realize he had family responsibilities? Part of him wanted to stay there for ever in companionable silence; part of him wanted to confront her with the situation as it was.

Eventually he roused himself. He sat up, wincing, removed the small stones that had embedded themselves in his back and pulled on his shirt. He scrabbled around in the grass and found Ella's amber beads.

'Here you are.' He reached over and put them into her hand. Her fingers seemed to caress him as they grasped the necklace and suddenly he felt a renewed rush of arousal. His eyes flickered to her breasts, still partially exposed; to her thighs, still gently parted; to her softly curving mouth.

'Oh God,' he moaned. 'I still want you.'

'Do you?' Ella's voice held amused surprise. 'You've become very demanding. No wonder Cressida looks so pale.' Charles scowled.

'It's not a joke.'

'Isn't it?' Her face turned to his invitingly and he met her lips with fervour; relishing her taste and her smell;

feeling for the curves of her body. Then he pulled away with a groan.

'It's no good.'

'It is a bit soon, perhaps,' said Ella agreeably.

'It's not that!' he said savagely. 'It's the whole situation. Oh God, how can you just lie there humming? Don't you realize we've just committed adultery?'

'In some cultures', said Ella, 'what we've just done would be considered normal.'

'Yes, well, we're not in other cultures now, are we?' said Charles tetchily. 'Oh God!' he groaned again. 'What are we going to do?'

'Go back inside,' suggested Ella. 'Or stay outside for a while.'

Charles sat in silence for a while. A blackness descended on him.

'Perhaps we should go inside,' he said eventually. 'We must have been out here for at least an hour.'

'All right.' Ella got nimbly to her feet; Charles struggled up heavily. They walked through the field wordlessly. Charles' steps got slower as they went; as they came in sight of the house, he suddenly stopped.

'What about the future?' he said desperately. 'What are we going to do?'

'The future?' said Ella. 'Well, I'll be in Italy, of course. I haven't an idea what you'll be doing. I think I might go out there quite soon,' she added. 'I have a feeling I'll get bored with England before too long.'

'But what about me?' As soon as he said it, Charles felt like a spoilt, whiny child.

'What about you?' Her eyes met his with a mixture of amusement and pity. It was clearly a dismissal. But he couldn't bear to give up.

'Couldn't we see each other some time?' He was begging. It was pathetic.

'If you happened to be in Italy,' Ella said thoughtfully, 'I don't see why Maud shouldn't invite you to stay at the villa. I'm sure she'd be glad to.'

As he stared at her, a delightful vision sprang into Charles' mind; a picture of a double life, spent between England and Italy; between Cressida and Ella. He saw Maud Vennings' villa in his mind's eye; a large, elegant house on the hillside, populated with artists and musicians; himself a regular part of the coterie. There would be workshops and discussions; long leisurely meals; nights spent with Ella. Perhaps he would take up painting again. As long as he came back each time with a few prints, Cressida would never suspect anything. He would hire someone to take over the day-to-day running of the shop, releasing him for as many trips a year as he liked. Perhaps profits would suffer a little – but they could afford it.

'I'll come as soon as I can,' he said joyfully.

'As you like,' said Ella. 'There's no rush.'

Before Charles pushed open the door to his bedroom, he looked down at himself and brushed a few blades of grass off his trousers. With any luck, though, Cressida would be in bed already. The thought of joining her there no longer dismayed him. He felt ridiculously good humoured and unreasonably pleased with himself. In his own mind, he was once again someone to be envied, with both a beautiful, rich wife, and an exotic yet undemanding mistress. It would all work out splendidly.

He opened the door cautiously and was surprised to see the light still on. Then he looked over at the bed. Cressida was in bed, asleep, but propped up against the pillows, as though she had been reading and fallen asleep over her book. Except there was no book to be seen. Charles went nearer and saw that a piece of paper had fallen out of her fingers onto the bed cover. Had she been writing letters at that time of night? He wouldn't have been surprised. Cressida corresponded with an incredibly large number of people, from old school friends to distant aunts.

He picked up the sheet of paper and began to skim it casually, kicking off his shoes as he did so. *Dear Mrs Mobyn.* It was from Cressida's portfolio manager, Mr Stanlake. He always refused to call either of them by their first names. Charles grinned to himself. Dry old stick. *You may recall that a while ago I wrote to you, explaining again the meaning of the term 'unlimited liability'.* Charles yawned. Some technical matter. He read the first paragraph without giving it his full attention; his thoughts were still outside, with Ella.

But suddenly, as his eyes moved down the page, he let out a cry.

'What the fuck . . . ?' The noise awoke Cressida, who opened her eyes in a fluttering motion. She focused her gaze on Charles, and then took in the letter with a little cry of alarm.

'Charles,' she said weakly. 'I got that letter today. I've been trying to show it to you . . .'

'Have you read it? Have you seen what it says?'

'Well, yes . . .' said Cressida hesitantly. She gazed at him hopelessly. His eyes met hers for a second, then fell back on the page again. He read the letter urgently from beginning to end, desperate for another meaning, for a conclusion other than the one he'd drawn.

When he'd finished, he looked up, with unseeing eyes. A hot, pounding blackness seemed to be rising up in his head. Stanlake's dry, well-chosen phrases ran relentlessly through his mind. *Next demand . . . one hundred thousand . . . future uncertain . . . particular syndicate . . . one million pounds . . . possibly more . . . staggered payments . . . commitment unlimited . . . will understand . . . thought it fair to warn you . . . unlimited liability . . . unlimited liability . . . unlimited liability . . .*

His hands could barely hold the paper still. He felt sick and shaken. A million pounds. The guy had to be joking. He looked down at the page again. *Your next demand will be, I am told, in the region of one hundred thousand pounds.* Charles' mind distractedly flicked over Cressida's portfolio. They could probably manage that. If that was all it was. But his eyes drew him on. *As I explained at our original meeting regarding this matter, your commitment is unlimited.*

Charles was not usually given to panic. But he could feel his breath coming more quickly; could feel sweat breaking out on his forehead. Cressida was a Lloyd's Name. Christ. Jesus Christ; he'd had no idea. Why the fuck hadn't he known? Why the fuck hadn't she told him? *Unlimited liability.* Unlimited. What, until they didn't have anything left? Until they'd sold the house? Got rid of the car? His eyes fell again on the sentence in the middle of the page. *I am informed that the sum total could be as much as one million pounds, possibly more.* But they weren't millionaires. OK, maybe on paper – but it was the house and the Print Centre that accounted for most of that. *One million pounds, possibly more.* More than that? More? The phrase *bottomless pit* sprang into his mind; he had a sudden vision of a fiery hell; of suitcases, full of money, being thrown down to burn in the flames.

He couldn't think where to place his thoughts; how to anchor his panic. For a moment he just stood, swaying slightly in the silent night, feeling almost heady with terror. Then gradually he became aware that there was something ominously niggling at his thoughts. His eyes focused again on the letter. *At our original meeting regarding this matter.* What meeting? What fucking meeting?

Suddenly he felt Cressida's eyes on him. Her pale face looked tired and anxious. Had she known about this for a long time? Had she known but not told him?

'How long have you known about this?' he snapped.

'Only today,' stammered Cressida. She felt cold inside the bed. Charles had read the letter but he hadn't laughed at it; he hadn't shaken his head and pointed out the foolish mistake made by some clerical member of staff; he hadn't tossed it aside carelessly to deal with tomorrow.

'Well, what meeting is he talking about?'

'I don't know.' Cressida felt a sudden wave of panic, as though she'd forgotten to do a vital piece of home-work. Was this something she was supposed to know about? Had she had a meeting with Mr Stanlake? She screwed up her pale face and desperately tried to re-member. But all her encounters with Mr Stanlake seemed to have merged into one hazy picture in her brain.

Charles sat down heavily on an armchair and began to read the letter through again from beginning to end. Cressida gazed at him silently, not daring to rub her sleepy eyes or push her fingers through her rumpled hair. Her gaze wandered uncertainly through the room, landing indiscriminately on corners of wall-paper, pieces of furniture, on the top of Charles' head and away again. She wondered what time it was. Far away was the sound of a clock ticking; otherwise there were no sounds in the house. Everyone must have gone to bed.

'Unlimited liability,' Charles suddenly said, in a voice which trembled with suppressed emotion. 'Do you know what that means?' Mutely, Cressida shook her head. She thought she did, but she wouldn't risk saying anything. 'It means they can keep asking you for money for ever. For ever!' Charles' voice rose. 'Do you appreciate what that means? For us? For the twins?' Shakily, Cressida got out of bed, went over to the chair and knelt at his feet. She was shivering, and would have liked a dressing-gown. But if she went to put one on, Charles might react badly.

'Perhaps they've made a mistake,' she said, in a wobbly voice. 'They've never done anything like this before.'

'I don't know.' Charles threw the paper onto the

ground exasperatedly. 'Fuck knows. Jesus Christ, Cressida, why didn't you tell me you were a Lloyd's Name?'

'I don't know,' said Cressida confusedly. 'I didn't think it was important. And anyway . . .'

She pulled up short and gasped. A sudden recollection suffused her cheeks with pink.

'What? What?'

'I don't know,' she said, flinching from his gaze. 'But I did have a meeting with Mr Stanlake a few years ago. I've just remembered.'

'And?'

'And I think it might have been about being a Lloyd's Name.'

'What? When? Why didn't you tell me?'

'It was just after we got engaged. It was only a very quick meeting.' Cressida paused, and tried desperately to remember. 'I was up in town to look at wedding dresses.'

'Get to the point.' Charles' voice was hard.

'Well,' Cressida swallowed, 'Mr Stanlake said something about paying some extra bills or something out of a separate bit of my money. Another special bank account or something. I can't remember exactly.'

'Extra bills? What extra bills?'

'I don't know.'

'You never fucking know anything. Christ almighty. Was he talking about Lloyd's losses?' Cressida's cheeks turned pinker.

'I'm not sure. I think so,' she said hurriedly. 'Something like that.'

'What? Why are you looking like that?' Charles stared at Cressida's blushing face and blinked as it loomed in and out of his weary vision. 'What aren't you telling me? Why do you think it was Lloyd's?'

Cressida stared back at him miserably. She could hardly bear to tell him what she had just remembered. But the idea of lying to him didn't even enter her thoughts. 'Well,' she began hesitantly, 'I've remembered something else Mr Stanlake said.'

'What? For Christ's sake, what?'

'I'd just told him I was engaged, and shown him the ring.' Automatically, she looked down at her engagement ring. 'And he was saying how nice it was,' she continued. Charles stared at her with incredulity.

'What the fuck's that got to do with anything?'

'Well, it was the thing he said next,' stammered Cressida. 'He asked about you, and about the wedding and everything, and then he said, "You know, I wouldn't advertise the fact that you're a Lloyd's Name if I were you."'

There was a short silence. Charles felt a very slow, frighteningly powerful surge of fury rise through him. For a few moments he couldn't quite think what to do with himself.

'You mean,' he said eventually, in an over-controlled voice that was barely above a whisper, 'you mean that you deliberately kept the fact of your being a Name secret from me?'

'No!' Cressida's face was aghast. 'I mean, I didn't know it meant anything then. I went off to have lunch with Sukey and go to Liberty's . . .' Her voice tailed away.

'And then?' prompted Charles, his face menacingly polite. Cressida swallowed.

'And then I forgot all about it.'

'You forgot all about it? You *forgot* you were a Lloyd's Name?'

'Yes. No. I mean, I sort of knew, but I didn't think it was important . . .' Her voice tailed away again.

For a moment, Charles' astonishment almost abated his anger.

'How could you not think it was important? Haven't you heard about Lloyd's?'

Cressida hung her head and his impatience with her increased. 'Haven't you heard what's happened to people?' he shouted. 'Didn't you realize what it meant for us? Haven't you got a brain?'

'I know, I know,' exclaimed Cressida, giving a sudden sob. 'I sort of knew, but I just didn't think any of that would happen to us. Mr Stanlake said he thought everything would be all right.'

'Well, fuck Mr Stanlake!' shouted Charles. 'And fuck you! You never bothered to listen to anything, or ask, or find out what was going on, did you?' He suddenly brought his face close to hers. 'You never bothered to understand your finances, you always left it up to your fucking father, or me. Well, you can sort this fucking mess out yourself. I've had enough of it.'

'Charles . . .' She gazed up at him with huge, frightened eyes.

Charles felt as though he'd stumbled into some horrible nightmare; some grotesque fantasy with no way out. Only five minutes ago he'd been so arrogantly pleased with himself; it had all seemed as though it was falling into place. He'd constructed for himself a large-scale plan of life for the future – taking for granted his wife, his income, his life as it was now – and embellishing it with even more delights; adding the little extras which would bring it to perfection. A continued affair with Ella; an acquaintance with the great Maud Vennings; a familiarity with Italy: he had imagined all these – even in the few minutes he'd had since parting from Ella – with an intense, desperate vividness. But suddenly all that seemed laughable; the stuff of schoolboy dreams. He could take nothing for granted. What was life without money? Come to that, what was his wife without her money? Could he still love her if she were not a source of riches, but a drain; a burden? Charles eyed Cressida afresh. Her limbs were lanky under her nightdress; her voice high and irritating. Her face was pale and tired. As he looked at her, a sudden vivid vision of warm, brown, coconut-scented skin appeared in his mind and he experienced a shocking, almost painful desire for Ella.

'I'm sure it'll all get sorted out,' said Cressida uncertainly.

'Are you?' said Charles sarcastically, hating her for not being Ella. 'Good. Well then, perhaps I'll leave you to it.' She gazed at him speechlessly for a moment, then burst into tears. Charles' stomach turned. The sound of Ella's bubbling laugh flickered through his head; her gently mocking eyes sprang up in his mind's eye.

'Shut the fuck up,' he shouted. 'Shut up. I can't bear that noise.' Her sobs increased. 'Shut *up*, I said. *Shut the fuck up!*' He raised his hand and brought it slamming down on the side of her face.

Cressida gasped, and put her hand up to her cheek. The side which Charles had hit was already bright blotchy red, but the rest was drained of colour. Charles didn't change his expression. Then Cressida rose unsteadily to her feet and backed away into the bathroom. The door closed and Charles heard the sound of Cressida vomiting. Then the taps were turned on. She had not locked the bathroom door; perhaps she was hoping he would come in after her. The thought made Charles scowl. He slid to the floor, picked up the letter and crumpled it.

'Fuck you,' he said. 'Fuck the lot of you.'

Chapter Ten

Annie was woken at seven-thirty by her electronic alarm clock. Its merry bleeping penetrated her dreams gradually; when she realized what it was, she reached out automatically to the left and was thrown into confusion when she hit Stephen's face. Eventually she found it, sitting on an unfamiliar table to her right. She turned it off, flopped back into bed and stared puzzledly for a while at a strange lampshade hanging from a white, well-painted, uncracked ceiling before it came to her suddenly that they were staying at Caroline's house.

And she had a peculiar feeling inside her, she realized. A bit like the ominous dread that one had on the morning of an appointment with the dentist – but this was positive rather than negative. She felt warm, cosy and encouraged. It wasn't just the bright sunlight visible through the chink between the curtains, and it wasn't just the knowledge that she didn't have to cook breakfast. She searched idly around in the recesses of her mind but whatever it was kept evading her. She looked around the room for clues, squinted at the clock and wondered why she'd set it so early.

Then suddenly it all came back to her in a rush. She'd set the clock early so she could take the children to church. The children. Nicola. School fees. Of course, Caroline and Patrick had offered to pay Nicola's school fees. And they'd accepted. Nicola would be going to St Catherine's. Annie sank back into her pillows pleasurably. Now that she was fully awake, she realized that she also had rather a piercing headache. But nothing could mar her happiness on Nicola's behalf.

169

She nudged Stephen with her foot. Sleepily, he rolled over until he was facing her.

'Wake up,' she said. 'Time for church.' Stephen screwed up his face in displeasure, opened his eyes a crack and groaned.

'I feel awful,' he croaked. 'Why do we have to go to church? We're on holiday.'

'We talked about it last night, remember?' Annie's spirits were irrepressible. 'It's good for the children. And I like going to country churches.' And I want to say thank you for Nicola's school fees, she added to herself. She heaved herself out of bed, ignoring the coloured spots that immediately appeared before her eyes, and added, 'I'll go and wake them up.'

Stephen groaned again, but it only made his head feel worse. He rolled onto his back and closed his eyes. Memories of the previous day began to filter slowly into his mind. They were here to play tennis, of course, and that had been fairly pleasant. They had also drunk a lot. Stephen didn't want to think about how much. And then there had been that deal with Patrick. Or was that a dream?

He opened his eyes and looked around. He could vividly remember sitting in Patrick's study, agreeing to take out a mortgage of eighty thousand pounds on his house. It wasn't a dream. It had been a real, big-time deal. He tried to recall the feeling of exhilaration he had experienced; the buzz of confidence which it had given him. But what began to go through his mind instead was suspiciously like alarm.

As Annie came back into the room, Stephen started guiltily, as though she could read his mind.

'How did the children sleep?' he asked hurriedly.

'Not very much,' she said, grimacing. 'I think it's been one long midnight feast. Nicola wasn't at all impressed when I told her to get up.'

'Perhaps we should let her sleep in,' said Stephen weakly.

'Rubbish,' retorted Annie. 'I told her we were going to church. And the walk will wake her up.'

'You seem in a very good mood today,' said Stephen curiously.

'Do I?' said Annie, smiling. 'I suppose I'm still reeling over the school fees.'

Stephen gazed at her blankly for a second – and then remembered. Of course. Caroline's announcement last night.

'Yes, that's wonderful news,' he said, trying to work up some enthusiasm. But he couldn't get out of his mind the deal he'd done with Patrick. He felt he was in out of his depth. This was really business more for high flyers like Charles than people like him. He preferred things simple. And he had a growing sense of unease about taking out a mortgage when he didn't really – despite what Patrick said – have the means to pay it.

He looked at Annie's glowing face and decided not to say anything about it yet. Perhaps he would have a quiet word with Patrick later on and see whether he could reduce the loan, or maybe go into it more gradually. Patrick would be understanding. They were friends, after all.

The church at Bindon was fourteenth century and tiny. As Stephen, Annie, Nicola, Toby and Georgina hurried through the churchyard – with only a minute to go – Stephen said, 'Bets on the congregation in there already. I say six.'

'I say ten,' said Annie, giving him a reproving look.

'I say fifty,' said Nicola, who was used to a full, thriving family service at St Mary Magdalene in Silchester.

'It's not the same here,' said Georgina kindly. 'I say four.'

'Oh dear,' said Stephen.

171

'I say forty-four,' put in Toby, enunciating carefully. 'I say forty-four.'

'Do you, Tobes? And do you know why you say it?' said Stephen, grinning at him.

'Forty-four,' said Toby obstinately.

Georgina was closest. There were, in fact, three members of the congregation already present at the service as they all trooped in. Two of these were Don and Valerie, who waved excitedly and gestured at the pew behind. Thankfully Stephen had already led the children into a pew on the other side, so Annie was able to smile and gesture apologetically back.

'Dear God,' said Georgina, sinking to her knees beside Annie, 'please help me do well at the East Silchester gymkhana. Help me learn how to do a French plait. And help Nicola not be too scared to jump Arabia.'

'Dear God,' said Annie clearly, 'please help some of Nicola's friends realize she isn't as old or as experienced at riding as them, and that jumping without a riding teacher there isn't a very good idea.'

'Oh, OK,' said Georgina equably, without moving.

Afterwards, they waited politely in the churchyard until Don and Valerie appeared.

'Smashing to see you,' said Don. 'It's a sweet little place, isn't it?'

'Lovely,' said Annie enthusiastically.

'Yes, it's a pretty village altogether,' said Don. 'Isn't it, Val?'

'Ooh! It's lovely!'

'The spot where we live has very good views,' added Don. 'Why not come back and see for yourself? We could have a bit of coffee and I could show you round the hotel.'

'Well,' said Annie doubtfully. She glanced at Stephen.

'Ooh, do come!' exclaimed Valerie.

'Do we have to get back?' Annie said to Stephen, raising her eyebrows.

'Can't think what for,' said Don jovially. 'Only thing

you've got to do today is play Caroline and Patrick. And I doubt they'll start without you!'

There didn't seem any answer to that.

'If you don't mind,' said Georgina suddenly, 'I'll go back. I want to look for costumes for our play.' Stephen looked at her in unwilling admiration. She was smiling politely, yet implacably, at Don.

'Could you take Nicola and Toby back too?' said Annie.

'Of course,' said Georgina. 'I was going to anyway. I need Nicola to help me.'

Nicola flushed with pleasure, and Annie smiled at her. 'Be careful!' she shouted after them, as they ran off through the churchyard.

'They'll be all right,' said Don comfortably. 'Cars hardly ever pass through here. It's a lovely spot. You wait till you see the view from the hotel.'

At first, Annie was too busy wondering how on earth Don was going to turn this wreck of a house into a hotel to notice the view. They had toiled for ten minutes up a steep, private track, which Don assured them at intervals of thirty seconds he was intending to modernize.

'It stands to reason,' he said, each time. 'You've got to have good access to a place like this.'

Finally they reached the house. Don swung open the door, then told them to stand in the porch and look out over the hills.

'Whenever I have my doubts,' he told them, 'I just stand here and look at that view. This is what it's all about.' The others dutifully turned and followed his gaze. But Annie was staring, aghast, at the dark, dank corridor that gave off the front door.

'Lovely, isn't it?' said Don, smiling down at her.

'Oh, yes,' she said, faintly.

'Over there', he said, pointing, 'is where the new generator's going to go.'

'You aren't wired up to the mains?' said Stephen in surprise.

'Well, no,' said Don, his face dropping slightly. 'Actually, it's been a bit more of a problem than I thought it would.' They all gazed silently at the patch of land for a few seconds. Then Valerie clapped her hand to her mouth.

'Ooh I know!' she said brightly. 'What about that coffee?'

Annie followed Valerie into the kitchen.

'It's quite a big project, this hotel,' she said conversationally. 'But I expect it's quite fun, getting it all going.'

'I expect so,' said Valerie, putting on the kettle. 'I don't really see much of it, being in London all the time.'

'Don't you come down here at weekends?'

'Sometimes. But it's a long way away. And I often have to work at weekends.'

'What do you do?' asked Annie.

'I'm personal assistant to an advertising account executive,' said Valerie.

'Ah yes,' said Annie, none the wiser. 'And is that a very demanding job?'

'It is if you want to get on, like me,' said Valerie. 'A lot of girls treat it like, you know, a normal job. But if you want to get promotion quickly, you have to put in the extra hours. It pays off in the end.' She uttered the words glibly, as though this was a message she had memorized.

'Gosh,' said Annie. 'I suppose you're right. And what are you aiming for?' Valerie looked at her blankly, as she spooned instant coffee into mugs.

'Well, you know,' she said. 'To get on. While I'm still young. Before I'm too far into my thirties. Before I settle down and have children.' She giggled, rather embarrassedly. 'You have to plan your career break in advance, you know. If you want to keep a toe on the career ladder. You can't take time off just like that.'

'Wow,' said Annie. 'I am impressed. I never thought ahead like that. I just went ahead and had children when I felt like it.' She stared at Valerie, intrigued, as she poured hot water on the coffee. 'I was never very good at planning ahead. When I married Stephen, that was it, I wanted a baby straight away.' She laughed. 'I expect you're made of sterner stuff.'

'Ooh,' giggled Valerie. 'Well, actually, I haven't ever thought about it.'

'But you obviously do want children? And your . . .' she glanced at Valerie's left hand, 'your boyfriend?'

'Ooh,' exclaimed Valerie again. 'I haven't really had many boyfriends. I had one at university, but he went to live in the States. And what with my job, I don't really have time to meet new people.'

'That's a shame,' said Annie.

'Not really,' fluted Valerie. 'The modern girl doesn't need a man. Men hold you back and let you down. A job doesn't. I don't need a man; I'm independent. If men ask me out,' she giggled, 'I usually say I'm too busy. That puts them in their place.' Annie stared at her in slight puzzlement.

'But you want children one day,' she said.

'Ooh, yes,' said Valerie. 'Just not quite yet. I want to wait till my career's more firmly established.'

'And before you have children, you'll want to find a man?'

'Ooh, yes,' said Valerie, and giggled excitedly.

'And are you so sure', said Annie bluntly, 'that you'll find one?'

Stephen and Don were standing in the room that would become the hotel lounge. It was a long, low room, with bare boards and recently plastered walls.

'Well, this is a good-sized room,' said Stephen cheerfully. 'You should fit a lot of guests in here.'

'Yes, I suppose so,' said Don. 'It's funny, sometimes I

175

forget that it'll be full of guests. I've got used to it being empty.'

'I suppose it's quite a good investment just as a house,' said Stephen.

'That's right,' said Don. 'It wouldn't really matter if it never opened as a hotel. Apart from the fact I wouldn't have any income!' He gave a chortle. 'But then, who needs money when you've got views like this?'

'I suppose so,' said Stephen, following Don's gaze out of the window.

'Thankfully I haven't got a mortgage to worry about,' said Don. 'Not yet, anyway. I may need one later.'

Stephen's insides contracted at the word mortgage. He was dreading having to ask Patrick to rethink the deal they'd made; reduce the loan he was taking out; basically chicken out of the world of high finance. It looked so feeble. And he was sure Patrick would shake his head at the opportunity Stephen was missing. But he couldn't help his nature, Stephen thought to himself. He was just more cautious than Patrick. And he was naturally nervous of debt. Which was all a mortgage was, really. Debt. It was a word that conjured up for him pictures of poorhouses, disgrace, wrecked lives. Ridiculous these days, when *everybody* seemed to have a mortgage. But that was just the way he was.

'Of course, that rascal Patrick tried to convince me to take out all kinds of fancy loans,' said Don amusedly. 'You know what he's like when he's got you cornered.' Stephen gave him a look of astonishment.

'Not that I'm knocking him,' said Don quickly. 'I know he's a friend of yours. No offence.'

'Oh, no, no,' said Stephen. Suddenly he wanted to hear more. 'What sort of deal did he try to do with you?' he said casually. 'Just out of interest.'

'Oh, he had some idea I should take out a mortgage on this place and let him make some money with it. I told him plain. I said that if he was about to start up a

176

business like me, he'd be looking to decrease his debt, not increase it.'

Stephen felt a sudden wave of reassurance. So there was someone else in the world who didn't see a mortgage as a desirable accessory to life.

'He nearly got me,' said Don, grinning. Stephen's heart started pounding.

'What did you do?' he said, trying to sound unconcerned. Don looked surprised.

'Well, I told him I'd take it away and think about it. Then, of course, I called him up the next day and told him no thanks.' He gave Stephen a beady look. 'I never sign anything on the spot.'

Stephen felt a wave of mortification rush over him. That's what he should have done. He should have told Patrick he'd go and talk it over with Annie. If he'd done that, if he'd left it a day, he would have quickly come to his senses; and now he wouldn't be in this mess. He looked at Don's amiable, sunburnt face. Don would never have allowed Patrick to talk him into signing. Don would have been cautious and prudent.

'Is anything wrong?' said Don. Stephen felt a stab of panic. He couldn't let Don – or any of them – find out what a fool he'd been.

'No, no,' he said quickly. He smiled – unconvincingly he felt – and searched desperately in his mind for a way to change the subject. Don eyed him warily.

'I wouldn't like any of this to go back to Patrick,' he said. 'I have actually done some business with him since then – and I do think of him as a friend.' There was a pause, and Stephen realized that Don was looking at him expectantly.

'Oh, of course,' he said hastily. 'I won't say anything to him.'

'That's all right then.' Don grinned toothily. 'Aha. I think I hear our coffee coming.'

The beaming smile with which Stephen greeted Annie as she came into the room bearing two mugs of coffee hid a thumping heart and a sensation of sickness. He felt despair at himself. How could he have been so stupid? How could he have been so thoughtless? How could he have done something as momentous as that without even consulting her?

'Have some coffee,' said Annie. 'Careful, the mug's hot.' He smiled shakily at her, taking in her wispy brown hair, her cheerful, blue T-shirt, tucked into a floral, cotton skirt, her simple plimsolls. He looked down at himself, his old tweed jacket, unfashionable trousers, battered Oxford shoes.

What had he been thinking of? It was laughable to think he could ever be like the rest of them: rich, worldly, fashionable. He should have known he was on dangerous territory as soon as he entered Patrick's sumptuous study. He saw it clearly now. Patrick was the sort of person who would do something like take out a huge mortgage and invest it – and would probably make his money twice over. He would pick the right investments, time his manoeuvres well, use his hunches to good advantage. But Stephen was the type for whom such an enterprise was bound to go disastrously wrong, no matter who was advising him, who was carrying out his investments. He saw, with fatalistic clarity, scenes of stockmarket crashes, company failures, panicked decisions. It was no good. If he had been the sort of person who was going to make a lot of money in life, he suspected he would have made it before now. And if he wasn't, then it was probably better not to try. Better just to carry on as they were.

'You're looking very serious,' said Annie, smiling at him. 'Is everything all right?'

'Oh yes,' he said, effecting a cheery voice. *Please God, don't let her find out what I've done; how stupid I've been. Please let me somehow sort it out on my own.* He took a sip of heartening coffee and looked up, smiling gaily, distractingly at her. 'Yes, everything's fine,' he said. 'We were just admiring the view from here.' She turned her head to look, as he had intended, out of the window, and exclaimed with pleasure. It was so easy to deflect her, Stephen thought, watching the back of her head. She was utterly unsuspicious; she would be the easiest person in the world to deceive. But far from reassuring him, this realization suddenly made him feel like weeping.

Charles woke to blinding pain and a weight of misery around his chest. A pulse in his temple throbbed; with each throb the brightness from outside seemed to pierce his eyelids more strongly. He didn't dare open his eyes, but lay motionless, gradually locating other areas of pain in his body and wishing he could fall back asleep.

He remembered everything. It was almost as though he had never fallen asleep; as though he and Cressida were, in his mind, still in the middle of their conversation. Or rather, their fight. Now, he realized – from the weight on the mattress; the taut line of the duvet; the light sound of her breathing – she was in bed beside him. She must have stayed closeted in the bathroom for a good hour. He had sat up for a while, waiting for her to reappear, then unwillingly crawled into bed.

He didn't open his eyes. He didn't want to see her. An unbearable combination of guilt and anger was creeping through his body. He had screwed Ella. Oh God. He had wanted to screw her again. He still did. Cressida had a right to hate him for that. But then – she didn't know about it. And it was *her* financial arrangements that were going to ruin them. Ruin them completely.

A vision of the future stretched ahead in Charles' mind; a dark, black road of debts and demands; of uncertainty. Unlimited liability; unlimited uncertainty. If Mr Stanlake's letter had stated the worst, if it had mentioned a definite total sum to be paid, then they would have had something to latch onto. They would have despaired for a while – and then set about tackling the situation. But the letter had mentioned only possible figures. Probable figures. Estimated figures. For how long would they wonder? How long before the next demand? The next set of estimated figures? The next smoothly ambiguous sentence, assuring them that the final demands might not be as large as expected – although, of course, they might be larger . . .

It was the uncertainty that would be the debilitating, wearing, endlessly nagging factor in all of this. It was the not knowing; the continual threat; the knowledge that the sword was hanging over them – but might never fall. It was the hope. Perhaps worst of all was the hope. The tiny, insidious flicker of hope that it would all turn out much better than they had expected; that this time next year they would be laughing about it all. He could feel it now, unwanted, unlooked for: a flame of hope that he couldn't get rid of; that would stay alive inside him, no matter how hard he tried to suppress it.

Cressida gave a little sigh in her sleep, and Charles' thoughts immediately changed track. A painful wave of resentment ran through him. This was his wife's problem, he thought, as though realizing it for the first time. Hers. Not his. It was she who had received the letter. Dear Mrs Mobyn, it had begun. His own fucking name. His own fucking stupid wife.

He lay perfectly still, trying to think rationally about it all. But nothing could stop the increasing surges of anger which filled his body with silent, furious, pumping adrenalin, driving reasonable thought from his mind. She was a Lloyd's Name and she hadn't told him. She'd allowed him to marry her, buy a house, behave as if nothing was wrong – while all the time, this disaster had been just waiting to happen. Everything they'd done in the last three years; all the money they'd spent; that holiday to Antigua . . . Charles could hardly bear to think about it. He'd been so confident, so sure of the future. If he'd only known. If he'd only fucking known. The stupid bitch.

He was fairly sure – no, completely sure – she wasn't lying when she said she hadn't realized what being a Lloyd's Name meant. Jesus, he should know she was thick. He was continually re-amazed at how completely – unbearably it seemed now – stupid she was. Even now, he was pretty sure she didn't realize the full enormity of the situation. But that bastard Stanlake had obviously kept things deliberately quiet. Some bloody misguided loyalty to Cressida, no doubt. Thought Charles wouldn't marry her if he knew she was a Lloyd's Name. That must have been it.

Charles stared straight up at the ceiling. The quiet room was driving him mad; he felt constricted and trapped inside the bed. So Stanlake had thought he wouldn't marry Cressida if he knew she was a Lloyd's Name. Well, perhaps he was right. Perhaps he would have taken another look at her insipid pale looks; listened one more time to her imbecile, brainless conversation – and got out as quickly as he could. To think he'd actually found her stupidity attractive. Jesus, if he'd known all this was going to happen . . .

He felt suddenly wary, as though Cressida, slumbering next to him, could read his thoughts. He opened his eyes and swivelled them quickly towards her. But she was motionless, buried under a rounded duvet. Dust motes were dancing in the sun above her. Once upon a time he would have burrowed down underneath the duvet with her, gently waking her with little kisses and whispers, until she gave that sudden, delighted half-asleep giggle. Today he wanted her to stay asleep, away from his thoughts.

He eyed her blond hair against the pillow, immaculate even in sleep. He should have guessed she was a Lloyd's Name. Of course she was. She was exactly the sort of person who would be. If he'd only once thought to ask her, to check, to bring the subject up. But he'd taken to filtering out difficult subjects of conversation when he spoke to Cressida, just to avoid seeing that stupid frown of utter incomprehension.

Oh God. He should have guessed; he should have known. And if he'd known, could he have done anything? Could he have prevented this thing from happening? Could he have stopped it all in time? Charles gazed at the ceiling. He didn't, wouldn't dare find out the answer. The discovery that, by acting then, he could have avoided this black pit of despair would be too much to bear. A million pounds. A million pounds. Charles whispered it quietly to himself. It didn't really mean anything to him.

The duvet rustled and Charles felt Cressida turning over. She opened her eyes and looked at him, at first with her normal sleepy early-morning expression – then, as she recollected her thoughts, with sudden dismay. Her hand came up to her cheek and touched it lightly. She didn't wince as her fingers met the skin, but her touch was tender. Of course, thought Charles suddenly. That's where I hit her. He stared at Cressida, appalled. It was all so sordid. Her eyes scanned his face uncertainly, then she pulled back the bed-clothes and slowly got out of bed. She tottered to the bathroom, a tall, willowy figure in her long, white nightdress. Charles watched her numbly. He couldn't bring himself to say anything, call out to her or go after her. She was part of the nightmare. Until she spoke, none of it seemed real; if he ignored her, perhaps it would all go away. He turned over, buried his aching head beneath his pillow, and stared blankly into the mattress, wishing himself into oblivion.

Caroline and Ella were having breakfast on the terrace. Caroline had made what she considered to be the supreme effort of getting up, making some coffee, heating up some croissants, and taking it all outside, only to discover that Patrick wasn't hungry, Charles and Cressida were still in bed, Martina had fed the twins, and all the others had breakfasted early before going to church.

'For Christ's sake,' she said to Ella, gesturing to the breakfast table, 'you must tell them I did all this. I can't believe no-one's here to appreciate it.' She bit crossly into a croissant. 'These are good, aren't they?' she added. 'They're from the new pâtisserie in Silchester. You must try it out before you go.' Ella took a thoughtful sip of coffee.

'I probably won't be around long enough,' she said. 'I've decided to go to Italy sooner rather than later.'

'But you've only just come back to England,' objected Caroline.

'I know,' agreed Ella. 'But I think I've seen enough of it.'

'Seen enough of Charles, more like,' said Caroline bluntly. 'He had a bit of a nerve, didn't he? Dragging you off for moonlit walks in the middle of the night? I would have told him where to go.' Ella shrugged.

'It was nice to see him. No really,' she added, at Caroline's incredulous look. 'I needed to get him out of my system.'

'And have you?'

'Well,' said Ella, 'I'm not sure he was still in it. But if he was, he isn't any more.'

'Well, that's a relief,' said Caroline. 'As long as he didn't sweet-talk you back into liking him.' Ella's mouth curved in amusement.

'Perhaps he thought he did. He was very ardent.'

'Ardent?' Caroline stared at Ella for a few seconds. 'Ardent as in . . . ardent?'

'It was the middle of the night,' pointed out Ella. With a deft movement she brought her legs up beneath her cross-legged on her chair, and shook back her hair. Caroline clapped her hand over her mouth and gazed at Ella with sparkling eyes.

'I'm not even going to *ask* you my next question,' she said in an excited voice, 'because I don't want to know the answer.' She paused. 'Except I do,' she added hopefully.

'It's not important,' said Ella.

'How can you say that?' demanded Caroline. 'He's married now.'

'That's not my fault.'

'It's not his wife's fault, either,' pointed out Caroline. She took a gulp of coffee and lit a cigarette. 'Christ, I'd go barmy if Patrick did that to me.'

'You don't know what Charles did,' said Ella.

'No, but I can guess.' She gave a wicked cackle.

'It's nothing,' said Ella, spreading her hands deprecatingly. 'Over.' She poured herself a glass of orange juice. 'Poor Charles,' she added.

'Over?' said Caroline suspiciously.

'Maybe over,' conceded Ella. 'Maybe not. It's funny, I'd half-forgotten what he was like. I had a different image of him in my mind. Perhaps I'd created it on purpose. But now I feel I don't know him as well as I thought I did. And I would quite like to know him again. Know him as a person, rather than as a lover.' She gave a little smile.

'But what about his wife?' insisted Caroline.

'What about me? Where's the symmetry in all this? I might have a husband, or a partner that no-one knows about. Charles might be the other man as much as I am the other woman.'

'Have you got a husband?' asked Caroline curiously. 'You can't have. You don't look married.'

'No, not a husband,' said Ella, smiling down into her orange juice.

'But someone. There is someone.'

'There is someone,' agreed Ella.

'And don't you feel bad, betraying them like that?'

'Betraying? I'm not betraying anyone. A quick fuck isn't the same as betrayal.'

'Ah!' said Caroline triumphantly. 'So you did sleep with him.'

'I didn't sleep with him,' said Ella. 'I fucked him. Something else altogether. His wife slept with him. Or so I imagine.' Caroline looked at her slightly puzzledly for a moment, then leant forward.

'And what's going to happen now?' she said, lowering her voice unnecessarily to a confiding, gossipy tone.

'Now?' Ella's voice rang like a bell through the garden. 'I'm going to have some more coffee.' She smiled at Caroline and reached for the *cafetière*. Caroline took a deep drag of her cigarette and looked around the garden. Ella obviously wasn't going to settle down to a good girly chat. She frowned in slight annoyance, and stretched out a tanned leg from under her dressing-gown, admiring the smooth, brown skin against the white satin.

'Oh I don't know,' she said suddenly, heaving a great sigh. 'What's it all about, anyway?'

'It?' Ella looked at her quizzically.

'Life. You know.' Caroline waved her cigarette vaguely in the air. 'Where are we all aiming?'

'Well, that really depends on your point of view,' began Ella.

'I mean, take Patrick,' interrupted Caroline. 'All he wants to do is earn money.'

'And all you want to do is spend it,' suggested Ella.

'Well, yes,' said Caroline, in slight surprise. She caught Ella's eye and gave a sudden cackle. 'But what do I want to spend it on?' she added. 'That's the difference.'

'You're not having a mid-life crisis, are you?' said Ella, her eyes twinkling.

'Christ, no,' said Caroline. She took a deep drag. 'The thing is, Patrick and I had a bit of a scene last night. About us paying Nicola's school fees. It just made me think.'

'What sort of scene?'

'He was furious with me for landing him in it. Which I suppose is fair enough.'

'Hadn't you talked about it already?' said Ella in surprise.

'Oh no. It was completely spur of the moment. Anyway, if I'd asked him beforehand, he would never have agreed. Patrick's basically a stingy bastard.'

'Well, I think it's a wonderful idea,' said Ella firmly. 'Not that I approve of private education in principle. But Nicola's a little bit different. And surely you can afford it?'

'I would have thought so,' said Caroline. 'I mean, what if we'd had two children? We would have been able to afford it then, wouldn't we?'

'Or three children,' said Ella.

'Or five,' said Caroline. 'Some fucking chance.' Her face suddenly clouded over and she stubbed out her cigarette in silence.

Chapter Eleven

By one o'clock, Patrick was presiding over a barbecue.

'I can't bear barbecues,' said Caroline at intervals. She was reclining on a white lounger, eating a plate of chocolate-fudge cake and smoking a cigarette. 'Bloody awful things.' She glanced provocatively at Patrick every time she spoke, but his face remained calm.

'Barbecues are lovely!' protested Annie in amazement. She was handing out hot dogs in buns to the children and had a smear of tomato ketchup on her cheek. 'They're such fun. Those spare ribs smell delicious,' she added encouragingly to Patrick.

'They're just about ready,' he said. 'Who's for a rib?'

'Who's for a rib?' echoed Caroline disparagingly. 'Who's for a burnt bone with a shrivelled-up bit of meat attached?'

'Come on, Stephen,' said Annie. 'Have a spare rib. You've hardly eaten anything. And you need something after all that tennis.' She giggled. The match between her, Stephen, Patrick and Caroline had been a desultory affair, undertaken only because of Patrick's insistence. It had lasted a mere forty minutes, during which time Stephen and Annie had managed to win only two games, despite rallying cries from Don.

'In a moment,' said Stephen, taking a swig of beer. 'You go ahead.'

Stephen wasn't feeling hungry. Now that he had decided to talk to Patrick about backing out of the deal, he wanted to get it over and done with. He was sure Patrick would make him feel stupid for pulling out of such an opportunity; perhaps it would be easier to leave it till later or even phone him once they were at home. But the thought of prolonging his mortgage commitment – by even a few hours – made Stephen nervous. He had stood for a while by the barbecue, trying to seize his moment to talk to Patrick. But the barbecue was soon surrounded by children, prodding the sausages and asking for ketchup and no mustard and no onion and no lettuce.

He watched Nicola grasp her hot dog awkwardly and take a huge, unguarded bite, and he winced even before she did at the burning-hot sausage inside. She gasped, instinctively opened her mouth to breathe in cool air, and turned pink – not with pain, he knew, but with embarrassment at having been caught out. Stephen felt a chord of recognition within him. She was like him in so many ways. He would spill scalding tea over his hand at a tea party and smile as though it were nothing; he would turn down the wrong street and carry on rather than turn round. Of course, children always take after their parents, he thought, watching her as she quickly breathed in and out, trying to relieve the burning sensation in her mouth, then, adopting a casual air, took a great gulp of cold water. But what no-one ever tells you is that your children inherit just as many of your deficiencies and foibles as they do your better characteristics. He smiled at Nicola.

'Is that good?' he said.

'Delicious,' she said stoutly. 'Really yummy.'

'Not too hot?' he said, in spite of himself.

'Oh no,' she said, as he knew she would. 'Just right.'

Charles and Cressida were sitting near each other on the grass. They had somehow staggered through the morning, communicating in short, polite phrases; avoiding each other's gaze. When their eyes did meet, it was with disbelief. This couldn't be happening to them.

They had arrived downstairs for lunch with an assumed unity; had mustered up smiles and excuses for their lateness with enough good cheer to stave off curious looks. But the others seemed intuitively to know that something was wrong. No-one had come to sit near them; no-one had attempted to bring them into the general barbecue banter. A tacit, perhaps unconscious, avoidance area surrounded them; even Martina and the twins were sitting away from them, with the other children.

Cressida picked abstractly at blades of grass and took tiny bites of the chicken drumstick which Patrick had pressed on her. The food was tasteless in her mouth; her mind was black with misery. She wanted to sit calmly somewhere and think it all out; but her thoughts were too confused; everything seemed to go round in circles. And there seemed to be a missing piece; an unexplained factor which, if she only knew what it was, would slot in to make things clearer. Something – a thought; a memory; an observation – kept tugging at her mind. She groped through her thoughts unhappily, but nothing tallied, nothing made her start with recognition.

She had almost successfully managed to block from her mind the scene last night. Of course Charles had not meant to hit her; he had simply been strung up. It was really her own fault for falling asleep and letting him discover the letter without her breaking the news to him first. In retrospect, it occurred to her, perhaps she should have kept it a secret until she had visited Mr Stanlake and checked that it wasn't all some awful mistake. Perhaps it had been wrongly addressed to her. Perhaps it should have gone to some other client. She imagined Mr Stanlake smiling at her, tearing the letter up and promising her he would have a stern word with whoever was responsible for worrying her in this way. She would smile gratefully back at him, and ask him to make quite sure no mistakes like that could be made in the future. He would pat her hand and order tea.

This scene was so comforting, Cressida dwelt on it a little bit longer. After all, people made mistakes every day, she reasoned. They dialled wrong numbers often enough; why shouldn't they have sent out the wrong letter? She glanced surreptitiously at Charles' sullen face. How relieved he would be if she could tell him it was all a silly error. The more she thought about it, the more she was convinced that that was what it must be. The thought was cheering.

Charles, sensing Cressida's eyes on him, quickly looked up, and saw a little smile cross her lips. She was eating her chicken drumstick determinedly, apparently unconcerned by the whole situation. A part of him wanted to work up an outrage that she could behave so naturally, when they were on the brink of ruin. But his senses seemed numbed; he felt blank inside. He couldn't rouse himself to any strong feelings, one way or the other. When he deliberately reminded himself of the precise amount of money that they might eventually owe, and painstakingly translated that into terms of material goods, a huge grey terror filled him. But it was an abstract terror; it was almost as though he knew he should be terrified – so he was. In the same way that he had never quite been able to believe that all that money in Cressida's portfolio was his too, so he was unable to relate a demand for a million pounds to himself. Other people dealt in that kind of money. Not him.

Every now and again, he glanced over at Ella. The first time he had seen her that day, the sight had brought back, with a stab, a memory of the night before. Now he couldn't stop tormenting himself – prodding his own sore spot like a small boy with a bruise. But his senses were becoming numbed towards her, too. The more he looked, the more the pain was dulled. The passion of last night had slipped away; try as he might, he couldn't recapture it. He reminded himself several times that it was only twelve hours since they had made love so frenziedly, that he had sunk into her eager flesh with a strange, mixed feeling of familiarity and newness, that he had shouted, that she had cried out, that he had felt like weeping. But the more he reminded himself, the more it all seemed like a dream. The sensations became more shadowy; the memories of her skin, her hair – even her lips – receded in his mind. He felt hollow and bland; a nothing.

Patrick, standing behind the barbecue, watched Charles, moodily staring at the ground, refusing to join in the party. He and Cressida had obviously had some sort of barney last night – probably over Ella. Patrick didn't like to think what had gone on between those two last night. But even if the worst hadn't happened, deciding to go for a midnight walk with an ex-lover wasn't exactly normal behaviour for a married man. Especially a man married to such a lovely creature as Cressida. Patrick's gaze transferred compassionately to her. She was sitting all alone, like a pale moth on the grass, fiddling with the same chicken drumstick he'd given her half an hour ago.

At the sight of her, Patrick's antagonism towards Charles increased. He was still smarting from their encounter yesterday; still resentful at the way Charles had dismissed his offer. Since marrying Cressida, Charles behaved as if he had been born and bred into wealth; as if he was somehow superior to everyone else. Of course, it wasn't his money, everyone knew that. If he hadn't found himself a rich wife, he would still be in Seymour Road, relying on his pathetic hippy arts centre for a living. Cressida had pulled him up a few notches – and in principle Patrick didn't mind that. But look at the way he was treating her! Letting her go upstairs to bed by herself like that last night; disappearing outside with Ella; even now, ignoring her completely.

Patrick eyed Cressida's pale skin, her fluttering

eyelids, her delicate hands. She was a real lady, he reflected. She wasn't the sort to complain, or cause a fuss, or defend herself; she was the sort who would just suffer in silence. And she'd chosen as her protector that pretentious, arrogant Charles – who had only married her for her money, anyway. Patrick's chest burned in silent indignation, and without looking at what he was doing, he knocked a sausage onto the grass.

'Daddy!' cried Georgina. 'You clumsy!' She shrieked with laughter, and after seeing what had happened, Caroline joined in.

'Blast!' said Patrick, bending down and trying to pick it up with the tongs.

'That must be enough food now, anyway,' said Annie. 'Why don't you sit down, Patrick? You must be boiled.'

'Yes, come and sit down,' said Caroline, in a mollifying voice. 'Come and have a nice drink.'

As Patrick sat down, Don sidled over.

'I've been looking again at the chart,' he said.

'Oh yes?' said Patrick shortly. There had been a slight scene when Patrick announced that the finalists in the tennis tournament were himself, Caroline, Charles and Cressida. Don had looked shocked; Valerie had expressed voluble disbelief; Patrick had stalked off to light the barbecue.

'I see the way you've worked it out,' said Don. 'I suppose that is a valid method, although it's not one I've seen before.'

'Oh good,' said Patrick.

'And I suppose, with Val injured like that,' continued Don, 'we weren't likely to win all our matches.'

'No,' chimed in Caroline in a loud, sarcastic voice. 'And you certainly wouldn't have wanted to put her through a final. Not with an injury.' Don flushed slightly.

'What I was wondering,' he said dolefully, 'was

whether you wanted an umpire for the final. Since I won't be playing, I thought I'd volunteer.' He shifted morosely from one foot to the other.

'Yes, well,' said Patrick. He looked around at the others for help. 'What do you think?'

'Oh, yes!' said Annie. 'That'll make it really special.'

'And since we do have an umpire's chair ...' drawled Caroline.

'Exactly,' said Don. 'It'd be a shame not to use it.'

'Yes, you're right,' said Patrick, feeling an increasing enthusiasm for the idea.

The authentic Wimbledon-green umpire's chair that towered at the side of the tennis court had been an expensive purchase from a specialist sporting catalogue but was rarely put to use by anyone other than Georgina.

'We could get along the kids to ballboy,' said Caroline. 'Georgina, you were volunteering yourself the other night. How about it?'

'Actually,' said Georgina, 'it's nearly time for us to do our play.' She sprang to her feet, and called to the others. 'Get everyone sitting in a row,' she commanded Caroline.

'What about the ballboying?' said Caroline.

'Maybe,' said Georgina. 'Play first. We'll be down when we've put our costumes on.'

'All right,' said Caroline. 'There's no hurry!' she called after her. 'Why do kids always want to put on plays for their parents?' she addressed Annie. 'I was just the same.'

'So was I,' agreed Annie. 'I used to love charades. And we had a wonderful dressing-up box.'

Patrick seized his chance. Sauntering casually down to where Cressida was sitting, he smiled gently at her and said, 'The children are about to put on a play for us. Are you interested?'

'Our children?' Cressida seemed confused; her eyes darted about.

'They're inside, getting their costumes together,' explained Patrick. 'Georgina's been organizing them.'

'Oh, I see, yes, of course.'

'They'll be a while yet,' said Patrick, and sank easily onto his heels. 'Lovely day, it turned out,' he said, looking up at the sky.

'Yes, lovely,' murmured Cressida.

'I tend to lose my appetite in this kind of heat,' said Patrick. 'I don't know if you're the same.'

'Oh, yes,' said Cressida vaguely.

'And it makes it worse when you're the one in charge of the cooking!' He laughed pleasantly and eyed Cressida surreptitiously to see whether she was relaxing. He wasn't quite sure what all this was leading to; but somehow he felt an obscure need to show her that not all men were like Charles; that there were a few she could trust, perhaps even confide in.

Cressida stared fixedly at her fingernails and felt a pink tinge creep over her face. It had just occurred to her that Patrick's job was something in finance. Perhaps he would know whether the letter was a mistake or not. Perhaps she should ask him. It would be such a relief if he could reassure her. She opened her mouth to speak – and then shut it again. If she mentioned the letter, he might well ask to see it. Did she want him, a relative stranger, looking at her correspondence? Did she want him to know how much the demand was for? Could she perhaps bring up the subject in a more oblique way?

She glanced over her shoulder. Charles had got up, and was stalking off towards the terrace. No-one was near.

'Actually,' she said, 'there was something I wanted to ask you.' She blushed, and looked down at her skirt.

Patrick's heart surged with a mixture of pride and terror. Cressida had chosen him to confide in. He had been right. She needed someone she could trust. But what was he to say if she asked him about Ella? He quickly prepared a few anodyne phrases in his mind. Of course, it wasn't right for Charles to have gone off with Ella like that – but on the other hand, had anything really happened? And although he would have relished Charles' embarrassment at any indiscretions, he couldn't bring himself to say anything that would hurt Cressida.

'It's about a letter,' said Cressida. Patrick's heart sank. Had Charles and Ella been writing to each other all this time? Had the affair never ended? He inwardly cursed Georgina again for having told Ella it was all right for her to come and stay with them. As far as he was concerned, it was never OK for that Jezebel to stay with them.

'A letter?' he said, in light tones, ready to downplay its significance. 'I've never been one for much letter-writing myself.'

'But business letters,' said Cressida quietly. 'You do write business letters.'

'Well, yes,' said Patrick, surprised. Was she not talking about a letter from Ella, then? 'At least,' he added, 'my secretary does. If anything goes wrong, I blame her.' He gave a quick laugh. Part of him regretted having invited Cressida's confidences. Although, to be fair, he hadn't really invited them. But he had certainly welcomed them. And now he had a nasty feeling he didn't want to hear her troubles after all. What if she was involved in some sort of scandal?

'I received a letter yesterday', said Cressida, 'which I think might be a mistake. In fact, I'm sure it is a mistake. But I'd just like to be sure.' She brought her head up, and stared at him with large blue eyes. Then her expression changed, and her attention shifted to over his shoulder. Patrick turned round, and saw Stephen striding towards them.

'Hello, you two,' he said, in a determinedly cheerful voice. 'Patrick, might I have a quick word? You don't

195

mind, do you, Cressida?' Cressida's face had closed up.

'Oh, no, not at all,' she said politely. Stephen grinned.

'I think the youngsters are about to entertain us,' he said. 'But I wanted to catch you before they begin.' He stopped, clearly waiting for Patrick to rise to his feet. Patrick didn't know whether to feel annoyance or relief.

'All right,' he said eventually, struggling up and brushing down his trousers. 'I'll talk to you later perhaps,' he said to Cressida, then wondered whether that sounded compromising. But Stephen wasn't the sort to wonder why he and Cressida had been chatting alone.

They walked off together in silence, and Stephen's face grew more and more scarlet. He could barely bring himself to say what he was planning. The whole subject covered him with embarrassment and shame; he would almost rather have just swallowed the mortgage commitment, managed somehow, and said nothing. But a growing conviction that he needed to sort this all out as soon as possible, compelled him at last to speak.

'It's about that deal,' he said awkwardly. 'I've been having second thoughts.' He looked away, in acute embarrassment. Patrick's step barely faltered. He was used to this kind of thing.

'People do,' he said in a jovial tone. 'When did you ever make a big decision and not have doubts somewhere along the line? It's only natural. But I can assure you, you've really done yourself a favour.'

'Maybe,' said Stephen. 'But, actually, I don't think I really want to take out a huge mortgage. Not while I'm still doing my doctorate.'

'Hardly huge,' said Patrick. 'It's well within your means.'

'I know,' said Stephen. 'I'm sure you're right. But you know . . .' He forced himself to look at Patrick. 'I just don't feel comfortable with it. I'm not like you and

Charles,' he added. 'I'm not used to dealing in big sums of money, and I'm not used to borrowing. I just wouldn't be able to sleep at night. So,' he paused, 'I've decided I'd like to pull out.'

'You really have got it bad,' said Patrick, giving an easy chuckle. 'You'll be laughing at yourself tomorrow, when you remember this conversation. But don't worry,' his eyes twinkled, 'I won't hold you to it!'

'No, really.' Stephen's voice was firm. 'I want to cancel the deal.'

'Well, that might be a bit difficult,' said Patrick in a thoughtful voice. 'The problem is, you see, the penalty charges for early surrender. You might come out with quite a bit less than you put in.'

'But I only put it in yesterday!' Stephen's voice rose in outrage.

'I know, silly, isn't it? These funds are all structured the same. They reward people who stay the course and penalize those who leave early.'

'And what counts as early?'

'For you, anything before ten years. But don't worry. I'm sure it won't come to that. If you like, I'll go through your accounts with you and work out how you can be sure of meeting the mortgage commitment each month.'

'Patrick, you don't understand. I want to cancel the deal.'

'I know you do.' Patrick's voice was sympathetic. 'But if you cancel the deal, you'll definitely lose out. You'll have to pay your charges straight away. They could be a good few thousand pounds. I really wouldn't advise it.'

'Oh.' Stephen looked crestfallen. There was a short silence.

'Actually,' Patrick said, in a thoughtful voice, 'there is an answer.' Stephen looked up. 'You could switch into our guaranteed investment fund.'

'Guaranteed?' Stephen looked up. Guaranteed. It had a comforting ring about it.

'Oh yes,' said Patrick. 'Utterly safe. I don't know why I didn't think of this for you before. It's designed precisely for someone like you, who isn't keen on risk.'

'That's me,' said Stephen, making a half-hearted attempt to joke.

'I understand completely. You're not one of the big-shot investors of our time, are you?' said Patrick in a sympathetic voice.

'Not really,' said Stephen. 'That's just it. I'm not happy with debt. Never have been.'

'Well then, that's the answer,' said Patrick, in a pleased voice. 'What a relief! You leave it all with me. I'll put your investment in our one hundred per cent guaranteed fund, and you sleep easy at night.' He grinned at Stephen. 'That way, you can't fail to cover the mortgage payments.'

Stephen felt uplifted, despite his reservations, by Patrick's enthusiasm.

'And you think that would be a better option?' he said cautiously.

'Christ, yes. I should have thought of it before. You get the best of both worlds with this fund. Investment and security. I'll go through it all with you on Monday, shall I?' Stephen gazed at him.

'All right,' he said eventually. There didn't seem to be any choice in the matter. He would just have to trust Patrick and hope for the best.

They walked along in silence for a few moments.

'Out of interest,' Patrick said casually, 'why the sudden panic?' Stephen flushed.

'Nothing really,' he said. 'I'm just a bit uneasy with such a big debt.'

'But it's not debt if you're making more than enough to cover it,' said Patrick, grinning at Stephen.

'I know that,' said Stephen. 'But I started thinking, I

should have taken the papers away to think about yesterday, shouldn't I?'

'Not necessarily,' said Patrick easily. 'There's no point delaying something if it's to your advantage.'

'But most people would think about it overnight,' persisted Stephen. 'At least, that's what . . .' He broke off.

'Yes?'

'Nothing,' said Stephen. Patrick stiffened slightly.

'Has someone been talking to you?' he said casually. 'Giving you advice? I'm just interested to know,' he added, smiling at Stephen. Stephen looked uncomfortable.

'Not really,' he said. 'I mean . . .'

'Don't worry,' said Patrick. 'I know what it's like. People ask you not to let on what they've been saying.'

'Well, yes,' said Stephen. He looked away.

Patrick stared at Stephen, filled with a mounting, angry certainty. Charles. It had to be Charles fucking Mobyn. Patrick was almost sure of it. It would be just like that supercilious bastard to find out what Stephen had been talking about to him, and advise him to pull out. What the fuck did Charles know about it? A memory of Charles' smooth voice ran through his mind. *I think it's a bit much trying to do business with one of your guests. This is supposed to be a party, isn't it? Keep your charts for the office.* Bloody bastard. Thought he was doing Stephen a favour, no doubt. Thought he was getting him out of a fix. Well, he should fucking well mind his own business. Spend more time looking after his wife and less poking his nose where it wasn't wanted.

'You liddle pigs are too old to leev at home,' said Martina, waving her arms vaguely in the air. 'You must go to seek your fordunes. But beware of ze volf!'

Toby and the Mobyn twins, each clad in a pink T-shirt, stared at her, apparently amazed.

'Off!' hissed Georgina, from the side of the lawn. 'Go on, Toby!' Suddenly remembering what he had to do, Toby grasped a twin by each hand and led them off the lawn.

'Shall we clap?' whispered Annie.

'Yes, I think we should,' said Caroline, and began hearty applause.

'It's not over yet!' Georgina's blue eyes regarded them with disapproval.

'Oh, we know,' said Annie. 'We're just applauding the scene.'

The adults were sitting in a row of seats facing the lawn, each holding a drink. Annie and Stephen were in the middle of the row, but Stephen was not attending. The sense of enthusiasm which Patrick had transmitted to him during their conversation was quickly ebbing away and his situation was becoming starkly apparent to him. He was still committed to a huge mortgage. That much seemed plain enough. He couldn't afford the few thousand pounds, or whatever it was Patrick had said he would have to pay in order to pull out. But was this guaranteed fund really the answer? What was meant by guaranteed? Stephen felt confused. Patrick hadn't actually said anything about it. Everything was going too fast.

One of the twins appeared on the lawn. He stared vaguely at the audience and began to suck his thumb. He looks so sweet, thought Annie, and she turned to grin at Charles. But Charles was sitting, chin cupped in his hand, staring morosely at the ground.

'Hello, little pig!' Annie looked up in surprise. It was Nicola, dressed in what appeared to be a suit and tie, and with a moustache painted on her face. She grinned tremulously at Annie, then addressed the twin. 'Can I interest you in some extremely fine straw for your house? It's the finest straw around; you won't find better, mark my words.' She fumbled with her bad hand at the catches of the attaché case she was carrrying; the audience was silent. Finally the lid swung open, to reveal a caseful of straw. 'Look at that, sir,' continued Nicola. 'Finest quality house-building straw. Yours for only five gold pieces.' A snuffling sound came from the end of the row. Caroline was shaking with laughter.

'She's brilliant!' she exclaimed in a muffled voice.

'So is that a deal then, sir?' said Nicola. 'I assure you, straw is the best thing you can build your house out of these days. Bricks are old-fashioned. Straw's what you want.' She bowed to the twin, handed him the case and walked off the lawn. The adults burst into applause and Caroline burst into snorts of laughter.

'She's wonderful! She's just like you, Patrick!' Patrick's head jerked up in shock. Along the row, faces turned towards him, giggles were stifled; even Charles raised his head and gave a grin.

Patrick turned white with anger. Was that how everyone saw him? As a cheapskate salesman? He wasn't surprised at Caroline – it was the sort of comment he might expect her to make. But for her to say it in front of all of them – some of them clients – filled him with a hot, embarrassed fury. Especially Charles. Charles, who had told Stephen he should try to get out of the deal. Charles, who thought he was so fucking superior. Patrick could hardly bear to look at his smooth, tanned face. Stephen, after all, didn't know any better. But Charles did; and Charles knew Patrick had been desperate for the business.

And now they were all sitting there laughing at him. With the utmost control, he forced himself not to get up and walk out. He gave a stiff grin and took a swig of Pimm's. The other twin appeared on the lawn, and once more Nicola came on with an attaché case.

'Are you building a house, sir?' Her tone was confident now; she was clearly enjoying the humour of the part. 'Might I interest you in some lovely twigs? They really are the finest twigs for house building.

201

Completely wolf-proof. Guaranteed against wolves of all shapes and sizes. You won't have any complaints, sir.' She handed the attaché case to the twin; once again the audience collapsed in laughter.

'She's priceless,' said Ella, wiping her eyes.

'It's amazing, isn't it?' said Annie. 'I had no idea she could be so funny.'

Toby wandered onto the lawn.

'I want bricks,' he announced loudly.

'Not yet!' hissed Georgina. Nicola hurriedly made her entrance. 'Hello, little pig,' she said. 'Can I interest you in some twigs or straw?' There was a pause.

'Now!' hissed Georgina from the side. Toby's brow cleared.

'I want bricks,' he said.

'Not straw?' said Nicola hopefully. 'Or twigs?'

'I want bricks,' said Toby.

'What about some nice cardboard,' suggested Nicola.

'I want bricks,' said Toby. Nicola sighed.

'You're making a big mistake,' she said. 'Don't say I didn't warn you. Here you are.' She handed Toby a brick, and led him firmly off stage.

'Interval,' announced Georgina.

'Aren't they good?' said Annie, turning to speak to Cressida. But Cressida was staring straight ahead, with a taut expression and unshed tears glistening in her eyes. Annie quickly looked away, and inadvertently caught the eye of Patrick. His face was thunderous. She quickly looked away again. Stephen was talking to Don; Valerie seemed to be talking at Ella, who was looking surprisingly interested in whatever she was saying. She glanced at Caroline. But Caroline had also noticed Cressida, and was staring at her with blatant curiosity.

'Act two,' announced Georgina, in a ringing voice. She eyed Caroline sternly. 'And try not to laugh.'

Caroline took no notice. She was still gazing at

Cressida. The sight of the younger woman sitting wanly, almost in tears, had struck a sudden chord of compassion in her. She and Ella had been laughing gaily that morning about Charles — but neither of them had to go through what Cressida did. The poor thing had quite obviously found out about Charles and Ella; perhaps she was contemplating leaving him; perhaps divorce. Suddenly Caroline felt remorse for her treatment of Cressida. She'd always taken her to be a cold, stuck-up bitch, but here she was, in a dreadful state because of that stupid Charles. A dim sense of feminism rose up in Caroline's mind. Why should that poor girl suffer because of a bastard who'd only married her because she was rich anyway?

Suddenly there was a roar of laughter, and Caroline looked round to the lawn. One of the twins had come on, and sat down in a big cardboard box covered in straw. Georgina entered behind him, wearing a long, black cape and looking more like Dracula than a wolf.

'Little pig, little pig,' she intoned, 'let me come in.' The twin looked blankly at her. He was clearly too young to have been given any lines; but from the side of the lawn came Martina's voice, high and squeaky.

'No no, by ze hair of my cheeny cheen cheen, I von't let you in!'

'Then I'll huff and I'll puff and I'll blow the house down!' yelled Georgina, and charged at the cardboard box. The face of the twin crumpled with fear, and he let out a piercing wail. Georgina, regardless, began to blow as hard as she could at the box and the twin's wail turned into terrified sobs.

Suddenly the sound was joined by a cry from the audience.

'Leave him alone!' sobbed Cressida, tears starting to flow down her cheeks. 'Leave him alone!' She leapt up, rushed onto the lawn and scooped up her son, who began to sob unrestrainedly against her shirt. From the side of the lawn came more sobs, from the other twin, who had decided to join in with his brother. Without looking right or left, Cressida picked him up also, strode towards the house and disappeared in through the terrace door.

Charles remained motionless in his seat for a few seconds, then, as everyone turned to look at him, he stood up, muttering something, and went after her. The others sat for a few minutes in silence. No-one seemed quite sure what to say. It was an awkward moment. Then a voice came from the side.

'Oh dear,' said Ella in an expressionless voice. 'I hope I wasn't the cause of that.' Caroline looked at her sharply.

'So do I,' she said shortly. 'So do we all.'

Chapter Twelve

'I'm so sorry,' said Cressida to Caroline. 'I don't know what came over me. Too much sun, I expect.' The two women were standing by the tennis court, waiting for the arrival of their partners for the grand final of the tennis tournament.

'Too much bossing by Georgina, more like,' said Caroline. 'She's a little Nazi. In fact, it's me who should apologize, on behalf of her. She's already caused havoc once this weekend.'

'Really?' said Cressida politely. Caroline cursed herself.

'Well, yes,' she said awkwardly. 'Telling Ella it was all right for her to come and stay. She didn't say a word about it to Patrick or me.' She looked away uncomfortably from Cressida's face. How could she have been so crass as to bring up the subject of Ella? But Cressida had obviously got her feelings under control.

'Extra guests are always difficult,' she murmured. 'People don't realize; they just phone up at the last minute and ask if they can bring their great aunt, or their godson, and one can't just say no. It's very trying. I've taken to making an extra pudding or two each time, just in case.' She smiled tiredly at Caroline, who was overcome by a sudden, irrational feeling of guilt. Her eyes swept over Cressida's pale, drawn complexion; the shadows under her eyes; the slender hand gripping the tennis racquet.

'It's not really a problem for me,' she said frankly. 'Since I never do any cooking.'

'Really? But last night . . .'

'Caterers,' said Caroline. 'I thought you knew. Can

you see me making seafood tartlets?' Her eyes crinkled humorously at Cressida. 'I'm crap at cooking. When I first invited Patrick round to my flat for dinner, I hired a caterer to do Beef Wellington. They delivered it to the back door, and I brought it up the stairs, through the kitchen and out to Patrick. He thought I'd been taking it out of the oven!' She burst into raucous laughter, and Cressida gave a shocked giggle. 'He still thinks I made it,' added Caroline. 'You're the only person I've ever told. You mustn't tell him!'

'Oh, no, I won't,' said Cressida. She stared at Caroline, wide-eyed. 'Did he really believe you?'

'Oh yes,' said Caroline. 'Men are so blind. He didn't even notice it was on a foil caterer's tray.' Cressida broke into giggles again.

'That's amazing,' she said.

'Sometimes he asks for Beef Wellington again,' said Caroline, 'and I tell him I don't want to make it because I want to keep the memory of that dish special.'

'So you haven't ever had it since?'

'Never,' said Caroline. She took out a cigarette, put it in her mouth and reached for her lighter. 'The caterers went bust,' she said. 'And I don't want to risk using another firm. They might do it differently.' She caught Cressida's eye and they both broke into laughter again. Cressida gave a few broken, almost painful giggles as she watched Caroline light her cigarette. Caroline looked up.

'Would you like one?' she asked.

'A cigarette?' Cressida paused. 'I haven't smoked since I was at school.'

'Do you good,' said Caroline. 'Calm your nerves.' She offered Cressida the pack. After a few moments, Cressida took one.

'They're menthol,' added Caroline. 'You may not like them.' Cressida took a few hesitant drags.

'Minty!' she exclaimed.

'Nice, aren't they?' said Caroline. She grinned companionably at Cressida. 'They clean your teeth as well.'

'Really?' began Cressida, then saw Caroline's face. She laughed. 'I always believe what people tell me.'

'I'm the opposite,' said Caroline. 'I always disbelieve what people tell me. It's a good habit to get into.'

'But what if they're telling the truth?' Caroline shrugged.

'Then you'll find out soon enough,' she said. Cressida nodded puzzledly and continued taking puffs on her cigarette. Caroline watched her, inhaling with shallow little breaths and quickly exhaling again, and suddenly felt a strong, almost maternal fondness for her.

'Have you ever tried to make it?' said Cressida suddenly.

'Make what?'

'Beef Wellington.' Caroline inhaled deeply, and looked at Cressida sardonically.

'Me make Beef Wellington? You're talking to the girl who got straight Es in cookery. I told you. I'm crap at cooking.' She blew out a satisfying cloud of smoke.

'I could teach you to make it.'

Caroline looked slowly round at Cressida, suspecting a joke.

'Teach me? What do you mean?' Her voice came out more sharply than she had intended.

Cressida's face fell slightly; but she carried on, in a slightly hesitant voice, 'I could come round – or you could come round to me – and I could show you how to do it. I've made Beef Wellington lots of times. And I'm sure you could, too.'

'Come round to your house?'

'Not if it's inconvenient, of course,' said Cressida. 'I could easily come here.'

'No, no,' said Caroline slowly. 'I'm always popping into Silchester. It would be easy for me to come to you. And you really think I could learn to make Beef Wellington?'

'I'm sure you could,' said Cressida. She smiled shyly at Caroline. 'You could cook it for Patrick. As a surprise.'

'Christ, he won't believe his eyes!' said Caroline. She grinned at Cressida. 'I have to warn you, I'm a bloody awful pupil. But I'll make a special effort to listen. Are you sure you can bear it?'

'Oh yes,' said Cressida. 'It'll be fun!' Her eyes sparkled and she looked for somewhere to stub out her cigarette.

'Cressida! You're not smoking?' It was Charles' stentorian voice. The light in Cressida's eyes dimmed; her eyes darted about distractedly. Even her skin seemed suddenly lifeless.

'It's all my fault,' called Caroline loudly. 'Bloody nerve,' she muttered under her breath. Charles approached the court briskly.

'I didn't think you smoked, Cressida,' he said. 'It's an expensive habit, you know.' Cressida was silent. He stared at her expectantly, his eyes cold; his face hard.

'I just thought I'd try one,' she said eventually, in a voice that trembled slightly. Caroline drew breath, and looked with a sudden fierce hatred at Charles. He met her gaze challengingly – then, with a sound of impatience, turned away.

'Hello!' The cheery voice of Annie reached them. 'Everyone's coming,' she called. 'Patrick was held up by a phone call.' She was carrying a number of bottles and a plastic ice bucket. 'I thought I'd bring a few supplies,' she added. 'Does anybody want a drink? I've got lemonade, and orange juice.'

'We should have some water on the court,' said Caroline. 'I'll go and get some.'

As she left, Cressida suddenly felt exposed, as though an insulating barrier between her and Charles had been removed. She looked surreptitiously at Charles' face. It was still harsh, with taut lines and shadows that actually made him better looking. He looked . . . she groped in her mind for the word . . . moody. Mean and moody. Of course. The sort of looks one was supposed to fall desperately in love with. But Cressida had never been attracted to that sort of man. She had fallen in love with Charles because of his easy good nature; his wide smile; his even temper. She had felt safe with him; protected and secure. And now she was, in spite of herself, frightened. She didn't want to be alone with him again; she didn't want to listen to his shouts and threats; she didn't want to experience again that tense, miserable silence.

'Aha! Our worthy finalists!' It was Don, striding briskly towards the court, with a straw hat on his head and a clipboard in his hand. He walked over to the green umpire's chair and deposited his clipboard. Then he produced a tape measure, went to the centre of the court and ceremoniously measured the net.

'It's a bit low,' he called. 'Annie, would you mind adjusting it?'

'Gosh,' said Annie, getting up obligingly. 'This is all getting a bit serious.'

Cressida stared straight ahead, avoiding Charles' eye, as Annie wound the handle back and forwards. Stephen seemed a cheerful, straightforward man, she thought to herself. Lucky Annie . . .

'A bit higher,' called Don. 'No, a bit lower . . . slow down . . . up a bit more, yes that's right, stop, stop!' He beamed at Charles and Cressida. 'Might as well get it right before we start.'

'Absolutely,' said Charles, in a taut voice.

Caroline and Patrick were coming down the path towards the tennis court.

'Listen,' said Caroline. 'We've got to beat that little shit.' Patrick looked at her in surprise.

'Who, Charles?'

'Yes, of course Charles. He's a complete bastard.' Patrick's eye fell on Charles, on his blond hair and insolent tanned face, and he scowled.

209

'I couldn't agree more.'

'Well, then,' said Caroline, 'don't play your usual crap.'

'You've got a nerve!' said Patrick indignantly. 'Anyway,' he added, 'I thought you quite liked Charles.'

'He's a complete two-timing bastard.'

'Ah,' said Patrick. 'I thought he might be. How did you find that out?'

'Ella told me,' said Caroline over her shoulder. 'They did it last night. In a field.'

'In *our* field?'

'I know. Taking liberties a bit, I thought.'

Charles and Cressida had gone onto the court.

'Hello,' said Caroline briskly. 'Just going to limber up.' She took up a position by the court and attempted a few rather flashy stretching exercises. 'My hamstrings are out of condition,' she complained loudly, catching Patrick's eye. She flashed a look at Charles. He was standing, scowling at the ground. Miserable sod, she thought. Can't even enjoy adultery.

Charles was wondering whether he could bear playing this match at all. All the others seemed so fucking cheerful, while his mind was clouded over with bleak misery. The only other person who looked as downcast as him was Cressida. And she was beginning to annoy him beyond measure, with her fluttering eyelids, and her pale face, and that stupid outburst of weeping. Everyone obviously blamed him. Christ. That was bloody ironic.

'Ready,' announced Caroline. 'Let's knock up.'

Charles scooped up a couple of tennis balls and began slamming forehands angrily at Caroline, trying to relieve his frustration.

'For Christ's sake!' shrieked Caroline, as another ball went straight into the back netting. 'I'm not Steffi Graf, you know. Here, Cressida, you haven't hit a single shot.' She deliberately aimed the ball at Cressida, but it went in the net.

'Oh fucking hell,' she exclaimed.

'Ahem, excuse me,' said Don, waving to attract her attention. 'I'll have to warn you against bad language. It's against the LTA rule book.'

'What?' Caroline gazed at him in amazement. 'You must be fucking joking.'

'As well as being unpleasant for players and audience alike,' explained Don.

'Bullshit,' said Caroline. She turned to the audience. 'Is anyone offended by my language?' she asked loudly. There was silence.

'Actually, Mummy,' said Georgina politely, 'I am.'

'You don't count,' said Caroline. 'Anyway, I thought you were going to be ballboy.'

'We're not going to stay for long,' said Georgina. 'Nicola wants to have a go on Arabia before she goes home.'

'Well, come and be ballboy until then,' said Caroline impatiently.

'Actually,' said Georgina, 'we'll probably go straight away. We'll come back and see how you're doing a bit later on,' she added kindly. 'Come on, Nick,' she said.

'I don't understand it,' said Caroline, as Georgina marched off with Nicola and Toby. 'She was dead keen to be ballboy last week.'

'She's probably realized it's actually quite hard work,' said Annie, laughing. 'She's not stupid, your daughter.'

'Let's get cracking,' said Patrick impatiently. 'Who's got rough or smooth?'

'I'll toss,' said Don officiously. 'Heads or tails?'

'Tails.'

'No, heads. That means Charles and Cressida are to serve.'

'So we choose an end,' said Caroline. 'I'll let you decide.' Patrick stared at her crossly. He had never been able to understand the mentality that went behind choosing an end in tennis. What did it matter? It wasn't as if you were stuck there for the whole match. He gazed up at the sun, temporarily covered over with light, gauzy cloud, and looked back down at the court, none the wiser. What was it they always said? Let's have one in the sun. But which end was the sun? He looked around. Everyone was waiting for him to decide.

'Let's have that end,' he said perversely, pointing to the opposite end. If he couldn't decide on any reasonable grounds, he could at least make that bastard Charles walk the length of the court unnecessarily.

As Charles passed the net, he saw the figure of Ella, unmistakable in her blue dress, coming down the bank in bare feet. She sat down beside Martina and began talking to one of the twins. A cold fury went through him at the sight of her, unencumbered, free, with no responsibilities. She had the air of someone who is only pausing on the way to somewhere far more exciting; who has dropped in, considerately, to say a quick hello, but who is already anticipating leaving for much greater pleasures elsewhere.

And he had actually thought last night that he was going to be part of those pleasures. Watching her, it came to him that she didn't really care whether he visited her in Italy or not. She hadn't brought up the subject again, she hadn't given him any conspiratorial glances or expressive looks. She was just going to go off, to her idyllic Italian ménage, and leave him behind, with a wife, two children and possible ruin. Selfish bitch, he thought furiously.

As if aware of his thoughts, Ella directed her gaze towards him and took off her sunglasses to see better. Charles hastily turned his head away, and met the amused glance of Caroline, who was approaching the net.

'You're looking rather tired today, Charles,' she said. 'I hope you slept well.'

'Oh, yes,' said Charles hastily.

'Perhaps it was just the late night then,' said Caroline, following Cressida, who was walking round on the other side of the court, with her gaze. 'Ella tells me you made quite a night of it.' She brought her blue eyes round to meet his; her face was full of contempt. A jolt ran through Charles. She knows what happened last night, he thought. That fucking bitch Ella told her. Why? Why tell Caroline?

She was still staring fixedly at him, and he couldn't move his eyes away from hers. He felt pinioned, like a rabbit mesmerized by a snake. She had power over him, and she knew it. If she wanted to, she would have no hesitation in telling Cressida; perhaps even telling the whole assembled company. She was that kind of insensitive, vulgar, indiscreet woman. No wonder Cressida couldn't bear her. He should have listened to his wife; they should have refused the invitation to come here.

Eventually she let him go.

'I think they're waiting,' she said. 'We'd better go to our places.' Charles watched her sauntering off to join Patrick; her pony-tail bouncing, her tasteless gold bracelets glinting in the sun. What did she know of the troubles he was in? he thought viciously. She and Patrick hadn't a money trouble between them; they had the easy, lazy sybaritic life while he had nothing but worries. He walked to the back of the court and scooped up a couple of balls.

'I'll serve,' he said shortly to Cressida.

'The final of The White House tournament,' intoned Don, 'between Caroline and Patrick Chance and Charles and Cressida Mobyn. Linesmen ready.' He turned to the audience. 'Any volunteers?'

'That's your job,' said Stephen lazily, his arm around Annie. 'We're here to applaud. Anyway, you're the expert.'

'I suppose I am,' said Don, in a pleased voice. He adjusted his hat and sat back in his chair. 'Players ready.' He glanced from side to side. 'Play.'

Cressida stood at the net, staring at the grass in front of her. She felt completely detached from the game, detached almost from real life. She stood in the correct position, holding her racquet ready, listening vaguely to Charles grunting behind her as he served each ball. The sound made her flinch; it sounded so angry and brutal. And when the ball came thundering into the net beside her, she physically started. The sound of racquets against balls was growing louder and louder in her ears; the shots seemed to be whizzing past her faster and faster. It was quite a threatening game, tennis, she thought unhappily. Quite violent, in its own way.

'Double fault,' announced Don resonantly. 'Thirty-all.'

'Bad luck,' whispered Cressida. But Charles hadn't heard her. He was swiping angrily at the air with his racquet.

His next serve went in, but it was weak. Patrick took a swing at it, and sent it to Cressida, standing stationary at the net, staring miserably at the ground. Too late, she stuck her racquet out with an instinctive, schooled action. The ball went sailing past her and landed just inside the baseline.

'What were you saying about my usual crap?' said Patrick to Caroline. Charles glared at Cressida.

'You could have got that, darling,' he said, putting a jovial veneer on his voice.

'Sorry,' she said, in a voice barely above a whisper.

'Thirty-forty,' intoned Don. Charles scowled, and threw the ball up high. He came down on it with all his weight, and hammered the ball into the service court. Caroline valiantly hit at the ball as it came thundering towards her, and sent it sky-high. Cressida began to prepare automatically for an overhead, but from behind her came Charles' voice.

'Leave it! It's mine!' He ran forward, brought his racquet back and smashed it down wildly.

'Out!' Patrick looked up and gave Charles a smug grin. That would take the smooth bastard down a bit. 'Long by about a foot,' he elaborated. 'Bad luck. I think that's our game.'

Charles glowered silently at Cressida as they changed ends. Now she couldn't even play a decent game of tennis. For Christ's sake. That was about the only thing she was supposed to be good at.

A sudden memory came to him of a long-forgotten tennis game, which must have happened sometime before they were married. He had sat and watched Cressida, playing in the dappled shade of a cedar tree. Where had that been? He couldn't remember anything about it except the way she'd looked, wearing an old-fashioned-looking tennis dress, with a dropped waistband, like a Twenties flapper. And the way she'd played. Neat, deft, confident without being aggressive. Afterwards, when she'd played her final winning shot, she'd caught his eye and smiled shyly, twisting the pearls she always wore around her fingers. He'd really loved her then. Or he'd thought he did. Perhaps it amounted to the same thing.

Chapter Thirteen

As the games progressed, Cressida's confidence was in shards. She couldn't keep her mind on the ball; her racquet shook in her hand; her shots were lame and tentative; her reflexes seemed numbed and slow. As she prepared to serve, she felt, to her horror, warm tears rising up in her eyes. She brushed them away with the sleeve of her tennis shirt, then, to stop the others from noticing, quickly threw up the tennis ball and hit it blindly.

'Fault,' said Don. Cressida tried to compose herself for her second serve. But the sight of Charles at the net, with his taut, angry legs and unforgiving neck, completely unnerved her. She threw the ball too low and hit it weakly into the net.

'Fault,' said Don. 'Love-fifteen.' Cressida quickly turned away to pick up the balls for the next point. She really had to pull herself together. She was playing so badly; they were already four-two down; Charles was furious with her.

Normally, she would somehow have managed to block everything out and keep hold of herself. But at the end of the last game, as they both approached the net to pick up balls, Caroline had put a warm hand on hers and winked at Cressida encouragingly. 'Bloody men,' she had said. 'They're all the same. Don't let them get you down.' Cressida had smiled tentatively back; forcing herself to keep her face composed. 'And tell that husband of yours', Caroline had added in a louder voice, 'that if he shouts at you one more time, I'll kick him in the nuts.'

Caroline's warm, coarse friendliness overwhelmed

Cressida like a wave of sea water. It revived her temporarily – but left her shivering and tearful; unable to return to her dry, controlled composure. She slowly picked up two balls and took a deep breath. It wouldn't last much longer. The set was nearly over. At least – it would be unless she and Charles started winning a few games. She walked back to the baseline and bounced one of the balls up and down a few times, staring at it in miserable puzzlement. Was it wrong to want to lose this set as quickly as possible? She couldn't remember if they were playing just one or the best of three. Maybe they would lose this set and that would be it. Over. Suddenly she was overcome by a fierce longing. She wanted to get home, to safety and familiarity.

Patrick watched Cressida's anxious face as she stood, bouncing the ball up and down before serving. Even if he hadn't had his own grudge against Charles, he thought, the sight of that poor miserable woman was enough to stir any decent man's heart. So what if her tennis was a bit off today? At least she knew how to behave on the court. She was unfailingly polite and courteous; she added a real note of elegance to the game.

Eventually Cressida served to him, a poor, pathetic serve. Patrick considered putting the ball deliberately into the net, as a token gesture. But the sight of Charles' smug face was too much to resist. Approaching the ball ponderously, he whacked it at Charles as hard as he could. Charles quickly jumped aside – but not, Patrick noted with satisfaction, before a fleeting look of terror had crossed his face. So he wasn't as cool as all that. They both watched the ball skim down the line.

'Out!' said Charles triumphantly. 'Just outside.'

'Are you sure?' Don's voice came querulously across the court. 'It looked in to me.'

'It was out,' said Charles, a note of steel creeping into his voice. 'Wasn't it, Cressida?'

'Well,' said Cressida, 'I'm afraid I didn't really see it.'

217

'You must have done! Was it in, or was it out?' Patrick flinched at the hectoring tone.

'All right!' he said hurriedly. 'It was out! OK, Don? Fifteen-all.' As he passed Caroline, he muttered, 'Let's give them a few points.'

'Give that bastard a few points? You must be joking.'

'Not *him* . . .' said Patrick impatiently.

'Ahem,' interrupted Don. 'Mrs Mobyn is waiting to serve.'

Cressida's first serve went in the net. Her second was long and deep.

'Good serve!' exclaimed Caroline, glancing at Patrick. She shot a bright smile at Cressida.

'I'm sorry,' said Don in slight reproof. 'But that really was out. By quite a long way.'

'No it wasn't!' said Caroline.

'I'm afraid it was.'

'It bloody wasn't!'

'It was!' piped up Valerie, who was sitting on the bank near to the court. 'It was well out. Sorry,' she added to Cressida. 'But I did see it.'

'Stupid cow,' muttered Caroline. 'All right,' she said aloud. 'Our point.'

'Fifteen-thirty,' said Don reproachfully. 'Mrs Mobyn to serve.'

Cressida sensed the atmosphere had changed. Patrick and Caroline were looking conspiratorially at each other; they kept hitting the ball out and exclaiming too loudly. Suddenly she had won her service game.

'Well served, Cressida,' said Caroline as they changed ends. Charles looked at her suspiciously.

In the next game, Caroline's serve became surprisingly weak each time she served to Cressida. And with each shot she hit over the net, Cressida felt her confidence return. After a few successful forehands, she felt positive enough to come forward to the net and smack a volley across court, past Patrick and into the corner.

'Game to Mr and Mrs Mobyn,' announced Don.

'Four games all.' Charles looked from Caroline to Patrick and back again.

'You're giving points away,' he said suddenly.

'No we're not,' said Caroline briskly. 'Charles, it's your serve.' But Charles didn't move.

'You're trying to give us this game,' he said. 'What's the matter? Do you think we can't play tennis?'

'Charles,' said Cressida hesitantly.

'You're talking nonsense, Charles,' said Patrick.

'Like hell I am! I know what you're thinking. You're thinking poor old Cressida's playing utter shit, let's give them a few points.'

'You bastard!' exclaimed Caroline. 'How dare you say that?'

'It's fucking well true, though, isn't it? You and Patrick have decided to be charitable to us. Well, thanks very much, but no thanks. I think I can probably do without charity from the Chances.' He spoke the name scathingly, and a sneer came to his lips.

'What the hell's that supposed to mean?' Caroline suddenly challenged him, feet planted wide apart on the tennis court, hands on her hips.

'I'll leave you to work it out.' The two stared at each other in sudden fury.

'Now, calm down,' said Patrick quickly. He glanced towards the bank. Everyone was sitting completely still, staring agog at Charles and Caroline. 'Come on, Charles,' he said, trying to adopt a jovial tone. 'Play the game, and all that.'

'What would someone like you know about playing the game?' Charles retorted.

'Charles, really . . .'

'Charles, I don't think . . .'

'Take it easy . . .'

Charles ignored them all.

'What the fuck would someone like you know about playing the game?' he shouted. 'You fucking pleb *nouveau*, inviting us all here because you think we're

219

smart, you think we've got money, you think we might buy one of your sodding, stinking little investment plans.'

He stopped to draw breath. But a frenzied, furious voice stopped him. It was Caroline.

'You shut the fuck up!' Her voice echoed around the tennis court and there was a pause, in which everyone tacitly re-evaluated the situation. Stephen, who had been about to stand up, decided to stay put. Don, who had been about to utter a few calming words, closed his mouth and looked down at his clipboard. The others watched silently as Caroline walked slowly up to Charles. 'You fucking well shut the fuck up.' The words issued from her mouth in a slow, deliberate sequence. 'You think you're superior to us? You think you're a better person than Patrick? Well, at least he didn't marry me for my fucking *money*! And at least he has better manners than to go to someone's house, as a guest, and spend the night screwing around with some tart in a field!' Her voice rose to a shriek. 'Just because you went to some fucking public school, doesn't make you a better fucking person! Patrick's worth a million of you!' She turned to face Cressida.

'If I were you, I'd leave him,' she began. But Cressida was staring at her, white and physically shaking.

'What are you talking about? What field?' she whispered. Caroline gazed at her uncomprehendingly.

'You know – Ella,' she said without thinking. Too late she realized, as Cressida's face crumpled. 'Oh fuck! I thought you knew. Shit. I'm really sorry. I thought that's why you were looking so ill.'

Cressida felt as though she was in a nightmare. It was all happening. Their private life was being discussed on a tennis court. In front of an audience. She barely took in Caroline's renewed apologies. Her humiliation was complete.

Annie and Stephen, sitting on the bank, glanced at each other worriedly.

'Say something!' whispered Annie. 'This is awful!'

'I can't!' hissed Stephen. 'What am I supposed to say? Don should say something. He's umpire.' They both glanced at Don, who was studiedly looking down at his clipboard.

'Cressida, let's go,' Charles suddenly barked in a stentorian voice. 'We've had enough here.' Cressida didn't move. She didn't even seem to hear him.

'Cressida!' Charles was starting to sound rattled.

'Why should she go with you!' Caroline poked Charles in the chest. He staggered slightly, as though she had hit him, and glared at her. 'Why should she go anywhere with a two-timing bastard like you? Sorry, Cressida,' she added. 'I didn't mean to remind you.' Cressida looked up. Something like a smile appeared on her face.

'It's all right,' she whispered. Caroline grinned back at her.

'You stay here tonight with us if you want to,' she said. 'You don't have to go anywhere with him. You can stay all week if you want.'

Charles gave a short laugh.

'That's rich,' he said. 'Stay with Caroline and Patrick. See how many investment plans they can sell you in one week. You think they're your friends? You think Caroline's being nice to you? They'll be getting you to sign on the dotted line by breakfast-time tomorrow. Jesus Christ.'

'Stephen!' hissed Annie. 'Say something. This is getting really nasty.' But Stephen was listening, agog, as Charles turned to Caroline.

'You think your precious Patrick's so wonderful?' he said. 'Try telling that to all the people he's conned out of their money.' His eyes flickered contemptuously to Patrick. 'Salesmen are all the same. He'd sell you like a shot, if he thought he could get a good price for you. Fucking con man.' He suddenly rounded on Patrick. 'Why did you ask us here? Not because you like us, or you wanted to see us. Christ no. Just so you could try to flog me your sordid little fund. Just so you could notch up a few more thousands on the bedpost. Is that how you get your kicks? Is that what turns you on?'

'Is that why you asked us here too?' Everyone looked up, startled. It was Stephen. He had stood up, and was staring, bright red in the face, at Patrick. 'Is that why you asked me and Annie here? To sell us that investment fund?'

There was a flabbergasted silence.

'What investment fund? What are you talking about?' Annie stared at Stephen, but he avoided her gaze. Charles slowly swivelled to face him.

'Christ, he didn't get you, did he? Stephen?' There was a silence. Stephen looked down. Charles turned back to face Patrick.

'You little shit,' he said softly. 'Do you really think Stephen can afford to invest in one of your fucking so-called unique investment opportunities? Do you really think he can afford to risk his money on speculation like that? Christ almighty.' He turned to Stephen. 'How much did he get you for?' Stephen was silent. 'Oh Christ,' groaned Charles. 'It was the whole fucking whack, wasn't it? I can't believe he talked you into it.'

'Oh fuck off!' burst out Patrick suddenly. 'You've already done enough! I know you've been talking to Stephen. I know you told him he shouldn't have signed. You needn't pretend you don't know anything about it.'

'What do you mean?' said Charles impatiently. 'I haven't spoken to Stephen.'

'Don't give me that,' said Patrick furiously. 'I know you said something about taking papers away overnight; not signing straight away. I know you told him not to trust me.'

'I haven't said a word to him,' said Charles. They both turned to face Stephen.

222

'Actually,' he said, shamefacedly, 'it was Don I was chatting to.'

'Don?' Patrick's look of shock was almost comical. Everyone looked up at Don, still perched on the umpire's chair.

'Sorry, what was that?' he said, looking up from his clipboard. 'I was just checking the score. You know, we've already had eighteen double faults.'

'Weren't you listening?' said Patrick incredulously.

'I don't like unpleasantness,' said Don, pursing his lips, 'either on court or off. Was there something you wanted?'

Patrick was so taken-aback he could barely speak. 'No, no,' he said quickly. He looked about. 'Shall we carry on?'

'What do you mean, shall we carry on?' Annie's voice was clear and resolute. 'I think a few things need explaining. What's this investment fund?'

'It's nothing you need to worry about,' said Patrick quickly. 'Stephen, it's OK. I'll tear up the documents. Pretend it never happened. Cancel it.'

'Cancel it? Are you sure?' Stephen gazed at him in amazement. 'But you said I couldn't pull out.'

'He told you you couldn't pull out!' Charles jeered in derision. 'He forgot to tell you that you've got two weeks to change your mind. The cooling-off period. That's right, isn't it, Patrick?'

'What, really?' Stephen looked at Patrick incredulously. 'You told me it was too late! You said it would cost me a few thousand to cancel!'

'Oh dear!' Charles' voice was vindictively triumphant. 'It looks like our gracious host hasn't quite been doing the right thing by his guests. Aren't there some regulations somewhere about selling investments? Isn't there some sort of complaints procedure?'

'Look, I said we'll cancel the whole thing,' said Patrick, avoiding Stephen's eyes.

'You deliberately misled me. You conned me.'

Stephen tried to drum up some anger. But the relief he felt was so strong, it wiped out any other emotion. It was almost euphoria. The whole thing was cancelled. He was in the clear. It was all OK. Suddenly he felt his legs buckling underneath him.

Flopping down in the deck-chair, he met Annie's stern gaze.

'Not now,' he said.

'Yes, now! Tell me exactly what's been going on!'

'It was nothing,' he said. 'I just said I'd invest some money with Patrick. But I'm not going to now.'

'What money? We haven't got any money?' Stephen was silent.

'Oh, come on. You might as well tell me, because I'm going to find out somehow.'

'I was going to take out a mortgage,' Stephen said quickly. 'But it's all cancelled now. Isn't it, Patrick?' Patrick nodded, his face expressionless.

'A mortgage? What were you thinking of?'

'Oh, don't you start,' said Stephen irritably.

'How much for?' Stephen was silent again. 'Stephen . . .'

'Eighty thousand.'

'What?' Annie gave a shocked laugh. 'You're not serious.' Stephen shrugged. 'Eighty thousand pounds? Eighty thousand pounds worth of mortgage? When we haven't got any income?'

'Oh Christ! Shut up! Yes, I made a mistake. Yes, it was with a lot of money. Yes, I've realized in time. Could we just drop it?'

'Eighty thousand pounds,' said Annie wonderingly. She turned to Caroline. 'Can you believe it?' she said. Caroline tried, too late, to adopt an astounded expression. She gave Annie an apologetic look and Annie gazed at her with unbelieving realization.

'You knew all along,' she said flatly. 'You knew Stephen had signed away all that money. Didn't you?' Caroline shrugged.

'I can't help what Patrick does. I told him I thought it was wrong.'

'But we're supposed to be friends,' said Annie incredulously.

'That's what I said to Patrick,' said Caroline defensively. 'I said you were my only real friend.'

'Well, if I'm your only real friend,' said Annie, in a voice which was dangerously quiet, 'why didn't you tell me what was going on?'

'I couldn't,' said Caroline uncomfortably. 'Patrick said he'd lose his reputation if I went around telling people to pull out of deals.'

'So you think it's better for him to succeed in persuading people to take out mortgages when they can't afford to?'

'Well, you probably could have afforded it,' said Caroline, rattled. 'I mean, it's not that much. And with us paying Nicola's fees . . .' She stopped abruptly.

'Hang on a minute! That's why! That's why you offered to pay Nicola's school fees! I don't believe it!'

Nicola, running down the path to the tennis court to see who had won the match, heard her mother's distressed voice rising above the hedge, and didn't understand what she meant. Bursting out onto the bank, she looked around, from shocked face to shocked face, and, in a voice that trembled slightly, said, 'But I don't have school fees. I go to a state school. You don't pay fees at a state school.' She looked around, her glasses shining, but none of the adults seemed able to speak. Then Valerie took a breath.

'Your mummy was talking about a different school,' she said, in a sugary voice. 'A lovely school in the country, with kind teachers and lots of space to run about.' She smiled at Nicola.

'A . . . a special school?' stammered Nicola.

'Oh yes,' said Valerie gaily. 'A very special school. For special little girls.'

Nicola's face turned ashen, and she swallowed. She

looked from Annie to Stephen and back to Annie. Then she turned on her heel and ran back up the path, her bad leg dragging pathetically behind her. As she turned the corner, she gave a huge sob.

'Oh Christ,' said Stephen, getting up. 'Nicola!' he called.

'I'll go,' said Annie angrily. 'Haven't you done enough already?'

There was silence when Annie had left. Stephen looked around. Valerie was still sitting in her chair, watching the events with gleaming eyes. Martina and the twins were nowhere to be seen; Ella had also absented herself. Patrick and Caroline were glaring at each other; Cressida had quietly sat down on the tennis court, and was curled up, hugging her knees. She ought to realize, thought Stephen, that her skirt was a bit too short to be sitting like that. But his thoughts were interrupted by Charles.

'Stephen, you're a fucking moron!' he exclaimed. 'What were you doing signing something like that? You're supposed to be the bright one around here.'

'Yes, well, it's all right now,' muttered Stephen.

'But it might not have been all right! You might have been ruined! I can't even bear to think about it! I don't know what could have possessed you.'

'How about simple envy!' exclaimed Stephen in a sudden angry retort. 'How about the simple fact that everyone here is rich, and we're poor? How's that for starters?' Charles stared at him.

'I never knew you felt like that . . .'

'I never did feel like that! I really didn't. But look at us! We're approaching middle age, everyone's getting on in the world, and I haven't even got a job!'

'You've got your thesis,' said Charles awkwardly. 'That's more than a job. It's an achievement.'

'That's all right for you to say! But it doesn't pay the bills, does it? We're not all in your privileged position, Charles.'

'My privileged position!' Charles gave a short bitter laugh. 'Christ, you have no idea what my position is.'

'It seems all right to me,' said Stephen shortly.

'That's because you don't know anything about it.' Charles paused, and took a deep breath. When he spoke again, it was in a different voice.

'I might as well tell you,' he said. 'We're as good as ruined.' He exhaled sharply; there was a stunned silence. Caroline's eyes darted quickly to Cressida, but she remained motionless, her head bowed. The others looked uncertainly at each other. Charles looked up at the sky.

'It's almost a relief to have said it,' he murmured. Patrick looked at him curiously. Was the man serious? Was he mad?

'What is it, the Print Centre?' hazarded Caroline. 'It can't have gone bust, surely?'

'I wish,' said Charles bitterly. 'At least then I'd go bankrupt and that would be it. At least it wouldn't be unlimited.' He enunciated the word carefully, with a self-mocking despair. 'Unlimited fucking liability,' he added. 'Never-ending liability. Oh Christ!' He gave a despairing, shocking cry, which echoed round the court. Nobody moved for a few moments. Then Patrick spoke.

'Lloyd's of London?' he said quietly. Charles' head jerked up in surprise. 'How on earth . . . ?' His eyes swivelled round to Cressida, still sitting, curled up on the court, as though trying to block the world out. 'I suppose she told you,' he said contemptuously.

'Actually, she didn't,' said Patrick calmly. 'It was just a guess.'

Cressida slowly lifted her head. Her face was pale, and she was shaking. 'Do you mean', she said, in a voice barely above a whisper, 'that it's not a mistake?' Patrick's heart contracted.

'I'm not sure,' he said gently. 'But I should think it's probably not.'

'Of course it's fucking well not!' yelled Charles. 'You stupid bitch! Is that what you thought? You really are retarded, aren't you?' Cressida's face crumpled, and she huddled closer to her knees. Caroline looked indignantly at Charles, but naked curiosity kept her mouth closed.

'Go on, say it!' exclaimed Charles to Caroline, catching her expression. 'You think I'm an evil bastard who married Cressida for her money! Of course you do. Well, maybe I did. But all I can say now is much fucking good it did me.' Stephen flinched.

'Honestly, Charles,' he said solidly. 'You don't mean that.'

'Don't I?' Charles' eyes were glittering. 'What would you know? Christ, you start whinging about a mortgage of eighty thousand. Do you know how much we owe?' He paused for effect. 'I'll tell you. A million pounds.' He looked round, to see the effect he'd made. Caroline looked astounded. Patrick was looking unsurprised. Stephen was staring down at his knees uncomfortably. 'Maybe less,' Charles continued, in a calmer voice. 'Or maybe more. Our debt is unlimited. We could still be paying out when the twins are twenty-one. Christ knows if we'll be able to send them to proper schools. But I should think it's most unlikely.' His eyes glittered more brightly. 'How do you think that feels?' He looked around, and his glance fell on Stephen, bright red with embarrassment.

'You're the lucky one,' he said, without rancour. 'You've got friends who can afford to help you out.' He looked around. 'Has anyone got a spare million they can let us have?' he said, in a mocking voice. 'We'll be terribly grateful. And we'll try to pay it back. Honest.' He gave a short, painful laugh, tossed a tennis ball, and slammed it hard across the court. Then he threw his racquet after it, slumped to the ground and buried his head in his hands.

Chapter Fourteen

Nicola was sobbing uncontrollably when Annie found her, curled up on the ground, half hidden by a bush. She looked up, startled, at Annie's touch and tried to scramble to her feet. But Annie clasped her firmly in her arms and pulled her back. There was a brief, tacit struggle before eventually Nicola surrendered and buried her hot, wet eyes in Annie's shirt, shuddering and gasping for breath. Annie hugged her tight, not saying anything but rocking gently, stroking her hair, soothing away the sobs.

'Now,' said Annie, after a while, when Nicola seemed to have calmed down. 'What's all this about?'

'I d-don't want to go away!' Nicola's wail turned into a sob, and a fresh stream of tears landed on Annie's shirt. 'I don't want to g-go to a s-special school.'

'A special school?'

'You know, for people like me. For weirdos.'

'My darling!' Annie held Nicola away from her in shock and peered intently at her face. 'Is that what you thought? That we were going to send you to a special school?'

'Th-that's what the g-girls at school s-say,' shuddered Nicola. 'They say I'll b-be sent away to a special school for p-people like me. They say it all the t-time.'

Annie stared at Nicola in shock. Control your anger, she thought. It won't make it any easier for Nicola if you lose your temper.

'Listen to me,' she said, slowly and clearly. 'You aren't going to any special school. You're going to stay just where you are. Those girls are crackers.' Nicola gave a half giggle, but her eyes were distrustful.

'Valerie said . . .' she said.

'Valerie was talking about something else,' said Annie. She felt Nicola stiffen. 'Now listen,' she said. 'I'll tell you what Valerie was talking about. What we were all talking about. Then you can think about it. All right?' Nicola nodded, her body still tense. 'When you're a bit older,' said Annie, 'you'll go to senior school.'

'Marymount,' agreed Nicola.

'Maybe Marymount,' said Annie. 'Maybe somewhere else. Has Georgina told you about the school she goes to?'

'Yes,' said Nicola cautiously.

'Do you think it sounds nice?'

'Yes.'

'Well, just maybe, if you wanted to, you could think about going there.'

'St Catherine's,' said Nicola thoughtfully. Annie felt her relax slightly.

'That's right,' said Annie. 'But you'd have to think very hard about whether you want to go. It's a boarding-school.' Nicola nodded.

'I know,' she said. 'You sleep in dorms. And you have exeats.' Annie tried to read her expression, but the afternoon sun was glinting on her glasses.

'Well,' she said, 'we won't talk about it any more if you don't want to. There's heaps of time to decide.'

'Can I really go if I want to?'

'I'm not sure yet,' said Annie honestly. 'It depends on a few things. Would you be disappointed if you couldn't?' Nicola gazed at her for a while. She shook her head, then nodded, then giggled.

'I don't know,' she said.

'You silly cuckoo!' said Annie, starting to tickle Nicola's tummy. 'You silly cuckoo! Are you still ticklish here? I think you might be!' Nicola shrieked with laughter.

'Stop, Mummy!' she gasped.

'Sorry, I can't hear you,' said Annie. 'Did you say something?' Nicola roared with laughter.

'Stop! Stop!'

Eventually Annie relented. She put her hands above her head.

'Look! I've stopped.' Nicola remained keyed up for a few seconds, ready for another attack, then flopped down, still giggling. Annie looked down at Nicola.

'Shall we go back to the others? Or shall we stay here for a while?'

'Stay here,' said Nicola. She buried her head into Annie's lap and closed her eyes. After a while, she said, 'Why did Valerie say I was going to a special school?'

'She meant a lovely, pretty, friendly school,' said Annie. 'Special doesn't mean bad, you know. Lots of things are special because they're so wonderful.' She paused. 'Like you in that play this afternoon. You were special because you were so funny.' Nicola looked up, her cheeks rather pink.

'It was Georgina's idea,' she said.

'But Georgina couldn't have done it nearly as well as you.' Nicola went pinker and looked pleased. 'I think my favourite bit', continued Annie, 'was when you told the poor pig that the sticks were wolf-proof.' Nicola suddenly gurgled with laughter.

'That was so funny,' she said. 'And then the wolf just came and blew them all away.'

'Poor little pig,' said Annie.

'Silly pig, more like,' said Nicola robustly. 'He shouldn't have believed me. He should have thought, Will sticks keep the wolf out? No, they jolly well won't.'

'I know,' said Annie. 'That's what he should have thought. But, you know, not everyone's as sensible as you.' She smiled down at her daughter and gave her a sudden, fierce bear-hug. 'Not everyone's as sensible as you,' she repeated quietly. 'Not by a long way.'

After a while, Nicola got to her feet. She pushed her hair back and sniffed.

'I was supposed to find out who was winning the tennis match,' she said. 'To tell Georgina.'

'I'm not sure anyone did,' said Annie. 'I think they decided to stop.' And thank God you didn't come along any earlier, she thought, feeling suddenly ashamed of the ugly bickering that had gone on; the screams and fighting by people who were supposed to be civilized friends.

'Well, I'll go and tell them that,' said Nicola. She looked suddenly anxious to be away, suddenly embarrassed, perhaps, Annie thought. Well, she was almost getting to that awkward age of embarrassment. And maybe it started younger these days.

'You go off then,' she said. 'You can tell Georgina the score was quite close.'

'All right.' Without looking back, Nicola ran off, leaving Annie with a damp patch on her shirt and a feeling of emptiness where Nicola's head had rested in her lap. She sat for a few minutes more, with her head thrown back, feeling the sunshine against her face, letting her mind wander, until a cloud moved slowly over the sun, turning the air cool, and a gust of wind blew at her skirt.

Slowly, feeling old and creaky, she got to her feet, and brushed down her clothes. She walked slowly and unwillingly back to the tennis court, wondering what dreadful scene of confrontation would await her. But the only person there was Stephen, sitting in a deckchair, sipping at a can of beer.

She went and sat down beside him. For a while neither of them spoke. Then Stephen said, 'Is Nicola all right?'

'She's all right now. She thought we were going to send her away to some special school.' Annie sighed. 'Those girls at her school have been saying she's going to be sent away. To a school for weirdos. Can you believe it?'

'I can believe anything of that lot.'

'I told her she might be able to go to St Catherine's.'

'And what did she think of that?'

'I couldn't really tell.'

There was a short silence.

'Christ, I'm a fool,' said Stephen suddenly. 'I don't know what happened to me this weekend. I wanted . . .' He broke off. 'I don't know, I wanted to be rich, and successful, and, you know . . . like the others. I thought Patrick might make me a bomb of money, and we could buy a bigger house or something . . .'

'But I don't want a bigger house,' said Annie.

'No,' said Stephen. 'Neither do I. But it's easy to forget things like that.' He smiled foolishly at Annie. 'I'm not level-headed like you.'

'Oh, I'm not level-headed,' said Annie surprisingly. 'I have my own fantasies.'

'Do you?' Annie flushed.

'You know. Silly things. Clothes. Jewels.'

'I'll buy you clothes and jewels,' said Stephen robustly. 'I'll buy you all the jewels you can eat.'

'Will you?' Annie's eyes softened.

'You wait', said Stephen, 'till my thesis is published to widespread acclaim. We'll celebrate with a double order of clothes and jewels.' Annie giggled.

'How lovely. I can't wait.' Stephen took a slug of beer.

'I thought I might do some work on it tonight. I've had a few ideas.'

'Good idea,' said Annie enthusiastically. She looked around and surveyed the empty scene. 'Is the party over, then?'

'I suppose it is,' said Stephen, 'if all the guests have gone home.'

'Have they?'

'Don and Valerie have. They asked me to say good-bye to you. Actually, Don got in a bit of a huff. He thought we weren't taking the match seriously enough.'

Annie giggled. 'Poor Don. I don't think we came up to scratch.' She giggled happily for a minute or two, savouring the silly, childish humour; the warm afternoon sun; the peace of the moment. Then she gave a huge yawn, stretching and wriggling in her deck-chair. She looked at Stephen.

'Is it time to go home?'

'I think so.' Stephen stood up, held out his hands and hauled Annie to her feet. 'Let's get our stuff together. I don't want to hang around here any more.'

When they got up to the house, they found Caroline standing in the hall.

'Oh, Caroline,' said Annie nervously, 'we thought we might go quite soon.'

'Yes, I thought you might,' said Caroline pathetically. 'I suppose you hate me now.'

'Oh no!' exclaimed Annie. 'Of course not! We've had a lovely time. Haven't we, Stephen?'

'Lovely,' said Stephen.

'Even after what Patrick did?'

'Patrick didn't do anything,' said Stephen firmly. 'It was my own fault, for getting myself into something I didn't really want to be in. No harm done.'

'Oh good.' Caroline smiled widely at both of them. 'So we're still friends.'

'Still friends.'

'And you'll still let us pay for Nicola to go to St Catherine's?' Annie glanced at Stephen.

'Maybe,' she said cautiously.

'Oh don't say you won't,' wailed Caroline. 'Because then I'll know that you think I only offered because of what Patrick did. And it's not true. I love Nicola and I want her to have the best. Please? Say you'll let her go?' Annie smiled. Caroline was irresistible.

'Well, all right,' she said. 'If she wants to go, that is. It's her decision.'

'Of course she'll want to go.' Caroline was sweepingly buoyant.

'She may not,' warned Annie. 'We didn't exactly break the news to her very sensitively.'

'Oh.' Caroline looked crestfallen. 'Did she say she didn't want to go?'

'Well, not exactly,' conceded Annie.

'There you are then! She'll do so well there. I can't wait.' Annie rolled her eyes at Stephen.

'The woman's mad,' she said.

'I'm not!' Caroline looked at them both. 'I just don't want to lose my friends.'

'You won't lose us,' said Annie.

'But we do really have to go now,' put in Stephen. 'I'm sorry the party came to such an unseemly end.' Caroline shrugged.

'A party isn't any good unless it comes to an unseemly end. I hope you realize it was all carefully planned.' She broke into cackling laughter.

'Oh yes,' said Stephen. 'Just checking.'

As they went up the stairs, Patrick came into the hall.

'Are they off?' he said to Caroline.

'Yes,' she said. 'You'll be glad to hear they don't hold you any grudges. And you'll also be glad to hear they'll still let us pay Nicola's school fees.'

'Oh good,' said Patrick sarcastically. He caught Caroline's eye. 'Actually,' he said, in a different voice, 'that is good. She deserves a bit of a chance, that kid.'

'That's what I thought,' said Caroline. Patrick carried on looking at her.

'You really laid into Charles out there,' he said. 'I couldn't believe it.'

'He's a shit,' said Caroline briskly.

'I know,' said Patrick. 'But you didn't have to get involved.'

'He was slagging you off,' said Caroline. 'Of course I

had to get involved.' She looked at Patrick; her eyes were surprisingly bright. A second later, Patrick had enveloped her in his arms.

'I really love you,' he said. 'You know that?'

'I had heard a rumour,' said Caroline. 'But I never believe rumours.' Then she was silenced as he fastened his lips to hers.

'Very touching,' came a voice from the doorway. It was Ella. The sunlight was behind her, turning her hair into a halo and her face into a silhouette. 'Sorry to interrupt. I've come to get my bag.'

'Oh, are you going?' said Caroline, with an unconvincing display of regret.

'I think so,' said Ella. 'Don't you?' The two women looked at each other for a few moments before Patrick disentangled himself from Caroline's arms. He nodded brusquely to Ella and walked out of the hall.

'I'm sorry I called you a tart,' said Caroline in a rush. Ella shrugged.

'I don't mind. Words like that don't mean anything to me.'

'How can you be so calm?' Caroline stared at her in bemusement. 'After all that's happened!'

'What's happened? I fucked Charles. Nothing more.'

'That's enough to be going on with.'

'You've changed your attitude,' said Ella. 'Interesting.'

'Yes, well,' said Caroline in an uncompromising voice. 'We all change.'

Ella's eyes surveyed Caroline's face quickly and she gave a little nod.

'I see. I really am unwelcome here, aren't I?' Caroline was silent.

'All right. I won't take long to get my things together.'

'Then what will you do?' Caroline's curiosity overcame her.

'Do? I should think I'll go straight to Italy. I've had enough of this country.'

'Oh well ...' Caroline's curiosity vanished as quickly as it had arisen. Ella's life in Italy, as she had described it, was so far removed from Caroline's idea of what life should be like as to be uninteresting.

As Ella went towards the stairs, Caroline wondered whether this was really the same plump, friendly girl who had lived with Charles in Seymour Road and looked up to him like a god. They had all changed since leaving Seymour Road, she thought. Except perhaps Stephen and Annie. And, of course, they still lived there. Caroline stood and thought about this for a while, and almost felt as though she was on the brink of some startling revelation. But the effort of thinking it out was a bit too much. She shook her head irritably and looked around.

'Well, we're off now.' Cressida's tremulous voice came down from the landing. Ella looked at Caroline quizzically from halfway up the staircase and shrugged. The next moment, Cressida's blond hair appeared round the corner. She descended a couple of steps – then saw Ella and stopped. The two women stared at each other for a few seconds. Cressida recoiled slightly; Ella's shoulders became taut. Caroline was reminded of a couple of cats put in the same room with no warning.

Then Cressida smiled. It was the smile of a well-bred woman; a smile of duty; the sort of smile that could mask a thousand emotions.

'Goodbye,' she said. She paused, and seemed about to say something else – but then appeared to think better of it. Caroline nodded approvingly. There really wasn't anything else to say.

'Goodbye,' said Ella, in an easy voice. There was a slight pause, as neither seemed sure which way to move. But suddenly Ella bounded up the staircase, taking it two steps at a time. She reached the top and disappeared along the corridor. Cressida looked down, caught Caroline's eye, and smiled with unmistakable relief.

'You don't have to go,' said Caroline, eyeing Cressida's suitcase. 'You can always stay here.'

'I know,' said Cressida. 'But I think I'd like to get home. Try and sort things out.'

Charles came down the stairs, laden with bags. He looked anxiously at Cressida and then at Caroline. 'Thank you for putting up with us,' he said. 'And I'm sorry. That's all I can say.'

'Don't apologize to me,' said Caroline, more harshly than she had intended. To compensate, she gave him a kind look. 'Take care of yourselves,' she said. 'And let us know if – you know – if we can help or anything.' Charles nodded wordlessly.

Caroline followed them out into the drive to wave them all off in their Bentley. Charles' face looked haggard as he leant out of the window, and Caroline tried to find a spark of *Schadenfreude* to cheer herself up with. She usually found it possible to gloat over the misfortunes of even her closest friends. But somehow this situation was far too big for that. Just thinking about it caused the base of her spine to tingle unpleasantly.

When they had gone, she wandered aimlessly back inside and wondered what to do. Everyone was gone, or getting ready to go. But it was still warm. She might be able to fit in some last-minute sunbathing.

She went to the kitchen and poured herself a glass of white wine, opened a packet of peanuts and poured them into a bowl. For good measure, she added a jar of marinated olives. She put all of these, plus the bottle of wine, onto a tray and took them out onto the terrace. Her steamer chair was in just the right position to catch the rays of afternoon sun, and soon she was agreeably ensconced, her eyes closed and her feet up. At least it hadn't rained, she thought idly. They really had been very lucky with the weather. And tomorrow, with any luck, it would be hot again, and she could sunbathe topless.

When Stephen and Annie shepherded Nicola and Toby onto the terrace to say goodbye to Caroline, they found her asleep on the steamer chair.

'Never mind,' whispered Annie. 'We can each write her a nice letter.'

Out by the car, Patrick was waiting to see them off.

'Thanks for a lovely weekend,' said Annie. 'It really was.'

'Thanks, Patrick,' said Stephen, rather shame-facedly. 'Sorry about all that bother.'

'Don't be silly,' said Patrick. 'It's your right to decide what to do with your own money.'

'Well, yes, I suppose it is,' said Stephen.

They carefully manoeuvred the car out of the drive and drove off, still waving.

'Well, thank God for that,' said Stephen.

'For what?' said Nicola at once.

'Nothing,' said Stephen.

'For a lovely time,' said Annie. 'That's what you meant, isn't it, Stephen?'

'Oh, er, yes,' said Stephen. 'For a lovely time.' He put his foot down and the car leapt forward, as though as eager as him to get away; to get away from the lovely time, back to real life and home.

Last to leave was Ella. She put her bag on the back seat of her car and looked around for someone to say good-bye to. But no-one was about. Shrugging, she slipped into the front seat and drove quickly and neatly out of the drive. Her little car was soon zipping along the motorway; she opened the sunroof and began to hum. She had already forgotten Caroline and Patrick; Annie and Stephen; had forgotten about the tennis party. Her mind was on the hills of Tuscany, on her lover, Maud Vennings. Maud would now, perhaps, be sitting

outside her villa, sipping Strega, wondering if Ella was
going to return to her. Business in England, Ella had
told her. Unfinished business. But now there was
nothing to keep her.

THE END